MARYSUE
RUCCI
BOOKS

Tell It to Me Singing

– A Novel –

Tita Ramírez

MARYSUE RUCCI BOOKS

New York   London   Toronto   Sydney   New Delhi

**MARYSUE
RUCCI
BOOKS**

An Imprint of Simon & Schuster, LLC
1230 Avenue of the Americas
New York, NY 10020

First Marysue Rucci Books hardcover edition July 2024

MARYSUE RUCCI BOOKS and colophon are trademarks of Simon & Schuster, LLC

Simon & Schuster: Celebrating 100 Years of Publishing in 2024

For information about special discounts for bulk purchases, please contact Simon & Schuster Special Sales at 1-866-506-1949 or business@simonandschuster.com.

The Simon & Schuster Speakers Bureau can bring authors to your live event. For more information or to book an event, contact the Simon & Schuster Speakers Bureau at 1-866-248-3049 or visit our website at www.simonspeakers.com.

Interior design by Laura Levatino

Manufactured in the United States of America

10 9 8 7 6 5 4 3 2 1

Library of Congress Cataloging-in-Publication Data

Names: Ramírez, Tita, author.
Title: Tell it to me singing : a novel / Tita Ramírez.
Description: First Marysue Rucci Books hardcover edition. | New York : Marysue Rucci Books, 2024.
Identifiers: LCCN 2023047019 (print) | LCCN 2023047020 (ebook) | ISBN 9781982157319 (hardcover) | ISBN 9781982157326 (trade paperback) | ISBN 9781982157333 (ebook)
Subjects: BISAC: FICTION / Hispanic & Latino | FICTION / Literary | LCGFT: Domestic fiction. | Novels.
Classification: LCC PS3618.A4647 T45 2024 (print) | LCC PS3618.A4647 (ebook) | DDC 813/.6—dc23/eng/20231204
LC record available at https://lccn.loc.gov/2023047019
LC ebook record available at https://lccn.loc.gov/2023047020

ISBN 978-1-9821-5731-9
ISBN 978-1-9821-5733-3 (ebook)

For my parents
and in memory of Nina Riggs
(1977–2017)

She wanted a little room for thinking . . .

—Rita Dove, "Daystar"

Every person who lives outside his context is always
a bit of a ghost, because I am here, but at the same
time I remember a person who walked those streets,
who is there, and that same person is me. So sometimes
I really don't know if I am here or there.

—Reinaldo Arenas, 1983

(as published in Ann Tashi Slater, "Fata Morgana:
Reinaldo Arenas, Writers in Exile, and a
Visit to the Havana of 1987," *Paris Review*, March 4, 2014)

Tell It
to Me
Singing

Part I

1

The night before my mother's surgery, we stretch out side by side on her hospital bed watching her telenovela, *Abismo de pasión*. I'm trying not to crowd her too much, so I rest my left arm on my pregnant belly, which I can do easily since I'm right at six months.

On the show, Armando is frantically rifling through a filing cabinet in his office.

"What's he doing?" I say in English.

"Looking for the money," my mom says in Spanish. This is how my parents and I always talk to each other: in two languages. Sometimes three if you count Spanglish.

"So he was lying when he told Jaquelín he didn't have it?"

"Of course," she says. Her faded yellow hospital gown is making her look glaringly pale. Her hair, dyed a reddish brown, is a little flat in the back, and her eyes are droopy, probably from the Ativan the nurse gave her.

When she came in for the pre-op tests this morning, she was having chest pains and her blood pressure was too high, so they admitted her right there. No suitcase, no nothing.

Her GP was the one who found the aneurysm. She had gone in

for a slight cough; my mother's a hypochondriac who goes to the doctor for everything. They took an X-ray and found a bubble-looking thing in her heart. "Mirta," the doctor said. "Eso está caliente."

She called me from the parking lot of his office. "Mónica," she said. "They found something in my heart. He said it could be an aortic aneurysm." She hadn't even called my father yet. She wanted me to Google what the doctor had said and print out the results. When it's important, she wants printouts. Hurricane shutter installation, eye serum for mature skin, fungus on tomato plants—I've Googled and printed it all at her request. This time, though, I had already typed it in and was starting to read: abdominal aortic aneurysm, thoracic aortic aneurysm.

"I got it, Mom. I'm getting ready to know everything," I said.

Unlike my mother, I only watch *Abismo* on Fridays, when I go over to my parents' house for dinner. After we eat, we drink Cuban coffee and she catches me up on the plot for that week. Then we sit down to watch.

Tonight, Armando checks one more drawer and finds a manila envelope with several stacks of money. He calls someone on his cell and whispers, "I'll be there by five." I look at my mom.

"Sebastián," she says. "If he doesn't pay him by five"—she slices the air in front of her— "olvídate."

Armando's office door swings open and his assistant, Jaquelín, comes in with a tray of coffee. She's wearing a tight white dress and she bends over so her boobs are right in his face when she puts the tray down on the desk.

"Oh my God," I say. "She needs to get over this already. He's with Clara now. She knows that."

My mom lets out a little huff. "Mónica, she was pregnant with his baby. That's not an easy thing to let go of."

"But he never even knew," I say. Jacquelín lost the baby when she had to run through the jungle to escape the cult people. She never told Armando about any of it.

Armando sips his coffee nervously, keeping one hand on the manila envelope. Jaquelín asks him if he's okay and I want to ask my mother the same. She seems weird now, a little far away. She's not even looking at the screen.

"I'm fine," he assures her, but it's clear he's not.

I turn to my mom to ask her if she thinks Clara knows about his dealings with Sebastián, but her eyes are drooping more now, so I just stay quiet and let the Ativan do its job. She falls asleep, and a few minutes later the baby wakes up and kicks me in the side. I take my mom's hand and put it on my stomach. "Mom, he's kicking," I whisper, half expecting her to say what she always does when I let her feel him: "Mi niño, estoy aquí." But she's out cold, which is good. Better for her to get some rest.

My phone rings and it's Robert. He's probably driving home from the track and wants to check on my mom and to tell me how he did tonight. He's in this car racing club and he likes to talk about his lap times, which I barely understand. I usually listen, because that's what you're supposed to do when you're engaged to someone and carrying their baby. But I'm too worried about my mom. In ten hours she'll be asleep on a table with her sternum broken open. I silence the call and let it go to voice mail.

The lemon pomegranate lotion I bought her from the gift shop is sitting on the tray table next to me. My mom's a hand lotion junkie and I knew she would like this scent. As I'm softly rubbing it into her hands, Armando goes into an abandoned warehouse to deliver the money, but there's nobody there. Just as he's about to leave, a shadowy figure appears in the corner and the episode ends.

I haul myself out of the bed and tidy up the room a little more: water cups into the trash, pitcher back by the sink. Then I check to make sure my mom's suitcase is packed. I slip the lotion and the James Patterson book she's been reading into the front pocket and zip it up.

"Good night, Mom," I say to her softly. "See you tomorrow. I'll be here at seven with Dad. You're going to do great."

What I think is: *You have to do great. I can't imagine my life without you. Who would call me at 5:30 to pick up their dry cleaning at the place all the way in Coral Gables that closes at 6:00? Or teach me how to make the frijoles from scratch at Christmas? Or help me be a mother?*

I put one hand on my stomach. With my other hand, I stroke her arm softly. I think of my father at home, getting ready to sleep in their bed alone for the first time in thirty-five years. I don't go to church anymore, but I do sometimes pray. I close my eyes now. *Please, God,* I say in my head. *Please, keep her safe. I need her. I can't do this without her.* The *this* is the baby, but it's also everything. I press on my stomach and squeeze my mother's arm one last time.

2

My mom and I talk every day. She helped me figure out that I want to study interior design. ("A woman needs a purpose, Mónica.") And she was the one who finally convinced me to break up with Manny, who kept reenlisting in the Army instead of staying here to make a life with me. ("He's a patriot, which is honorable. But he will never love you the way you want him to.")

I lived with my parents until I was twenty-six—not because it was convenient and cheap, as I said to my friend Lisa, but because I felt like I wasn't *allowed* to move out. My mother wanted me to stay for the same reason every Cuban parent wants their daughter to stay: a woman should move from her parents' house to her husband's house. But, more than that, she wanted me to stay because I belonged to her. When I finally told her I had to leave, she nodded and said in English—as if I were a stranger, not her daughter—"Well, if that's what you feel is best." Then she pulled a dead leaf off the plant she had been watering, put it into the pocket of her shorts, and went to her room, where she stayed for the rest of the night and most of the next day.

The apartment I found was on the edge of Coral Gables, almost in Little Havana. It was two little rooms on the back of a larger house with a tiny airplane bathroom and half a kitchen. Manny called it the Mouse House, it was so small. But I didn't care. I loved it. I loved the plaster walls and the fact that it had hardwood floors instead of tile. I loved that I could be completely alone if I wanted to. A few months after I moved in, Manny deployed for the third time, so that's where I was living, thank God, when I broke up with him via Skype. I could never have survived that experience living in my parents' house. Every night for the next three months, I came home from work, drank three beers, ate a bowl of cereal, and cried on my sofa until I fell asleep.

When I could finally get through an evening without dissolving, Sandra at work started talking about the water delivery guy, Robert—how cute he was, how she thought he was flirting with me. We work at a small dermatology office and we both sit at the front desk. Sandra answers the phone and checks in the patients. I do the billing. When Robert leaned over the counter and asked for my number, she said, right in front of him, "¿Que te dije?"

I ignored her, hoping he didn't understand, and wrote my number on an appointment card.

"Sweet," he said. "You like sushi?"

That weekend we went out for dinner and had sex. I cried silently through most of it. If he noticed, he didn't say anything. On Monday he left a Deer Park spring water invoice on my car that said, *You like Mexican?* The next weekend we went for Mexican and had more sex. That time I only cried a little. Soon I wasn't crying at all. When I was with him, I was happy. We went Jet Skiing and out to bars for trivia nights and to the movies. We stayed home and cooked. He made me steak on the grill and I made him carne con papas.

A few months in, I brought him to my parents' house for dinner. They liked him instantly. "He has a gentle way about him," my mother said. "Like my father." Her only complaints were his tattoos, which were peeking out from the sleeves of his polo, and the fact that he's American. My father liked that he had a steady job and that he was going to school at night—at FIU, no less—studying finance and accounting. "Eso es una decisión muy prudente," my father declared when I told him. They liked the idea of their daughter being with someone who had plans, given that I'm still sitting here with no degree—just my forty-some-odd credits from Miami Dade College.

We'd been together for eight months when I suspected I was pregnant. I waited until the weekend to take a pregnancy test, to give my period a few more days to show up. Then, on Sunday morning, after Robert left for the track, I took the test. Positive. I didn't want to be pregnant—not with Robert's baby. But I didn't want to have an abortion, either. I was twenty-eight and Robert was a good guy. A great guy, in fact, with a decent job and a solid future.

Any other time I imagined having a kid, I saw Manny standing in the backyard on Nochebuena, drinking a beer with my father and Tío Fermín, watching the pig roasting in the Caja China. I saw a brown-skinned, curly-haired child running to catch up with the older cousins. But now it would be Robert, who, according to the pictures in his mom's house, was blond until he was ten. Maybe that kid in the backyard would be, too, if that was even possible.

Sitting on the closed toilet seat, looking at those two pink lines on the pregnancy test, I felt something inside me break. Having a baby with Robert meant I would never be with Manny again. It would excise him from my life in a way nothing else had, and the thought of that was like a punch I had to recover from before I could tell anyone what was happening.

The next Sunday night, I muted the episode of *Breaking Bad* we were watching and turned to Robert. "I need to tell you something," I said.

He took a sip of his beer. I wasn't having one. "Yeah?"

"I'm pregnant."

"Oh shit," he said, but couldn't stop himself from smiling. "Wow." He put his beer down. "Mónica. Whoa." He shook his head. "Damn. Sorry, I'm just really surprised."

"Me too," I said, wiping my palms on my shorts. "I thought we had been careful enough."

"You're sure? You, like, took a test and all that?"

I had taken another one that afternoon. "I'm positive."

"Okay, okay. So, what, uh, what are you thinking? What do you want to do?"

I wanted to click the back button and return to the previous version of my life, the one where I was just riding out the aftermath of Manny with this sweet guy who made me laugh. But, of course, I couldn't. So I said, "I have to keep it."

He took a long sip of his beer, nodding while he drank. "Okay."

"Listen, you do *not* have to stick around for this," I said, even though I knew he'd be sticking around for this. His own father had taken off when he was three. It was just him and his mom until he was in high school, when she met his stepdad.

He put his beer down hard on the table. "Mónica, are you kidding me? I am *not* taking off on my kid. Listen"—he took my hand—my clammy, sweaty hand—and held it between both of his—"I love you." It was the first time he had said it.

I had been thinking about whether or not I loved him for a

week. Whether there was a difference between loving someone and being *in* love with them. I wasn't sure how I felt. I liked him. I knew he'd be a good father. Beyond that, I didn't know. So, instead of saying "I love you too," I just kissed him and said, "Okay, thanks."

I told my parents a couple of weeks later, right at the end of our Friday night dinner. It was just the three of us. Robert was at the track that night. My mother closed her eyes and raised her face to the ceiling. "Ay, Mónica," she said.

I forced myself not to say "I'm sorry."

She got up from the table, lit the San Judas candle, crossed herself, and said, "¿Pero como pasó esto? Robert doesn't like to use condoms?"

I put my hands over my eyes. "Oh my God, Mom. Please. Who cares how it happened? You're going to be a grandmother. Aren't you happy about that?"

"We would be happier if you were already married," my father said. "When are you getting married?"

I took a deep breath. The kitchen still smelled like pork chops marinated in lime and garlic, garbanzos and white rice. "We haven't talked about getting married."

My mother said, "Are you joking?"

"We haven't even been together a year," I said softly.

My father shook his head in disgust and ran a hand through his hair, which was still mostly black, with a few silver strands here and there.

"And I feel like you should be with someone for at least a year before you decide to marry them."

My mother was still in her work clothes: black pants and a white blouse with tiny yellow flowers on it. There was a grease stain on one of the flowers, but I didn't tell her. She leaned in. "You don't think he wants to marry you?"

"I'm not sure what he wants." That wasn't true. Though we hadn't talked about it yet, I thought he probably did want to marry me.

"Well, you need to find out," she said.

My father said, "You need to talk to Robert. He needs to do the right thing." He pointed at me. "You're not going to be one of these single girls with a baby. That baby needs a father."

Something about that pissed me off. I was almost thirty years old. So I said, "That baby *has* a father. I'm just not married to him."

My father got up and poured himself a glass of Pepsi from the two-liter he always keeps on the counter. Then he went to the cabinet above the sink, took down a bottle of rum, and poured some in—something he rarely does. He took a sip. "Mónica, you're our daughter and you're pregnant. You need to get married. Think about what people are going to say about you."

"About *us*," my mother said.

"Look, I know it's a surprise, and it's not ideal, but I'm not a teenager. I can handle this. We'll probably move in together at some point." I realized it was true as I said it and I felt both relief and dread.

My mother started talking about my job, whether Dr. Peña would offer me maternity leave and for how long. My father mentioned that I didn't even have my associate's yet, and didn't I want to be an interior designer one day? As I cleared the last of the dishes and wiped down the table, I listened to all of it, thinking how right they were and how all of that sucked, but that maybe having a baby could also somehow be a good thing. When I finished, I got my purse. "I'm leaving," I said.

"You're not staying for the show?" my mother asked.

I shook my head. "No. I need to go." I walked past them and left without giving them a kiss goodbye—something I never do.

Then I did something else I never do: I didn't call or visit them all week. Every day I told myself I should call, but every day the mix of anger and fear paralyzed me and I just didn't. They didn't call me, either: they were punishing me. Finally, on Friday, I called before leaving work and asked if Robert and I could come for dinner. "Of course," my mother said. "We'll be happy to have you." When we arrived, my parents hugged and congratulated him and all they said to me was "How are you feeling?" and "When is your first appointment with the doctor?"

After dinner, my mom and I made coffee. Since Robert was over, I served it in the red espresso cups instead of just orange juice glasses.

My father and Robert took theirs out to the garage while my mom and I watched *Abismo de pasión*. By the end of the night it was like any other Friday. Except for the fact that it wasn't. As I sat there drinking my coffee, watching Armando and Clara kiss on the beach, I felt how different my life was about to become.

Robert suggested, a few weeks later, that I move in with him. "We'll be spending all our time together when the baby's born anyway," he said. Logistically, it made sense. The Mouse House was tiny. Too small for a crib, even. So, two months later, even though I wasn't sure I was ready, Robert's roommate moved out and I moved in.

The next weekend was our eleven-month anniversary and Robert announced he was taking me to dinner. He said he wanted to take me someplace that we never go to, so we went down to South Beach. We walked up and down Lincoln Road, looking at all the beautiful people in their beautiful clothes, the tourists and the beach kids with their skateboards and blown-out pupils. It was a nice night—not too hot, with a little breeze off the water a few blocks away. That helped with my nausea, which had kicked in hard by then. Everywhere we tried to eat was packed. Finally, we found a place that could fit us in. It was some kind of Asian place where the floor was covered in actual grass. They made us take off our shoes at the door and sit on a woven mat. There were no tables.

As soon as we were seated, I realized I had to pee. That was another symptom that had recently kicked in. I was about to get up when Robert said, "Well, I was going to wait until after dinner to do this, but I can't." He smiled and pulled a small white box out of his front pocket. *Oh my God*, I thought. *Oh my God*. It felt like an emergency was happening—a fire or a tornado—and I needed to get out. I actually looked at the door, but only for a second. I brought my eyes back to Robert's.

He smiled and held the ring out toward me so I could see it better. "It was my grandmother's," he said. "If you don't like it, we can get another one. I just didn't want to do this without a ring." Then he said the words, asked me the question.

I breathed slowly, deeply. I thought about how sweet and attentive he was—how he brought me crackers every morning to help with the nausea. I thought about how he was smart and funny and good in bed and, even though the car racing was a little stupid, he was also serious about getting his degree and making a good living. We had been together for only a fraction of the almost five years

I had been with Manny, but maybe that didn't matter. We were having a baby. We were already living together. I looked down and closed my eyes for a second. I saw my mother in the kitchen, lighting the San Judas candle. My father frowning, pouring that drink.

"Yes," I said, looking back up at Robert.

He slipped the ring on my finger, and then we were kissing. I kept my eyes open and all I saw were legs—of the servers, of the people coming in and going out. When Robert pulled away, he said, "I love you."

I took another one of those slow, deep breaths to steady my voice. "I love you too," I said.

3

Normally, only one family member is allowed in the pre-op area. But my mother shames the nurse into letting me in here. "Are you going to tell me that you're not going to let my *only* daughter, who is pregnant with my *only* grandchild, say goodbye to me before I go into open-heart surgery?" she says. My mother can be very persuasive. So I'm allowed in, but only while my father is out in the hallway with the surgeon.

"Mónica," she says. They've given her the first round of drugs. Her eyes are glassy and she looks like she's feeling pretty good.

"Yes, Mom?"

"Last night, while we were watching the show, I realized I need to tell you something."

She has a blue surgical cap on and it looks like it's pinching her forehead. I run my finger under it to reposition it a little. "Is this better?"

"I need to tell you. Please."

"Mom, you don't need to tell me anything. There's nothing you need to tell me. You're just a little high right now." I smile. "Everything's going to be fine."

She shakes her head. "No, no. I need to tell you. Watching the show last night was a sign."

She loves signs. "A sign of what?" I rub my arms, trying to warm up. "Are you cold? It's like thirty degrees in here."

"Listen to me," she says. "This might be my only chance."

"Mom, c'mon. Don't talk like that. Everything's going to be fine." I'm reassuring her and myself at the same time.

She pulls her hand out from under the blanket and grabs my arm. "Mónica. Please. Listen." She squeezes. "You need to know this." She's speaking English and I don't like it. I'm already scared about this surgery and what's wrong with her heart, and now she's doing this. She blinks slowly. She lets go of my arm but takes my hand. "Look at me, okay?" She looks right into my eyes, almost frantic. My heart starts going faster. "Mi niña, I have to tell you. Rolando will never tell you. And if I die, you need to know the truth. It's not fair to you."

"What truth? Mom, let's just relax. Let's take a deep breath." I take one to show her.

"Mónica, your father is Juan."

"What? What are you talking about?" What is she talking about? My father is Rolando. Rolando Campo.

She's still looking right at me. "I was pregnant and I never told him. Just like on the show."

"What show? *Abismo*?"

She nods. "I loved him so much and he never knew about you." Her eyes begin to water and she looks at my stomach. "But now *you're* going to be a mother. And you deserve the truth."

"What truth? What are you saying? What are you telling me?" My legs are shaking and I'm not cold anymore. What the hell is happening right now? There is no way she's telling me my father is someone else. No way.

The door opens and it's the nurse. "Time to go," she says.

"Wait," I practically yell. "No. Can we have another minute, please?"

"The doctor is on a very strict schedule this morning."

I lean over my mother. I can smell her breath, a little sour from the drugged sleep last night. "Mom," I say, in an almost whisper. "What do you mean Juan is my father? Who's Juan?"

She touches my arm. "I had to tell you. In case I die."

"But are you telling me Dad is not my father?"

My mother nods with her eyes closed. "My toes feel so good," she says.

My father walks in then and the nurse tells us we need to leave, that they're taking her in. He kisses my mother's cheek and says, "I'll see you in a few hours. Behave yourself, okay?" and laughs a little.

A wall of confusion rises up in front of me. I don't know what to say or do, especially with my father right there. I look down at my mom. I touch her shoulder. "I love you, Mom. I'll see you in a few hours."

The nurse wheels her out and I stand there, my entire body trembling. The term *tectonic plates* comes into my head and I start thinking it over and over. *Tectonic plates, tectonic plates.* I guess because the ground, or what I thought was the ground—the place or thing that was holding me—is no longer holding me. All I can think is that she was just super high. Just mixing up her telenovela—the fantasy world she loves to live in—with her real life. But something about her voice, her eyes—the way she looked right at me—made it sound like she knew what she was saying. And like what she was saying was the truth.

Mirta

I swore to your father I would never tell anyone, and I never did. Not even Teresita, and she's my best friend. For twenty-nine years, I've kept it all in. But I couldn't go into this surgery without telling you. What if I don't wake up? Rolando would have done what we planned to do all those years ago, which was to never say a word, to take it to our graves.

If I live through this, Mónica, I will tell you everything—all the things about my life you don't know, all the things you deserve to know. I will tell you about Juan and my life before you were born. I will tell you how I almost lost you because of how weak I became and because of the darkness that nearly consumed me. And I will tell you about your father—how strong he has always been, and how he saved me over and over.

4

In the waiting room, it's me and the fake plants and the brown carpet and my father, having no idea that my mother just said to me, "Your father is Juan. I loved him so much and he never knew." The words float through me like poison, burning up my insides. What could they possibly mean? There's no way they could mean what I fear they do.

My father yawns, takes off his glasses, and cleans them with the little black cloth he always keeps in his pocket. It says *Campo Optical*—his business, which he's owned since I was a kid—in gold letters. He chooses a *Time* magazine with Mitt Romney on the cover from the side table. It's from a few months back—a special issue about the convention, which my parents watched like it was the Olympics. A few minutes later, he asks me to text my brother, who has an 8:00 a.m. meeting and can't come until after that. "Tell him she's gone into surgery," he says. My father has a cell phone but refuses to carry it unless he's traveling.

"Okay," I say, but then I just stare at my phone without moving.

"Mija," he says, "she'll be okay."

Mija: my daughter. But what if I'm not his daughter? What if, somehow, that crazy, terrible thing she said was the truth? I can't bear to think about it.

I have to get away from this room—these plants and this carpet and my father's face. "Coffee," I say, slinging my purse over my shoulder. It's leather and big and heavy because I never clean it out and it feels good now, pulling on my shoulder, grounding me a tiny bit. "I'll go get us some coffee. Okay? And I'll text Pablo. I'll be back."

I ride the elevator with an older white janitor and his cleaning cart. I smile at him the way you smile at people in elevators and hope that I look normal and not like what I feel like. I hear my mother in my head again—*Your father is Juan*—and a wave of nausea hits me so hard I turn away from the janitor and gag in my mouth. *It was the drugs,* I tell myself. *She was just high and making no sense.*

I continue telling myself this the entire four hours of the surgery, until the doctor walks into the waiting room with a serious look on his face. Too serious. I bolt out of my chair. My father and Pablo are right behind me.

The doctor says the surgery itself went well. They repaired the aneurysm, replaced the valve, and everything was fine. But when they tried to extubate her, they couldn't. Her lungs are not functioning on their own, and her blood pressure is high and unstable. "We'll continue to monitor her and try again in a few hours," he says. "But the takeaway here is that the situation is not good." I nearly gag again. My head becomes a helium balloon about to float off my body and I have to sit down to keep from passing out. In the meantime, those terrible words she said before surgery slip away, a panel sliding off to the side, making room for this new thing: the very real possibility that she could die.

5

They have to put my mom in a medical coma, and that's when my father calls in the Stars. They're my parents' neighbors and a couple, and, amazingly, they're both named Estrella, though one goes by Yeya and one goes by Chichi. Nobody talks about the fact that they live together and wear matching rings. What they talk about is the fact that they're into Santería, which supposedly no one believes in. That is, until something goes wrong—lost job, cheating husband, medical coma—and then people are lining up around the block to get a live chicken shaken in their face.

Yeya, in her cargo pants and Keens, always looks like a fourth-grade teacher on a field trip. She has short gray hair and the straightest, whitest teeth I've ever seen. Chichi's more of a hippie, with her flowy skirts and Birks. They come in wearing matching fanny packs, carrying tote bags full of God knows what. Hopefully nothing alive. As they make the rounds saying hello to everyone, my father goes back to talk to the nurses, and a few minutes later one comes out to escort the Stars into my mother's room. They stay for twenty minutes, and when they walk out, they look assured. "Babalú-Ayé will help us," Chichi says, nodding.

Afterward, I ask my father if he knows what they did in there.

"Un despojo, I imagine. And I'm sure they prayed." I see the worry in his face, the uncertainty we're all living with, and I find myself saying my own little prayer that whatever they did will work. *Please, God. Or Babalú. Or whoever. Please,* I say.

And then, within hours, her numbers—all of them—are better. Every day she progresses a little more. Maybe whatever they did worked. Or maybe it's just my mother, fighting to come back to us.

The nurses tell us to stay positive, to just keep talking to her and doing the things she likes. So we play a little Celia Cruz or Celine Dion. My father brings un café con leche every morning and dabs a little on her lips around the ventilator. I rub the lemon pomegranate lotion on her hands. And whenever the baby kicks, I take her hand and place it on my stomach, saying, "Mom, here he is—tu niño."

There's no TV in here—it's the surgical ICU—so I've been bringing my laptop to watch *Abismo de pasión* with her. I set it up on the bed now. "Time for our show," I say.

Last week the shadowy figure in the warehouse pushed Armando down a flight of stairs and stole the money he owes Sebastián. Now Armando's wearing a neck brace and is paralyzed from the waist down. Tonight he's waiting for Clara, the love of his life, to arrive from Spain, where she's been visiting her sister. But her sister calls. Clara, it seems, is gone. "Desaparecida," the sister says, with the lisp—I guess because she's living in Spain, so that's how she talks now. She says it was the cult that took Clara.

"Holy shit, Mom. Now the cult has Clara," I say.

No response, of course. Just the Darth Vader sounds of the machines, and her lying there with the breathing tube down her throat, the IV in her arm, her hands so puffed up with fluids, they look like they're about to burst. God, all I want in the world right now is to hear my mother's voice—to have her say my name or call the baby "mi niño." To hear her complain about the tasteless American food, the nurse's attitude—anything. What she said before surgery feels like something that happened on a trip I took but can't remember. I've almost convinced myself she was just high and hallucinating on the pre-op drugs.

Almost.

And I've told no one. I considered telling Caro—she's my cousin, and we're close like that—but I don't want anyone in the family to know about this. I should tell Robert. But I can't and feel terrible that I can't. I feel close to him, most of the time. But the truth is I feel like he doesn't really get me or my need to be alone. Sometimes I lie and say I'm going shopping with my mom when really I'm just driving around, looking at houses I like or walking up and down the aisles of T.J. Maxx, not buying anything, just looking and thinking. He's sweet and funny and cute, and he's coming to the hospital almost every night, bringing us dinner, sitting with us. But there's only one person I could possibly tell: Manny.

Manny, who knows me better than anyone. Manny, who, because he was a medic in Afghanistan for three tours, might be able to tell me it was just the drugs, the confusion—anything other than my mother saying my father is someone else. I keep thinking about calling him. I know I shouldn't, but it's an emergency. I find his last text, from three months ago. He was just saying hi, just telling me he missed me. He had no idea I was pregnant, and I never responded.

I read his message again. Maybe I can ask him this one question about the drugs. The nurse here in ICU told me it was Versed and fentanyl. "Versed will make you sleepy and probably cause some amnesia," she told me. "Fentanyl is for pain." Maybe Manny will know more. Maybe he'll know about what can happen if you combine the two. I've thought about asking Dr. Peña at work, but she's a dermatologist and I don't know how much she knows about pain meds. Also, I don't want to tell her why I'm asking. I begin texting Manny—*Hey, something's up with my mom*—but then the door opens. It's my father, back from the cafeteria. He hands me a chocolate pudding.

"Oh wow, you're the best," I say, smiling at him. "Thank you."

He sits down next to me and pats my leg. "De nada, mija." He takes off his glasses to clean them with his cloth. He looks even more tired and worried than normal. He's sleeping at home now, not in the hospital, but he's still not getting enough rest. I stayed with him last night and I heard him up and down, getting water, sitting in the living room with the TV on, probably thinking what I can't stop thinking, which is *Oh my God, what if she dies? What will I do? How will I live?*

The pudding has a little mountain of whipped cream on top. I scoop it off and eat it all in one bite. "What did you eat?" I ask him.

"Sopa y un sandwich."

I look at him. He's in pants and a button-down because he went in to the optical for a little while this morning. "Dad, you should go home. You've been here since noon."

"I can't leave yet." He points at the laptop screen. "I have to see what happens." Some goons who work for Sebastián have kidnapped Armando and are dragging him into a dungeon-like basement. My father shakes his head. "I thought *I* had problems, with my wife being in a coma and everything. But this guy has it worse."

I laugh a little and squeeze his hand. "Her oxygen was eighty-nine. That's a really good sign."

"I know." He sneaks a peek at their wedding photo sitting on the bedside table. Caro brought it in the other day, along with photos of everyone else in the family. "So she won't be all alone," she said, reaching into her purse to pull out two eight-by-tens of her twins in their St. Brendan uniforms, and two wallet-sized pictures of her brother's kids. Eventually we had pictures of everybody taped up all over the walls, plus two San Judas prayer cards taped to the bed railings: one on the left, one on the right, right by her head. He's my mother's favorite and Caro knew she'd want him close by.

My father asks if I've updated Pablo on the oxygen. "He told me he was going to come today, but I think—"

"Let me guess: He had an important 'meeting'?" I do air quotes because my brother always seems to have a work commitment when something's going on with our family. He's been here three times in the week since her surgery. I've been here every day.

I eat the rest of the pudding and text Pablo about the oxygen. Then I text Caro the same update. *Will you tell your parents, too?* Keeping everyone informed—the people here in Miami plus my grandmother and the cousins up in Jersey—is so hard for my father; I can tell. He's actually been carrying his cell phone. If my mother weren't in the ICU, all the Miami people would be here, packed into the waiting room. Instead, everyone just calls and texts us all day long.

I take my mom's hand now and rub some of the lemon pomegranate lotion on. "Does this feel nice?" I ask her. "Don't worry, I'm doing your cuticles." I push them back softly but firmly, like she taught me to do. Her nails are bare—not even clear polish on them—and this unnerves me. She's a manicurist. Her nails are never bare.

The show ends and I pack up my laptop while my father kisses my mother good night. He touches her cheek and says something in her ear that I can't hear. I look away, partly to give him privacy and partly because it hurts too much to see it all: the tubes and wires and monitors keeping her alive. And him so scared.

When he's done, I give her a kiss. "Good night, Mom. I love you. Keep that oxygen up and that blood pressure down, okay? If you do, we'll see you in a couple days." I squeeze her hand, being careful of her IV, and my father and I walk out together, the glass doors of her room whooshing closed behind us.

Mirta

That lotion feels so nice, mi niña. Lemon always reminds me of my grand-parents' house in Cuba. They lived out in the country, on a small farm— too small to be seized by the government when Castro took over, thank God. It was just a few chickens and goats, and pigs my grandfather slaughtered himself and shared with the neighbors. Every summer my sisters and I went to visit and help my grandmother deep-clean the house. We picked all the lemons off the little stand of trees in the yard, then used the juice to wash everything—the windows, the floors. Even the walls.

The year I was eighteen, my sisters couldn't come because they had con-tracted a stomach flu and could barely get out of bed, so my grandmother asked the girl who lived at the next farm over to come help in exchange for some extra pork. Her name was Adelita and she was also eighteen. We became friends right away. One afternoon, when I rode back to her house with her, I met her brother. His name was Juan. He was two years older and more handsome than any of the boys I had known in school. Blue eyes, black hair, muscles from working the farm all day. He washed his hands at the kitchen sink before shaking my hand and saying "Mucho gusto" when Adelita introduced us. By the end of that week, he was visiting me at my grandparents' house. By the end of the summer, we were sneaking away to the field of coffee trees to do the things we couldn't do in my grandparents' lemon-fresh living room.

At the end of the summer, I went back to the city, but we continued to see each other as often as we could. Two years later we were married. I moved to their farm to live with him and Adelita, who was now my best friend. Their mother lived there too. Their father had died years before, fighting Castro, which was something that made Juan and Adelita very proud. So proud that they were continuing his legacy.

They were part of a group of counterrevolutionaries, people whose main goal was to resist Castro's government by causing mayhem and destruction. Adelita helped organize their meetings and transmit messages between them. When she told me what she was doing, I said I wanted to help too. I had grown up under the regime, with my teachers attempting to indoctrinate me. But my parents didn't believe in the Revolution, and neither did I. Now I was old enough to try to do something about it.

Chucho, Juan's best friend, ran a bakery in town and we had a code: an extra piece of bread in the bag meant there was a job to do. We were successful for about a year before the police arrested Juan and Chucho for setting fire to a sugarcane field. Chucho was given a joke of a trial and shot at the wall. We were so worried the same would happen to Juan. His joke of a trial resulted in a life sentence, which would only last, we knew, if he survived it. At the prison, they would not allow visitors, but he was able to sneak letters out. He wrote me saying, "Mirta, forget about me. There's no way I'll live through this. The food alone will kill me, if the guards don't. Go back to the city, to your parents, to your life. Do not waste it waiting for me."

But I couldn't—not for two years. Finally, Adelita and their mother, Dolores, convinced me Juan was right. He would never make it out. His life was all but over. "But yours isn't," Adelita said. I was only twenty-three, she told me, with my life ahead of me, waiting to be lived.

I left the farm then, telling myself Juan would die in jail, that I was doing what he asked of me. I moved back to the city and requested a divorce, which was granted because of his life sentence. When I received the papers verifying that the divorce was final, I couldn't even look at them.

My mother took them from me without saying a word and placed them in the box where she kept all the family documents.

I was assigned to work at La Periquera museum, where I led tours. On one of them, I met your father, who was escorting family visiting from La Habana. Afterward he asked if he could take me out sometime. "For a walk or maybe to eat some lunch." He had kind eyes and I didn't know how to say no, so I said yes.

We began dating and it felt okay. He had a gentleness about him that I liked, and he made me laugh—something I had not done much of in the past few years. He knew I had been married before, to a contrarevolucionario who was now in jail, and he didn't care. He loved me, he said, so I did what everyone told me to do: I married him. Within a month I was pregnant with your brother and living a whole new life.

6

I find Robert in the spare room with the iguanas. There are twenty of them, each about as big as my hand, in tanks all over the floor. He bought them off his friend Flaco's brother and he's supposed to sell them to this guy Laz from the track, but Laz isn't answering his texts.

Robert has one of the iguanas out. "Watch this, Mon," he says, and lets it walk from his hand up to the inside of his elbow. "Cool, right?"

"Super cool," I say. "Have you sprayed them yet?"

"No. I just got in here."

I get the spray bottle off the windowsill and walk around, spritzing each iguana, thinking, *How is this normal?*

Robert is making little kissing noises, trying to get the iguana to keep crawling up his arm. "I'm calling him the Hulk," he says. "'Cause he's the biggest."

"Oh my God, no. Do *not* name them."

"Why not?"

"They're not your pets. They're your . . . your business venture." I start tearing pieces off a head of lettuce he's brought in. "Have you heard from Laz?"

"No. He should have been home by now. I'll text him again."

He puts the Hulk back into his tank and feeds him a piece of lettuce. He asks about my mom and I think again about what she said to me before surgery, and then about how close she's come to dying since. But I force myself to focus on the positive, so I tell him about the plan to wake her up in a couple of days.

Robert walks over to the Hulk's cage and runs a finger down his back. "See you tomorrow, buddy."

"You *are* going to sell these, right?"

"Yes."

"All of them?"

"*Yes.*"

But what if he doesn't? Or what if he sells them all but wants to keep the Hulk? Then we'll have a newborn in *this* room, assuming Laz ever calls. And Robert will keep the Hulk where? In the living room? Our bedroom? A dull ache begins in my left temple.

Robert comes up behind me. "I know what *you* need." He's joking, but he's also pressing up against me. He starts kissing my neck. "You're in the second trimester. Isn't this supposed to be when you're into it?"

"I'm really tired. I need to take a shower."

"Okay," he says, the disappointment in his voice clear. I feel bad, but not bad enough to change my mind.

When I get out of the shower, he's already asleep, thank God, so I lie there reading a pregnancy chat thread about toxins. Somebody mentions reptiles. Reptiles, apparently, can give you salmonella, which can cause a miscarriage.

I sit up. Oh my God, how did I not know this? I Google *reptiles and pregnancy* and read the first three hits, panicking. I learn that as long as we wash our hands after handling the iguanas and don't let them walk on the kitchen counters, we should be fine. I feel calmer, but I still want Robert to know all about this. I text him the articles so he can read them in the morning.

It takes me a while to fall asleep, and when I do, sure enough, I dream I have a miscarriage. There are birds in the room while it's happening. They're big and dark and they're trying to get out. They keep flying into the window, their wings spread out like capes, banging into the glass. Meanwhile, I'm in the bed with all this blood. It's pooling in the sheets and blankets, in my underwear, everywhere. I keep looking for the baby, but I can't find him. I search through all the blood, afraid he's drowning in it. I scoop and scoop with my hands, feeling for his little arms, his bulbous eyes. When I wake up, my fingers feel tingly, as if I was doing the scooping in real life. My heart's going crazy, and my bladder is about to pop. Robert's asleep on his back, his arms above his head like he's cheering. He's snoring loudly.

In the bathroom, I turn on the light to inspect the toilet paper after I wipe. Everything looks fine, but I'm too awake to sleep, so I make some tea and turn on HGTV. The baby starts moving, pressing into my right side. I press back. I love it when he does this. "Hi there," I say to him. I talk to him a lot, sometimes out loud, sometimes in my head. Usually when I'm driving home from work, I tell him about my day: how many patients yelled at Sandra because Dr. Peña was running behind, how many times I had to call Blue Cross for a clarification. Or I'll put on NPR and tell him about whatever's happening in the world. Normally it's horrible stuff like George Zimmerman or the embassy in Libya. But sometimes it's a six-year-old violin prodigy playing with a professional orchestra or twin parrots who sing Dolly Parton songs. I make sure to tell him that kind of thing too.

Robert also talks to him every night. One night, after we ate Chinese food, the baby started kicking me like crazy. So now when Robert's talking to him, he calls him Taz, like Tasmanian Devil. He'll pull up my shirt and flick my stomach. "Hey, Taz," he'll say. "This is your dad speaking." I don't call him Taz. I call him "mijo."

I look at my phone, scrolling to that last text from Manny. It came in one night when Robert and I were out playing pool with Flaco and his girlfriend. My phone dinged from inside my purse and Robert asked who it was—something he does all the time because he was cheated on really badly by his last girlfriend.

"Caro. I'll call her later," I said, and dropped the phone back into my purse. I took my shot, which sucked because my hands were shaking so bad. After about ten minutes I went to the bathroom to read the text again. *Hey, just thinking about you,* it said. *Miss you.* It made me mad and broke me into pieces at the same time.

He was deployed for a lot of the five years we were together. He served three tours in Afghanistan; one was the Army's choice, two were his. When he reenlisted the first time, he said it was because he felt like he hadn't finished his job.

"But this could go on forever," I said. We were on our way home from dinner with his sister and her girlfriend.

"I know. But it just doesn't feel right to be here, doing regular stuff, going to fucking Cheesecake Factory, when they're still over there doing that." We were stopped at a light, but he wouldn't look at me. "I'm sorry, Mónica. It's hard to explain."

I put my hand on the back of his neck. "I know. I know it is."

By the end of his second tour, he had lost three friends. One stepped on an IED, one died in a firefight, and another one drowned in a ditch filled with water when he got blown out the back of his Humvee.

Some nights Manny would move in his sleep, kicking his legs and mumbling, louder and louder, until he'd shout himself awake. One time he brought his arm up and pounded it back down on the bed an inch from my face. I learned to wake him up when I felt the kicking. Eventually, I stopped asking him if he wanted to talk about it and I would just put him back to sleep like a child, running my hands softly down the side of his face, his back, his arms.

He got his crane operator's license as soon as he came back from the first tour and the hours were long, the jobs always far away, up in Broward or down in the Keys. And he worked a lot of overtime. If he got home earlier than 8:00 p.m., he'd go to the gym. It felt like he was hiding. From me. From the pain of losing his friends. And losing his father.

On our first date, he'd told me that he was enlisted and was supposed to be gone already but they had given him a deferment because his dad was doing chemo and it didn't look good. "It's kind of a last-shot thing," he said. I thought it was weird that he would tell me that on our first date, and I asked him about it a few weeks later. "It didn't feel like a first date," he said. "It felt like I had known you my whole life." When he said it, I realized I had felt the same way.

After his second tour, I told him I wanted to get married, start a family. He said he wanted those things, too, but then he'd take more overtime shifts and avoid me on the weekends. When he re-enlisted a third time, I was so mad I didn't talk to him for a week. I stuck with him for half of the tour until I realized my mom was right about his commitment to me, and I was afraid of him coming home and doing it all again. I Skyped him one Sunday night and told him I needed to break up. He didn't fight me, and that hurt almost more than the breakup.

I drink the last sip of my tea, now cold, and put the mug down on the side table. It's one of the few pieces of furniture in the house that's mine. I wanted to bring my sofa, but Robert hated it. He said it was too close to the ground. "I feel like a grasshopper every time I sit in it. And it's too hard," he said. So I sold it and now I'm here with Robert's overstuffed couch and black lacquer coffee table. I want to redecorate so badly it's killing me. Every time I sit in here, I think about the Mouse House, how much I loved it, how it was mine and no one else's.

The miscarriage dream floats by in my head: the birds, the blood, the baby. I try to push it away and instead think about the baby as a little boy, with flat, wide fingernails like my brother's and Robert's gray-green eyes. I think about my mother lying in the ICU. For the thousandth time this week I replay her last words to me before she went in: *Your father is Juan.* I tell myself, again, that it was the drugs. It had to be the drugs.

I look down at Manny's thread again, reading and rereading. *No,* I tell myself. *No. That's over. I'm here now, with Robert.*

The HGTV show is wrapping up and I decide to go back to bed. I shift Robert to his side so he'll stop snoring and curl up around him. *I'm here now,* I say again in my head. I make it a little chant—*I'm here now, I'm here now*—that I say over and over until I fall asleep.

Mirta

*The Mariel boatlift started in April of 1980, and your father said this was
our chance to get away from the food rationing and the lack of money and the
block captains who reported you for reading the wrong kinds of books. I hated
the Revolution just as much as he did, but I wasn't as sure about leaving.
My parents didn't want to go. Neither did my sisters. But Rolando did, and
he was my husband, the father of my baby. It had been five years since Juan
had gone to jail, three since I had left the farm. I had convinced myself that
Juan was probably dead and I had cut all contact with his sister, Adelita. I
had to—it was too painful. I had a new life now, with Rolando, who finally
convinced me to let him apply for the boatlift. Two months later, we left.*

*We had been living in Miami for almost a year when I finally agreed
to the English class Rolando had been wanting me to take. On the first
night, I walked into the classroom and someone called my name. "Mirta,"
the woman said, and it was like a bell ringing inside me. I looked toward
the voice and there was Adelita, sitting in the first row. Next to her was
Juan. He looked up from the desk and I saw those eyes that were blue like
the water in Varadero and that black curly hair. And a mustache he had
not had in Cuba. "Oh my God," I said.*

*Adelita got up and put her arms around me. "Mirta," she said, into
my hair. "No lo creo."*

We walked back out into the hallway and Juan followed. He did not hug me or even touch my hand. The look on his face told me he was afraid to. I guess he had seen my wedding ring.

"You told me they would kill you," I said to him.

"They tried to. But it didn't work." He smiled. "He let a bunch of us out in '79. There were some negotiations—those people who went to see him."

"What people?"

"El Comité de los 75. They negotiated our release."

Adelita looked up at him. "Thank God," she said, touching his arm. Then she looked at me. "When I found out he was being released and sent to the States, I went to see your grandmother. But"—she shook her head—"she told me things had changed for you."

I gripped the notebook I had brought with me and the metal spirals cut into my hand. "She never told me," I said. Not that it would have mattered. By 1979, I was already married to your father, and had I known Juan was out, it would have killed me.

"When did you leave Cuba?" she asked.

"August of last year. I came on the boatlift," I told them. "With my husband and my son."

She leaned in and smiled. "You have a son. How old? What's his name?" We had been best friends. Of course she wanted to know everything.

"His name is Pablo." I took out my wallet and showed them the pictures I kept in the plastic sleeves. His first birthday. His baptism we did here in Miami a month after we arrived. "He's almost two now."

Juan was quiet at first. He shifted his weight and looked away, down the hall. I could feel him taking it all in: the way in which my life had changed, how far apart we were now. Finally he said, "That's wonderful. I'm sure he makes you very happy." I wasn't sure which "he" he was talking about.

We spent the rest of the class sitting in the hallway, talking about the old days when we all lived on the farm together, then about what we were doing now. Adelita was working at a laundry near their apartment. Juan was working with their cousin, laying tile and digging ditches for a communications company in the evenings. They lived together, along with their mother, who had been diagnosed with lung cancer and was undergoing chemotherapy. Juan's face—that face I thought I'd never see again—darkened with pain as Adelita talked about her prognosis, which was not good.

At the end of the hour, the other students came filing out of the classroom and the three of us said goodbye. Adelita asked me for the notebook I was holding and wrote her phone number down on the first page, which was still blank, since we never went to class that day.

"Call me," she said.

I sighed and shook my head. "I'm not sure." She was a reminder of all that I had lost. Not just Juan but also a purpose. There is meaning in being a mother, of course; you'll know this soon enough yourself. But it isn't the same as working for the freedom of your country.

Adelita hugged me. She asked Juan for the keys to the car, then squeezed my arm before walking away.

Juan turned to me. "Are you coming back next week?"

I looked in the direction of the parking lot, where I knew your father was waiting for me. "I don't know."

"I'll be here," Juan said. "Please, Mirta, come back."

7

On Friday, I'm at my desk, drinking a Diet Dr Pepper—my favorite—and working on last week's claims, when my father calls to say they're going to wake her up. They've been weaning her off the oxygen for a couple of days now. I tell my office manager, Val, what's happening and she says, "Go."

By the time I walk through the doors of my mom's room, they've got the breathing tube out and she's sitting up. The doctor is in there, along with my father and Caro, who must have taken the day off. I wish I had done the same.

"Mom," I say, rushing over to hug her. She shrinks a little in my arms, as if she's afraid of me, so I step back. Her eyes seem lost and sad. She looks so strange it scares me, but she's awake and that's all that matters. I swallow three times to get rid of the knot in my throat.

My mother looks down at her lap and, in this tiny, scratchy whisper, says, "No lo creo."

My father smiles. "Yo también no lo creo. Pero here you are. Alive."

Dr. Summers says, "Mrs. Campo, don't strain your voice if it hurts to talk." He smiles at her. He's in his sixties. American, but not intimidating.

My mother closes her eyes, then opens them and, in Spanish, says to Dr. Summers, "I thought he was dead. But then there he was. With Adelita right next to him. I couldn't believe it."

Dr. Summers looks at my father for a translation, but my father just frowns.

"You thought who was dead?" I say. "Mom, what are you talking about?"

She doesn't answer.

My father puts his hand on hers and smiles. "Mirta, listen," he says in English, I guess because Dr. Summers is here. "You're in Baptist Hospital. Te operaron, remember? It's 2012. You're waking up now."

My mother looks at me, at my belly.

"Mom, it's me, Mónica." I try Spanish, just to make her feel better. "Yo soy Mónica. Yo soy tu hija." I put my hands on my stomach. "Y aquí está tu nieto. Tu niño."

"Mónica," she says. "Mi hija."

"Sí. And Dad's here too." I look at my father.

"Rolando," he says, and points to their wedding picture in its frame.

My mother looks at the picture and then at my father again. Her face softens into recognition. "Rolando. Sí, Rolando."

She looks at Caro. "Carolina," she says, smiling a little. She's always loved Caro, who is a better Cuban daughter than I am: she's married to a Cuban guy and they have two little girls in Catholic school who they take to church every Sunday.

Caro smiles. She's wearing her brown hair highlighted and straight these days. Today she has it up in a high ponytail, which makes her look more twenty-five than thirty-five. "Hi, Tía Mirta. It's so wonderful to have you back."

My mother starts to cry.

Dr. Summers says, "That's fine. Many patients experience a variety of emotions coming out of sedation. You're doing great. And we have an excellent team here taking care of you." He pats her shoulder and smiles. "Well, I'm going to go finish my rounds. Welcome back, Mrs. Campo. We missed you."

The nurse asks my mother her full name, if she knows what year it is, and who the president is. She answers all the questions correctly and rolls her eyes on the last one, which I take as a good sign. Her vitals are fine except for the blood pressure, which is a little high. "We'll keep an eye on that," the nurse says. "And I'll let Dr. Summers know."

A few minutes later my brother shows up. It takes my mother a minute, but then she says, "Pablito." She never calls him that. Except when she's coming out of a coma, apparently.

My father pulls the pictures off the walls and shows them to her one by one. First, Caro and Mike and their girls. Next, Caro's parents, Tío Fermín and Tía Gladys, and her younger brother, Eddie. We show them to her slowly, so she won't be too overwhelmed. She keeps zoning out and then zoning back in, asking who each person is, except when we get to the picture of Caro's older brother, Fernando. He and his wife are chiropractors in Sarasota and sell blue-green algae out of their office. The picture of them Caro brought is from their website: them in lab coats with their clinic's motto—*Maximize Your Life!*—written underneath. When my mother sees it, she twirls her index finger next to her temple. "Locos," she says, and we all, even Caro, start laughing, the relief in the room like a drug making us all high. For a moment I almost forget how close she came to dying.

Mirta

I did come back as Juan asked me to, many times. But I never actually
went to class. Your father would drive me to the school and I would walk
through the double doors, then wait until he drove away to walk right back
out to Juan's car waiting for me in the teachers' parking lot. We would go
to Tamiami Park to sit at the picnic tables and talk for the two hours I was
supposed to be learning English. It was a little like the old days in Cuba
when we'd go into town to sit on the stone benches in El Parque Calixto
García.

Then one night we went to the motel. By then he had already taken my
face in his hands to kiss me and I had let him. I did it without thinking;
in situations like that, there is no thinking. So when he pulled into the
parking lot of the Palmetto Motel, I said nothing. I followed him into room
four, where I let him unbutton my shirt and put his hands on me and say,
"Mi belleza, mi belleza," over and over.

On the ride back to school, he held my hand, rubbing my thumb with
his. He parked and I slipped back inside and waited, like always, to see the
blue Corolla pull up five minutes later. "¡Mami!" your brother called from
the back seat. For the next two months, that's how it went. Adelita stayed in
the course and learned how to ask where the bathroom is and how to order
a sandwich. I learned how to lie to my husband without looking nervous.

8

Now that my mother's awake, everybody's blowing up my phone, wanting to know when they can come, what they can bring. Tía Gladys leaves me two messages about the arroz con pollo she's dropping by tonight. And Tío Fermín calls to ask when visiting hours are, because God forbid he look them up himself. All four of my father's cousins from Jersey call in succession, wanting the update and asking why my father isn't calling them back. I text one and tell her to tell all the others: my mother is still in the surgical ICU and only about half there. Most of the time she's either asleep or loopy on the drugs and saying weird shit. I don't say *shit* in the text.

That night, when Robert gives her a kiss hello, she says, in Spanish, "I'll get the chickens. You get the donkey. And Adelita will get Fresa."

He looks at me.

"Mom?" I say. "What are you talking about? Who's Adelita? Who's Fresa?"

"La vaca," she says, with her eyes closed.

"'La vaca,' like *moo*?" I laugh a little, but she doesn't.

Robert says, "The cow?"

I put my hand on her arm. She smiles at my stomach and says in English, "Let's do the baby shower at Caro's house. We'll do it how the young people do it with the men there, too, if you want." Then she tears up. "I'm sorry, mi niña. I'm sorry I did this."

"Mom, you didn't do anything. We'll let you get some rest. I think you need it."

In the waiting room, we sit with my father and Pablo and Maritza. I serve the arroz con pollo. My phone pings three times in a row and Robert asks, "Who's that?"

"My other boyfriend," I tell him. It's what I've started saying every time he asks me who's texting. It's just my mom's best friend Teresita, asking for an update.

He rolls his eyes and asks me what my mom was talking about with the cow and the chickens and all that.

"No idea. And I don't know who Adelita is, either."

"What?" my father says and puts his fork down.

"Mom was talking about someone named Adelita."

"And a cow and some chickens," Robert says.

"When?" my father asks.

"Just now."

He frowns, picks up his fork to keep eating, but puts it back down again. A minute later he gets up without saying anything and walks out the door.

The next day she goes to the step-down unit on the sixth floor. It's the halfway point between the ICU and a regular room, which means she has a TV. That night, I turn on Univision and turn up the volume so we can hear the *Abismo* theme song, which she loves. As the actors' faces and names come flashing across the screen, I try to give her the CliffsNotes version of everything she's missed. When Jaquelín comes on-screen, I take it as a sign.

"Mom," I say. "Um . . . before surgery, you said"—I freeze, trying to find the words—"you said you had the same problem as Jaquelín."

"I did? What problem?" She's slurring from her bedtime dose of Ativan.

"A problem with a baby. With a pregnancy."

"I had no problems with my pregnancies."

"No, no. You said you didn't tell someone you were pregnant. You don't remember?"

"No." Her eyes droop, heavy. Her chin is dropping in real time.

"You also said Juan is my father. Do you remember saying that?"

"I didn't say that. I would never have said that."

"You did. You said Juan was my father and you loved him and never told him. Is that—what does that mean?" I lean in, touch her hand. "Mom?"

"There's no way I said that."

"I promise, you did. . . . Mom?" I squeeze her shoulder softly. "Mom?" But she's totally out.

I try to watch the rest of the show but all I can think about is what she said. Or, rather, what she didn't say. She didn't say, *That's not true.* Or *Who's Juan?* Or *Your father is your father.* All she said was that she didn't say it.

In the elevator, I find myself scrolling back to Manny's last message. I read it again. In the lobby, the doors open and I step out and begin typing. *My mom had heart surgery and something is happening. Just want to ask you a couple questions. Can I call you?* I press Send before I can have another thought. My heart thumps so hard it's difficult to breathe.

Right when I get outside, my phone rings and it's him. Jesus Christ. I stop walking and stare at the giant pineapple fountain in front of the hospital, trying to slow my heart. The fountain is lit up so the pineapple looks like it's sparkling, the water flowing off of the leaves and into the pool, which, I realize now, has a rubber ducky floating in it. I nod at the ducky and answer the phone.

"Are you okay?" Manny says, and I can feel every cell in my body.

"I've been better. But at least my mom's out of the coma."

"Holy shit. Was that after the surgery?" His voice sounds exactly the same: deep and a little loud. Assured.

"Yep. For a week. It was like medical Whac-A-Mole. They'd get one thing stabilized, then something else would tank." Because of his medical background, I give him the detailed version.

"Oh, babe," he says. "I'm sorry." *Babe.* I haven't actually talked to him in over a year. I didn't even know if he was here, in the States, or back there again, doing another tour.

He asks me about her numbers—O_2, blood pressure, heart rate—and I picture every part of his face in my mind. The freckle on his bottom lip, right where you would put lip liner if he were a woman. The little black pelitos between his eyebrows that he would sometimes let me tweeze if he was stoned or just in a good mood. My legs are shaking so bad I don't think I can walk to my car, so I sit on one of the benches by the entrance.

"And what about you?" he says. "How are you doing?"

"I'm, you know—" I look up at the sky. The moon is a sliver.

"Shitty?" he says. He was never one to sugarcoat anything. When they were sent to Kunar Province, he didn't try to convince me that what he was doing was safe. I knew about the raids they went on, the gun battles in the Korangal Valley.

"Yeah, pretty shitty." A family of smokers walks out. Mom, dad, two teens. They all light up. I scoot down the bench to get away from them. "Actually, I called because I want to ask you a question about medication. What do you know about fentanyl?"

"Do they have her on it for pain?"

"No. They gave it to her before surgery, I think, and also something called Versed? She said something super weird in pre-op and I'm trying to figure out if it could have been the drugs."

"What did she say?"

I lower my voice. "She said my real father is Juan." Saying the words out loud makes my stomach churn.

"Who's Juan?"

"I have no idea. She was talking about a character on her telenovela who hid a pregnancy and she said she did the same thing. And that my father is Juan. Do you think she could have been hallucinating? I looked it up and it said there's a small chance."

"Sure. Fentanyl's an opioid and some people do have adverse reactions, but it's not common. It's more likely to just make you high as hell. Was there anyone else in the room with you? Was your father there?"

"No, no. That's the thing: she said my father would never have told me. It felt like she was telling me a secret. I asked her about it again tonight, and she said she didn't remember saying it. Then she fell asleep."

"She probably *doesn't* remember. The Versed would have wiped all that out. It's basically a roofie; it'll relax the hell out of you, but you won't remember shit. Sounds like you need to talk to her again. How's her cognition when she's awake?"

"It's whatever. Better, I guess. But it's hard to get her alone. My father's pretty much there all day. Or the nurse, or the respiratory therapist, you know . . ."

"Yeah, maybe just wait till she gets out? I think it's possible that with the fentanyl she was really high and—who knows?—maybe she was just saying crazy shit."

"You think?" A tiny blip of hope flashes through me.

"It's possible. People say anything on opioids."

The smokers have finished up and left but now there's a woman dictating a text about the Airbnb she owns. Out of nowhere, the baby kicks me, almost like he's reminding me, *I exist and you shouldn't be doing this.*

"Okay, yeah," I say. "Thanks for . . . I just . . . I needed to talk to someone about this. And I thought maybe you would know about the drugs and everything."

"No problem," Manny says. "Keep me posted, okay? Let me know how things are going?"

"Okay," I say, like an idiot. "I'll let you know." I'm not even sure if I say goodbye. I know I touch the button on my phone and sit there, shaking a little, feeling what I always feel: the excitement, the sadness, the anger. And, of course, the love. After all this time, it's still there, at the center of me, like a river that won't dry up.

Mirta

I made a mistake, Mónica. A mistake that changed my life. When the English class ended, we tried to stop seeing each other, but we couldn't. Always one of us would call the other and we would end up meeting at the motel on his lunch break. If Pablo was asleep, I would carry him into the room, put him on the bed, and Juan and I would slip into the bathroom.

If Pablo was awake, we would put him in the pool. Juan would take off his work boots and sit with his feet in the water, his pants rolled up around his calves. In the grass behind him, the hibiscus bushes bloomed—those huge red flowers that looked like mouths. He would bend down to splash Pablo and I would catch myself pretending we were a family. Then I would snap back to reality, aching with the joy of seeing his face and the regret of ever having let him go.

Some nights I would tell Rolando I was going to visit my friend Josefina from English class, when really I was going to the motel to meet Juan—sometimes to make love, but sometimes just to be together, eating the arroz con leche I had made for him. Sometimes, of course, we did both.

For months, it went on like this—my double life. And it wasn't just Juan I was seeing behind your father's back. I started spending time with Adelita, too, at the laundromat where she worked. She would let me do my sheets for free and we would stand at the counter and talk while Pablo drove his carritos all over the blue plastic chairs. Sometimes, on her days off, I would go to their apartment. We'd drink coffee and practice English. I would bring a bag of toys for Pablo and Adelita would teach me the sentences the English teacher had taught her. I was so happy to be seeing her, to have my friend back, that I didn't even feel bad about the fact that your father had no idea.

9

When they move my mom to a regular room, everyone my parents have ever known shows up. The ladies from my mother's salon, the people who work for my father at the optical. The old tías and tíos who might not actually be blood relatives. And my parents' old friends from Cuba who have moved here over the years.

They gather in the waiting room, taking turns coming in to see my mother, bringing her all manner of contraband food: croquetas and pastelitos and, of course, café. Nearly every person who arrives walks in with una colada de café and the tiny plastic cups to serve it in.

My mother smiles and says, "Gracias por venir," and tells each of them how she almost died. How she was in a coma for a week.

"A medical coma," I say.

"Yes, a medical coma," she says. "But still."

"Thank God you're okay," they all say, then head back out to the waiting room to drink the rest of the coffee and gossip.

Pablo calls it the Cuban National Convention—only it's happening for a week, not a day. He comes every other day, always has Maritza with him, and stays an hour, maybe two if there's food. I come straight from work every day and stay until my mom goes to sleep.

One night I come back from the bathroom and there, sitting in the corner, is Manny.

"Fuck, what the fuck?" I whisper.

He looks up then, blinks hard at my stomach, and comes over to where I'm standing.

"What are you doing here?" I say. He's holding a small arrangement of flowers with a balloon that says *Get Well Soon*.

"Damn," he says, shaking his head at my stomach. "That's a surprise."

"I know. I didn't tell you."

"No, you didn't." Anger flashes across his face. "Why didn't you tell me?" He looks at my hand. "And married? Are you married?"

"Engaged. I'm sorry. I just didn't think it was relevant."

"I'd say it's pretty relevant." He's wearing shorts and a white button-down, untucked. And, of course, a baseball cap. Yankees, not Marlins, for his father, who lived in New York.

"I'm sorry."

"No, *I'm* sorry. I wouldn't have come if I'd known. But you didn't let me know—about anything. I called the hospital to check on your mom's condition and they said she was stable, so I thought it would be okay to drop these off." He holds out the flowers to me.

My father comes into the waiting room then. Tía Gladys and Teresita, my mom's best friend, are sitting two chairs away, pretending not to stare. They know exactly who this is.

Manny says, "Your father told me you'd be right back."

"You talked to my father?"

"He looked even more surprised to see me than I thought he would. Now I know why."

"He didn't know we'd been talking." I can't believe Manny's

actually standing in front of me. I haven't seen him in person for almost two years.

"So, who's the lucky guy?" he says. "Is he here? Do I get to meet him? Say congratulations?" He looks around at everyone in the waiting room, scans their faces. They're all my parents' friends except for a family of American people over by the vending machine.

"His name is Robert. Robert Copple."

"Like 'Bond. James Bond.' Is he a spy?" He puts his hands in his pockets and leans against the back of a chair no one's sitting in. This is Shitty Manny. Threatened Manny.

"He's racing tonight."

"Racing?"

"He races cars."

"For a living? He's a race car driver?"

"No. For a living he delivers for Deer Park. But he's working on his bachelor's. To do financial planning." For some reason I feel like I have to tell him this, to make Robert sound more legit, maybe to make my decision to marry him and have this baby sound more legit.

"So, what, he just races cars for fun?"

"Yeah, like, for his hobby."

"Great. Cool." He points to my hand. "And you're engaged."

"Yeah."

"Wow. Big news. So when are you due?"

"January twentieth. It's a boy."

"Great, great." He won't look me in the face. "So, um, your father said your mom might go home by the end of the week?"

"Hopefully. The blood pressure is still a problem. And they still have her on a cannula at night."

"Did she have any comorbidities they didn't know about?"

"Not that I know of. She just—I don't know. Her body just couldn't take it, I guess. It was weird. I mean, her blood pressure's been a problem for years now, but that's the only thing."

"Is she walking around?"

"She walked to the nurses' station this morning. Then she had to take a nap."

I watch Teresita leave for my mom's room. Great. Now I'll get to hear about how Manny didn't respect me enough to commit and how Robert is a wonderful man who loves me.

He adjusts his cap. "So any more info about the thing she said?"

I check to make sure my father's out of earshot. "I haven't been able to ask her again. She's been pretty out of it. And now"—I look around the waiting room—"I mean, forget it. Somebody's always in there." Also, I'm scared to ask her again. I don't say this to Manny, but I want to.

Now we're quiet. I could ask him about work. I could ask him about his family. I could ask him if he's engaged too. But I know he's not. He wouldn't be here if he were. And I don't want to ask him anything except the one thing I can't ask him, which is why I wasn't enough to keep him home. God, his beautiful face. My back starts to hurt a little, so I shift my weight from one foot to the other.

"Okay, well, sorry to barge in," he says. "Please give your mom my best."

"Of course. No problem. Thanks for coming."

He looks down at my stomach for another split second. And then he leaves. No kiss, no hug. He doesn't even say goodbye. He just walks toward the door while I stand there, trying not to cry.

Mirta

One night, Juan and I were at the motel, lying in bed, drowsy, about to get dressed, and someone knocked at the door. Juan thought it was the manager. There were a lot of comings and goings at the Palmetto. Probably a lot of people doing what we were doing, or worse. The person knocked again, and Juan put on his pants.

From the open door, Rolando could see me lying in the bed. A moment later he was in the room, yelling at me to get up, then pulling me out of the bed himself. I weighed nothing in those days, and when he yanked me up, I lost my balance and fell into the dresser.

"¡Súeltala!" Juan yelled, but Rolando wouldn't let me go.

Rolando gathered my clothes and grabbed me again. I twisted and turned, trying to get free, but he was holding me too tight. He dragged me, naked, into the street while I screamed for my clothes and he screamed back, terrible things, awful things. You can imagine.

The car was in the middle of the parking lot, still running. Rolando shoved me in, threw my clothes in my lap, and reached down to the floorboard for something. I got my underwear on, my shorts halfway up, and then I heard, "Mami."

I had no idea your father had brought him. I didn't know what I thought: that he had left him alone at the apartment? That he had called Gladys to come over? No. He had lifted him out of bed and put him into the back seat asleep. Now he was awake and looking at me.

I have never felt more ashamed in my life.

Across the parking lot, I heard yelling and saw your father hit Juan in the ribs with a stick. He did it again and Juan doubled over. I pulled my shorts all the way up, put my shirt on, and ran to Rolando. I tried to push him away, but he pushed me right back. The stick in his hand, I saw now, was the miniature bat the cousins from New Jersey had brought Pablo when they came to visit. It was about as long as a man's forearm—small, but big enough to hurt. It said Yankees on it in blue.

When Juan slumped to the ground, your father started kicking him. Juan curled up right there on the sidewalk, his body closed like a fist, his arms around his head. He wasn't even trying to fight back. Rolando hit him and hit him with the bat. He kicked him too. He called him a piece of shit, un cabrón, un pendejo. He yelled at him to get up and fight like a man.

The door to room three opened and two men came out. They screamed at your father to stop, telling him that they had called the police, he'd better stop. But he didn't stop. He just kept going, hitting Juan over and over on the shoulders, kicking him in the back, in the legs. Juan was making terrible sounds, like an animal, and I felt like I was the one being beaten. I stood there and screamed at your father to get control of himself.

Finally, a police car turned into the parking lot with its lights on. Two policemen got out, and when they saw what was happening, they ran, not walked, over to us. It took both of them to pull Rolando away, to get that little bat out of his hand. When they did, I realized he was crying.

As soon as they had him, I threw myself down to Juan. He was still curled up, his arms covering his head. Up close, I saw that he had lost control of his bladder. I stroked the back of his head like he was a child. "It's over," I said. "It's over."

But he wouldn't move his arms from his head. He wouldn't uncurl. He was making a different sound now, a nnn-nnn-nnn sound, like a machine. I rubbed his back and whispered, "I'm sorry."

One of the policemen came over to me. "Can you tell me what happened?"

Behind him, still in the back seat of the car, your brother was crying, calling me, banging his hand on the glass.

The policeman looked back at the car. "Is that your child?"

"Yes."

"You need to get him out."

"I know." I pointed to Juan; he was still making that sound. "I just need to help him here for a second."

"Señora, go get your child," the policeman said.

So I stood up. As I did, I heard the policeman say to Juan, "We've got him. He's in the car. We're taking him away."

I crossed the parking lot to get Pablo. His tete was still attached to the string pinned to his pajamas. I put it back in his mouth and he sucked and cried while I patted his back and tried not to think about what a bad mother I was. On the other side of the parking lot, Rolando was sitting in the back of the police car, nodding as the other officer talked to him.

The ambulance arrived a few minutes later. They worked on Juan— something with his left leg, his left arm, heart, lungs. They lifted him onto the stretcher. His face was scratched and swollen from being on the pavement. His right arm was cut and bleeding.

"I'm so sorry," I said. "I don't know how this happened. I'm so sorry." But he wouldn't talk to me. As they wheeled him away, he turned his face to the sky.

10

A couple of nights later, Caro beelines it for me. "Oh my God. Manny came here? Why didn't you tell me?"

I pull her out of the waiting room into the hallway. "Who told you? Your mom or mine?"

"Both."

"I have to pee. Come with me to the bathroom."

Inside, I check all the stalls to make sure we're alone. "Yeah, he just showed up."

"Like, out of nowhere?" We pee and she flushes and leaves her stall. It takes me another minute to get my leggings up.

"Yeah," I say. "That's what he does."

"How did he even know about the surgery?"

We're at the sinks, washing our hands now and talking through the mirror. I deliver the lie I've had prepared for two days. "He probably heard from his aunt. She does her hair at my mom's salon."

I wish I could tell Caro everything. But she doesn't understand my thing with Manny. She never has. Caro's a good girl who would never text her ex-boyfriend behind her fiancé's back. Especially while pregnant. "So, how was it to see him?" she asks, reapplying her lip liner.

"It was okay. You know, a little weird."

She pauses, holds her lip pencil in the air like it's a pointer. "A little? You guys went out for like five years. Did he even know you're pregnant?"

"Nope."

She turns away from the mirror and looks at the real me. "Are you okay?"

I am definitely not okay. "It wasn't great," I say, "but I don't have a choice, right?"

"He came here for you. Obviously. But you know what?" She points to my stomach. "You've moved on."

"Yep," I say, but I can't look at her—the mirrored her or the real her—when I say it.

We're cleaning up the dinner Tía Gladys brought and a report about a political prisoner in Cuba comes on the TV. Apparently, he died of a hunger strike. My mother says, more to the window than to anyone, "Adelita and Dolores said they would kill him. We thought he was gone. Dead."

Gladys pops the tops back on the Tupperware. "You thought who was dead?"

Before my mother can answer, my father says sternly, as if he's talking to a child, "Mirta, please. We're here in the hospital, finishing up dinner. Gladys made us a beautiful meal." He turns to Gladys and makes a production of thanking her.

She smiles. "De nada, Rolando. It's my pleasure."

My mother says, "Sí, Gladys. Gracias. Era muy rico."

My father turns off the TV, thanks Gladys again for the food, and then says we should all go so my mom can get some rest. He walks Fermín and Gladys out, almost like a security guard, hands hovering near their lower backs.

A few minutes later he wants me to leave with him, but I want to stay and talk to my mother.

"I'm going to watch *Abismo* with Mom," I tell him. "I promise I'll leave as soon as it's over." He looks like he wants to say something, but he doesn't. He just kisses us each goodbye and leaves.

Clara is back from the cult and now engaged to Sebastián, the guy Armando owed the money to. My mom can't believe they're engaged, but Clara is just pretending to be in love with him in order to save herself and Armando, who is still in the dungeon cell in Sebastián's hacienda.

"Pobrecita," my mother says. "What is she going to do? She's trapped."

I'm eating the chocolate pudding that came with her hospital dinner and drinking a Diet Dr Pepper. "She'll figure it out," I say. The baby wakes up and starts kicking. "Mom, look." I point to my stomach.

"Oh!" she says. "Let me touch him!" When she places both hands on my belly, I'm so relieved I almost laugh out loud. "Mi niño. I can't wait to hold you," she says. She looks at me. "You used to do this too. Always after I ate."

"I guess he likes pudding." He kicks and flips around, and she moves her hands all over my stomach, feeling him do it.

"Mónica, I need to ask you a question," she says, her tone completely serious now. "What was Manny doing here?"

Here we go, I think. "Nothing, Mom. Just delivering his good wishes." I point to his flowers, which I placed on the windowsill. "He brought those."

She doesn't even look at them. "You're with Robert now. He's a good man. He's the father of your baby."

"Manny was just being nice. We knew each other for a long time. Hey, I got a new lotion," I say, hoping that will divert her attention. "It's the same brand as the lemon pomegranate but cherry." I get it out of my purse and put some on. "Can you smell it? It's really strong. What do you think?" I place my fingers under her nose. "Too much?"

"Ay, que peste." She waves it away. "Listen to me, Mónica. Manny is in your past. You're going in a different direction now. Robert is your future."

"I know, Mom. Believe me, I know."

The last scene of the show is Clara on the back patio of the hacienda, staring longingly into the night. Suddenly her phone rings and it's the only person she hates more than Sebastián: his mother. I look at my mom with an Oh-my-God face.

"Hello, Clara. I have a proposal for you," the mother says, and the episode ends right there.

My mother shakes her head. "Whatever that is, it's not good."

"Totally." I gather my courage one more time. "So, um, let me ask *you* a question, Mom. Before you went into surgery, you said that Juan is my father. What did you mean? What was . . . what were you talking about?"

She's wearing her own pajamas today, not the hospital gown, and she fiddles with one of the buttons on the top. She shakes her head. "I don't know. Did I say that? I—I don't know. I don't remember saying that."

"You did. You said Juan is my father and you loved him."

She shakes her head. "No. I don't know. I must have been talking out of fear."

"That you would die in surgery?"

"Yes."

"You said you were just like Jaquelín on *Abismo*—that you never told," I say more insistently. "What did you mean, Mom?"

She looks everywhere but in my eyes. "They gave me those drugs. I remember that, and they told me they would make me feel strange. But I don't know what I said, okay? Everything is fine now. I'm done with the surgery. I'm getting better. Everything is fine." She finally looks at me. "Everything is fine. Okay?"

My stomach starts to feel shaky. "Okay," I say, even though it doesn't seem like everything is fine. It seems like everything is weird and potentially terrible.

Then she says, "I'm tired," and it's clear she's done for the night. "Hasta mañana," she says, and closes her eyes. But she looks uncomfortable.

"Mom, are you in pain?"

"No. I just—" She waves me away. "I just need to rest. Just go. Please."

This is super strange. She always wants me here. When I'm at work, she calls me and asks when I'm getting here. But now she wants me gone, out of her sight. Because she's lying to me. I feel it. Or I think I feel it. She's still lying there with her eyes closed, her face turned away from me.

"Okay," I say. "Okay."

And I walk out, just like she asked me to.

Mirta

For a week, I tried to see Juan; I wanted to talk to him about what happened, to apologize again. But his mother wouldn't let me. Every time I called the house, it was always "He's sleeping" or "He's at the doctor." Finally, I appealed to Adelita. I talked her into hiding a key for me, and one afternoon I left Pablo with Gladys and went over to the apartment myself.

"Hola," I said as I came in. Adelita had warned him that I would be there around three, when she and their mother would be gone. He looked up at me from the sofa, his left leg up on the coffee table, covered in bruises. The cuts on his face were scabbing over, but, just like his leg, his left arm was purple and green from the shoulder all the way down.

"You shouldn't be here," he said.

"I shouldn't? I love you. I'm worried about you. And I'm so sorry he did this to you." My voice broke then and I started to cry. "Yes I should be here."

"It's not right."

"Since when?"

"Mirta, you have your husband. You have your life."

"My life includes you."

He shook his head. "Either you leave Rolando or you leave me. But are you really going to leave Rolando? He's the father of your baby. He can provide for you. I lay tile. Dig ditches. I can barely provide for myself."

I had never worried about any of this. Rolando having a better job meant nothing to me. The only thing that meant anything to me was Juan. Juan and your brother. I loved your father as the father of my child, as a friend, but I had realized, over those last few months, that I did not love him as a husband.

"We're leaving anyway," he said. "We're going to Puerto Rico. Mamá's cancer is going to kill her. She knows that, and she doesn't want to die here. If she can't die at home, she at least wants to die on an island. We have a cousin down there. Her husband can get me a job."

I felt slammed to the ground, and all I could think to say was "Don't you love me?"

He looked me in the eyes. "I love you with my whole soul. But I am not the man for you." He looked out the sliding glass door, at the traffic on Bird Road. "It's a complicated situation, and I need to do what's best for everyone."

"What about what's best for you? What do you want?"

"What I want doesn't matter. You deserve a man, not whatever I am. Whatever I've become."

"What are you talking about?" But I knew what he was talking about. I knew he was ashamed that he hadn't defended himself, that he had lost control of his body and had to say to the paramedic, in his broken English, "Sorry, I need clean up."

He adjusted his leg on the table and winced in pain. "You deserve a man," he said, "and Pablo deserves a father. Rolando is his father."

I felt like I was about to split open with pain, that I would die right there. Part of me wanted to. I didn't want to go back to knowing no one but Rolando's relatives, to not making even one phone call all day long except to his cousin or his brother's wife. And worst of all, to living without Juan.

I moved closer to him on the sofa. "I could come with you. I could bring

Pablo." But even as I said the words, I knew that wasn't true. Your father loved Pablo madly. What would he do if I tried to take his son? I didn't know how the laws worked over here. Could a husband take a child from a wife if she had done what I had? The thought of that—of losing your brother—brought me back to my senses. I wouldn't have done it to your father, anyway. He was a good man and he didn't deserve any of this.

"Please, Mirta," Juan said, his eyes closed. "You need to go now."

I stood up and my whole body felt oddly cold all of a sudden. I looked at him one last time. His eyes—that strange blue. His hooked nose. The birthmark in the shape of a half-moon on his neck. I will never touch him again, I thought, and I was right.

11

Laz, the iguana guy, still isn't returning Robert's calls. "Maybe we need to find someone else," I say. It's Saturday and I'm heading to the hospital. I check once more to make sure my phone is zipped into the innermost pocket of my purse. Last night Manny drunk-texted me. Twice.

2:21 a.m. You don't know how much I care about you monica

3:02 a.m. sorry but it's true

Robert was still asleep when I read the texts this morning and I took the phone into the bathroom and read them over and over again, fear and anger and excitement swirling inside me.

Now I watch Robert pack his bag for the track. He and Flaco are racing at ten and then Flaco's coming over to work on the cars. "I'll try Laz one more time," he says. "And I'll ask Flaco if he knows anyone else. His brother sold some snapping turtles a couple years ago, so he might know someone."

"Thanks."

"Come here." He kneels down in front of me and lifts up my

shirt. "Taz, this is your father speaking. I promise I'll get rid of the iguanas before you get here." He looks up at me. "We have three months, you know."

I shake my head. "Not really. We need time to air that room out and to decorate. You can't just throw a nursery together."

"You can't?" He counts off on his fingers. "Crib, changing table, rocking chair. Done."

"Okay, but I need those cages out of there so I can see the room empty and figure out a color scheme and where the furniture is going to go and what kind of textures I want."

"Textures?"

"Yeah, textures. Like, I want a sheepskin rug because that seems like something a kid would eventually want to sit on. And I don't want the room to be all blue and filled with airplanes and footballs. I'm thinking maybe a light gray with orange accents. And we're on a budget, so, like, I need time to look."

He stands up off his knees. "If I still worked at the futon place, I could get us a great discount on some stuff."

"Uh, no," I say. I roll my eyes at him.

He laughs. "What? Why?"

"Oh my God, please. I want some good vintage stuff, if I can find it on discount. Except for the crib. We'll get that new. But I need the room cleared out."

He holds up his hands, surrendering. "I promise they'll be gone soon. Definitely by November."

"What? Robert, they *have* to be gone by November."

"Okay, okay. I promise."

He pulls me in for a soft kiss and then he just holds me for a minute, rubbing my back. It feels nice to be close to him. It almost makes me feel like telling him what my mom said about

Juan, how she kicked me out last night. But those texts from Manny are burning a hole in my purse, making me feel guilty and slimy and unsure of everything in my life—a feeling that is more and more present these days. So instead of saying *Listen, this weird thing happened with my mom* and opening myself up to him, I just pick up my purse and say, "Good luck today. Break a leg," which is our little joke.

"No, thanks," he says.

My father's in my mom's hospital room, sitting in the pink pleather chair next to her bed, working on his laptop. My mother is reading her James Patterson book. She seems more like herself.

"How's my baby?" she asks. *My baby.* That's what she calls him when she's not calling him *mi niño.*

"Good. Asleep right now, I think."

"Bueno," she says, and points to the door. "¿Viste a Pablo?"

"He's here?"

My father nods. "He said he was going outside to make a call for work."

"Y Maritza?" I ask. "She's not here?"

My mother says, "She's doing her nails. I hope with Letty. I told her not to trust anyone but Letty until I get out of here."

The only time Pablo and Maritza are apart is when she's having her nails or her hair done. They live *and* work together—at this knockoff insurance company where the boss is an old guy named Al who drives a Jag and never shows up before eleven. Maritza does accounts payable and Pablo sells insurance. He comes back into my mom's room. He's in his black pants and a white polo shirt with the company logo on it.

My father tells us the doctor came by this morning and said my mom can go home within twenty-four hours, as long as she has supervision.

Pablo looks up from his phone. "Can't they send a home nurse?"

"Not full-time," my father says. "The insurance won't pay for that."

"What are we going to do?" I ask.

"Well," my father says, "that's why I brought it up. Do you think you can get time off work? I really need to get back to the optical."

I look at Pablo.

He shakes his head. "I have a lot of new prospects going right now. And I don't have regular benefits, you know, like vacation time. Mónica, can't you do it? Take some vacation time?"

"Yeah, I can, but I'm trying to bank some for when the baby comes, to add it to my maternity leave. I only get FMLA, and it's unpaid."

My mother says, "It's okay. I'm sure Caro can help."

"She works until three," I say. "Plus she has the girls." Amanda and Ashley are thirteen months apart, in first and second grade, and they're in everything—soccer, gymnastics, swimming, even Girl Scouts, which neither Caro nor I ever did because it was "para los Americanos."

My father gets up and pours himself a cup of water from the hospital pitcher. "We'll figure it out," he says, which we all know means Mónica will do it. I don't mind taking care of my mom, but I need the maternity time, and I need somebody to realize that.

"Maybe we can split it," I say to Pablo. "Like, you do a couple days, I do a couple days."

"I'll call Caro," my mother says. "Maybe she can come over in the afternoons after she picks up the girls from school. It will be nice to spend some time with them." This is not true at all. She just doesn't want Pablo to do it. He can't cook. Or clean. His version of doing the dishes is to put everything into the dishwasher without a drop of water on it. My mother scrubs the dishes clean before she puts them in. If Pablo comes to take care of her, he'll spend the whole time on the phone with work or texting Maritza. He won't watch her shows with her or clean out the pantry while she sits at the kitchen table telling him what to keep and what to throw away. He never does anything like that. He just comes and goes as he pleases, with his free pass to live his life however he wants to. Then, when he does show up, it's like Jesus Christ himself has arrived. I once saw my mother make him an entire meal when she was in the middle of cleaning the bathroom. She just got up, left the Clorox by the toilet, and began chopping onions for the sofrito.

My phone buzzes. It's Manny. I read it as fast as I can. *Hey, really sorry about previous texts. Gimme a call when u get a min?*

Right then the doctor comes in to talk about my mom's blood work. His name is Dr. Layne and he's tall and Bahamian and looks so much like Kobe Bryant it's freaky. His wife is a pediatric oncologist who runs marathons. They have two daughters: one in med school at UM and one in college in New York. "Fashion—that's her thing," he said yesterday, when my mother kept him here for twenty minutes asking questions about his life, which is what she does with everyone. As a result, I know the entire life stories of the day nurse, the night nurse, and all the CNAs.

Dr. Layne starts telling us about my mother's platelets. All I can think about, though, is my mother refusing to talk to me last night and Manny texting me. I need him to please leave me alone. Except I don't want him to leave me alone. But I'm engaged to Robert, who loves me, and loves the baby, and wants to get married as soon as possible. And my mother wants me to get married, and so does my father, and Tía Gladys and Tío Fermín and Caro, and even Sandra at work. Everyone. Everyone wants me to get married, but I can't imagine doing that—not now, not with Manny texting me that he cares so much about me, and my mother acting so strange, lying, I think, about what she said before surgery.

Dr. Layne is talking about when my mom might go home and my heart is beating harder and harder, my hands are tingling, my arms are heavy, and now my head feels unattached to my body. I take a step toward the bed and lean against it, take a deep breath, let it out slowly, take another one. But it does no good. I know I'm going to faint about three seconds before it happens, but I can't say anything: my mouth won't work.

I wake up throwing up. I'm sitting on the floor, my father behind me holding me up under my arms. Pablo and Dr. Layne are squatting down in front of me. I'm puking into my own lap, drunk-girl style. I touch my stomach, press a little. *Mijo*, I say to him in my head, *are you okay?* I want to ask someone if I hit my stomach or fell really hard, but I can't talk just yet because of the puking. And because my mother is yelling "¿Que pasó? ¿Que pasó?"

The doctor stands up and presses the nurse call button. When they answer, he says, "This is Dr. Layne. Can we get some help in here?"

A minute later a nurse is in the room. She asks my father what happened.

"No se. Se desmayó." Then to the doctor, he says, "She's pregnant," as if he's blind.

The nurse brings over the kidney-shaped plastic thing for me to puke into, but I'm just dry heaving now.

My mother is going nuts in Spanglish. "Mónica, are you okay? Mónica? ¿Rolando, que pasó? Ay diós mío, what happened to her?"

I point up toward her bed. "Calm her down. Please. Somebody."

Pablo stands up. "Mom, relax, okay? The doctor's here."

"Mirta, todo está bien," my father says. He turns to me. "Mija, you're okay," he assures me, but I can see the concern on his face. He runs his hand down the back of my head like he used to do when I was little.

"Did I fall? Did I hit anything?" I ask.

"No, you fell on top of me. Thank God." He says it in English and, because of his accent, it sounds like *thang gah.*

"Oh, no. I'm sorry. Are you okay? Did I hurt you?"

"No, no. Don't worry. I caught you."

The nurse wipes up the puke on the floor. She hands me a bunch of paper towels for my pants and my shirt.

Dr. Layne is standing off to the side, letting the nurse clean me up. He tells my mother everything's okay, that I just fainted. "She's probably dehydrated, probably just under a lot of stress. Everything's fine."

Nothing is fine, I think. *Not one thing.*

Dr. Layne says, "Let's get her into the chair, okay, Dad?"

My father nods and he and Pablo pull me up to the pink pleather chair.

Dr. Layne squats down in front of me and shines a light in my eyes. "How far along are you?"

"Twenty-seven weeks."

"Have you ever fainted before?"

"Once when I got my wisdom teeth out. After the anesthesia." I don't tell him about the time I fainted after Eric Mendoza kissed me on our first date—how I came to in his arms. I threw up then, too, all over my parents' driveway.

Dr. Layne has the nurse get all my vitals and call in a Code 9.

"A Code 9?" my mother says in English. "What's a Code 9? Is that bad?"

"It's what we call it when the family member of a patient needs to be treated. We'll get someone up here to take her down to the Emergency Department. They'll want to get a fetal heartbeat and do an ultrasound. Maybe a head CT. It's not recommended for pregnant women, but they may want to rule out anything neuro- logical. Just to be on the safe side."

"A head CT?" I say. "Do I have to?"

Dr. Layne scratches his ear. "Legally, you can refuse any treat- ment you want."

"No," my father says. "You're not refusing anything."

I never do. I never get to.

The nurse comes back in with two gowns and explains that one is for the back and one is for the front. "That way nothing shows," she says, pointing to her own butt.

"Thanks." I go into the bathroom to change. Everything looks fine—no blood in my underwear.

When I come out, my father is on the phone. "Okay. See you soon," he says in English, and hangs up. "Robert's bringing you clothes."

"You called Robert?"

"Of course I called Robert. You fainted." It's the same voice he used to tell me I wasn't refusing anything.

The door opens and a short blond guy comes in pushing a wheelchair.

"Okay," Dr. Layne says to me. "Here's your ride."

Before I get in the wheelchair, I say to my mom, "Listen, you need to keep your blood pressure down, okay? I'm just going to go get checked. I'll be back in a little while."

TELL IT TO ME SINGING

Her face is filled with anguish. "I dropped you," she says. "You slipped into the water. I'm sorry. It was just for a moment. I'm so sorry."

What I want to say is *What are you talking about? What the hell is going on with you?* But instead I adjust my two hospital gowns and say, "Mom, I just fainted. It's okay. They're gonna check me out. I'll be back in a little while, I promise." I squeeze her hand. "Just relax. Please. Your blood pressure."

The guy's name tag says *Jason Mead, Transporter.* I sit down and off we go, my father walking right beside us.

Mirta

Rolando and I talked about what happened, but only briefly. He asked me if I was going to leave him for Juan, if I wanted a divorce. He knew Juan was my first husband, that Adelita was his sister. I had been completely honest with him about my life when we met. I had even shown him the one picture I had of the farm. In it, Adelita and I were standing in the field, squinting into the sun with the cow, Fresa, behind us.

"No, I don't want a divorce," I told him. And I didn't. There was no reason to divorce him. Juan was gone; everything was over. Adelita had called me the week before to say goodbye, and I was so sad I could barely speak. I had already lost her and Juan once, and now I was losing them again.

"Can we stay in touch?" she asked. "I'll pay for the calls."

But I said no. It was time to let go, to stop lying. I had no choice. I had to stay and make a life with your father, who was a good man, and had loved me once. I only hoped it was possible that, even after everything, he still might.

For weeks he didn't want to talk to me. I still washed his clothes, made his meals, packed his lunch for work. But he slept on the sofa and I slept in the bedroom. One night I came to him, knelt down in front of the sofa, and tapped him on the shoulder until he woke up.

He sat up halfway. "What is it? Is it the baby? Is he sick?"

"He's fine," I said. Then I said, "I'm sorry. I'm very sorry I lied to you."

He looked at me for a moment, then lowered himself back down and turned his back to me. I stayed there, waiting for him to say something else, but he wouldn't. After about a minute he said, "Go back to bed, Mirta," and I did.

A few days later I missed my period. I told myself it was nerves, but by the Monday after Thanksgiving, when it still hadn't arrived, I feared the worst. I bought a pregnancy test, which I had learned about from the television. In the commercial, when the water in the little vial turned blue, the woman smiled and threw herself into her husband's arms. When mine turned blue, I sat on the closed toilet seat and cried while your brother watched Mister Rogers *in the living room. I could hear the trensito going around the track and I thought about how God must be punishing me. There was no way it was Rolando's. We hadn't made love since the night of our anniversary, which was way back in September.*

I started vomiting not long after that, but I hid it from your father. I also tried to hide my exhaustion: in the afternoons when Pablo took his nap, I would lie down and fall asleep instantly, until I heard him wake up. And even then sometimes I couldn't get up. Part of it was the pregnancy, but the other part was just a darkness I couldn't get out of. I was so sad. And angry. With Juan for leaving. With your father for catching me and ruining my life as it had been, although it was clear to me now that it would have been ruined anyway as soon as I realized I was pregnant.

Finally, one morning, your father came into the bathroom while I was throwing up. "Mirta," he said. "You're sick?" He stood behind me, gathering my hair away from my face. It was the first time he'd touched me or shown me any affection since the night he caught me with Juan.

I was kneeling in front of the toilet, heaving and heaving, nothing but yellow liquid coming out of me. All I could do was shake my head back and forth.

"You're not sick? Why are you vomiting?"

I looked at him between heaves, but I couldn't bring myself to say the words.

He let go of my hair and stepped back. "You're pregnant."

I nodded.

He stayed quiet for a minute, then he walked out. He went to work without showering, without brushing his teeth or drinking even one cup of coffee. He just put on clothes and left.

That night, after I put your brother to bed, I found Rolando sitting at the kitchen table, smoking and having a drink. I could tell by the color it was mostly rum.

"You need to get rid of it," he said.

"What do you mean 'get rid of it'?"

"I mean get rid of it."

"¿Un aborto?"

"Sí."

The thought of having this child who was Juan's and not Rolando's was gut-wrenching, but the thought of getting rid of it was worse. I could never have lived with that. "No, Rolando. I won't do that. I'm a Catholic," I said.

He laughed. "Oh, are you? Yes, you are such a good Catholic." He put his cigarette out in the ashtray. "You'll get rid of it or I will divorce you. Catholic or not."

I sighed. "No," I said. "I'm sorry."

His face started to crumple into the sadness I imagine he had been feeling since that night he caught us. He lit another cigarette and smoked silently, taking a few sips of his drink. Then he shook his head in disgust and got up from the table. He picked up his keys and wallet and left the house. I have no idea where he went. All I know is that he came home the next morning, walked into the bathroom while I was throwing up, and got into the shower. From behind the curtain, he said, "We will have the baby. We will tell no one that I am not the father. Including Juan."

The thought of never telling Juan he had a child made me feel ter-

rible. But I told myself it was for the best, that he and Adelita and their mother were gone, that I had no way of contacting them even if I wanted to. I needed to move forward, to find a way to live this life with Rolando and Pablo and this baby growing inside me.

I pulled a few squares of toilet paper off the roll to wipe my mouth. "Okay," I said. "I swear I'll never tell."

12

The ER nurse is a guy named Milko. He has sculpted brows and like ten Livestrong bracelets on, all in different colors.

"Milko," my father says. "¿Eso es un nombre Cubano?"

"Claro," Milko says, smiling. "I came over when I was thirteen." He takes my vitals. They're fine, except for my blood pressure, which is a little high. "Probably just nerves, right?"

I say, "Yeah. I think—I hope—this was just, like, an anxiety thing. That happens, right? People faint from anxiety?"

He nods and touches my shoulder. "All the time."

"Okay," I say. "Okay, great." I feel better, less worried. "The doctor upstairs said something about a head CT. Do you think I'll need that?"

"I doubt it. It's contraindicated for pregnancy. Unless, like—" He points to his own head. "¿Te golpeaste la cabeza?"

I look at my father. "No, right?"

"No. She didn't hit her head. Or anything else." He smiles at me and rubs my arm. "I told you I caught you, mija." My mother's words—*Your father is Juan*—float through my head, and the place on my arm where my father touches me feels like it's crackling.

The doctor comes in to see me, then sends me for labs and an EKG, just to rule out anything bad. When I come back, Milko says, "So you need to have a full bladder for the ultrasound. They get a better picture that way. Which means we need to give you an IV."

"Why can't I just drink a bunch of water?"

He looks away for a second. "It's just a precaution. In case you need an emergency D&C. You can't have anything in your stomach."

"What's a D&C?" my father asks.

I know what a D&C is. Caro had one after she miscarried a few years ago.

"'D&C' is short for dilation and curettage," Milko says, switching into a professional voice. "It's a procedure to remove the contents of the uterus in the event of a miscarriage."

I think of my dream and the salmonella thing. I made Robert read the article before he left for work that morning. When he went into the bathroom, I texted him two more and yelled, "Read those too," from the living room. He came out telling me I didn't have to do anything else with the iguanas and promising to wash his hands every time he fed them.

"And no more petting the Hulk," I said.

"And no more petting the Hulk."

Milko gets the IV in me and I put my hands on my stomach and press around again. *Come on, mijo,* I think. *Wake up. Please. Please just let me know you're okay.*

A little while later, Robert comes in. He's wearing shorts and an old green tank top with grease stains all over it. He says hi to my father and shakes his hand. My father eyes his tattoos for a second; they're all tribals except for the dolphin on his right shoulder.

Robert loves dolphins. "They're very gentle animals," he told me once. "But they'll fuck you up if you mess with them."

"Hey, baby," he says to me now. "You okay?" He looks worried. "Have they checked the baby yet?"

"Not yet. As soon as this IV is done, I'm going for an ultrasound." I point to his shirt. "Why are you filthy?"

"Me and Flaco were working on his injectors. He wants to put in that 450 Walbro before next week."

"Cool," I say. I have no idea what a 450 Walbro is.

"Why do you have an IV? Are they hydrating you?"

"It's just a precaution, in case I need a D&C."

"A what?"

I try to say it exactly like Milko did. "It's a procedure to clear out the uterus in the case of a miscarriage."

He leans in. "Do they think you miscarried?"

"No, no. They're just going to check."

"I think what you said was right," my father says in English. "Your nerves are getting on top of you. You got a lot on your mind. Your mother, the baby, all that." He waves his hand in the air to indicate *all that*. If he only knew.

When Milko comes to take out my IV, a woman comes in right behind him. "Ms. Campo?" she says. "I'm Tanya. I'll be doing your ultrasound." She's American, white, about sixty. She has her hair in a French braid.

My father extends his hand. "Rolando Campo," he says, like he's at a business meeting. "I'm her father."

"This is my fiancé," I say, pointing to Robert.

"Nice to meet you all. I'm just going to take Ms. Campo down to get a peek at the little one. Dad, you're welcome to come too."

My father and Robert both take a step forward.

"I think she meant Robert," I say.

My father looks around at all of us. "No, but can't I come too? It's not a . . . a personal procedure, is it? It's just with the thing on the stomach, right?" He swirls his hand around in front of his own stomach, giving himself an ultrasound.

Tanya looks at me. "Okay with you?"

It's not, but I can't say that. I sneak a look at Robert to make sure he's not mad. He looks okay.

"Sure," I say. I just want to get in there and see the baby.

In the ultrasound room, which barely fits the four of us, Tanya puts the sheet on my legs so she can pull up my gown. My bladder is so full I'm about to pee all over this table and now my giant stomach is out for everyone to see, complete with the brown line down the middle and the belly button that looks like a marble. My father keeps his eyes on the screen and a second later, there he is: the baby, with his big round head, his curved body, his arm-looking thing, his leg-looking thing.

"There's my Taz," Robert says, smiling. "Ain't he cute?" He takes my hand.

The baby's heartbeat is like a thumping drum coming through the speakers. I close my eyes and let the relief wash over me.

"That's unbelievable," my father says. He was amazed enough at the printouts I brought home after our first ultrasound. Now he's crying, I realize. He's trying to hide it, but he's not doing a very good job. He wipes his eyes. "I'm sorry, mija," he says to me in English. "Just very emotional."

Tanya smiles at him. "That's your grandson," she says, and something catches in my chest. I focus on the baby. If I don't, I'll end up in tears like my father, but for a very different reason.

Tanya moves the wand over my stomach. "Heartbeat is 153. Not too fast, not too slow."

Robert says, "And everything else? The movement looks good? All that?"

Tanya says, "Yep. Let me just take a couple measurements."

My father asks her how it works and she explains—something about sound waves and sonar technology created for ships. She runs the wand over my belly, typing stuff into the computer as she goes. My phone rings. It's in my purse, on a chair in the corner.

Robert lets go of my hand. "You want me to get that?"

My father says, "Get it. It's probably Mirta."

But I don't want anyone near my phone—not after those drunk texts from last night. "Just leave it," I say. "I'll call her in a minute if it's her."

"I got it, I got it," Robert says, reaching into my purse. *No*, I think. *Please no.* I'm stuck on the table, my belly still exposed and covered in the slimy stuff. I'm stretching my arm out, my hand, my fingers moving in the air. *Please, please.* "I got it," he says, pulling the ringing, vibrating phone out of my purse, turning it over in his hand, and looking at it. He looks up at me.

I try to look innocent, but I'm half hanging off the table, my arm stretched out so far it looks like I'm trying to rescue someone who's fallen out of a boat. It rings one last time. He hands it to me. The screen says, MISSED CALL MANNY.

"That's weird," I say.

Robert cocks his head at me. "Yeah?"

"Yeah."

"Why's he calling you?"

"No idea."

My father says, "Who was it?"

Robert looks right at me. "No one important."

"It was Manny," I say, and look into my father's eyes, pleading with him silently not to mention the fact that Manny showed up here the other night.

My father frowns but doesn't say anything, thank God.

And thank God for Tanya, who starts cleaning up my belly and then hands me a pile of tissues. "Here, sweetie," she says. "You can just finish up."

"Thanks." I clean up my stomach with the precision of a surgical nurse preparing for a transplant. The phone, lying next to me on the table, vibrates *and* does the special voice mail ring. In my head, it sounds like a train whistle. Robert won't look at me and my father won't *stop* looking at me. I could really use a meteor right now. Or the ability to turn invisible. As Tanya wheels me back to my bay in the ER, I consider jumping up and pulling the fire alarm on the wall. Instead, I count the little diamonds on my hospital gown and think about what an asshole I am.

My father goes out to the waiting room to call my mother, and Robert says, "Aren't you going to listen to the voice mail?"

I shrug. "I'll listen to it later."

"You should listen to it right now," he says.

My stomach starts shaking from the inside. What am I going to do if it mentions the texts? Or says anything like what the texts say? I press it as close to my head as possible while the message is playing. Not that it matters. Manny's voice is so loud that Robert can hear every word. Miraculously, it just says, "Hey, can you give me a call? Hope your mom is doing okay."

Robert crosses his arms in front of his chest. "How does he know about your mom?"

I shake my head, buying time. "His aunt. Probably his aunt. She goes to my mom's salon for her hair."

"So are you gonna call him?"

"Nah. I'll drop him a text, tell him everything's fine."

He gives me a once-over just as the doctor comes in. She says my labs and EKG look good, that I'm fine: it was just a mild anxiety attack, and Milko's on his way back in with my discharge papers. She hands me an info sheet about strategies for handling stress.

"Thank you," I say. I grip the info sheet and smile, trying to look and sound as normal as possible.

I have to convince both my parents and Robert to let me drive myself home, but eventually they say okay. Once I'm out of the parking lot and sitting in the traffic on Kendall Drive, I pull up the drunk texts, replay the voice mail, and then press Call.

It rings twice before he picks up. "Hey," he says. "How's your mom?"

I tell him about the blood work being good and the oxygen and blood pressure starting to stabilize. "Last night she slept without the cannula."

"Fantastic. Sounds like she'll be out soon."

"Yeah. Hopefully."

"So listen," he says. "I may have had a few drinks last night and sent you an inappropriate text message or two. I'm really sorry. I got a little too worked up about how things have changed."

"Yeah, I'm just, you know, in a different place now."

"Obviously."

"Yeah."

"I'm really sorry I did that. It won't happen again. I'll just stop contacting you." He sounds so fine with it that it hurts. It reminds me of when I broke up with him and he just nodded and said, *Okay.*

I close my eyes, but have to open them again because I'm driving. I don't cry but I do have a closing feeling inside. A folding in, then over. In, then over. It's almost worse than crying. "Great," I say, trying to sound as okay about it as he does. "Thanks. And thanks for your information about the drugs. And your concern about my mom."

"No problem. Good luck with everything, okay? I'll, uh, *not* talk to you later."

"Okay," I say, quieter than I meant to.

"Okay," he says. "Bye."

Mirta

I was sad, and sick, for the first few months of my pregnancy, just like you were, but then the sickness got better and I tried to be better, happier. We started talking about buying a house. With the baby coming, we agreed we would need three bedrooms and we didn't want to rent anymore. "It's just throwing money away," Rolando said, so we started looking. One house we looked at smelled like cat pee so badly we didn't even go past the front door. "Well, if I was looking to buy a barn, this would be perfect," your father said. I laughed, and Pablo did, too, even though he didn't really understand the joke. We stood there bathed in that terrible smell, laughing. It was the first time we had laughed together since the night at the Palmetto.

Finally, we found the house we wanted. Fermín helped us move in and Gladys sent over arroz con pollo for our first night there. We fed Pablo, put him to bed, and then sat down to eat, resting our plates on moving boxes. Afterward, you were rolling around inside me, kicking and kicking.

Rolando pointed to my stomach. "Pablo never did that," he said.

"Yes he did. You don't remember?"

He shook his head. "Do they all do that?"

I shrugged. "All of mine do." He was silent. I knew he was thinking about whose it was. It was mine, yes. But it wasn't his.

He carried his plate to the kitchen without finishing his rice. I came in behind him and opened the box we had labeled Cocina. The cafetera, which I had packed last night, was right on top.

"I knew because you started fixing yourself up," he said.

At first, I didn't know what he was talking about.

He went on. "I noticed there were days when you had done your hair, and your face was fixed up with more makeup than usual. At first I thought it was for me, and I got excited. But then nothing was changing between us. You were still going to bed before me and not wanting to touch me, and I started to wonder."

"Oh." I stood there, holding the cafetera in its box, not knowing what to say. He said that one morning he saw me in my underwear and noticed that I was shaving, keeping myself up better than I normally did. Not my legs and my underarms—I shaved those every day—but my bikini area. It had never occurred to me that he would notice such a thing.

"I watched you for a few weeks," he said. "And then one night I decided to follow you when you went to visit 'Josefina from English class.' I left the baby sleeping and followed you out of the apartment to what I hoped would be some woman's house. But no." He shook his head. "When you pulled into the parking lot of the motel and went into that room, I felt like someone was kicking me in the stomach. I almost got out of the car right there, but I couldn't move. I went home to wait for you, but after twenty minutes of sitting on the couch, getting more and more angry, I decided you were my wife and I needed to go get you. So I put the baby in the car this time and drove back."

I hadn't moved an inch while he was talking. In fact, I had been so still that I had forgotten to breathe and I suddenly found myself very dizzy.

Rolando took a step toward me, worry all over his face. "¿Mirta, que te pasa?" he said, the alarm in his voice clear.

I couldn't answer, I was feeling so dizzy.

He took the cafetera out of my hands and made me sit down. He got me some water from the sink in one of the paper cups Gladys had sent. It said Happy New Year! *I sipped the water slowly and started crying.*

Everything had piled on top of me in those moments when he was telling me how he knew. The guilt and shame, the anger, the sadness. I felt terrible for what I had done and yet still I wanted to be doing it. I missed Juan so much that my bones hurt with missing him. I still couldn't believe I was going to have to live without him for the rest of my life. I cried and cried and your father just stood there, not touching me.

Eventually, he put his hand on my back and pulled me toward him. He was wearing the Campo Construction T-shirt that Fermín had given him on our first night in Miami. I let my cheek fall against the cotton, let him press my face into his stomach, let him say "Shhh" to me as he stroked my hair. I was very sad and I needed very much for someone to care for me. For the second time in my life, that person was your father. To this day, he's never told me he forgives me. I don't think he does. Acceptance and forgiveness are not the same thing, you know, but sometimes they are close enough.

13

At home, my mother situates herself in the living room while my father unpacks. He's trying to put away the facial products she made me pack when they admitted her on the spot. "Which one goes in the drawer?" he asks her. "¿El vitamin C serum o el pore refining cream?" Only my mother takes pore refining cream to open-heart surgery and only my father takes the time to put it back for her.

I follow him into the bedroom to help. "I'll do those, Dad. You do her clothes."

Her suitcase is sitting open on the bed, one wheel gone and a block of wood in its place. The wheel fell off on one of their trips to Jersey. Pablo laughed, telling him to just throw away the suitcase and buy a new one. But my father would never do that. He never throws anything away until it's completely useless.

He puts her slippers in the closet and all the clothes into the hamper. "By the way, the home health nurse called," he says. "She's coming on Monday at nine. You'll be here then, right?"

"Yeah." I tell him how I'm going in on Monday afternoon to pick up a laptop so I can work part-time from here. "I was thinking I'll just sleep here during the week and go home on the weekends. Is that okay?"

"Of course. Is that okay with Robert? For you to sleep here?"

"It's fine," I say, even though I haven't even told him yet. The truth is that part of me is relieved. I'm having trouble being with Robert these days. I'm uncomfortable all the time, afraid of something I can't name. And I don't feel it as much when I'm not with him.

"Okay, mija. Gracias," my father says. "It's a big help to have you." He sits down on the bed and I can see the weight of everything we've been through settle in him. I bet he could sleep for two days straight right now.

"I'm so glad things are going back to normal," I say.

He takes out the cloth for cleaning his eyeglasses. "Me too," he says as he wipes one lens, then the other. "Me too."

In tonight's episode of *Abismo*, Armando is still in a wheelchair and is now hooked on the painkillers that Sebastián's goons have been providing him for the neck injury. He lies on the dirty mattress in the dungeon cell, begging the guard for more pills.

My mother takes a sip of her coffee and turns to me. "Mónica, why don't you want to get married before you have the baby? Di'me la verdad. Is it because of Manny?"

Shit. I look at the wall behind her, not at her face. "No, it's not. It's because I don't want to do it all fat and pregnant. If I'm going to do it, I want to do it nice. I want to lose the baby weight and wear a nice dress and have a party."

"Bueno, just go to the courthouse downtown." She gestures with an upturned palm at the window, as if downtown were just down the block. "And then have the reception later, after the baby comes." I'm surprised she wants me to do it at the courthouse and not in church. But maybe she doesn't want her knocked-up daughter walking down the aisle at Saint Timothy for all her friends to see.

"Listen," I say, "I want to get through the first few months with the baby. And then I want to take some time to lose the weight so I can look good in my wedding pictures." I want all of this, yes, but what I really want is to be sure. That's what I'm not telling her, or Robert, or anybody: that there is a little part of me that still isn't sure. "I mean, what's the rush, Mom? I'm already pregnant. It's not like we're fooling anyone here, right?"

She sighs. "No, mi niña, you're not fooling anyone," she says in English, and takes the last sip of her coffee.

Mirta

Two months after we moved into the new house, you were born: a head full of black, curly hair just like Juan's, and gray eyes I was terrified would turn blue. Thank God they didn't. It was hard enough knowing that when I touched you I was touching him. Your skin, your fingernails—all of you was part Juan. It was all I could think about, and it made being married to your father so hard all over again.

By the time you were three weeks old, I cried all the time. My body had stopped making milk, and it took me three terrible days of you crying nonstop to figure that out. On the third day, your father made me call the doctor. You had an appointment that afternoon and I was trying to bathe you. I was convinced they would think I was a bad mother if I brought you there without a bath. I had you in the kitchen sink and you were screaming and writhing, your arms and legs twitching. I was trying to hold you, but you slipped. Your head went under—I don't know for how long. Long enough to hear the silence. Long enough for there to be the whisper of a thought about what would happen if you weren't there. About how quiet it would be. About how I wouldn't have to look at that face that was Juan's. Those long fingers that were Juan's. Your brother said something, probably "Mami, can I help?" or "Mami, can I see?" and I pulled you up out of the water, up to my chest, soaking my shirt completely, you coughing, and— thank God—screaming.

*I began to cry then. Loudly. Your brother stared at me. "¿Mami?"
he said, but I could not answer him. I could not do anything but stand
there, holding you, shaking, my mouth open, yelling almost, I was crying
so loudly. You had been under the water for maybe two seconds, but I will
never forget it, and I will never forgive myself. What if I hadn't pulled you
up? When I think of those two silent seconds, I am filled with the shame
that I immediately felt in that moment. Dark, ugly shame that still burns
me inside and out.*

*I needed help, so I called Gladys. She brought me a Valium and we sat
together until it started working. When I told her I had an appointment in
an hour, she said, "Bueno, let's get ready." She took me to the bedroom, told me
to get in the shower. When I came out, dressed but with my hair still wet and
stuck to my head, she told me to dry my hair and do my makeup. I could not
imagine doing that, but something told me to try it, that she was in charge
now. It felt so good to have someone else in charge. The Valium was in full
effect, and I could feel it like a coating all over me, soothing me so that I could
think just the tiniest bit. I went back to the bathroom and did the best I could.*

*Gladys drove us all to the pediatrician, where they gave you a bottle of
formula right there in the office. You drank the whole thing and then fell
asleep in my arms.*

*You slept until nine o'clock that night, woke up, took another bottle,
and went back to sleep. It felt like a miracle, or at least like a gift from
God—something small He was giving back to me, after everything else He
had taken away.*

14

It starts out small. First, it's Teresita, who comes by the next day around lunchtime. The three of us sit on the back patio talking and eating ham and cheese sandwiches on Cuban bread. My mom is relaxed and happy. She presses the heart-shaped pillow they gave her at the hospital to her chest when she laughs at one of Teresita's stories.

The next day Blanca Pérez comes and brings two of my father's cousins who don't even live here but are visiting from Jersey, and soon every tía, tío, cousin, and friend who came to the hospital either calls or shows up. It's like the Bat-Signal went out and— *boom*—here comes the croquetas. The more people who show up, the more anxious my mom gets, especially if I forget to ask them to take off their shoes.

On Thursday afternoon, Letty from her work arrives with pastelitos and a plant. I'm in the kitchen putting the pastelitos on a plate and making coffee—because now I'm a waitress, too—and I hear my mother say, "I'm going to ride the gray horse this evening. I'm going to take her out to the fields." I get a sinking feeling in my gut and sneak into the hall so I can hear better.

"You're going to ride a horse?" Letty asks.

"She's Adelita's, but she lets me ride her. She's probably grazing in the yard right now. She doesn't like the barn very much. Probably because of Fresa."

"Mirta, what are you talking about?" Letty says.

My mother stays quiet for a second. Then she says, "The doctor said I could start back part-time in three weeks. I need to call Janet to tell her to start booking my appointments."

Letty lets it go, but I wish she wouldn't. I wish she would keep asking my mom what in the world she's talking about and who Adelita is. She probably thinks my mother is still on pain meds and high right now. But she hasn't been on anything heavy since she left the hospital.

After Letty leaves, I find my mother in Pablo's old room, which she now calls the White Room. I redid it for her a few years ago. She said she wanted an all-white reading room, so I gave it to her: white bookshelves, where she keeps all her crime thrillers and romances. White furniture, white walls. I even put a white flokati rug down over the tile. I find the room simultaneously soothing and sterile, but she loves it. It was after I did the room for her that she told me I should be a designer. "You're quite talented, Mónica," she said. "You really should go to school for this." That night I looked up the interior design program at Miami Dade College.

She's sitting in the chair in the corner now, holding a book: another James Patterson—one of his romances—but she's not reading. Her eyes are closed, her head back. I go to step out of the room, thinking she's asleep, but she opens her eyes just then. "I'm just resting," she says. "It's hard to visit right now. It tires me out."

"Why don't you go lie down for a while?"

"No, let's do our walk now. I'll rest after." She tries to get up, but the chair is too low to the ground. It takes a minute because of my belly, but I get her up. I put an arm around her back and side.

She feels thin. Or thinner than normal. I know she probably likes that—she's always been uncomfortable with how much weight she carries up top—but it saddens me to think of her losing weight because she spent two weeks in a coma being fed through an IV. I feel a prickle in my eyes at the thought of this and have to blink away tears.

Out on our walk, the sky is a little cloudy, so it's not too hot. There's even a breeze blowing through the big palm in the front yard. Next door, Hugo is spraying the weeds growing through the cracks in his driveway. He fought in the Bay of Pigs, which my parents find admirable, but he's the neighborhood complainer, so they usually avoid him. We say "Buenas" and immediately cross the street so we don't end up in a thirty-minute conversation about the rude people down the block.

"So," I say, "did you have a good visit with Letty?"

She nods and tells me about how Letty's son lost his driver's license paddle boarding in St. John's but a woman found it and returned it to him through Facebook.

"Oh wow," I say. We keep walking, past the Stars' house. Their Jack Russell barks at us from the front window. Everything seems so normal suddenly and I feel close to her, so I tamp down my fear and say gently, "Mom, I heard you mention something about Adelita to Letty. Who is she?" I'm thinking maybe if I start with Adelita we'll get somewhere.

We have to walk out into the street for a minute to avoid a sprinkler. When we get back on the sidewalk, her face is soft, sad. "She was my best friend a long time ago, in Cuba," she says.

"Did she live on a farm?"

She stops walking.

"Are you okay?" I put my hand on her shoulder. "Mom?"

She nods and closes her eyes, pinches her nose. "I'm having these memories. They're so strong."

"You feel like you're there on the farm with her?"

"Yes."

"Is she still there, in Cuba?"

"No, she's not."

I look at her face, her faraway eyes. I ask where Adelita is, if they're in touch anymore.

"I'm sure this is something from the anesthesia," she says. "It'll pass."

"You don't think we should ask about it? Maybe at your follow-up?"

"No, I don't."

I almost say *I do*, but I know it won't do any good. With the exception of coming to this country, my mother has never done anything that wasn't her idea.

We finish the walk in silence. At home, I tell her Pablo and Maritza are picking up El Rinconcito for dinner. "Why don't you tell me what you want before you go rest and I'll text him."

She waves her hand. "Whatever. I'll take anything."

There is no way this is true. "You want the garbanzos?" She usually gets the garbanzos.

"Yes. The garbanzos. Y dos croquetas. De pollo."

"I know." For some reason she hates their regular croquetas and always gets chicken.

"And don't get tostones. Theirs are too salty. Get maduros."

"Okay. Anything else?" There's usually something else.

"Well, I could eat some arroz con leche."

I review her order to make sure I got it right before texting it to Pablo. Otherwise, I'll be driving back to El Rinconcito to get what I got wrong.

"Is Robert coming?" she asks.

"He was going to," I tell her. "But they're having a special thing at the track tonight. Like an audition to train with a guy who was in the Daytona 500."

"Bueno. Tell him I send my best wishes." She's never cared or asked me one thing about Robert's racing. This is clearly her putting in a plug for him.

"I will," I tell her, and send the text with our food orders to Pablo. Then I ask her if she's okay.

She won't look at me. She just nods and heads down the hall toward her room, her slippers making the same scratching noise on the tile I've heard my whole life, only softer and slower. When her door clicks shut, it feels like she's pushing me away again, like that night at the hospital when she just wanted me to leave. It's as if she's on a boat and I'm on the shore and only she can control whether or not I can get to her.

El Rinconcito gets her order wrong. They give her regular croquetas.

"Shit. Here, Mom." I try to hand her half of my sandwich across the table. We're in the dining room because we won't all fit in the kitchen.

"No, but what are *you* going to eat?" she says.

"I'll eat your croquetas." I like them fine. Not as much as I like what I ordered, but whatever. I don't feel like going back to the restaurant.

She accepts and we spend the whole dinner talking about Pablo and Maritza's trip to the Keys. The boat broke down and Maritza's cousin, who used to be a flight attendant, kept everyone calm, offering drinks and sandwiches from the cooler while her dad radioed for help.

My mother says, "You think that's bad? Try being stuck in the belly of a shrimp boat with a four-month-old."

Maritza looks at us like *What?* and my brother explains: "When we came over from Cuba. We took a boat."

"Not just any boat," my father says. I look over at Pablo. Here comes his Mariel boatlift speech. "We were members of one of the greatest exoduses in the history of North America," my father explains to Maritza, who actually seems to be listening. "Over 125,000 Cubans came to Miami within the span of six months." She asks him why so many people came at that time, but before he can answer, my mother takes back over.

"The captain was a man named Captain Hooper," she says. "We owe him our lives. He didn't speak any Spanish, but he kept us safe." She tells Maritza the story Pablo and I grew up hearing, about how he sent all the women and children down below, where they normally kept the shrimp. How bad it stank and how she kept trying to nurse Pablo, but all he did was cry. "They gave us food. Vienna sausages, apples, and Coca-Cola. I had never tasted an apple. I loved it, but with the waves, I got so sick that I threw everything up into the bucket that was being passed around. I haven't eaten an apple since."

"Wow," Maritza says. She's playing with one of her earrings, which are long gold ropes that almost touch her shoulders. "That sounds terrible. My parents just came, like, on a plane." Her parents are Colombian and rich.

My mother worried they were making a mistake. But when the boatlift started, my father put their paperwork in and eventually they were transferred from their home in Holguín to a holding camp called El Mosquito. They slept in tents with no place to go to the bathroom and got one box of uncooked rice and one egg a day. My father didn't eat for three days so he could give her his food and she could keep producing milk. All of this to then get on a boat with her baby and travel to a country where she didn't speak the language and would have to figure out how to live for the rest of her life. Without her family, mind you; neither one of her sisters were able to come and, because of that, her parents refused to leave. It hits me now, in a way it never has before, how unreal it all must have been. And terrifying.

My mother moves her fork around her plate in a little circle. "A storm came and he sent the men down, too, and that's when I knew we would die." She turns to Pablo. "Your father found me sitting on the ground, praying el rosario. I used my fingers, then yours, for beads. The woman sitting next to me kept saying, 'We're going to be free. We're going to be free.' But all I could think was we were going to die."

"You've never told us this part," I say.

My father wipes his mouth with his napkin and folds it into exact thirds. "It's not important. We got here safe, and that's what's important."

My mother keeps going. "I kept thinking the water would rush into the hole above our heads and fill the room where we were sitting. We would drown. *You* would drown," she says to Pablo. "You would float right out of my arms and there would be nothing I could do." Her eyes turn glassy with tears.

"It's okay, Mom," I say.

She doesn't say anything at first; she's just looking into her plate. Her lips are moving but nothing is coming out. But then she says, "Rolando, take the baby. I need to throw up."

"¿Qué?" he says.

She looks up.

He folds his napkin one more time. "Mirta."

"Mom," I say. "Are you okay?"

"No." She sniffs away tears, blinks a few times. "But, yes, I'm fine." She puts the top back on the garbanzos. "Let's get this cleaned up. I want to save these. And the rice. The maduros too. We can eat them for lunch." I look over at Pablo. He gives me an *I don't know* with his eyes and we all let the moment pass, one more time. My father puts the extra food into the fridge while Pablo and Maritza throw away the garbage and I go pee.

When I come back, Pablo and Maritza are out on the patio. He's smoking his e-cigarette thing. She doesn't smoke, but she never leaves him alone, so she's out there, too, scrolling through her phone.

I go out and sit down with them. "So you like that thing?" I ask him, pointing to the e-cigarette.

"No, I hate it." He nods at Maritza. "But she won't let me smoke anymore."

Maritza tilts her head at him. "Baby, please. Number one, it's gross. Number two, it's unhealthy."

"And that's healthy?" I ask.

He shrugs. "Healthi*er*."

Robert used to smoke when I met him, but he quit when I got pregnant and now only does it when he drinks. "So, how about that thing with 'Take the baby'?" I ask.

Maritza looks up from her phone. "Oh my God, that was weird, right?"

"She's been doing that," I say.

"Doing what?" she says.

"Saying weird shit. She says she's having memories of her best friend from Cuba. Adelita." I turn to Pablo. "Have you ever heard of her?"

"Nah. But that's probably just the pain meds."

"She's done with pain meds. All she takes is Tylenol."

"It's probably just the stress, then. Too much going on, too many visitors. Total Cuban National Convention."

I roll my eyes. "You have no idea."

Maritza says, "I'm sure she's, like, super overwhelmed with all the people showing up."

I shake my head. "She's been saying weird shit since before."

"Before when?" Pablo asks. He takes a drag of the e-cigarette and the tip lights up blue.

"Before the surgery."

"What did she say?"

I put my hand on my stomach. *Do I tell him?* I'm not sure I can, especially in front of Maritza. God, I wish she weren't here. I know I need to tell him. I'd definitely want him to tell *me*. "She said this thing to me before she went into surgery about 'Your father is Juan.'"

Maritza leans in. "What? That's super weird."

Pablo goes to take a drag but stops. "Our father?"

"She said *your*. Like mine. I asked her about it the other day and she just played it off, said it was the pre-op drugs, which, you know, *did* fuck her up that morning. But it was strange, I'm telling you."

Pablo says, "Oh, they had already given her drugs? Then it was that."

Maritza says, "When I had my appendix out, they gave me Dilaudid and I ended up hallucinating these spiders with different-colored legs. They were really scary but also really pretty at the same time."

I ignore her. "So you don't think we should talk to Dad? About the Adelita stuff? Or maybe tell the doctor about it?"

"Mónica, you know Mom. She's a hypochondriac on a good day. You throw in open-heart surgery, and forget it. She'll be fine once she gets back to her routine, back to work, chismeando with the ladies and whatnot."

The baby kicks me twice right then and I wonder if he's agreeing or disagreeing. I tap my belly twice. *I don't know, mijo*, I think to him. *I just don't know.*

Mirta

For weeks after, I couldn't stop thinking about it—that moment when you were underwater, those thoughts I had had. I was full of fear, so afraid of myself that I wouldn't bathe you alone; I made your father help me. There were moments when I wondered how I was going to live with you for the rest of my life knowing you were Juan's. Even after you started eating and sleeping, I was still buried under that darkness that had fallen on me when you were born. It had taken me prisoner and kept me from feeling any joy at all. I couldn't take care of myself, and your father finally noticed.

One Saturday morning when I was washing dishes, he said, "Mirta, how long has it been since you showered?"

I was too tired to think up a lie, so I told him the truth: I couldn't shower because I couldn't hold my arms up for that long.

He got up from the table, put Pablo in front of the TV, and took me into the bathroom. You were asleep in your crib.

He got us both undressed and then into the shower. He washed my body, then my hair. "Is that it?" he asked.

I pointed to the crème rinse bottle. He read the instructions, put it in, waited the three minutes, and rinsed it out. When we got out, he dried me off and brought me by the hand back to the bedroom.

"Let's get dressed," he said, opening my underwear drawer. He pointed in. "Which ones?"

I took out a pair of underwear and a bra. He sat me down on the *bed and helped me put them on as if I were a child. I could see that he was scared, and that made me feel scared. And guilty. I don't think I had realized until then how bad I had gotten. He asked me where to find shorts and a shirt, brought them over to the bed, and helped me put those on too.*

I thought of how Gladys told me to do my hair and makeup before we left to the doctor's, how that helped a little. After your father got me dressed, I went back to the bathroom and tried to do that. I couldn't dry my hair completely. Holding the brush in one hand and the hair dryer in the other—I just couldn't. But I got one side done. Same with the makeup. I put on eye shadow and a little blush, but nothing else. I'm not sure I got anything on my lips, but I did try, which I hadn't done in weeks, not since that day with Gladys. When I came out of the bathroom, your father was sitting in the living room with Pablo, watching TV and giving you a bottle.

"Let's get out of here," he said.

"What?"

"You spend too much time indoors. You need to get out, get in the world."

It's true that I spent all day every day inside. I believed that it was dangerous to take a baby out before three months. But even if I didn't, I couldn't have gone anywhere because of the sadness. I was living with two kids and the people on TV. Jane Pauley, Donahue, Bob Barker y las novelas. I watched all the soaps in those days. Let me tell you, I learned more English from General Hospital *than from any book, class, or tape. It was the only company I had. I had made no new friends here in Miami, and the few friends from Cuba who were here worked during the day. Gladys came over every once in a while to drop off a bag of hand-me-downs or a box of old kitchen stuff she thought I might need, but she was very busy with her own life: she had the kids and she was helping Fermín run the company back then. Not that I minded. Those first years I had the feeling she didn't really like me—that she was one of those people who thought they were better than us because they had been here for twenty years and we had come on the boatlift three years before. We were refugees. They were exiles. As if we hadn't all left our homes and part of ourselves behind.*

Your father turned to Pablo and asked him if he wanted to go to the park. Of course, the answer was yes. "Get your purse," he said to me. "What do we need for the baby?"

"Pampers, another bottle, clothes."

"Bueno," he said, putting you up on his shoulder to burp you. "Get that stuff too."

I went into the kitchen to make the bottle, and then into your room to gather the other things. As I packed the diaper bag, I could feel something shift—a leaking of the ugliness out of me.

An hour later, the sun on my face, the breeze blowing through my half-done hair, Pablo screaming in delight as he went down the slide, I felt a bit more of the ugliness leak out. It was only a little—nothing big. But it was something. It was the beginning of the end of that darkness.

15

My father's in the living room watching a special report called *Who Is Mitt Romney?* He wants to vote for him but doesn't know what a Mormon is. Not that it matters. Obama might as well be wearing fatigues and smoking a cigar. I've tried to talk to them, but they won't listen. Like most of the older Cubans, they've voted Republican from the moment they became citizens.

My mom and I are in their bedroom watching *Abismo.* Clara is riding in a Hummer limousine with Sebastián's mother—who, it turns out, hates her own son but wants an heir very badly. So badly that she is willing to pay off Clara if she gets pregnant and signs over all custody of the baby to her. This was the proposal she was talking about the other day when she called. They scream-whisper about it in the back seat of the limo.

"She'll never do it," my mother says from her side of the bed.

I adjust the pillows, trying to get some support for my lower back. "She'll never do what?"

"Give up the baby."

"You don't think so?"

"No woman could do that."

"Mom, women do it all the time."

"Young girls. Girls into drugs." Then in English she says, "Clara's not that young. She's not with drugs."

"*On* drugs."

"*With* drugs. *On* drugs. Whatever. You watch," she says, switching back to Spanish. "She's not going to give up that baby." She nods at my belly. "Would you?"

I put my hand there. "Of course not. But I'm in a different situation."

"So why do you think Clara will?"

"I don't know. She seems pretty into it. Armando can get his surgery with that money."

A commercial for Tide comes on: just your average happy Hispanic family playing softball and getting filthy.

"I won't do it," my mother says into her lap. "Even though he threatened me."

"Who threatened you? What are you talking about?"

She turns her head toward me. She looks a little surprised, a little scared. She's coming back from wherever she was. "¿Que? No. I—"

"Mom, what is all this? What are you talking about?"

"Look," she says, and points to a CoolSculpting commercial on the TV. "That's what Teresita did where they sucked the fat off her stomach."

She's stalling. "Mom," I say again, "come on. What were you talking about just now?"

"Ay, Mónica. Nada, okay? I don't know what I said. I just said I would never give up a baby like Clara."

"No, Mom. You said you *won't* give it up. Even though somebody threatened you. It sounded like you were having one of those episodes, those memories. Who threatened you?"

She sighs and looks toward the window. "Tu papá."

"Dad threatened you? Like, physically?" I can't believe this. He's never touched her.

"He threatened to divorce me."

"Why?"

"Es muy complicado. All this happened a long time ago. And it's not important anymore."

"What 'all this'?"

She shakes her head.

"Complicado how?"

She glares at me and says, in English, "Can you please let it go?"

"Mom. All the memories and everything? I'm thinking we need to talk to the doctor about it. Maybe it's not just the anesthesia. I think you should see a neurologist. Or maybe a psychiatrist."

She looks at me, a little scared, I can tell, but also angry. "No," she says, sternly. "I don't need a psychiatrist."

"But you keep having these episodes."

"It's fine. They'll go away," she says. "And I will not be going to a psychiatrist, so don't bother making the appointment."

It's the most herself she's been since before the surgery, and for a moment I see a spark of the old her: the woman who was in charge of everything, from who hosted Thanksgiving to what color I should paint my bathroom—that thing about her I both admire and resist, and that's been absent since she woke up.

"Could you get me some more water, please?" she says.

I go to the bathroom for the water, and when I get back, her eyes are filled with tears. Now I feel bad. I don't even under-stand why she's crying, and I feel like if I ask, it will make things worse.

Jesus is hanging on the cross above their bed. He's looking down, of course, and for a second I think he's looking at my mom. Maybe *he* can do something about whatever the hell is going on. I stand there trying to figure out what to do, what to say.

"Let's just watch the show," she says.

I go back to my side of the bed and try again to get the pillows right. It's impossible and I sit there with my lower back aching, trying to remember exactly what she said. Something about a baby. And my father threatening her. Somehow I know this is related to what she said in pre-op. It's just a feeling, nothing I can explain, and I don't know what to do except sit there in silence with her watching the show. On-screen, Clara and Sebastián are on horseback, riding through a field. Sebastián is smiling this huge smile, but Clara's back there with her eyes closed, looking like she might be praying for help. A few minutes later, I sneak a look at my mom and she looks the same way.

On my way out, I stop in the living room to tell my father goodbye. I don't tell him exactly what my mother said, about him threatening her, but I do tell him she had another episode.

"Something's wrong with her," I say. "Like, for real."

"Mónica, the woman was in a coma for eight days. They told me that for every day you're in a coma, it takes two days to come back to normal. She just needs some time to readjust."

I do some quick math in my head. Sixteen days for readjustment. She's been awake for fourteen. She should be almost there by now. Physically, she *is* improving. She can move around better and she's getting her strength back little by little. But cognitively it seems like she's getting worse. "Dad, what about the other night when she asked you to take the baby? That seemed like an actual delusion."

"That's nothing to worry about." He looks like he doesn't totally believe it himself.

"Nothing to worry about? Yesterday they sent a male home health nurse and she thought he was one of the bad guys on *Abismo*. I had to make the guy show her his ID badge. And has she told you about the memories of her friend Adelita? How intense they are? I really think she needs to see someone."

He sighs. "She won't go."

"Can't we make her go?"

"Are you kidding me? Your mother is half mule. You know that."

I shake my head. "God, I know."

He turns off *Who Is Mitt Romney?* "Okay, I'm done with this. It doesn't matter who he is," he says. "What matters is who he isn't." He walks me out to my car and places a hand on my back. "Go home and relax, mija. Have a good weekend with Robert. You deserve it."

When I get home, Robert's sitting on the sofa eating ribs and watching a Chris Rock stand-up special. "Hey, baby," he says. "Want some? I made homemade sauce. And I washed my hands before."

"I'm good." I go into the kitchen for some water and it's like someone committed a murder in there. A half a slab of ribs is still sitting out on the counter—not on a plate or a cutting board or even a paper towel. A slash of sauce runs from the sink almost to the coffee maker. All the stuff to make the sauce is still out: vinegar, sugar, ketchup, molasses. I put my hands on my stomach. "Since when do we have molasses?" I say. "What is this, a fucking Cracker Barrel?" The empty aluminum foil box is on the ground next to the garbage can, along with a couple of used paper towels. Worst of all, he's used one of my wooden spoons from the blue and yellow pitcher. The spoon is so glued down with barbecue sauce that I have to pry it off the counter. Something in me clicks open.

I walk into the living room holding the spoon. "Why did you use this?" I know I'm not being rational.

He pauses the stand-up. "What do you mean?"

"I mean these spoons aren't for cooking."

"What are they for?"

"Decoration."

"Then why are they there?"

"I just told you: for decoration."

"That's stupid."

"No it's not."

"Why would you have spoons that you don't use?"

"For decoration."

"Well, how am I supposed to know that?" He takes a rib off his plate, takes three quick bites, like a rat.

"Because I never use them."

"Yes you do," he says with his mouth full.

"No I don't."

"You use one every time you make tacos."

"No. I don't." I go back to the kitchen and take out a wooden spoon that looks almost identical to the one in my hand, except the wood is a little more frayed. I come back to the living room, holding both of them. "I use this one," I say, holding out the frayed one.

"Where'd you get that?"

"From the drawer next to the stove. The one with all the cooking spoons in it."

He shrugs. "I didn't know that was there. I just used the first one I saw."

"Obviously." I go back to the kitchen, put the older-looking spoon back in the drawer, and close it a little too hard.

I hear him say, "Dude, what the hell?" and put his plate down on the coffee table. He comes into the kitchen. "It's just a spoon. I can wash it off. I can buy you a new one if you want. What's the big deal?"

The big deal is that I have a baby growing inside me that I'm going to have to raise in three months. With Robert. Who's currently raising iguanas. And Manny, who didn't care enough to stick around the first time, now can't stop caring about me. Meanwhile, my mother might be losing her mind or hiding something about my father, or both, and all I want right now is to be back in the Mouse House, lying on my sofa, alone.

Robert picks up the aluminum foil box and throws it in the trash, puts the cap back on the molasses, and puts it away.

"Sorry," I say. I cover my face with my hands. "I'm just a little overwhelmed right now. I'll be right back." I go to the bathroom, wash my face, and tell myself to calm down. I put my hands on my stomach. "Mijo," I whisper to him, "what the fuck am I doing?"

When I come back to the living room, Robert puts his hand on the back of my neck and pulls my face into his chest. "Sorry I made such a mess," he says. "I'll clean it up. And I'll buy you a new wooden spoon. I promise."

"It's okay. You don't have to."

"Oh, I'm going to. I'm buying you a whole pack of wooden spoons. In varying sizes." He smiles and I punch his chest, but not hard.

We clean up the kitchen and watch the end of the special. I

know the whole time that he's going to make a move on me. He rubs my leg while we watch; he touches my lower back while I'm brushing my teeth. When we get into bed, he reaches across and puts a hand on my belly, then rubs it down to my thigh. I just take a breath. I don't want to have sex with him. But I feel like I owe him. Because I texted Manny and then he showed up at the hospital and drunk-texted me and called me. And because I was an asshole about the wooden spoon. So when Robert puts a finger into the top of my underwear, I let him pull them down. We never do get my tank top off, but I don't think he cares. He tries to wait for me but I tell him it's okay. I just want to be done, to not be having this day, this week, this month, anymore. Right after he comes, as he's still breathing in my ear, I think of this thing Manny told me once. He said he loved to hear me laugh. I push away the thought and get up to go pee. I stay in the bathroom a long time, hoping that when I get back, Robert will be asleep.

Mirta

I knew your father was right—that I needed to get out of the house more. So once you were three months old, I started taking you and Pablo to Tropical Park in the mornings. It helped me, having that place I could go where Pablo would have something to do and you could sleep in your stroller. And I could sit on a bench in the shade and breathe.

And then one day I met Teresita. She came up and sat down next to me and just started talking. You know her; that woman would talk to a rock if there was nobody around. She was pregnant with Elizabeth and I asked her how many months she was.

"Only six, but it feels like twelve," she said.

"You're not feeling well?" I asked, and that was it, we were off. All you need is two women talking about being pregnant and you're there all day. By the end, we were talking about our hemorrhoids right there on the park bench.

When it was time to go, we couldn't get the boys out of the sandbox. Pablo and Alex had become fast friends, just like we had, and they wanted to stay, of course. Teresita had to pick Alex up and carry him, screaming, to the car. I tried to do the same, but I couldn't because I was pushing the stroller and, of course, you woke up and started crying. Now Pablo was screaming that he didn't want to leave and you were crying and people were looking. I yanked him by the arm but he buckled his legs so I had to drag him down the path to the parking lot. "¡Vamos!" I yelled, not realiz-

ing that his shorts, which were from the bag of hand-me-downs Gladys had brought over that week, and a little too big, had slid off and were down around his ankles. How had this gone so wrong so fast? I didn't know. I just knew I had to get him to the car. I bent down and pulled his shorts off. Now I was the crazy, screaming mother dragging her half-naked child down the path.

Teresita put Alex into the car and came back to help me. I was so ashamed. I shook my head. "No, thank you. I'm fine," I said. What a joke. I wasn't fine. I hadn't been fine for months.

"Here," Teresita said, taking the stroller. "Let me take her for you. That way you can get him."

I nodded my thanks, worried that if I opened my mouth to speak again, I would cry. Or maybe scream. I picked up Pablo and carried him to the car.

Teresita strapped you into your car seat and then stood there while I put your brother's pants back on. She wiped the sweat off her forehead, blew air out of her mouth. "Ay, chica," she said, pointing back to the path. "That happens about twenty times a day at my house. It's nice to know mine isn't the only one." She smiled kindly.

I swallowed, blinking my eyes to get the tears away. "Gracias," I said.

"It's nothing." She touched my arm. "See you next time." She went back over to her car and got in, her big belly grazing the wheel as she leaned up to pull the gearshift on the steering column.

I was so embarrassed, thinking about how the other mothers had seen all that and were judging me. I felt that a lot in those days: other people's judgment. Probably because we were Marielitos, something I wasn't proud of back then. Castro had called us worms and the Americans here thought we were the trash he sent over. And even some of the Cubans didn't think much better. So maybe it was a little of that. But I was judging myself so much too. Just look at my life: I had two babies from two different men. I had gotten dragged into the street naked at a motel. And I had terrible *thoughts sometimes about leaving. Just getting on a plane to Puerto Rico and going to find Juan, to live with him forever in some secret place. But then, in the very next second, I would look at you and Pablo and know that I could never leave you.*

Before that night in English class, I had accepted my life with Rolando. He was a good husband and a good father and I was content. But then Juan came back into my life and I felt more than contentment. I felt true happiness again. Juan elevated my spirit, my soul. Now, without him, I felt shrunken and sucked in on myself, with nothing to do all day except take care of you kids, and nothing else to think about except how much I missed him, how much I wanted to be back in Cuba. Leaving the park, all I could think about was the old days living on the farm, working with him and Adelita and the other people in our group, passing on messages from Chucho at the bakery, trying to actually do something to save ourselves.

Instead of turning left to go home, I turned right, got on the expressway, and drove in the direction of the last place I had been happy. I pulled into the parking lot, parked in my space in front of room four, and stared at the door, the peeling blue paint. The gold number shining in the sunlight. I began to cry. To sob. My head on the steering wheel, my hands curled into fists in my lap.

From the back seat, I heard, "¿Mami?"

I said nothing.

"¿Mami?"

I didn't want to hear him. I wanted to be inside there, under the sheet, pressed against Juan, not even making love, just lying together, watching the smoke from his cigarette snake up to the ceiling. I pounded my fists into my thighs, over and over, and Pablo said my name louder and louder. "Mami," he said. "Mami. Mami. Mami."

Finally, I turned around and screamed, "What? What do you want?" so loud that he jumped. His eyes filled with tears right away. He looked so scared. Very soon, he was crying so hard that he was hiccupping and not breathing very well. I sat there turned halfway around in my seat, watching him cry, paralyzed. I knew I was supposed to do something but I didn't know what.

By now you had started crying too. The sound was filling the car and I didn't know how to stop it and that made me want to die. What good was I? As a mother, I was a waste. A failure. As a wife—forget it. I was nothing. Nothing. And everyone was crying. And it was so loud. Nobody would stop. I couldn't stop. Pablo was trying to talk but he was crying so hard, I couldn't understand him. You were screaming. That horrible sound, the sound of a screaming baby. There is nothing like that in the world. I was trapped in that car. In the parking lot of the Palmetto Motel. It was hot. The air-conditioning was broken. The windows were down and we were all screaming and crying. I had started to yell, "Shut up!" over and over. A man came out of the office. I saw him coming over and I knew I couldn't take one more person knowing what an awful mother I was. I put the car in reverse and backed out. I pulled right out without even looking and almost got hit—a yellow van had to slam on its brakes—but I kept going, away from that man. I found my way to 836, got on, and drove. The more I drove, the calmer I got. You calmed down a little too. But Pablo kept crying, on and on, for a long time. I just kept saying, "Please, Pablito, please," because it was all I could say. I should have pulled over and gotten him out. I should have held him and stroked his hair and told him I was sorry, that everything was okay, and offered to take him for ice cream, or back to the park, or anything but what I did, which was to drive to the airport and back and just wait for him to calm down, which he eventually did, and then, by miracle of God, he fell asleep, and so did you, and then there was quiet, and I just kept going, all the way up 836, onto the turnpike and away from everything, at least for a little while.

16

Sunday night, my mom says she's feeling up to it, so we invite every-one over for dinner to celebrate her coming home. Caro brings la-sagna and a salad. Gladys brings flan and CONGRATULATIONS! party ware. We're thirteen total, so the guys bring in the patio furniture.

My mother tries to set up the food, but we tell her to rest. "Let me just do the napkins," she says, and starts putting one down, along with a plastic fork, at everyone's place. My parents, Gladys and Fermín, and Caro and Mike sit with the girls at the dining room table. At the patio table, it's Pablo and Maritza, me and Rob-ert, and Caro's brother, Eddie. Usually he brings some girl in a skirt the size of an Ace bandage, but tonight he's alone.

The whole night is easy. Everyone has their shoes off, so my mom's not worried about them tracking in dirt. She just sits at the table sipping the red wine my brother brought and looks happier than I've seen her since before the surgery.

At one point Caro and I slip down the hall so she can give me the update on the fight she's having with Mike. They own a McDon-ald's in North Miami and he wants to buy another one down here, but she doesn't want him to because they'd have to borrow against the house to do it. "It's over," she says, and takes a sip of her wine.

"What? What's over?"

"The fight. It's over. We made up. For now. He agreed to wait until January so we can see how well the North Miami store did this year."

"Great. Are you guys okay? You seemed okay at dinner."

"Yeah, we're okay. He's just so impatient. I keep telling him we need to be careful and not get in over our heads. If it fails, you know, we could lose the house."

"Totally makes sense." I feel like an idiot who's saying nothing of value. But I don't know what to say; I've never been even remotely in the same position. I'm currently paying rent to my boyfriend. Fiancé.

"I mean, honestly, I'd rather borrow from my parents if we have to."

"Do you think they'd be up for it?"

"My father's already offered, but Mike doesn't want to do it. You know how he is: Mr. Independiente." She means this literally. Mike's parents moved to Orlando his senior year of high school and he stayed here to work full-time and put himself through college. "Hey," Caro says, "anything more from Manny?"

I look her in the face so she won't know I'm lying when I shake my head and say, "Nope. Nothing."

She nods. "Good." We walk back down the hall to rejoin the party.

Maritza is on the sofa with the girls, talking about some Justin Bieber song. She plays it on her phone while the girls sing along and try to teach her the dance from the video.

Fermín says, "Ay, por favor. That's not music. Rolando, put on some Hector Lavoe."

As soon as he does, Fermín has Gladys up and dancing, their

hips and legs and feet moving so in sync it's like they're one person. Pretty soon somebody's moved the coffee table out of the way and we're all up, Caro and Mike over by the TV, Pablo and Maritza by the sofa, Eddie trading off the girls. Even my mother and father, doing a really easy one-two. Last Thanksgiving—Robert's first with us—he couldn't believe it when we turned on the music and started dancing after dinner. Now he's used to it—not that we do it at every family gathering or anything, just parties and special times. And tonight does feel special. It feels, finally, like things are turning around.

Robert takes my hand and does his white-boy pretend salsa, joking around because he can't really do it but is giving it his best shot anyway.

He points to my stomach. "Lil Taz is gonna have my moves."

"I hope not." I laugh and give him a kiss.

When the song ends, everyone claps and then the girls insist on putting on one more Justin Bieber song and my mother says to me, "Vamos a hacer el café."

In the kitchen, I get the big cafetera out since we're so many people, but when I go to pack the coffee in, a piece of the gasket falls off in my hand.

"That thing is a piece of junk," my mother says. "I knew it wouldn't last. I'll get the other one." She goes into the garage, and I follow her.

"What other one?"

"The old one." She points to the boxes that have been on the shelf my entire life but that I've never paid any attention to.

She wants the one that says *Cocina* on the side. I take it down and she starts taking things out of it: yellow-and-white-checkered kitchen towels and an old pressure cooker, a red spiral notebook, and some recipe books that I'm surprised she owns. My mother doesn't use recipes and disdains any woman who does. They must have been a gift she never threw away. The notebook is strange too. I open it: in her handwriting, a phone number on the first line, then lots of English sentences with Spanish translations. "Is this from a class?" I ask.

"Sí." She takes it from me, looks at it for a long second, then puts it down. She finds the cafetera, which she's kept in its old, worn box. "Okay, vamos." She starts back to the kitchen.

"Wait. Aren't we going to put this stuff back?"

"No, no. We can put it back later."

"Are you sure? I can put it away real quick for you."

"No, no, vamos," she says, almost hurrying away. "We need to make the coffee."

"Are you okay?" I say.

"I'm fine," she says. "I'm feeling a bit weak, that's all. I should probably sit down."

"Okay." I leave the box where it is.

We make the coffee, and the entire time she's making the espumita, she's far away and silent. When the coffee's ready, she comes back. "Let's use the saucers and everything," she says as she pulls the red cups down out of the cabinet. "We're celebrating. Right?"

"Right," I say, though ever since we went into the garage, it feels like almost the opposite—like we're mourning.

Mirta

Meeting Teresita was the thing that helped me the most to get out of my depression. Women need friends. Maybe men don't, but women do. And having her in my life—to talk to on the phone, to drink coffee with while the boys drove their carritos on the living room floor, to sit with at the park—helped me tremendously. I would call her and she would answer the phone, "Dímelo cantando," just like my mother always had, and that made me happy. Over the next few months I began to feel less alone and more able to do things. I could take a shower in the mornings now, do the shopping and the laundry, keep the house up a little more. Things were getting better, it seemed.

Then, one night, they got worse.

The phone rang and a man who said he was with the FBI asked me if I knew Juan Viera de Céspedes. I was making dinner, and I dropped the tomato I was holding right onto the floor. "Yes," I said. "I do." I was too afraid to say no. If he was calling my house to ask me this, he must have known the answer was yes. But why was he calling my house to ask me this? Was Juan in trouble? Was I in trouble? The FBI. Calling me. This made no sense.

"Excellent," he said. "When can I come by to ask you some questions? Is tomorrow morning okay? Ten o'clock?"

He arrived the next morning at 9:15. Your father had been gone for an hour, thank God, but still, the breakfast dishes were all over the table and nobody was dressed. But I had to open the door. What was I going to do? Leave an FBI agent standing on the doorstep? He had a mustache and wore glasses and was about my age.

"¿Señora Campo?" he said.

"Sí."

He showed me his identification. "Agente Daniel Fernández."

I brought him into the kitchen. You were lying in your playpen and Pablo was sitting at the table, eating his tostada and leche con chocolate. I moved it all to the living room and turned on the TV for him. Then I went into the bedroom and changed my clothes.

Agente Daniel Fernández was still standing in my kitchen when I got back. I offered him un cafecito and I was so nervous as I made it that I kept forgetting how many spoons of coffee I had put into the cafetera. Of course, you started crying.

He didn't even ask; he just reached into the playpen and picked you up. "Let's see if we can make you happy," he said. "My son likes the one-two-three." He pulled you away from him. "One," he said. He pulled you to his chest. "Two." And then up over his head. "Three!" You stopped crying.

"Thank you," I said. "How old is your son?"

"Almost seven months." He repeated the one-two-three a few more times while I made the espumita and the coffee brewed.

When it was done, I put his on the table and he handed you back to me. He took a sip and pulled a little spiral notebook and a pen from his front pocket. "Señora Campo, did you have a relationship with Juan Viera de Céspedes from January to October 1982?"

I looked down, stunned. In the living room, someone on Sesame Street *was counting to ten, first in English, then in Spanish. I closed my eyes. When I opened them, he was looking me straight in the face.*

"Yes." I thought maybe this was about the night Rolando caught us. "My husband knows all about this," I said.

"Yes, I know. I've read the police report from the night at the Palmetto Motel. Did your husband and Juan ever communicate with each other beyond that night?" So it was about that.

"No."

"Okay. Do you know where Juan is now?"

"He moved to Puerto Rico."

"He shared that information with you?"

"Yes. The last time I saw him, he told me they were leaving. Him and his sister and his mother."

He wrote something in his notebook. He was left-handed and I could see the letters smearing a little on the paper as he wrote. "And do you know anything about his move? Why he was leaving?"

I told him everything I knew: about Dolores having lung cancer, about her wanting to die in Puerto Rico instead of here, because at least it's an island. I mentioned the cousin getting Juan a job and the fact that Adelita went with him.

He took another sip of his coffee. "When Juan told you he was moving to Puerto Rico, that was the last time you saw him?"

"Yes."

"Was that at his apartment?" He checked his notebook. "Bird West Apartments, apartment 204?"

The image of Juan on the sofa that day, his leg and arm bruised from what Rolando had done to him, bloomed in my mind. I heard his voice in my head saying, "We're leaving." I looked at Agente Fernández now, here in my kitchen. "Yes," I said. "The last time I saw him was at his apartment."

"And you visited him there frequently?"

"I visited with his sister. We were friends. We knew each other in Cuba."

"You did? His sister Adela?" He wrote something down in his notebook.

"Adelita, yes." I didn't tell him that Juan and I had been married and then divorced. Or that we had, at one time, all lived together on their farm. That felt like something that belonged to me and I didn't want him to have it. He already had so much, it seemed.

He asked me if I knew how Juan spent his time, who his friends were.

"I know he had friends," I said. "But I never met any of them. Our time together was very limited, you know." I looked away, embarrassed.

"I understand," he said.

I knew he used to visit Chucho's mother. Chucho was an only child and Juan had promised him that if he made it out of prison, he would look after her. Luckily, her neighbor in Cuba convinced her to leave on the boatlift so he could do just that. Now she lived in a little apartment on Miami Beach and he would go visit her every other Saturday. I told Agente Fernández all of this and watched him write it down. "He is a very loyal person," I said. "When he makes a commitment to someone, he keeps it."

"Yes. I've heard that." Daniel Fernández smoothed his mustache with his fingers. "Señora Campo, did he ever talk to you about what he was doing here in Miami?"

"What do you mean? He was working for his cousin, laying tile. And he had a second job digging holes for a telecommunications company. They needed money for their mother's medical bills."

He nodded and asked me what I knew about the cousin, and then I knew for sure this wasn't about that night at the Palmetto—that it was about something else, something worse. I didn't want anything to happen to us, so I told him what Juan had told me about an American who used to show up sometimes at their jobsites, how Juan thought his cousin might have been buying or selling drugs. He wrote that down. He asked me if I had ever seen that person, the American, if I knew anything about him, what kind of car he drove—anything.

I tried to think back. I didn't want to think about that time, of course. When I did, all I could think were thoughts that hurt me. I saw his shoulders hovering over me in the dark; I felt his eyebrows, which I used to trace with my fingers when we made love. "No. He never told me anything about him. I know he would show up and Orlando, the cousin, would go smoke a cigarette with him in his car. That's all I know."

He filled up pages in the little notebook, writing and writing. "Bueno," he said. "That's all my questions for now." He stood up.

I said, "Can I please ask you— Why are you here? Am I in trouble? Is Juan in trouble?" I was holding you in front of me, facing him, almost like you were a shield.

He looked down at you, gave you his finger to grab. "No, Mirta. May I call you Mirta?"

"Yes."

"You are not in trouble. Juan, however, is a person of interest in an investigation."

"Investigation of what?"

"I am not allowed to disclose that information at this time."

"Drugs?" I said. "Did he get involved in drugs with Orlando? I told him not to. He said he wouldn't."

"I really can't discuss the investigation." Daniel Fernández took his card out of his wallet and laid it on the table. "Please," he said. "If you think of anything about Juan that was in any way out of the ordinary, anyone he knew or interacted with who seemed a little strange or different, will you call me? Or if you think of anything else that might help me get

in touch with him?" Pablo laughed at something on the TV. Big Bird was singing and clapping. Pablo clapped along with him.

I said yes, I would. Daniel left and I hid the card in the back of my wallet, where Rolando would never find it. That night, I served dinner and said nothing about the FBI agent who had sat in his chair for an hour that morning.

17

Gladys calls and tells me she'll be over at six to drop off dinner. My father is staying late at the optical so he won't have to work this weekend when I won't be around. I'll be at Robert's, spritzing and feeding the iguanas with gloves on because he left for Marco Island this afternoon with Flaco, Flaco's brother, and their girlfriends. I was supposed to go, too, but I secretly didn't want to, so I used my mom as an excuse. Now I'll have the whole weekend to myself.

Gladys arrives dressed like she's going to the Oscars, in a full-length black gown, with her hair and makeup professionally done.

"Whoa," I say. "Look at you!"

She smiles. "Fermín is being honored by the South Florida Contractors Association." She hands me three Tupperwares of food: white rice, black beans, and picadillo.

My mother's on the sofa watching a *Golden Girls* marathon. She looks over. "My God, Gladys," she says. "You didn't have to do this."

"It's nothing," Gladys says. "Listen, I didn't put any raisins in the picadillo. I couldn't remember if you did yours with or without."

"Without," my mother says. "Juan doesn't like them. Neither does Adelita."

Gladys looks at me, as if I can explain. But I can't explain. Because I can't speak. Everything inside me is exploding. There's no way she meant to say "Rolando." My father loves raisins, especially in picadillo. It's been a point of contention between my parents my whole life. She meant to say "Juan." Whoever Juan is. *Your father is Juan. I loved him so much and he never knew.* No. Oh my God. And he knew Adelita somehow.

Fermín honks the horn for Gladys and she leaves. I take the food into the kitchen and stand there staring at the spoon rest. The penguin on it has a yellow bow tie on. I focus on the bow tie while I breathe deeply and try to calm the buzzing feeling in my arms.

That's it, I say in my head, maybe to the baby, maybe to myself. *I have to know.*

I serve up the food and my mom and I eat it in front of the TV.

It's the episode where the Golden Girls' house is burglarized and a young George Clooney is one of the cops. When they knock on the door, my mother says, "The police took him while we were gone. Adelita found the note."

Go, I say to myself. *Do it.* Instead of breaking her out of the moment, I try to keep it going, to see what else she'll say. "Where was it?" I ask her. "The note."

"In the kitchen drawer. He had hidden it."

"What did it say?"

She goes quiet. She's looking at the television but not really.

I take the remote and mute it. "What did the note say?"

"It said, 'Say nothing.'"

"Who wrote it? Who was the person who got taken by the police and left the note?"

I can tell she wants to answer but is afraid to. Her eyes are darting around, past my face, above my head. She touches her mouth, then her hair. I'm pretty sure she's back from the delusion.

I try to play it cool. "Adelita read the note that said, 'Say nothing.' Did that really happen? Was that real?"

She nods a tiny nod.

"It was? It was real?"

Another tiny nod. Still not looking at me.

"Who did they take, Mom? Who did the police take?" Because I know, somehow, that if Juan is the person the police took, then everything she said the morning of her surgery is true. And my life as I knew it is over and the me who was me will be gone.

She presses her fingers to her lips. She looks sad. Finally, she says, "Juan. They took Juan."

I'm actually short of breath. I'm afraid I'll faint. *Go,* I tell myself. *Ask her.* "Juan who doesn't like raisins?"

"Yes."

No, I hear myself say, maybe out loud. But I have to keep going. "In the hospital, before the surgery, you said—"

"I know. I know what I said." Her shoulders are slumped forward, almost in defeat, her hair hanging in her face a little.

"You do? You said you didn't remember."

"I don't. But I remember thinking I wanted to say it, that it was time."

"Mom—" *Go.* "Mom, who is Juan?"

"You want to know? You want to know the whole story?"

"Yes," I say, even though I don't. But I know I have to. I've been hiding from this for weeks, I realize. Maybe even using the stuff with Manny as a way to avoid it.

She sits up a little straighter, looks me in the face, like she's squaring off with me.

"Juan Viera de Céspedes was my first husband. We lived on his mother's farm in Holguín. Adelita lived there too. She was Juan's sister—and my best friend."

The baby kicks. It's like he's listening too.

"Your father didn't want me to tell you," she says. "He wanted me to just leave this part of my life in the past."

"Mom, what—"

"We got a divorce. But only because he was put in prison and I thought he would never get out. He had been working as a counterrevolutionary. Against Castro, you know, to undermine the government. He was caught and imprisoned, and I thought I'd never see him again. But I was wrong. Like a miracle, he reappeared in my life. He had been released from jail and sent to Miami. His mother and sister came later, on the boatlift, just like us. I didn't know any of this, but then I ran into them in the English class I had signed up for."

I point in the direction of the garage. "The one where you used that notebook?"

"Yes." She folds and refolds the lip of the green throw lying across her lap. "The moment I saw him, I knew."

"Knew what?"

"That I still loved him." She looks at me with what I guess is her version of a game face. "Mónica, I made a bad decision. I began to see him behind your father's back."

I try for my own game face, but I can feel how big my eyes are. "You mean, like *see* him see him?"

"We would meet in the afternoons. In a little hotel on Eighth Street. Eighth and 32nd Avenue. The Palmetto Motel. I'll never forget it. It had the most beautiful hibiscus bushes. It still does. It's not called the Palmetto anymore. They converted it to a Quality

Inn or something like that. But it's there, just bigger, you know—with two stories now."

I'm almost speechless with shock, but not quite. "You cheated on Dad?" I say.

"Yes."

"In a Quality Inn on Eighth Street and 32nd Avenue?"

"Yes."

I don't even know what I'm feeling. I'm so afraid of what she's going to say next. Oh God, what is she going to say next?

"Your father caught us at the hotel. He dragged me naked into the street and he tried to kill Juan."

I put my hand to my mouth. "He shot him?"

"No, thank God. He didn't have the gun back then. He beat him. Somebody called the police. They arrested your father, but they let him go later."

"How old was I? Does Pablo know any of this?"

"You were not born. Pablo was too young to know anything." She looks at the TV for a second. All the Golden Girls except for Sophia are pacing around the living room. I almost want to get up and do the same thing, but I'm not sure my legs will work. "That wasn't the end," she says. "I—I did not protect myself." She clasps her hands in front of her chest, right where her scar is. "I got pregnant, and Rolando knew he wasn't the father. We had not . . . been close for a while."

I'm holding my napkin, ripping it into little pieces in my lap. I ball up the pieces and put them in my pocket.

"He wanted me to get an abortion," my mother says. "He threatened to divorce me if I didn't."

"You said he wanted you to give it up."

"Give it up, abort it. Same thing. I couldn't do it."

"So what happened to that baby?" I say. I hold all the fingers of my left hand with all the fingers of my right hand. I squeeze really hard, hoping that, somehow, that baby is not me.

She closes her eyes. "That baby is you."

At first, I say nothing. I might hear nothing and see nothing, too; I'm not sure. All I know is that the baby—my baby—is kicking and kicking, pushing on me from the inside out, moving me toward the truth of all of this.

"I'm sorry I never told you. Your father didn't want me to. He would be very upset if he knew I'd told you now."

"Which father?"

A look of pain comes over her face. "Juan had no idea."

"You never told him?"

"I only saw him one more time after that and I didn't know I was pregnant yet."

"Just like Jaquelín on the show."

"Just like Jaquelín on the show."

My face has completely stopped working. Time feels nonexistent and warped. I'm asking all these questions because I want to understand but also because I want to keep my grip on reality. Is it possible this is all a hallucination—that I've dreamed myself into my own telenovela? Like my mom mixing up the male nurse and the bad guy on *Abismo*? I look at the TV for relief or help of some kind. Something to ground me. But even *The Golden Girls* can't do it. I half expect my mom's house to turn into theirs. For her beige camelback sofa to morph into the art deco rattan set with the flower print cushions. And then, who knows? Maybe Clara and Sebastián and the goons will come knocking on the door. I rub my hands down my thighs a few times, just to feel that I exist. Finally, I say, "I can't even believe this."

My mother's eyes are filled with tears. "I know. It's very hard. Very complicated."

The anger hits me and I say, "No shit, it's very complicated. Why didn't you ever tell me? How could you never tell me?"

"Your father made me promise. He felt it was better that way. Easier."

"To lie to me my whole life?"

She doesn't say anything. She just closes her eyes.

"So why are you telling me now?"

"I have no choice. I told you when I was on those drugs. You were going to keep pressing me and pressing me." She rubs her forehead. "And with these memories taking ahold of me . . . it's just all too much. Maybe we *should* have told you from the beginning. Maybe you deserved to know. Especially now that you're going to be a mother."

"And Dad knows it all? He knows Adelita is Juan's sister? That you guys used to live on the farm? All of it?"

"Yes."

"That's why he can't take it whenever you mention her."

"Yes. I'm sure he doesn't like for me to talk about her. He believes that time of my life should be forgotten. And it probably should. It's all over. Done. Juan is dead. He died a long time ago. Rolando is your father. He will always be your father."

I want to ask what happened to Juan, how she knows he's dead, but I can't. Because all of a sudden I'm not paralyzed anymore and my chest is an accordion squeezing open and shut, and I feel like I'm going to die if I don't get out of here.

I stand up and go pack my clothes and the week's worth of toiletries I brought. And then I leave, rolling my suitcase through the living room as fast as I can. I don't say anything. No *Goodbye*. No *I need some air.* No *How could you do this to me?* Not even *I can't believe you.* I just walk out.

My mother calls to me: "Mónica, por favor." She yells, "¡Mónica! ¡Mónica!" her voice cracking as she says my name, over and over, but I don't care, I can't, I just have to keep going, keep walking, practically running now, probably dropping a trail of bras and underwear all over the front lawn. I shove my suitcase in the back seat, get in, and go.

Mirta

Teresita and I were sitting in the living room, drinking coffee and talking about the fact that her baby was upside down and a week late, when Daniel Fernández called again. I spoke to him in the kitchen, bouncing you on my lap. I tried to keep my voice as low as possible so Teresita wouldn't hear. He told me Juan might be in danger and he needed my help.

"What kind of danger?"

"We haven't verified the intelligence yet. It's from a source who has not always been reliable. But if the information is solid, then Juan may be the target of violence, depending on where he is right now."

"I told you where he is. He's in Puerto Rico."

"Not anymore."

"Not anymore? Do you think he's back here?" I didn't want that. I didn't want him to be in Miami. But more than anything, I didn't want him to be in danger.

"Mirta, what can you tell me about Lou Quintero, the owner of the laundry where Adelita worked?"

"Not very much," I said. Lou was half-Venezuelan, half-American. He owned an office cleaning business and that laundry, which Adelita basically ran for him. They were dating, but he was a dog, and I didn't like him. I told Daniel all of this.

He asked me a few more questions that sounded like he thought maybe Lou was into drugs. So many people were back in those days, with the

Cocaine Cowboys and all that going on. I told him no, she had never said anything about that. And then I said, "Agente Fernández, can you—"

"Daniel."

"Daniel. Can you tell me anything about Juan? Are you sure he didn't get involved in drugs?"

"I can tell you there is a drug trafficker involved in this investigation, yes. But it's not as simple as that. I'm sorry. I know this is hard for you. When I can tell you more, I will. In the meantime, it would be better for you to keep this to yourself."

"My husband does not know I've talked to you."

"Good," he said. "Let's keep it that way. And if you think of anything else you remember about Lou that seemed different or off in any way, please give me a call."

I promised I would.

When I came back to the living room, Teresita took one look at me and said, "You look terrible. Who was that?"

I put you down on the floor with the boys, who were playing carritos, driving them across the living room rug.

"You're not going to believe this," I said, and then I told her all of it. Almost all of it. I didn't tell her Juan was your father. I had made a promise to Rolando and I planned to keep it. I felt like that was my one duty in all of this. I could not love him as he loved me; I could not give him my soul. I could only give him my respect, and sometimes, when I needed to be touched, when I was feeling close to him, and I knew he missed it, I could give him my body.

"Oh, Mirta," she said. "No wonder you've been having such a hard time." She knew about Gladys having to rescue me that day you almost drowned, about the hours I had spent crying in my room while you slept in your crib and Pablo watched cartoons in the living room. "You love Juan?"

I closed my eyes for a moment. "Very much."

"*And you have no idea what happened to him?*"

I shook my head. "All I know is that they went to Puerto Rico. But now it sounds like he's not there and something bad is happening." I tried not to cry, but it was no use. Tears spilled down my face as I told her how Daniel wanted me to stay in touch, to call him if I could think of anything else that might help him find Juan. "But I can't. I knew almost nothing about his life here. We didn't have a lot of time to spend together, you know?"

She put her hand on mine. "Of course, of course."

"I'm so afraid," I said. I wiped my tears with my fingers, but they just kept coming. "What if something happens to him?"

Teresita put one arm around me and rested the other on her giant belly. "They'll find him," she said. "Don't worry. That's their job."

18

The beautiful hibiscus bushes are still there, right out front near the pool. I sit in my car staring at them, the flowers so red, like mouths screaming out at me, *That baby is you, that baby is you.* I think, *That baby is me,* and I know I can't go back to Robert's right now. Robert's is not home. Home is the Mouse House, but it's gone. All I have is this. When I remember the iguanas, and the fact that I should be spritzing them right now, I say "No" out loud and get out of the car.

At the front desk, I ask about rates. All they have available are the suites, but there's a special: $119 a night for military personnel. I put my hand on my stomach and tell the guy my fiancé is military. I get the rate.

So now I'm sitting on the bed in room 107, my purse in my lap, wondering if my mother was ever in this actual room. I talk to the baby. "Mijo," I say. "Everything is terrible. Terrible." I feel so alone, so tripped-out and scared. Home is not home and my father is not my father and my hands are trembling, my arms feel like rubber doll arms, just dangling at my sides. I need to do something, to call someone, to get some help. For one second I think, *I should call*

Robert, but immediately I know I can't. He won't know what to say or how to help me. He'll tell me to calm down, that it's going to be okay. But it's not going to be okay. Nothing is okay. Except the baby. The baby is okay. *The baby is okay*, I say in my head, over and over, trying to calm myself. *The baby is okay, the baby is okay.* I repeat it again and again, but it doesn't help. Nothing helps. I can't calm myself. I need someone to help me figure out how to do this, how to live through this. Manny. He won't tell me to calm down or that it's going to be okay. I need to call him. I'm not supposed to, but I need to. It's all I can think right now, so I do it. I pull out my phone, find his name in the "Recents" list, and tap it.

It takes him four rings to answer, but then he picks up and says, "Tell it to me singing." It's an old joke between us: the English translation of "Dímelo cantando," which is how his grandmother and so many old-school Cubans answer the phone.

I tell him everything. I can hear him breathing, taking it in. And then I tell him where I am.

"Why?"

"I don't know. I had to see it." I start crying.

"You're in the parking lot?"

"No. I got a room."

More breathing. "Is anybody with you? Are you alone?"

"Yeah."

"Yeah you're alone?"

"Yeah."

"Okay. I'll be right there."

"No, I—you don't have to—"

"Where is it again?" I can hear him moving around, probably getting shoes, keys, wallet.

I give him the address and the room number and he asks me to turn on the TV. *How do I turn on the TV?* I think. *What do I need to do that?* The remote. I need the remote. It's on the bedside table.

The TV screams on. "It's on." I am almost not crying.

"Find something stupid to watch. *The Kardashians* ó algo." I hear the chiming of the truck starting.

I find a show about former beauty pageant winners who are now rich moms. "I got something," I say. "It looks really stupid."

"Great," he says. "I'll be there soon. Watch TV till I get there, okay?"

I nod but say nothing.

"Okay?" he says again.

"Okay." I kind of yell it—not because I'm angry but because I can't control my voice or my body right now.

"I'll be there," he says, and something in me slows down.

Manny will be here. Manny, who would not stay with me, who would not quit going to war and just be with me. Commit to me. Get married to me. But he's coming here, to the Quality Inn & Suites, which used to be the Palmetto Motel, where my mother cheated on my father with her first love, who had been her husband, and got pregnant. With me. And now I'm pregnant. And engaged. To Robert. Robert, who is sweet, and who loves me, and who I didn't call. Oh God, I should have called Robert. I know that. But I couldn't. I can't. Not right now.

Maybe I should call Caro. No. She'll offer to come get me. Then I'll have to tell her everything. And if I do and I tell her I called Manny and that he's on his way, she'll ask me if I think that's a good idea. And I know it's not, it's a bad idea, but right now I don't care about good ideas or bad ideas. Right now I'm trying to understand how my parents kept that secret my whole fucking life.

The rich beauty moms, who are all white and blond except for one who is Black but really light-skinned, are going to a roof-top bar in Manhattan. I watch for thirty seconds but then I have to get up and move. I cannot stay still. If I stay still, the reality of what's happening, of my self—the self I had just two hours ago—dissolving will consume me. I try to listen to all the voice mails my mother has left, but after the first "Mónica," I have to press Stop. I can't stand the sound of her voice right now.

The room is a studio suite, which means there's a sofa—dark blue with gold flecks—with a coffee table and a matching chair. There's also a little kitchen with a table and two chairs, a mini-fridge and a mini-sink, which looks recently cleaned. The bed also looks clean—white sheets, white pillows. In the bathroom, everything is fine. Basic, beige, with the little strip of paper across the toilet, even. I pull back the shower curtain: clean tub. No hair, no pubes.

The sofa has two throw pillows that I arrange behind my back when I sit back down to watch the beauty moms again. Right as I do, my phone starts pinging repeatedly: Robert, power-texting me pictures of them at a bar eating oysters and drinking Coronas. At the end he sends a text that says, *Miss you babe. Wish you were here. Call me before you go to sleep.*

"Oh my God," I say out loud.

When Manny knocks on the door, I say, "Who is it?" even though I could look through the peephole if I really wanted to.

"The boogeyman," he says.

I open the door. He's holding a six-pack of Heineken in one hand and a bottle of Diet Dr Pepper in the other. "I can only stay a minute," he says.

I laugh a little. "Thanks for coming."

"Nice neighborhood. Did you see the place down the block? They have hourly rates and video movies."

"I love video movies," I say.

He's wearing shorts and a black T-shirt that's tight enough to show off his chest and his biceps. And a Yankees cap that he takes off and puts on the kitchen table. His hair is longer than I've ever seen it. He normally wears it shaved down, Army regulation–style.

"You have hair," I say.

He pats his head. "I'm putting the 'fro' in Afro-Cuban."

He's not full Afro-Cuban, but he's definitely a little mixed—darker than me, with tighter curls. When my mother described him to Teresita, before she'd met him, she said, "Bueno, es un poco—" and then she rubbed the back of her wrist with two fingers: Cuban for *Black.*

"It looks good," I say. I open my Diet Dr Pepper and sit down on the sofa "crisscross applesauce," as Caro's girls say.

He sits down next to me. I can smell him—his bath soap, his detergent. "So where's . . ." He points to my stomach with his beer.

"He's out of town."

"So you called *me.*"

"I panicked."

He takes a long sip. On TV, the beauty moms are drunk and arguing about somebody named Angelica—whether or not they should have invited her. "This *is* stupid," he says.

I start flipping channels. When I see Clara's face, I stop, almost out of habit. She's screaming at Sebastián that he could never be half the man Armando is. I keep flipping.

Manny makes me stop on *Jaws 2.* A bunch of early-eighties teens are sailing in a harbor, throwing water balloons at each other. He says, "All the hot ones are gonna die."

"They are?"

"Never seen this. But I'll bet you twenty bucks." He takes another long sip of his beer.

"Thank you again for coming here. I didn't mean to blow up your night." My voice breaks on *night* and that's it, I start crying. Hard. Harder than I've cried since my mom's surgery. I put my face in my hands and then I feel Manny's hand, warm and heavy, on my back right between my shoulder blades. He leaves it there as I cry, ugly and loud, everything in me just coming out in one long wave. It's Robert and the baby and the surgery and the delusions and now this—this thing where I am not my father's daughter, which is breaking me open in a way nothing ever has, not even losing Manny. It's a loss I can't explain, that I can barely understand.

We stay like this—me bent over a little, sobbing, him touching just my back—until I stop heaving. Until I'm sniffling but not crying anymore.

"I need a tissue," I say, and go to the bathroom. I don't want him to see my face. I close the door, blow my nose four times, and wash my hands. When I try to leave the bathroom, I can't. Something about the smallness of the room is comforting and the idea of leaving it is too much. I close the toilet seat and sit down.

After a few minutes, Manny knocks. "You okay?"

"Come in."

He opens the door. "You gonna puke?"

"No."

"You gonna shit?"

"No. It's—" I look around. "I just need to be in here right now."

He nods. Leans against the doorjamb. His phone buzzes in his pocket. He checks it, texts the person back. I'm thinking it's a girl, whoever he's seeing now.

"It's Robbins," he says. "He's on his way down. Won't be here till midnight." Robbins is from his first tour. He was also a medic but now he does IT in Orlando and comes down for the weekends sometimes. He had a lot of trouble when he got back: DUI, wife left him, de todo. He's got two little kids that he sees every other weekend.

"Okay. Sorry I fell apart. Thanks for—" I wave my hand in the direction of the other room.

He comes into the bathroom, squats down in front of me, and puts his hand on the back of my neck. He looks me right in the eyes. "Mónica," he says. "Please." For that one moment, the world feels right. Even though I know that us, here, in this bathroom, in this room at this hotel, is wrong. Very wrong.

"I can't believe my father's lived with this for twenty-nine years," I say.

"I couldn't do it."

"He wanted her to get rid of me."

"Yeah. Well, imagine. Your wife pregnant with some other dude's baby." There's a flicker of something in his face.

"Do you think it kills him to look at me? That I'm, like, some walking reminder?"

He shifts his weight, still in the squat, and laughs. "No, man. I think he loves you to death."

I remember the moment during the ultrasound when he started crying. That felt real. That felt like he loved me.

"I left my mom alone, you know. She called me like ten times but I haven't listened to the voice mails. I have no idea if she's okay. Her blood pressure is probably 180 over a thousand."

"Doesn't work that way," he says, smiling. "The bigger number's always on top. Can she get up and down off the sofa? Get to the bathroom by herself?"

"Yeah. But we're not supposed to stress her out. She's already super weird."

"Super weird how?"

I tell him about Adelita and the farm, her going in and out.

"That actually sounds a little like TBI."

"There's a condition called postsurgical delirium," I say. "But it usually goes away in a few days."

Manny says. "She should see someone."

"I know. But she's being stubborn."

He smiles. "Claro." He points at me. "We gonna be in here for a while? I can bring the drinks in."

"I think I'm good now."

We go back into the room and he says, "Have you eaten? Wanna go to Versailles? It's just right there."

It's true, it's just a few blocks away. But there will be so many people—the tourists eating their Cuban sandwiches, the regulars ordering from the ventanita. I can't do it. I feel like anyone who looks at me will somehow instantly know everything. I shake my head. "I think I have to stay here. But you go."

He frowns. "You could go home? You still in your little place?"

I look away from him, to the TV. Jaws is in the water now. People are screaming. "We moved in together. I'm at his place now."

"So why can't you go there?"

I keep looking at the TV. "It's complicated."

I can tell he wants to ask, but he doesn't. "So you're definitely staying here?"

"Yes."

He pulls out his phone. "Then I'm ordering a pizza."

Manny tells me stories about work: the one guy who calls his girl-friend three times a day; the one guy who's had too many DUIs and has to wear an ankle bracelet, so they call him Plug-In. He hands me a piece of his crust without me having to ask and it al-most feels like the old days at the Mouse House when things were going well. He'd come over straight from work on Friday, shower, and stay until Monday morning, when he'd kiss me goodbye before the sun was up.

Every once in a while, we'd go out to a bar or a club. There was a place in Wynwood that would do '90s nights and we went there for my birthday one year. My friend Lisa and her boyfriend, David, came with us and we danced to Britney and Backstreet Boys, old Missy Elliott and Tupac. David bought us a round of birthday shots and then we went out to the dance floor and stayed there for the rest of the night, sweating and dancing, laughing and singing. At one point Manny turned me around, held me from behind, his cheek right up next to mine, his mouth next to my ear, and said, "I love you, babe. I always will." I believed him.

At about eleven, he gets a text from Robbins saying he's twenty minutes away. "I guess he made good time. I gotta go." We get up off the sofa. "You sure you're okay?" he says.

"Yep. Doing great. Just great." I put my hands on my waist—what's left of it.

He pulls me to him, holds me really, really tight, his whole body pressed up against mine; it's always been a thing of ours, hugging this way. It's hard because I'm so big in front, but somehow he manages. I move my arms up around his neck so that now his face is next to mine, touching, his skin on my skin. This is really not okay, I know, but nothing has felt this right in months. He tightens his arms, pushes into me a little, and that's when I stop thinking altogether. My mouth is right next to his, then on his, then open, his tongue making its way in, soft, hot, his hand on the back of my head now, his thumb behind my one ear, stroking me there, just a little, just enough. We kiss, my hands all over his shoulders, up and down his arms. Finally, I pull away.

"Sorry," he says. "I don't know what happened."

I look down. "Me too. I'm a fucking mess. I don't know what I'm doing."

"I'll go," he says, backing up, opening the door.

I watch as he gets into his truck. A white guy with long brown hair comes out of the room next door. He's barefoot and watching where he walks, so he doesn't see me standing in my doorway. He gets two Publix bags out of his car and goes back into his room.

I go back into mine and pace from the door to the bed, trying not to think about the last five minutes. I rub my stomach and apologize to the baby for kissing Manny. I feel like I have to for some reason. "It was an accident," I say. "I don't know what happened."

I have to call Robert. If I don't, he'll think something's wrong. I sit down on the sofa and press the heels of my hands into my eyes for ten seconds. I call him and he answers on the second ring. "Hey. Did you get my pictures?" He's a little slurry—*pictures* comes out *pishurs*.

"Yeah. Super fun."

"Everything okay?" Oh God. It's like he knows.

"Everything's good. Just tired."

"How's the Hulk?" Fuck. The Hulk. I never spritzed them.

"Good. Everything's good." I exhale a long breath as quietly as I can. "I'm about to go to sleep. Are you in for the night? Back at the room?"

"Yep. This place is great. They have a hot tub out by the pool. I wish you were here," he says. "I miss you."

I stare at the microwave on the mini-counter. "Me too. Miss you too."

"Give the Taz a flick for me."

"I will."

"Wait. Lemme talk to him. Put the phone up to your belly." I do it. I even raise my shirt. I feel like I should, after everything that's happened. I hear him telling the baby about going snorkeling, how he's going to take him when he's older. "Good night, buddy," he says. "I'll see you soon."

"Hey," I say, to let him know I've pulled the phone away from my stomach.

"We went snorkeling."

"I heard."

He tells me a long story about the charter company and how they found a reef, how they saw a whatever fish. It was green and blue and something. I'm barely listening. He wishes I had been there. He wants to take me too. Finally he says he's beat, that he's going to go to sleep. "I love you, baby," he says. I see Manny's face, feel his finger behind my ear.

"Love you too," I say, the guilt aching in my chest.

Mirta

One morning, about a week after Daniel the FBI agent called, the phone rang again. It was Juan. "Mirta," he said. "Listen to me. Don't talk. Just listen."

When I heard his voice, I almost fell to the ground. I stretched the phone cord from the wall to the kitchen table and sat down. "Okay."

"Do not talk to anyone about me. You could get hurt. If anyone asks about me, say you don't know anything. I moved to Puerto Rico. That's it. Do you understand? Say yes or no."

"Juan, where are you? You're not in Puerto Rico. I know that. The FBI has—"

"No more talking, Mirta. No more. You could be hurt. Your family could be hurt."

"Please, tell me. Are you okay? What's going on?" I couldn't even think, I could barely speak. I couldn't believe I was hearing his voice.

"Ya, Mirta. No more. Remember? Say nothing." Of course I remembered. It was our pact in Cuba when we were working with Chucho and Adelita and the rest of the group. Say nothing, *we reminded each other at the ends of all our meetings.* If they catch you, say nothing. No names, no dates, no locations. *It's what he wrote on the note to let us know he'd been caught, and I suspect it's what saved Adelita and me and the other people in our group, one of whom was Chucho's girlfriend. The other two were guys from Banes who didn't come around very often. The police must*

have thought Juan and Chucho were a duo and that the women in their lives knew nothing about their activities.

"I remember," I said to him now. "'Say nothing.'"

"Promise me. Don't tell anyone anything. Not even that I called."

"I promise."

"Good," he said, and hung up.

I sat there with the phone against my ear, trembling, trying to figure out what had just happened. It took me a minute to be able to stand up and hang the phone up on the wall. As soon as I did, there was a knock on the door.

It was Daniel. "Was that him? On the phone?" He was almost yelling. He didn't ask to come in; he just walked right through the front door, past Pablo watching TV, past you in your playpen, into the kitchen. I followed him in there. He looked tired. Like he had slept in his car. Or not slept, more like it.

"Mirta," he said, "you need to tell me the truth. Was that him?"

I had no idea how he knew about the call. I didn't know anything about how they can listen to your phone and all that. The fact that he was even asking me this scared me. How did he know what I was doing in my kitchen?

"No," I said.

"Who was it?"

"My husband."

"Your husband? For real?"

I looked out the window behind him. Say nothing. *Juan had said I could get hurt, that my family could get hurt, if I told anyone anything about him. "Yes," I said. "He forgot his lunch," which was true. I pointed to the Tupperware filled with last night's ropa vieja sitting on the counter.*

Daniel ran his fingers through his hair. It looked greasy, unwashed. "Mirta, listen to me. Juan got involved with some very dangerous people. I need to find him. I couldn't get into the line fast enough. If there's any way you can help me—"

"I can't," I said, shaking my head. "I can't."

"I think people are trying to kill him. Do you understand? And I'm worried they're going to try to hurt you too."

Say nothing. *I looked at the floor.*

He waited.

I said nothing still.

Finally he said, "Please, if you change your mind, will you call me?" He took out his wallet, put another one of his cards on the table.

He walked out the front door. A minute later I ripped the card into pieces and fed them to the garbage disposal.

19

I wake up at 8:37 to someone knocking on the door. It's Mr. Publix Bags from last night, shirtless, smoking a cigarette. He has a
little beer gut and his hair is in a ponytail. It's graying a lot at the
temples, I see now. From the wrinkles on his face, he looks about
fifty-something. "Oh," he says. "I was looking for Sean."

"No. Sorry. Maybe you have the wrong room?"

"He was here yesterday. With his girl, Jo. But you're not Jo."

"No," I say. "I'm Mónica." What am I, an idiot, telling this guy
my name?

He puts out his hand, a regular gentleman. We shake hands.
"I'm Rack," he says.

"Rack?"

"It's a nickname. Got it in prison. Long story." Fuck. What? He
smiles and I see that one of his side teeth is missing. His eyes are
a really pretty blue, though, which makes me a little less scared of
him. "So you don't know where Sean went?"

"Nope. Sorry. I got in last night." It's October, so it's warm out
but not deadly. The sun is, though. I shield my eyes with my hand.

"Cool," he says. "Where you from?"

I almost say, "Here," but I don't want him to know that much about me. "I—I'm just visiting."

"Gotcha. Well, if you need anything, I'm just next door. Me and my girl, Suzie. She's sleeping in. I'm an early bird. Morning light's good for the brain, you know. Sometimes I wake up before dawn, go down to the beach, watch the sunrise. That's why I moved here. I was living in Lake City, but, man, that place is a hellhole. It's landlocked. Too constricting." He swings his arms open, crucifixion-style. "I need freedom. I need sky. Coming down here was the best decision I ever made." He takes another drag off his cigarette, exhales off to the side. "You like donuts?"

"Yeah."

"There's donuts in the lobby. But only on the weekends. Weekdays it's just coffee. Not half bad, either."

"Thanks." I look away, trying to indicate that the conversation is over. I close the door an inch. Nothing.

"You staying long?"

I don't like all these questions. Without thinking, I put a hand on my stomach to protect the baby. "I'm not sure what—"

"'Cause they have a weekly rate."

"Oh. Thanks."

He takes another drag. Smooths back his hair in his ponytail. "Okay. Well, looks like I woke you up—sorry about that. And you with a little one on the way." He points to my stomach. "You need your rest."

"No problem."

"I'll just go ask William if he knows where Sean went." I have no idea who William is.

As if he's read my mind, he says, "Front desk guy."

I nod.

He doesn't move. He takes another drag and knocks twice on the doorjamb. Points to himself. "Rack."

"Rack," I say.

"Mary?"

"Mónica."

He snaps his fingers. "Like on *Friends.*"

"Yep."

"Okay," he says, taking a step back.

My phone starts ringing. He looks into the room. "Better get that."

I nod and start closing the door. "See ya," I say.

The phone is my mother. I let it go to voice mail, then count them up: six total, including the one she just left me. I get back in bed and pull the covers up to my chin before listening to them all. The ones from last night are pleading and in Spanish. The one from just now is angrier, in English: "Mónica, please call me as soon as possible. Thank you." The I'm-in-trouble feeling runs through me.

Part of me wants to call her back so that I can get out of trouble. Part of me wants to call her back to make sure she's okay. And part of me wants to stay in this bed and never see or talk to anyone in my life ever again. While I'm trying to decide what to do, the phone rings again. Robert. At nine in the morning, on vacation. Shit.

"Are you okay?" he says.

"Did my mother call you?" I stare at the ceiling.

"I just hung up with her."

"Sorry. She must have forgotten you're out of town. I'm okay."

He says, "What happened?"

"I'll tell you everything when you get home."

"No, baby. Tell me now," he says. "And then call your mother."

I roll over and look at the window. The curtains are closed, but there's a sliver of space between them where the sun is shining in. I stare at the sliver and force myself to speak. "Okay, well. Last night my mom told me she had an affair with her first husband, who I didn't even know existed, and she got pregnant with me, and my father knows and raised me as his own and they never told me."

Robert is silent.

"Hello?" I say.

"Holy shit."

"Yeah." Telling him—saying it out loud for the second time—doesn't make me feel like crying. It makes me feel an even worse feeling: an almost out-of-body, this-isn't-me thing that scares me.

"Why didn't you tell me when I called last night?"

"Because I didn't know how to talk about it. And I didn't want to bother you. You were drunk and having a nice time."

"Damn. Did you sleep at all?"

"Yeah, some."

"Listen, I can come home right now. I can literally pack up and get—"

A flash of panic goes off inside me. I cannot see him right now. Not after last night, that kiss. "No, no," I say. "I'm fine. I'm just shocked, but I'll be fine." I throw the covers off and close the curtains all the way. I want the world out of here.

"Are you sure?" he says.

"Positive. I'm, like, freaked out, of course. But I'm dealing with it. I'll see you tomorrow. We can talk more then. I promise."

"Well, your mom thinks you're lying dead in a ditch. Go call her before she has another aneurysm."

In the bathroom, I count the washcloths, then the towels. I stare in the mirror, lift up my shirt to see my giant stomach. "Mijo, what is happening?" I say. I press, seeing if I can get him to press back. "I don't really understand what's happening. And I need to call your abuela. And I did something I shouldn't have done."

I take one of the washcloths off the shelf above the toilet and squeeze it over and over. I need to call her. I need to get it over with.

She picks up on the first ring. "Why didn't you call me back? I was so worried. My blood pressure went to 172. I almost called 911."

Oh God. I knew it. I tell her I'm fine, not to worry about me.

"Of course I'm worried about you. You're six months pregnant and you ran out of here and left me. Have you talked to Robert? He's worried too."

"Robert's fine," I say. "Is your blood pressure down?"

"It's better."

"Good. I'm hanging up now. Please don't call me again. I don't want to talk to you right now."

"For real?" she says in English.

"For real."

"Ay, Mónica, que falta de respeto."

I don't say anything back. I just touch End. It takes two tries, actually, to hang up because my hands are shaking so much. I've never done this to her. Even when I was a teenager, I never disrespected her this much. But not telling me the truth for my whole life is also una falta de respeto. Of the highest degree.

I sit there for a minute, dazed, sweating a little. I need to get food and go spritz the iguanas. If Robert comes home to a roomful of dead lizards, he'll kill me. I brush my teeth, put my hair up in a bun. The whole time, I just keep thinking about my mother saying *That baby is you.*

I change into shorts and a T-shirt, but then, when I go to pack everything up, I do the opposite. I open the top drawer of the dresser and put in my bras and underwear. Pj's, T-shirts, and shorts go in the second drawer. Jeans and leggings in the third. I had just done laundry at my parents'—I was going to take home a suitcase full of clean clothes. Now I'm unpacking them all into this faux bamboo dresser. I remember what Rack said about the prices for the week. On my way out, I stop in the lobby and ask William for the military rate. I charge it to the credit card I've been trying to pay off for three years.

I'm in the bedroom, trying to decide whether to take this book that Caro lent me about a woman who went on a life-changing trip to India. Suddenly, I hear Robert's keys in the door. "Hey, baby," he calls from the living room. What the hell? I thought I had convinced him to stay until tomorrow. I actually count the Mississippis it takes him to get to the bedroom. Seven. Now here he is, sunburned and smiling, holding out his arms. He gives me a kiss and a big hug. I half hug him back—just forearms on his back. I'm still holding the life-changing book.

"Hey," I say, "what happened? I thought you guys were going Jet Skiing today?"

"I went for a little while. But I couldn't stop thinking about you, so I took off." Oh my God. Why is he so nice? I wish he wasn't so nice. "Mónica, I still can't believe you didn't call me last night when she told you. I would have come home."

I drop the book onto the bed and shake my head. "You were already too drunk to drive. And there was nothing you could do."

"I could have been with you. I could have helped you." He touches my arm, rubs it up and down. "How are you doing?"

I'm losing my mind. I feel like a pretend version of myself. I feel sick because of what happened with Manny. I should never have called him. Definitely never let him come over. I should have called Robert. Or Caro. Or no one.

I nod at Robert. "I'm okay. The baby's okay. Even the Hulk is okay." I smile and tell him how I washed all their water bowls and then went to Publix a little while ago to get them new lettuce. I did it out of guilt, of course. The bowls weren't that dirty and the lettuce we had was only a little brown, but I felt bad about never showing up last night.

"You didn't have to wash their bowls. I would have done that. Did you use your gloves for everything?"

"Yep."

"Good. Good." Then he looks at the bed, where my work clothes are lying out on hangers, and my suitcase is open, a bunch of clothes already in there. He points and says, "What's going on?"

I dig my nails into my hand. I don't want to say it. I don't know *how* to say it. I take a breath and blow it out slowly, my cheeks expanding, then contracting. "I—I need to move out for a while."

"Into your parents'? Did something happen to your mom?"

I shake my head the tiniest bit. "I'm not moving in with them. I'm moving out," I say quietly. "On my own. Into a hotel."

He frowns and leans back. "Into a hotel? Why?"

God, how do I explain this? I glance around the room, at the black dresser and matching nightstands that aren't mine. "I don't exactly know. But I know I need to be there."

"Where?" he says.

"At the hotel. Where my mom went with Juan. Where my father caught them. It used to be called the Palmetto Motel, but they remodeled it and now it's a Quality Inn & Suites. It's on Eighth

Street. But it's good. Clean. It has these really pretty flowers outside. Hibiscus bushes. My room is a suite. It's nice. It has a sofa
and a kitchenette, with a little fridge and a microwave, you know,
and I like it." I'm talking and talking. I can't stop. I'm nervous, trying to convince him, trying to make this make sense. "And there
are donuts. In the lobby, on the weekends. But no breakfast. The
breakfast part is closed. I don't know why."

He looks away from me to the left, then the right, as if he's
looking for someone who can help him understand this. "What?
Mónica. For real?"

I thought explaining that it's the place my mom used to go
with Juan would help him understand why I need to be there—like
it would justify me needing to be there and not here. But I see
now that it doesn't. It just makes me sound unhinged. "I'm sorry. I
don't know how to explain it. I think I need a little space to digest
everything that's happened to me. It's a lot, you know?"

"I know it's a lot. But why do you need to digest it somewhere
else?" His voice gets softer. "Why can't you digest it here? With me?"

"I'm not sure. Maybe I wasn't ready to do this."

He cocks his head. "Which this?" he says, a little edge in his voice
now. "The having a kid? The moving in? Or the getting married?"

"The moving in." I say it small. "I just kind of feel, like, trapped
or something."

He puts his hands up in front of him and backs away a little, the
confusion in his eyes turning to anger. "Oh, I'm trapping you now?
Are you kidding me?"

"No," I say. "No, you're not trapping me. I just feel, like, con-
stricted." I cover my face with both hands and talk through them.
"I'm not sure. I mostly feel crazy. Like nothing makes sense. Like I
just need to be alone for a little while to figure things out."

"Like what? Like what do you need to figure out? Like whether you want to be with me?"

"More like *how* to be with you. Or anyone. I mean, I need—"

"Because it's so hard to be with me?"

"No, it's just that—"

He walks out of the bedroom. Shit. This is going about as bad as it could. I stand there for a moment staring at the metal mini-blinds that I hate. I imagine closing my suitcase, picking up my work clothes, and walking out the door. But I know I can't do that. I know I need to follow him through the house and try to make this better, so I do. He stops in the living room to pull his cigarettes out of his overnight bag. I thought he only smoked when he drank. I guess he also does it when he's furious.

We step out onto the patio and the neighbor's dog starts barking. Robert lights up, blows the smoke away from me, into the yard. The sun is high in the sky, beating down on us. He starts pacing the patio. "So you're moving out. Are you giving me the ring back? Like, are we done?"

I close my eyes and stand very still. "No. No. I just need to be on my own for a bit. I need to think about everything that's happened. I'm sorry."

"I'm sorry too. I'm sorry I'm not whatever it is you need me to be."

"It's not that." I don't know if this is true, but it's what I say.

"It *is* that. I'm not what you want. I know that. I don't know what you *do* want, but it seems like I'm not it."

I try to make my mind blank, to not let myself think about what I want. But a moment from last night flashes through my head. It's not the moment when Manny said he was coming over, or even the kiss. It's the moment in the bathroom, me sitting on the closed toilet, him squatting down in front of me, his hand on the back of my neck, looking into my eyes. It's the moment when everything felt right.

The dog stops barking and takes it down to a whine. Robert takes an angry drag.

"Listen," I say, "I can't explain to you how crazy I feel."

"So you're going to a hotel to get less crazy? What are you, fucking rich too?" Before I can even answer, he says, "Mónica, you're pregnant. You can't be living in a hotel on Eighth Street."

"It's fine. I told you. It's not some roach motel. It's a Quality Inn." I try to think about what else I can say to make him feel better, to make this feel like less of an emergency between us. "I just need some time, okay? A week. I'll be back in a week."

He takes another deep drag. "Time for what?"

"To think. To get used to everything. You have no idea what this is like."

He flicks the cigarette ash onto the patio and rubs it out. "That's why I came home. To help you, to try to support you through this. And now you're taking off on me."

"I'm not taking off on you."

"What do you call packing your shit and moving into a hotel? I call that taking off."

"Okay, fine. I'm taking off. But only temporarily. I just need to gather—"

He crosses his arms in front of his chest. "Whatever, Mónica. Just go. Go do what you need to do."

Mirta

Only a few days after Juan called me, Daniel came to tell me he was dead. We were sitting at the kitchen table. He had his pen out, capping and uncapping it nervously. "I'm sorry, Mirta. I know how you felt about him."

I tried to say, "No," but there was no sound to my voice. I covered my face with my hands, almost as if I was trying to shield myself from what he was saying. My chest felt like someone was grinding their fist into it. "What happened?" I asked.

"The people he got involved with. They are very dangerous, as I said. They found him."

"They killed him?"

"Yes."

"How?" I needed to know everything. For some reason, I needed to understand exactly what had happened to him. I took my hands off my face.

"They shot him."

"Was he in Puerto Rico?"

"Panamá."

I couldn't hold my tears. I did not want to cry in front of him, but I couldn't help it. All I could think was that maybe I could have saved him. If I had told Daniel that he had called, maybe I could have saved him. You were in your playpen, and your tete had fallen out, so you began to cry. I couldn't move. Daniel reached over and put it back in for you, but you didn't want it; you just kept crying. So he picked you up, bounced you, rocked you a little. He did his one-two-three and it worked. I just sat there, tears pouring down my face. I felt that a part of me had been removed, and I didn't understand how I was supposed to live now. I thought of Adelita and Dolores and the feeling in my chest got worse. I asked him about them.

"Dolores passed away last year."

"Thank God. And Adelita?"

"Someone will be notifying her as soon as possible."

I nodded. And then a sob grabbed me and I began to cry very hard.

Daniel stood up and said something to you about going to see what was on TV. He took you into the living room. I heard him talking to your brother, but I don't know what they were saying. After a few minutes, I washed my face in the sink, dried it with the dish towel, and went in there. Daniel was sitting on the floor with you in his lap, playing cars with Pablo.

"Thank you," I said to him.

He stood up and handed you back to me. "I'm very sorry," he said one more time before leaving.

I watched from the doorway as he got into his car but didn't go anywhere. Instead, he lowered his head as if he were praying. Sure enough, a few moments later, he crossed himself and started the car. I thought maybe he had been praying for Juan's soul, and this made me feel less alone—to know that there was someone else besides me right now who cared that Juan was gone from this earth forever. I took a moment there at the front door, lowered my own head, and did the same.

20

I'm driving back to the hotel when my phone rings. I think maybe it's Robert, and I don't want to talk to him. I don't want to face what I've done, what I'm doing.

But it's Caro, calling to ask for my help on her bedroom. They've been redoing it for a year, but she takes forever to make decisions, so she just bought the rug last week. Now she wants to buy the bed. "I was thinking West Elm," she says.

West Elm. It feels so far away. Not literally. Literally it's down by Dadeland Mall, which isn't that far from Robert's house, but the *idea* of West Elm, or anything besides the fact that I am not my father's daughter, feels so far away. *That baby is you.*

It takes me a minute to think about it and to say, "Don't buy anything online. You need to go there so you can see the construction up close."

"You wanna go with me a little later? I can pick you up." She means pick me up at Robert's, of course.

"Do you have a minute to talk?" I say.

"What's up?"

"You might want to sit down."

"Is it the baby? Is something wrong?"

"No, it's not the baby," I say, and then I tell her. Everything.

"Oh my God, Mónica," she says. "Mónica, oh my God."

It's the third time in two days I've told the story—to Manny, Robert, now Caro. As I tell it—the farm, the affair, my father catching them—I feel ashamed on behalf of myself and my parents, like we're this defective branch of the family. We're the trashy people who end up naked and screaming in the street, pregnant with the wrong guy's baby.

Caro says nothing about this, of course. She just asks if I'm okay.

"I don't know. Not really."

"Are you at home? Is Robert there? Oh no, wait. He's in Marco Island, right? Do you want me to come over? I can come over. Just let me tell Mike."

"No!" I say. "Don't tell Mike. Don't tell anyone. I'm not home. I'm out. Doing errands."

I pull up to a light and a woman is standing on the grass, holding a sign that says, ANYTHING HELPS. I remember what Sandra said once on the way back from lunch when we saw a woman standing at the exit of 826. "Where is her mother?" she said, and the sadness in her voice filled the car for the rest of the ride. I feel it now. *Where is her mother? Where is the person who was supposed to take care of her, to keep her safe from harm?* A voice deep inside of me says, *Gone,* and my eyes begin to burn.

"Listen," Caro says. "Don't worry about West Elm. We don't have to go today."

My first thought is *Oh, thank God.* The idea of walking in there feels really scary. The only place I make sense right now is at the hotel, where I want to stay forever. I think about that—about walking in the door with my suitcase and my work clothes, taking off my shoes, getting into the bed and staying there for the rest of the day, the rest of the night until . . . until when? I don't know. In some ways that feels safe and comforting. But maybe it's too safe. It occurs to me that I could get stuck in that bed, consumed by this feeling of aloneness, of alienness, and that's even scarier than the world.

So I tell her I'll do it.

I find her checking the price tag on a glass dining table. "Hi," I say, and give her a kiss hello. She's in jeans and sneakers and still looks amazing: weekend makeup, her hair down and pushed back off her face with what I'm sure are designer sunglasses. I point to the dining table. "I thought we were looking for beds."

"We are. I'm getting there." She puts her hand on my arm. "How are you?"

"Well, I pretty much never want to see or talk to my parents again. And I moved out. From Robert's, I mean."

"What? Why?" The look on her face is surprise and concern but the tone of her voice—especially the *Why?*—feels judgmental, like she can't believe I've done this. "Are you breaking up with him?"

"I don't know. No. I just can't be in that house right now. I said I'd be back in a week."

"Where are you staying? With your parents?"

I tell her about the hotel.

She cocks her head. "The exact same one?"

"Remodeled. But yes."

She's quiet. "You know that's weird, right?"

"Yeah, I do." I almost tell her that it's the only place I feel at home right now, that it's been three months and I still feel like a visitor in Robert's house. And now I feel the same way in my parents' house.

"Does your *mother* know you're staying there?"

"No, and don't tell her."

"I won't."

"And don't tell *your* mother any of this. Not yet." The thought of Gladys and Fermín finding out after all these years is awful. Assuming they don't already know. My mother said she swore to my father she'd never tell anyone. But did *he?* I imagine him confessing to Fermín—going over there to cool off after one of their fights and letting it slip: "Mónica no es mío." The thought makes me feel sick.

Caro says, "Don't worry, I won't tell my mom. I promise."

"Thanks."

"But what did Robert say?"

"He said to do what I need to do."

"So he's okay with it?"

"No. But . . ."

She raises her eyebrows. "Oye, chica, that guy really loves you."

I bow my head, unable to even keep her gaze. "I know."

A salesgirl with thick Cleopatra eyeliner walks up to us, smiling. Caro ignores her. "Mónica, let me ask you something. Is Robert Mr. Mónica?"

Cleopatra looks at Caro, then at me. She's waiting for my answer too.

I sigh. "I mean, I love him. He's a great guy. I'm just not sure I'm *in* love with him."

"Bueno," Caro says. "You better figure that out. You can't just string him along, you know?"

I do know. And I knew this is what Caro would say.

Finally, Cleopatra speaks. "Are you ladies looking for anything in particular?"

"Beds," I say. "Please."

In the bed section, an older woman with a scarf knotted at the side of her neck is talking with a sales guy. He's explaining something about kiln-dried wood and she's nodding. Then she talks and it's a metallic buzz. The scarf is covering a tracheotomy voice box thing.

Cleopatra is talking up the tufted headboard on the bed we're looking at, but all I can hear is the sound of the woman's voice as I think about last night: crying so hard for so long with Manny's hand on my back, and then I kissed him and I'm pregnant, and Robert came home early to support me because he's such a good guy. But I'm such a bad person, and I don't know if he's Mr. Mónica, I just don't know, I'm worried he's not. And this woman with her throat, Jesus Christ, that sound, I can't take that sound. I'm starting to feel lightheaded—I can't get a full breath, I need to breathe, I cannot faint in West Elm. And then it's not the tracheotomy sound anymore, it's my phone, or actually it's both—the trach *and* my phone—vibrating and ringing from inside my purse. *Find the phone, find the phone,* I tell myself, so I search my purse and find the phone, just as it stops ringing. It was Pablo. Who never calls me.

I'm still lightheaded, so I try for a deep breath before saying to Caro, "Excuse me for a minute. Pablo called. I don't know why."

"Of course," she says.

I go over to the bath section and call him back. He answers on the first ring. "Hey," he says.

"Hey. What's going on?" I feel a little better, less lightheaded.

"Didn't you tell me something about a Juan—something Mom said before surgery?"

My shoulder blades tighten. "Yeah. Why?"

"She won't shut up about him. And Dad just stormed out."

Two women walk by me pushing strollers with toddlers in them and I have to scooch in to let them by. "What do you mean 'stormed out'?"

"I mean they had a fight and he got in the car and left."

"Did he say anything?"

"Not to me. They were in the bedroom, so I couldn't really hear them at first. But then I heard him yell, 'How could you do that?'—or something like that. A minute later the door opens, he comes out, gets his keys, and dips. She's in the bedroom llorando como una loca, talking about how he left her, he's never coming back. I thought she was talking about Dad, but then it's Juan left her, he's never coming back, he's gone forever." The baby moves inside me—just a shifting in my lower belly. I put my hand there. *Mijo, this is bad,* I think to him.

"Where is she now?" I ask Pablo.

"Taking a nap. She took a Xanax and passed out."

"Can you hang out there for a while?"

"Yeah, but I gotta be at Maritza's parents' by seven."

I sigh into the phone.

"Sorry, dude. Today's her father's birthday. They're doing a dinner for him."

"Fine. I'll be there as soon as I can," I say.

"What's with this Juan guy? Is that who she was talking about before surgery?"

"She didn't tell you anything?"

"No."

I can't tell him right now, not in front of these bamboo bath accessories and the woman with the trach box just around the corner. "I think he's someone from when she was young. Before she was married to Dad."

"Like an old boyfriend?"

"I'm not sure." Now I'm lying to my own brother.

He says, "Man, do you know what's going on with her?"

This pisses me off. She's been weird for weeks and he's just now clueing in. "Yeah, I do," I say. "I told you she's been wacko ever since she woke up from the coma. On the patio. Remember?"

"I just thought she was getting better. But she's obviously not. This is some crazy shit: she mentioned the FBI."

Maybe I heard that wrong. "What did you say?"

He repeats it: she mentioned the FBI. "She said something like 'The agents will know. They're looking for him,' and I go, 'What agents?' and she goes, 'Agente Fernández del FBI.'"

"Was she talking about Juan right then?"

"Yeah, I think so."

So there's more. How the hell can there be more? "Listen," I say to Pablo. "I'm in West Elm with Caro. I need you to hang out for like another thirty. I'll be there as soon as I can." He says fine and we hang up.

When she sees me, Caro's eyes widen at the look on my face. I barely register that I'm moving, but I tell her I have to go, and when she asks if everything is okay, I shake my head and tell her the truth: "I don't know. I have no idea."

My father's car is gone and Maritza's Lexus is on the street. Inside, Pablo and Maritza are sitting next to each other on the sofa, watching YouTube clips of the *The Apprentice*. He loves *The Apprentice*. He thinks Donald Trump is a genius.

I give them each a kiss hello. They keep watching like there's nothing wrong. Like the world isn't collapsing, one weird comment at a time.

"Mom's not up yet?"

"Nope," Pablo answers. I want to tell him everything she told me last night, but not with Maritza there. I need to be alone with him, but I don't know when that will ever happen. I feel a twinge of anger, and maybe even jealousy of their bond. And of his oblivion, how he moves through his life without feeling like he doesn't know anything about himself anymore.

Donald Trump yells, "You're fired!" and Maritza stands up. "Okay, babe, we gotta go," she says.

He puts his phone away. "Yep. Okay." The twinge of anger gets stronger. Of course he's just leaving me here to deal with this. And where the hell is my father?

"Nothing from Dad?" I say.

"Nah. He's probably just doing his thing." His thing, which he's done our whole lives, is to take off after a fight and not come back—sometimes for hours, sometimes for the whole night. So many times they would have a fight, he would leave, and we wouldn't see him until the next day. We assumed he went to the optical, to sleep on the sofa in the back office. But now, with secrets coming out everywhere, I find myself wondering if that's true.

As Pablo and Maritza are walking out the door, my phone rings. It's Manny. My stomach jumps—part happiness, part fear that, somehow, they know it's him.

"Is that Dad?" Pablo says.

I bump it to voice mail, hide the screen. "Robert."

Pablo says, "I'm sure he'll be back for dinner."

Maritza slips on her shoes by the door and says, "By the way, my sister has some maternity clothes for you. She's bringing them tonight."

"Thank you," I say. "Please tell her thank you."

As they're backing out of the driveway, I play the voice mail Manny just left. "Oye, I'm just calling to see how you're doing. Me and Robbins are here in the Grove getting food, so just call me when you get a minute, okay?" Listening to it, I feel a jolt of happiness followed immediately by shame.

I text back that I'm at my parents' house and can't talk. *Some weird shit about the FBI and Juan.*

He writes back, *WTF?*

Idk, I type. *My mom's sleeping. More later.* I sit down in the living room and turn on HGTV. It's the show with Vanilla Ice renovating houses. Halfway through, my mother comes out of her room wearing her blue bathrobe and slippers. Her hair is sticking up on one side and she has a crease down the side of her face. "Pablo?" she says as she comes down the hall. When she sees me on the sofa, she turns around without saying a word, goes back into her room, and locks the door.

"Mom," I yell.

Nothing.

I go down the hall to her room. "Mom," I say, louder.

The shower starts.

"Oh my God, Mom. Please. Open the door." She's not supposed to shower alone yet. She could get dizzy and collapse. I imagine her falling, hitting her head, blood, all of it. I start knocking and yelling, "Mom! C'mon, please. Mom!" I know she can hear me. If she's conscious, that is. I stop knocking so I can hear if she falls. I have my phone in my hand, ready.

I don't know why she's doing this, and that alone—the fact that I don't understand her right now—makes everything feel even more strange and awful. I feel like I'm just out here on my own, with no one. Not even the one person I thought would be connected to me forever.

Eventually, I hear the water stop. A few minutes later, the hair dryer, then the creak of her closet doors. Finally she comes out.

She's wearing a pair of seafoam-green pants and her "look professional" shirt from when I was a kid. It's a yellow button-down with pink squiggly lines that she wore to every parent-teacher meeting I ever had. I can't believe she still has it. All of this plus a pair of dingy white pumps and a white belt. She even has the dingy white purse to match. And then there's her face: heavy eye shadow. A ton of blush. Her hair looks semi-normal except it's blown out all big. She looks like an extra in a music video from the '80s.

"Josefina is picking me up at six," she says.

"Who?" She heads toward the kitchen, her heels clacking on the tile floor. I catch her at the door to the garage. "Mom."

She doesn't respond, just heads into the garage, and goes for the *Cocina* box—the one we got the cafetera out of the night everyone came for dinner. It's still out, still sitting on the floor from when she rushed me back into the kitchen that night.

"Mom," I say again. "What are you doing?"

She starts looking through the box, pulls out the red spiral notebook. "We're going to study," she says. "And then we're going to Casablanca's. Josefina really likes their papitas."

She's so far into this—dressed up in these clothes, talking like this—that I wonder if this is some kind of dementia. Or even Alzheimer's. My heart clenches at this thought, at the possibility that we missed the signs and now she's this bad. "Mom, Casablanca's is closed," I say. "Remember? The guy went to jail? Now it's a Chuck E. Cheese." I touch her arm. "Remember?"

She opens the notebook, stares at the page full of her handwriting. *My name is Mirta Campo.* Mi nombre es Mirta Campo. *Where is the bathroom?* ¿Donde está el baño? She looks back at me, her face filled with sadness and what looks like regret. She closes the notebook, holds it in two hands like it's a platter. "I didn't know what to do," she says, and I know she's back.

"About what?"

"About everything."

"Pablo said you were talking about Juan and the FBI. Was he a criminal?"

"Not exactly." She looks down at herself—the outfit, the shoes—then over my shoulder. "Sometimes I lose myself."

"I know."

She puts the notebook back in the box and asks me to put the box back up on the shelf. I do it and then I lead her out of the garage, back into the house. "Let's sit down," I say. We go into the living room and I fix up her pillows on the sofa, take off her white pumps. I ask her if she's hungry, if she's thirsty. She says she would love a glass of water, so I go into the kitchen and get her one. When I bring it back out, she's just sitting there. The TV's on but she's not watching it. I hand her the water. She sips it slowly.

I sit down next to her on the sofa, put my hands on my stomach, and press a little on either side. *Mijo, your abuela is not okay,* I think to the baby. *And neither am I.* I'm still so mad and hurt by what they did to me, but I have to put that away for right now. I have to find out the whole story: what happened with Juan and the FBI. The baby presses a foot into my side: "Do it. Find out," he's saying. I press on his foot and turn to my mother. "Okay, Mom. Start from the beginning, please, and tell me everything."

Part II

21

I hear my father's key in the door and my stomach drops. He's back from wherever he goes when they fight. It takes him eight Mississippis to get to the kitchen, where I'm warming up Gladys's raisin-less picadillo from last night. By the time he gets in here, I'm shaking a little, afraid I'll look at him and see that his face is in no way my face.

He doesn't greet me like he normally does. No kiss. No "Hi, mija." Just "Mmm" when he smells the ground beef. Then, as he sits down at the kitchen table, he says, in English, "Put me a few raisins in?"

I can't look at him. I'm feeling so many things: fear, anger, even embarrassment for some reason. I stare down into the picadillo. "I don't know if we have any, but I'll check." I go to the pantry and stand there, my back to him. I move a few things around, half-heartedly looking for what I know is not there. I hear him sniffle, then sniffle again.

"Mónica," he says, his voice breaking.

Everything in my body locks up. I still don't turn around, afraid that if I do, something terrible will happen. I will burst into flames. Or a giant sinkhole will open in the kitchen floor and suck us in—

the table, the stove, everything. So I stand still and say, "We don't have any."

"Mónica."

"I can get some next time I go to Publix." I suck my cheeks in.

"Mónica."

"You probably shouldn't tell her, though."

"Por favor, Mónica. I'm very sorry you never knew. I was afraid that if you found out, you wouldn't love me as much. Or, worse, you'd think I didn't love *you* as much."

I finally turn around. His glasses are off and tears are falling down his face. He pulls a napkin out of the penguin napkin holder and wipes his eyes, his cheeks. Seeing him cry makes me want to cry, too, but, honestly, it also makes me mad. Like: Who is he to cry? Who are either one of them to cry? I'm the one who got lied to for my whole life. Was it just going to go on like this forever? Was this kid going to be born and live his whole life having no idea about this other guy—my real father, his real grandfather—who was some criminal on the run or whatever he was?

"I'm sure you have a lot of questions," my father says. He gets up to pour himself some Pepsi from the two-liter on the counter. Then he adds some rum from the cabinet above the sink.

"Mom told me everything. I know he's dead. I know about him getting mixed up with the drug dealers and the FBI coming to see her."

"What?" He places his glass very softly on the table, gets up, and goes into the living room. I follow him.

My mom is on the sofa. She's changed out of her 1980s clothes and she's watching *Sábado gigante*.

"Mirta," he says, "what is she talking about with the FBI coming to see you? And drug dealers?"

My mom's eyes look older than they did a few weeks ago, her skin a little sallow. "You told him?" She doesn't sound mad. She sounds almost curious.

"I had no idea you'd never told him that part."

My father takes a step toward her. "What the hell is she talking about?"

"Juan was involved in something illegal—something with bad people. I never found out what. The FBI was looking for him. I told them I knew nothing. A few weeks later, they came and told me he was dead. The bad people he got involved with killed him. That's all."

"That's all? That's *all*?" He's starting to raise his voice. "You had FBI agents showing up at the house and you never told me?"

"Just one," she says. "Agente Fernández. He was very kind. He had a son."

"What the hell else was going on that I didn't know about?"

"Ay, Rolando. Nada, okay? Nada más."

Now he's going and going, yelling at her about how stupid she is and who knows what Juan was into. "Obviously he was dangerous," he says. "We all could have been killed, Mirta. Do you realize that? Do you realize the kind of danger you put your children in for that man?"

"He was a brave, honorable man," my mother says. "A patriot. And they killed him like a dog in the street." Her eyes fill with tears.

"Well, I am your husband! I am the man who has put a roof over your head and taken care of you and your children for thirty-five years. I can't believe you never told me about this." He shakes his head. "You have no respect for me. You never have."

I've never seen him like this before. He's breathing hard, his chest rising and falling. His hands, I notice, are fists.

My mother is crying now, wiping her eyes with her fingers.

I turn to my father and try to use the calmest voice I can. "Dad, sit down. Her blood pressure."

Something like fear flashes across his face. "Oh, for God's sake." He backhands the air between them. "I can't believe you're crying over some farm kid from thirty years ago." He walks out and I hear the bedroom door slam.

My mother covers her face and cries silently. I just stand there. I'm stuck like this—unable to touch her or to comfort her in any way. It's all too weird, too much of a reminder that she's not who I thought she was. That neither of them are.

On the way to the hotel, I think about my mother's periods of silence and distance when I was a kid—the way, for days, she'd just be gone. Not literally. But she'd be lost inside herself, not looking at any of us, not really. I could feel my father trailing behind her, trying to get her back, and then, after a few days, giving up and moving into his own space.

So then we were all like parts of an atom. My father, my brother, and me, a proton, a neutron, and an electron all floating away from the nucleus, which was, of course, my mother. It's always been my mother. We'd spend a few days like that—everyone taking care of themselves, not talking very much, just existing in our own worlds—and then something would shift and we'd all slip back into our normal orbits. My parents would be okay again, laughing, talking. He'd touch her on the small of her back when he walked into the kitchen in the evenings. She'd step back into it, put her cheek out for a kiss hello, and I would feel my insides settle back down. I didn't recognize this then. Only now.

I wonder if those periods were about Juan. Maybe they were days of mourning that she—and the rest of us—had to ride out. Or maybe they were days of regret, the weight of this unplanned life pulling her away from us. It was a life where she was married to her second choice and living in a country she never thought she'd live in, much less raise her children in. Whatever they were, they make sense now.

The dome light in Rack's car is on. It's an old brown Camry with a dent on the passenger's side. I have no desire to see or talk to anyone right now, but what if they wake up to a dead battery and then I'm the asshole who didn't tell them? I know I'll never be able to sleep if I don't go over there.

I knock three quick knocks.

He yells, "Just a minute," and then opens the door pulling a shirt on. He has a gut but his arms and chest are kind of muscly, especially for an older guy. "Mónica," he says.

I point to his car. "Your dome light's on."

"Oh, man. Thanks."

"No problem," I say, and go to walk away, but he says, "Suzie, this is Mónica. Mónica, Suzie." Suzie's lying on the bed, drinking a hard cider out of the bottle. She looks about twenty years younger than him. Her hair is a shiny brown bob and she's wearing blue scrubs. "Nice to meet you," she says.

"You too." I look around the room. It's clean—no socks or shoes on the floor, no clothes scattered on the sofa—but the walls are lined with moving boxes and garbage bags full of clothes. They must be living here.

"Mónica's next door," Rack says. He's walking around the

room searching for his keys, looking on the dresser, the counter. "Is it just you there?"

"I—uh, my boyfriend is with me." I don't want them to know I'm staying there alone.

"The guy in the truck? With the Army stickers?"

"Yeah." What is he, a cop?

"Saw him leaving last night. Was he deployed?"

"Afghanistan. He was a medic."

"God bless him," Rack says.

Suzie doesn't take her eyes off the TV but she says, "Is he out now?"

"Yeah. He's a crane operator now." I have no idea why I tell them this. It just comes out.

Rack says, "Dangerous work. Not easy, either."

"Yeah. No," I say, trying to figure out how to stop talking, how to get back to my room.

"And what about you, Mónica? What do you do?" He smiles a little and it makes his question feel more friendly than nosy. Or creepy.

"I work for a dermatologist."

"Are you a nurse?" Suzie asks. The show on the TV is the kind of police show where there's one of every different kind of person—white, Asian, Black, Hispanic—and they're all beautiful.

"No," I say. "I do insurance."

Rack points to Suzie. "Suzie's in school full-time. She's gonna be a nurse."

I raise my eyebrows in an *Oh?* kind of way. "Cool." I look at her scrubs again and feel a tug of envy. She's doing things, going to school. I mean, given the moving boxes, she seems to be living in a hotel, but at least she's not on hold because she's pregnant and paralyzed by the knowledge that her entire life was a lie.

Rack says, "I'm between careers right now. Currently, I'm in the entertainment industry."

Suzie laughs.

"I work the door at a couple clubs. Getting a late start tonight, actually." He finds his keys behind a bowl of oranges they have on the counter. "Got 'em."

"Okay, well—" I give a little partial salute, which I'm pretty sure is the stupidest thing I've ever done. I take another couple of steps back. "Have a good night."

Suzie says, "You too. Nice to meet you."

Rack comes out behind me and gets into his car. "Nighty-night," he shouts from the driver's seat. "Thanks again." He points to the dome light.

"No problem," I say. Their vibe is really not what I thought it would be. They're less like creepy losers who're going to ask you for twenty bucks and a ride to Ft. Lauderdale and more like just chatty American neighbors. Maybe they're simply down on their luck moneywise and, with her going to school, they can't afford rent or something.

I think about how neat their room is. I've only been here twenty-four hours but I've already got stuff all over the place. So I hang up the work clothes and unpack my suitcase. I stack the *What to Expect* book and the life-changing-trip-to-India book on the nightstand neatly. As I'm finishing up, throwing away my food wrappers, putting my dirty clothes into the plastic bag in the closet, my phone pings. It's Caro sending a picture of a bed Cleopatra showed her after I left. She wants to know if I like it and whether my mom is okay. *Why was Pablo calling?* she says.

I just say my mom was having one of those episodes and he didn't know what to do. I tell her we're trying to get her to see someone but she's refusing.

I'm going over on Monday. I'll try to talk to her then.

Thanks, I say. *Maybe if it's you, she'll listen.*

NP. Are you okay? Do you want to talk?

I tell her no, that I'm tired and headed to bed, which is not totally true. I *am* tired but I feel like talking to Manny. I text him. *Sorry I missed your call. Can you talk now?*

He texts back right away. *Can't. Out.*

I bet he is. It's Saturday night, after all, and Robbins is here. They're probably down on the beach. Or maybe somewhere in the Design District. I can see him—black button-down and jeans, getting some girl to dance with him, getting her number. Who knows where he'll end up later.

I text back, *No prob. Talk to you later.*

Call u tomorrow, he says. *XO.*

I think about what Caro would say about this, especially the XO. The only person who might understand, I realize, is my mother.

22

I hide out at the hotel all day on Sunday, going crazy on my phone searching for information about Juan Viera de Céspedes of Holguín, Cuba. My fantasy is to find a picture of him, though I'm not sure I'm ready for that, and read an explanation of exactly why the FBI wanted him, how he ended up in Panama, and who killed him. Without ever having to talk to or interact with anyone. I Google and Google. There's information about the prisons in Cuba and even about a group of political prisoners who were released in 1979, but his name is nowhere.

My mother calls around three. She leaves a voice mail. "This is Mirta Campo. I lied to you," she says. Then she hangs up. I play the message two more times hoping that I misheard it.

I call her back. "Mom, are you okay?"

"Hola, mi niña. Yes, I'm fine. Tired, of course, but that's normal, after everything I've been through. ¿Por qué?"

"You just left me a voice mail where you identified yourself as Mirta Campo and said you lied to me. And then you hung up."

She lets out a kind of half breath, half snort. "No I didn't. That's ridiculous."

"What? Mom, that just happened. I have the voice mail on my phone."

"Well, I—I must have been mistaken. How are you feeling? Is the baby okay? When is your next appointment with the doctor?"

I want to refuse to answer, to say that we're not talking about me right now, that we're talking about her, and how something is not right with her brain. But I don't have the energy. So I just say, "My next appointment is Friday. And I have to go now. I need to be somewhere."

"What are you doing? Where do you need to be?"

I *need* to be at Robert's, being his fiancée and letting him support me through this. I *want* to be nowhere, with nobody, except maybe the one person I'm not supposed to be anywhere near. Manny called around noon, after Robbins left, and I told him about my mom in her '80s clothes finally telling me everything. After I hung up, I told myself that was it—no more calling, no more texting. I'm trying so hard to leave it alone, to forget about Friday night, that kiss and what it felt like. "I'm going out with a friend," I say to my mom.

"Qué friend?" she asks. She has no idea where I am, that I haven't seen or spoken to Robert since yesterday afternoon when I left.

"I need to go, okay? I need to go."

"Okay," she says. "Will you call me tomor—"

"Bye." I throw the phone onto the sofa next to me. My face and neck are tingling. "God, I can't believe her," I say to myself and to the baby. I am simultaneously furious and worried. I have never wanted so desperately to run *from* something and *toward* it at the same time.

———————

On Monday I call in sick and spend the day in the room, watching daytime TV. When I need something to do, I take out the garbage and dust all the surfaces using a hotel washcloth. I wipe down the bathroom and the kitchenette area. I'm a housewife with no house.

Robert starts texting me. I text back to say I'm fine, but when he calls, I don't pick up. I feel awful, but I can't. I avoid him and almost everyone else. Sandra from work calls late in the afternoon but I let it go to voice mail. Caro texts to check in and I don't write her back.

At night, I watch *Abismo de pasión*. It's strange watching it without my mother. So strange that when Sebastián kidnaps Clara and throws her into one of the dungeon cells, I almost call to say, "Oh my God. Did you see that?" But I don't. I just sit there drinking my Diet Dr Pepper. By the end of the episode, Clara's on a hunger strike, and I remember what my mother said in the hospital when she saw the report about the political prisoner in Cuba. "We were afraid he would die," she said. That "he" was Juan, I know now. My father knew this then, of course. That's why he was pissed and trying to get us all out of there before she said anything else. A feeling of shame, and stupidity, washes over me and any urge I had to call my mother evaporates.

On Tuesday morning I call in to work again and say it feels like a stomach flu, that I'll probably need a few more days. That night Clara breaks out of the dungeon jail and ends up like me: hiding out. The only difference is I'm in the hotel where I was conceived and she's in a nearby convent disguised as a nun. When one of Sebastián's guards comes snooping around, he somehow doesn't recognize her, even though all the other nuns are old and wrinkled and she looks like a runway model wearing a habit. She spends her days alternately baking bread and crying over Armando. And praying the rosary. I wish I had a rosary—not because I'm feeling particularly close to God but because I remember it being calming, almost meditative, to say all the prayers.

Caro calls me just as the show ends. I let it go to voice mail. She says she talked to my mom but it did no good: she's still being stubborn. She also says she's going to buy the bed Cleopatra recommended. *I have no bed,* I think. *And no home.* I am untethered and floating, like an astronaut who's come undone from his spaceship umbilical cord, and all I can think about is how unreal everything feels. How, for my entire life, my parents knew I was Juan's and never even considered telling me. Or did they? Did they ever talk about it? Did my mother ever bring it up? Probably not. Why would she? It would only cause problems, like she said. And Juan is dead, so it's not like they were depriving me of the opportunity to meet him. But still. They let me live for twenty-nine years thinking I was my father's daughter. But I'm not. Which means I'm only Pablo's half sister. And I'm not Caro's anything.

This hits hard. So hard, I have to stand up and walk around the room. I pace around, shaking out my arms. I get a glass of water with lots of ice and drink it all at once. I pace more and think about the fact that I am in no way related to any of my family on that side: Caro, her brothers, Tío Fermín, and Tía Gladys. "I'm not a Campo," I say out loud. I look down to my stomach. To the baby. I press my hands into my sides. "Mijo," I tell him. "I'm not a Campo. And neither are you." For some reason it feels like my fault. "I'm sorry," I say. "I'm sorry you're not a Campo." My eyes fill with tears and my throat thickens. I stand there holding my stomach. "I'm sorry," I say, over and over to him. "I'm sorry."

I turn everything off and get into bed, under the covers; I don't pee or brush my teeth or anything. I need to be in the bed, hidden—hiding, maybe—from all of this: my mother, Manny, Robert, and, most of all—worst of all—the fact that I'm not a Campo. Because if I'm not a Campo, I realize, what am I?

Mirta

The night after your fifteenth birthday, I served your father his café in the living room and, instead of going to wash the dishes, I sat down next to him. "Rolando," I said, "I want to talk to you." I paused, took a silent breath. "Maybe we made a mistake. About Mónica. She's fifteen now. Maybe it's time for her to know."

He looked up from the newspaper he was reading. "To know what?"

Saying it felt like jumping into a dark pit. I didn't know where I would land. "To know about Juan."

"No," he said.

"Why not?"

"Can you imagine what that would do to her? To find out that she's someone else's?"

I leaned toward him, put my hand on his knee. "She's not someone else's. She's yours. You're her father. You always have been. But that's only part of the truth. Maybe she should know the entire truth."

"What good would that do? It would only confuse her and make things a mess."

I wondered if he was afraid you'd want to find Juan, to meet him. So I said, "He's dead, you know."

He squinted at the paper. "No, I don't know."

"Yes. He died," I said, more quietly than I meant to. I still couldn't think about it without a soft throb of pain in my chest.

"*How do you know?*"

"*Adelita called me.*"

Now he looked at me, frowning, his eyebrows pulled together like drawn curtains. "When?"

"*Years ago. When the children were babies." It was a small lie.*

Rolando didn't say anything about Juan being dead. Not "I'm sorry to hear that" or "That's a shame," but when he looked back down at the paper, he nodded solemnly. After a few seconds he said, "There is no need for her—for anyone—to know anything. End of story."

Years later, when you were having such a hard time with Manny, with him coming home and leaving again, choosing his duty over you, I wanted to tell you that I knew what it was like to love a man who lived by unshakable beliefs. A man who was loyal and brave, almost to a fault. Juan would have burned those fields and set those bombs with or without me. If I had asked him to stop—if I had told him I was afraid I would lose him—he never would have listened. He knew he was risking losing what we had, that he could be killed or thrown in prison for the rest of his life, but that was not enough to stop him. That was the difference between us. If Juan had said, "Let's stop this, it's too dangerous; we could lose each other," I would have. But he wouldn't. He couldn't, just like Manny. I didn't tell you any of this, of course. I held my tongue as you told me that Manny was going back again and then I told you what I knew: that a man like that will never give up on his beliefs for you or anyone.

And then you told us you were pregnant. I was in shock, but soon all I wanted to do was tell you about Juan. I couldn't, though. Rolando would kill me. And besides, we had been lying to you for so long. Maybe Rolando was right. Maybe it was best to just leave it alone, let you go on with your life with Robert and the baby, making your own little family.

And then they said I had to have surgery, and I knew I could die. It happens, you know. People go in and they never come out. And if I died, you would never know. That information would be gone when Rolando was dead. Not one other person on earth knew—and never would if I didn't tell you. Which I guess I did when they had me on those drugs. I truly don't remember anything I said before the surgery, but it was very clear that I had told you something, and it was the one thing I promised your father I never would.

23

I'm eating Domino's for dinner on Wednesday night, watching Clara confide in a fellow Sister about her true identity, when someone knocks on the door. I think it's Rack and Suzie, who offered to get me Tylenol because I've had a headache all day, so I open the door without even asking who it is.

It's Manny. I'm flooded with happiness. Then guilt.

"I can only stay a minute," he says, and walks right in, a box of pastelitos in one hand and a six-pack in the other. He's shaved his head back down again, but he's got a little scruff, so all the hair on his face and head is about the same length. Unfortunately, the effect is sexy as hell.

Meanwhile, I haven't showered or washed my face in two days. I've been wearing the same leggings and T-shirt since Monday, so I don't smell great, either.

Still, he gives me a kiss hello on the cheek like we're just friends. Like Friday night never happened. He hands me the box of pastelitos. "Just making sure you get your proper nutrition."

"Thanks."

He looks at the TV for a minute. "Is this the one with the vampires? My mom watches the one with the vampires."

TITA RAMÍREZ

I laugh and turn it off. "No vampires. Not yet, at least." I'm embarrassed, so I say, "I got into it watching with my mom."

He pops a beer. "They didn't have any Diet Dr Pepper at the gas station. Sorry."

"It's okay." I point to the can I'm drinking from, sitting on the coffee table. I bought a twelve-pack yesterday.

He sits down at the kitchenette table, takes a swig. "So. You living here?"

"Maybe. For now."

"You all right? Sandra said you haven't been to work all week." A car door slams in the parking lot.

"You talked to Sandra?"

"I called."

"When?"

"Today."

I give him a look like *What the hell?*

"I was worried about you, genius. You're MIA." It's true that I told him I'd keep him posted but then I didn't. He opens the box of pastelitos, gets the coco out, hands it to me. It's my favorite. He takes a guayaba, his favorite.

"So what's up?" he says. "Are you having a nervous breakdown?"

I feel like I am. Last night I stood in front of the bathroom mirror for twenty minutes, trying to see where my mother ends and Juan begins. My cheekbones and the shape of my mouth are both hers. But my eyes are rounder than hers, my nose thinner. Does that mean they're his, I wondered. "I'm trying to figure some stuff out," I say to Manny. The A/C in the room switches on, drowning out the sounds of the parking lot.

"What kind of stuff? Family stuff?" He takes a swig of his beer. "Or, like, other stuff?"

"A little of everything. I just feel like I need some time to get my shit together. The Juan thing has me pretty fucked up. You know—all the lies, deceit, betrayals. All I need now is some vampires."

He laughs and I take a bite of my pastelito. I've been living on McDonald's and Domino's for days. I know I need something more nutritious. Maybe a carrot.

"What about, uh, the race car driver?"

"I told him I needed a little break."

He takes a bite of his pastelito, chews. "Sorry about the other night. It just happened." He rubs a hand over his head and looks down like he really is sorry. But then he looks back up at me through his eyelashes: not *so* sorry.

"I know. Me too."

Somebody knocks on the door.

"You expecting company?"

"It's the neighbors. They're bringing me Tylenol."

"Who?"

"The people next door." I get up and open the door.

It's not the neighbors. It's Robert. Still in his Deer Park uniform, but with the cap turned backward. He hasn't shaved in a couple of days and his eyes look tired. I'm so surprised I can't speak.

"Hey," he says. And then he sees Manny. "Who's this?"

Manny looks at me.

I fight the urge to run out the door, or at least throw myself on the ground the way you do in a bomb attack. "It's Manny. He came by to make sure I was all right."

"To make sure you were all right?"

"Yeah."

"How did he know you were here?"

My heart speeds up. "Because I told him."

"When?"

"The other day."

"The other day when?" He looks at Manny again. Manny's still looking at me.

"When he called to check on my mom and left that voice mail. I texted him back."

"He called to check on your mom two weeks ago. The day you fainted." He puts his keys in his pocket and crosses his arms. He smells like cigarettes.

"Yeah, I hadn't called him back. He was worried, so he texted me and I just texted him back this weekend. Just to say I'm okay."

"And now he's here with you? In a hotel? Having a beer?"

I look at Manny. He's leaning back a little in the kitchen chair, legs crossed, beer in hand. God, this looks bad. I turn back to Robert. "What are you doing here?" I ask.

"Are you fucking kidding me, Mónica?" Robert steps toward me, into the room. He takes two more steps in and then he's right in my face, with his stubble and his bloodshot eyes, and now I can smell the alcohol too. "What the fuck is this?" he says. "What the fuck is going on?"

Manny stands up from the table. "Relax, bro." *Oh fuck*, I think, and my stomach clenches. They're about the same height; Robert's maybe an inch taller, but Manny's thicker. The room feels really small right now. Probably as small as it felt the night my father caught my mother and Juan in this same hotel.

Robert says, "No, I'm not going to relax, *bro*." He points to my stomach. "That's my baby."

"Yeah, I know."

"So what the fuck are *you* doing here?"

Manny says, not super convincingly, "I just came by for a visit, make sure she was okay. I brought her some food."

"Brought her some food? That's not your job. That's *my* job. I'm her fiancé. You're just—"

Manny raises his eyebrows at him, then his chin, just a little, and I see a look I know well. He's not exactly feeling threatened, but he's not okay with what Robert's implying. "I'm just what?" Manny asks. It feels like he's closer to Robert, but I'm not sure he is.

"You're nobody," Robert says. "You're nobody to her."

"I think you might want to talk to her about that." Oh my God. Fucking Manny.

Robert looks at me.

What do I say? What is Manny to me? He's the love of my life. But it doesn't matter, because, although he loved me, and may still love me, he would not show up for me. He's a risk—good in a crisis but not in the day-to-day. Not like Robert, who is safe and reliable. Even now, Robert's here, sad and mad and drunk because he loves me and wants to be with me and show up for me. Robert is my fiancé. Manny is my nothing. That's what I should say. That's what I'm supposed to say. But I can't. It doesn't feel right. So I say the thing that's true: "I don't know what anybody is right now. I don't even know what *I* am."

"I'll tell you what you are," Robert says, raising his voice. "You're my fiancée. So I don't understand what the hell you're doing here with him."

"I told you—I need some time to process everything that's happening. To figure myself out."

"No you didn't. You didn't tell me shit." He's slurring, so *didn't* sounds like *din*. "And you won't fucking call me or text me or anything. You're completely gone. I came over here to see what's going on with you and I find this." He waves his arm around the room and loses his balance. He falls forward and has to grab onto the back of a chair. "I mean, fuck, Mónica. You're pregnant with my kid," he yells. "Did you fucking forget that?" I've never seen him like this before. I've seen him angry, but not like this.

"No, I didn't forget that," I say, raising *my* voice now. "Of course I didn't forget that. I know I'm pregnant with your kid. And I know I said I'd marry you." I pull my hair back off my forehead, hard, and take a deep breath in. "But I'm just not sure about that right now. I'm not sure that's a good idea."

There's a silent beat while he takes that in, and I imagine it as a sharp object piercing him.

"Why not?" he says. His voice is soft, almost pleading. Not like he's begging but like he genuinely wants to know why not.

Out of nowhere, I think of this old woman I saw at the gym a couple of months ago, in the locker room, naked, her ass all old and wrinkly and covered in cellulite. I thought, *What if my ass ends up looking like that? Who will love me? And, more importantly, who do I want to love me when I look like that? Do I want it to be Robert? Do I want to be that old with him?* I tried to imagine being that old with him and I couldn't. But I was already pregnant and we were already living together, so I just pushed the thought—the whole memory—away. Until now.

The base of my throat feels weird, jittery, almost like I could cry, but I don't. I think I'm numb from the shock of him being here. "I don't know," I say. "I don't know exactly what I want right now. I just need some time to think about everything."

He points to Manny. "Is it because of him? Because of *this* guy? Who dumped you how many times? Five? Six? And now you're shacked up with him in this place?"

Manny steps forward. "What happened between me and her is none of your business."

"It is when it's still going on. When she's wearing my ring and carrying my baby."

There's a knock on the door and then I hear Rack say, "Mónica?"

Right. The Tylenol. I open the door. "Hey, thanks."

He's holding a Publix bag. "Everything okay?" He scans the room, sees both Manny and Robert, and pushes the door open so it'll catch on the rug and stay open.

Robert turns around and looks Rack up and down. He's taller than all of us—well over six feet—and wearing a tank top, so you can see all his tattoos. "Who's this?" Robert asks.

"I'm Rack," Rack says. "You're the medic, right?" He points out to the parking lot. "Saw the truck."

Robert says, "I'm her fiancé." Then he looks at me. "Why does he think I'm the medic?"

"You're not the medic?" Rack says.

I'm screaming in my head, *Rack, shut up. Please shut up.*

Robert points to Manny. "He's the medic."

Rack says, "Who's he?"

Manny says, "I'm a friend."

Robert says, "Yeah, friend," and shakes his head.

Rack looks at me. "Mónica, you okay? Everything cool?"

"Yeah, um, it's just—"

Robert asks again, "How does he know he's a medic?"

I shake my head and shrug. "I don't know. Just a mix-up of information."

Robert doesn't buy it. He looks at Manny. "How many times you been over here?"

I can't believe he's putting this together. How can he be drunk and putting this together?

Manny doesn't say anything, but I see the face he gives him and it isn't good. It pretty much tells him the truth. Great.

"So this *is* what it looks like. You're totally fucking cheating on me."

"I'm not cheating," I say. "I asked you for some space. I told you I needed to be on my own for a little while."

Robert steps toward me. "You told me you'd be back in a week. Were you just gonna fuck this guy for a week and then come home like it was nothing? What kind of whore are you, anyway?"

"Uh-uh," Rack says. "You're not gonna talk that way around here." He gets Robert by the shoulder and starts pushing him out. "Need you to leave the premises right now."

Robert flings his arm up. "Don't touch me." He looks at me, points at Rack. "Is this another one of your boyfriends? Are you fucking him too?"

Rack gets him by the front of the neck and pins him with both hands, hard, against the open door. Robert's head knocks against the door. "You better watch your mouth, son," Rack says. The Pub-lix bag is hanging off his wrist, swinging in front of Robert's chest.

"Rack!" I yell. "Leave him alone."

Robert's trying to pry Rack's hands off. "Get your hands off me," he yells.

"Whoa, man," Manny says, "let him go. Let him go. He's just talking shit."

Suzie comes in right then. "Dad! What the fuck?"

"This guy's using inappropriate language," he says, and lets Robert go.

Suzie grabs Rack by the back of his shirt. "Get the hell out of here," she says, and pushes him out the door like she's the one who's the bouncer. "What if he calls the cops?" she hisses.

Rack doesn't say anything, just lets her push him away, into their room. When I hear the door close, I realize that she called him "Dad."

"Who is that guy?" Manny says.

I don't answer. I'm shaking so hard I can't talk. I sit down on the sofa, cross my arms in front of me, and squeeze to calm down. Finally, I manage to say, "He lives next door."

"He lives here?" Manny says.

"Yeah, I think so." The A/C cuts off and it's weirdly quiet for a second.

Manny looks at Robert. "You all right?"

Robert glares at him.

"Are you okay?" I ask him. My head is throbbing so hard it scares me.

He shakes his head, his eyes more disappointed than angry now. "I don't know who you are, Mónica. You're not who I thought you were." He shoves his hands into his pockets, turns around, and leaves. A few seconds later I hear the low rumble of his souped-up car as he pulls out.

Manny closes the door. He picks up his beer and downs it, then opens another one. He sits down next to me and takes a long sip. He won't stop bouncing his leg and he keeps pulling his shirt away from his side, like he's hot and trying to cool off. His forehead's a little sweaty. He motions next door with his head. "That guy. ¿Qué carajo?"

I shrug. "I don't know." For some reason I'm not surprised by what Rack did. He's a weirdo, and nosy as hell, but I get the feeling he's actually pretty nice. And what Robert said wasn't nice. It *was* understandable, though. Of course he thinks I'm ignoring him because of Manny, especially after what Manny said tonight.

Manny says, "You okay?" He puts a hand on my knee. I want to take it but also to push it off. I'm pissed that he sold me out. I wish he could have kept his mouth shut. I almost say that to him, but I don't. It's not his problem that I'm engaged and that I called him—twice—for help. It's mine.

The throbbing in my head has subsided but it still hurts really bad and Rack took the Tylenol. "I need to lie down."

"Go ahead. I'll hang out here on the sofa. Just to keep you company."

"I think I need to be alone."

"You sure? I mean, like, what if he comes back?"

I shake my head. "He won't."

"How do you know?"

"Pretty sure Suzie won't let him."

His leg is still shaking a little but he's not doing the thing with his shirt anymore. "I don't know, man. Ten cuidado con eso. That's all I'm saying."

"I will."

He finishes his beer in three gulps, picks up his half-eaten pastelito. "I'm done with mine. You?"

"Done."

He picks mine up, puts it into the box. "Maybe you'll want it later." I think he's stalling but I can't be sure. Until he starts cleaning up the crumbs off the table. Then I know he is. "You sure you're good?" he says.

"Yeah, I'm good."

He picks up the rest of the six-pack and says, "Okay, I'll text you later," before walking out.

I lie down on the sofa, being as still as I can so the baby will wake up. I take deep breaths and try to stop thinking about Rack pinning Robert to the door. I'm worried about Robert driving; he's drunk and probably shaken up. I'll text him in a little while to make sure he made it home.

Finally, the baby presses a foot into my left side, then my left ribs. I press back. "Hi, mijo," I say. "I can't believe you slept through all of that." Hurting Robert like that was maybe the worst thing I've ever done to another person. And then having them both—Robert and Manny—here together was a bad dream come to life, a re-creation of my mother's sordid past, complete with unplanned pregnancy and love triangle. Except that my mother's choices were clear: she had to stay with my father. She had no other option after Juan left. My choices, on the other hand, are not so clear. They're murky. And for some reason the Juan thing is making them murkier. How can I know what I want if I don't even know who I am?

24

The next morning the Publix bag is hanging off my doorknob. Inside is the Tylenol and a note written on yellow legal paper.

Monica,
I'm very sorry for my behavior with your fiancé last night. I
should not have put my hands on him. I should have practiced
B.O.B. (Brain Over Body). I let the anger I was feeling in the
moment overtake me and I should have taken a moment to count
to ten. I hope I didn't offend you and if I did, I am very sorry. I
hope you can forgive me.

Rack

I toss the note, the Tylenol, and the Publix bag onto the passenger's seat and spend the drive to work wondering what I'm going to say to him and Suzie next time I see them. I barely know him, and he was acting like my father. If my father was a middle-aged club bouncer.

At work, Val tells me Sandra's out today so I'm covering the front desk alone. We have two new patients scheduled first thing, and they're both late, so when Manny texts me saying *You okay???*,

I can't text him back right away. He texted me the same thing last night but I ignored it. I texted Robert instead to check on him. It took him a while but he finally wrote back *Fine. Home.*

I get the new patients done and check in a couple of regulars, then write back to Manny and tell him I'm fine.

No more trouble from next door?

Nope. I consider telling him about the note but it's too much to explain by text.

Good. Gotta get back to work. I'll text you later. XO.

It's been four days since I've talked to anyone in my family. I have a string of missed calls and messages from my mother, and two from my father. I consider calling my mother, then decide I can't. One thing at a time. At five, I force myself to leave, even though I have a good two hours of billing to catch up on. I just want to be at home, or at what counts as home right now, under the covers, alone.

As I pull in at the hotel, Rack comes out of their room holding a potted plant. Shit.

"Mónica," he says. He's wearing a Pink Floyd T-shirt and his hair is down. "I've been waiting for you to get home. Did you get my note?"

"Yeah."

Rack looks down at the pavement. "I'm really sorry." He hands me the plant.

"Thanks."

"It's the least I could do." He snaps his fingers. "Wait. We actually got some extra Breadibles too. Let me give you some."

"I'm fine, it's okay." I have no idea what Breadibles are.

"No, come on. They were BOGO and we'll never eat this many before they go bad."

"What are Breadibles?"

"Gluten-free bread."

"Oh." I can't believe I'm in a hotel parking lot talking to a convicted felon about gluten-free bread. I know I should be more afraid of him, but there's something about him: his eyes, but also the way he's always so polite and friendly. Except when he's strangling people in my room.

A maid comes out of the room two doors down. Rack waves and says, "Hi, Ana!" She waves back as she takes some towels and shampoos off her cart. Right then Suzie pulls in and parks next to my car. She gets out holding a bag of Pollo Tropical.

"I'm apologizing to Mónica," Rack says.

"You were supposed to wait for me." She turns to me. "We're so sorry he overstepped his boundaries. It'll never happen again."

"You have my word," Rack says.

"Thanks."

"Come on in," he says to me. "I'll get you the Breadibles. They're really good."

I try to just hover at the door, but Rack can't find them right away and Suzie says, "Come in, come in."

Their room smells flowery and sweet, like the Renuzits my mother used when I was a kid. Suzie puts the Pollo Tropical on the counter. Now the room smells flowery and sweet and delicious. My stomach growls. Hopefully nobody heard it. "My dad's a great guy," Suzie says. "But he can be a bit of a bruiser sometimes. Especially when he thinks someone's in trouble."

Rack's looking through the cabinets above the sink. "Well, it *is* what I do for a living." He smiles. Then he gets serious. "But that's no excuse. Actually, have you ever read this?" He gets a book off the dresser and hands it to me. *Being Your Best You* by Roger Morgan, who looks like somebody's creepy white-guy uncle. "There are some good ideas in here about how to be successful in life. It's where I learned about B.O.B."

Rack finds the package of Breadibles and puts it on the table. He gets out two ciders and holds a bottle of water out to me.

"I'm okay," I say.

"It's important to hydrate. Especially in your condition. Come on."

I take it. "Thanks."

"Sorry about the mess. It's laundry day." The "mess" is just piles of folded clothes all over the bed and a clothesline running from a lamp on one side of the room to a lamp on the other. Two sets of scrubs and three white button-downs hang off of it.

Suzie points to them. "School clothes and work clothes. I do cater-waitering on the weekends."

Rack pulls a chair out for me at the table. "Please. Have a seat."

I sit down and he sits across from me. We're all quiet for a second, then Rack says, "Have you heard from your fiancé? He okay?"

"Yeah. He made it home."

"Good. He was pretty boozed up. I worried about that afterward. Did he call you?"

"I texted him just to make sure."

"And he texted you back?"

I nod. "I didn't think he would. I thought I was going to have to stalk him on Facebook to figure it out."

"Facebook," Rack says. "Can't do it. Too many ghosts. Too

many people from prison I really don't need to be in touch with."

I sit back in my chair, as far as I can, away from him, the thought of him actually having been in prison freaking me out. I open my water and take a sip. No one is saying anything, and the vibe is weird now. "So, where do you wo—"

"It was racketeering," he says.

"What was?"

"What I went to prison for."

"Is that, like, money laundering?"

"Sort of. A lot of times 'racketeering' means mob. But that wasn't me. Not really. Yeah, I roughed a couple people up. But it was mostly about getting my hands dirty with company money. Just making bad decisions."

I don't know what to say.

"I was sentenced to four years, served twenty months. They were long months, though. It was federal. I'm still on parole." He nods at Suzie. "That's why she got so mad at me for roughing up your guy. If I get in trouble, it's over."

Suzie says, "I was worried he'd call the cops. Do you think he will?"

"I doubt it." Although I also never would have thought he'd show up here drunk and call me a whore.

"God, I hope he doesn't," Suzie says. She gets up and starts unpacking the food. "Hey, are you hungry? You want to stay? We have more than enough."

Rack says, "Have you tried this Pollo Tropical stuff?" He gets *Pollo* right but pronounces *Tropical* in English like *tropical fish.*

"You guys should eat. I'm good." I gather up my purse, the Breadibles, the plant.

Suzie brings the rice and beans to the table. "Come on. Nothing says 'Sorry I tried to kill your boyfriend' like chicken and black beans."

I laugh.

"Seriously," she says. "We're not going to have room in the fridge for the leftovers. It'll just go to waste."

"Okay, sure, thanks."

"Great," she says, and brings everything else to the table.

While we eat, I check out their setup. They've got stacks of plates and bowls and silverware—all real, nothing disposable. On the counter next to the sink is a hot plate, a toaster, a little basket of off-brand spices. There's a pile of restaurant napkins in a sandwich-size Tupperware container—the real one from the lunch box. "Oh wow," I say, pointing to it. "I haven't seen one of those since second grade."

Suzie smiles. "I know. I got it at Goodwill. Like most of our stuff."

Rack says, "I found that hot plate for seven dollars at the Goodwill down in Kendall."

I tell them about the Salvation Army store on Bird and 97th where I got the sofa I had in the Mouse House.

Rack says, "Good to know. When we get enough money to get out of this place, we'll be on the hunt for furniture. We hocked everything we had when we got evicted."

Suzie explains how it happened: she was working full-time and doing school at night, but they got behind on rent, so now she's going to school full-time and working part-time. "The faster I get my degree," she says, "the faster we get out of here."

I think about my summer class that I gave up on.

Rack looks over at the clock on the bedside table. It's 7:31.

"Oh!" he says, and gets up to get the remote. "Do you guys mind? I'll keep it low. Promise." He gets the TV on just as Alex Trebek is coming out onstage.

Suzie says, "He can't live without it."

I laugh. "It's like my mom with her telenovela," I say. Or me, now.

Rack sits back down with us. He's excited because "U.S. Presidents" is one of the categories.

Suzie rolls her eyes and says, "He can name them all. In order."

"Impressive," I say.

"Learned them in prison," Rack says. "Had a lot of time on my hands."

I ask Suzie how much longer she has to go in school.

"This semester, then one more. We should be out of here by next summer, assuming we can find some place affordable. It's so expensive down here."

"I know," I say. "I used to live in an efficiency off the back of someone's house and even that was a lot."

"Where do you live now?" she asks.

Rack is mumbling answers to the TV. I can barely hear the questions, but apparently he can. It's like he's tuned to a special frequency.

"I live at Robert's. We moved in together when I got pregnant."

Rack says, "Which one's Robert?"

"The one you tried to strangle." I smile a little and take a bite of chicken.

He bows his head. "I'm really sorry. I just don't like to hear that kind of talk. You seem like a good person and he was not treating you with respect."

"He was just drunk. And mad. Really mad. He's a good guy, actually. He loves me a lot."

Rack says, "He's . . ." He points to my stomach.

"Yeah."

"But the other guy?"

"He's my ex. We were together for a long time."

He looks away from the TV and right at me. "And things are a little complicated right now."

"Yeah."

He wipes his mouth with a napkin. "Me and my ex—not Suzie's mom; my second ex—me and her had a complicated thing for a few years. Couldn't quite say goodbye. I knew it wasn't gonna work, so I moved on. Married my third wife, had two kids, the works. But Number Two was something else. I believe some people are just carved into our souls. She was one of those people for me."

Carved into my soul. Exactly. "Sucks," I say.

"Yeah. So you and what's his name?"

"Robert."

"Robert. You taking a little break? That why you're here?"

Suzie whacks his arm. "Dad, you're prying."

He laughs. "My mom said she should have named me 'Why?' because that's all I ever said. I always wanted to know more."

I think about telling them more. My mom, Juan, the FBI. But I don't. I just say, "Yeah, we're taking a little break. I have a few things to figure out." Alex Trebek loads a new board and I imagine a category called "Mónica Campo's Crazy Life" with answers like "The biological father she never knew she had" and "The love triangle she inadvertently found herself in."

I ask Rack about his job, and Suzie says, "He bounces at a lesbian bar."

"And then on the weekends I'm at Butter down on the beach," Rack says.

"Is that a lesbian bar too?" I ask.

He shakes his head. "Little bit of everything there."

We finish eating and *Jeopardy!* ends. Rack turns off the TV and cleans up the dishes, washing and drying at the mini-sink while Suzie and I close up what's left of the food and throw away the trash. I ask her, "Do you have any particular floor you're interested in?"

"I think Emergency Department. I like the pace. And the variety. You're always learning something new, you know? Or maybe the ICU."

"My mom just spent a month in the ICU. Very different pace."

"She did? What for?"

Rack turns away from the sink. "Is she okay?"

Now I tell them: about the aneurysm, the coma. Then, for some reason, I tell them about the crazy-talk memories. I don't know why. There's something about them that makes me want to tell them about my life. Maybe because they aren't actually *in* my life. I don't tell them everything. I just say that she's been slipping back into the past, being unaware of the present for a few minutes at a time.

"Like Alzheimer's?" Suzie says. "Like how they can't remember five minutes ago but they can tell you what kind of cake they had at their tenth birthday?" She holds out a garbage bag and I put the trash from the table in it.

"Kind of." I think of my mom all dressed up in her '80s clothes. What's weird, I realize now, is that she even *had* those clothes. That's not like her. Normally, she cleans out her closet every couple of years. She must have been saving them.

Rack turns off the water and hangs the towel off the front of the sink to dry. "Do the doctors have any idea what it is?"

"We're trying to get her to go see someone, but she's refusing."

"My mom would do the same thing," Suzie says. She points to Rack. "And so would he."

He gives her a look.

"Thanks so much for dinner," I say. "I really appreciate it." As much as I wanted to be under my covers tonight, this was actually kind of nice.

"Anytime," he says. "And remember, we're right next door if you need anything, okay? Just call. Room 108."

This makes me feel good. Safe, even.

25

I've ignored so many of my mom's calls by now, she's stopped calling for a few days. When I listen to her latest message, it says, "Juan is alive. Call me."

She must be having another episode, and I can't handle it right now; I don't have time. I'm behind on work because of my OB appointment this morning. It was my first time going without Robert, which felt strange, and sad, but there was no way I was going to bring him right now.

I call my mother as I'm walking to my car after work.

"Mónica, hablé con Daniel," she says. No "Hi, how are you?" And she sounds completely sane, not like she's having an episode at all.

"Daniel who?"

"Daniel Fernández."

"From the FBI?"

"Yes, I called him." An alarm bell sounds somewhere deep inside me.

"Why?"

"All he ever told me was that Juan was killed and there was drugs involved. But I never believed that Juan got into drugs. He wasn't that kind of person. And he never would have risked going back to jail. Not for that."

"But, Mom, why do you need to know all this now? It's done, it's over."

"Because now I'm telling *you*. And you deserve to know the whole story."

"You called the FBI agent from thirty years ago? He's still there? How is he still there?"

"Yes, he's still there. He's retiring next year. His son is getting married in two weeks. Not the son that's your age. He has two more children, a girl and another boy. It's that boy. He met his fiancée in law school; they're both lawyers. They're doing the wedding in Connecticut because that's where she's from." Of course my mother knows all this. She was probably on the phone with him for an hour. Who cares about his son? She called him to talk about Juan. I can't believe she called him to talk about Juan.

Sandra comes out of the building. I wave from the car like everything's fine. Like I'm not talking to my mother about how she contacted the FBI to find out about my real father, who I didn't even know existed until two weeks ago. "So he remembered you?" I say.

"Actually, he remembered *you*. I reminded him how he used to hold you and do the one-two-three and he remembered that. Can you believe it?" She sounds excited, like she's won a prize of some kind. "He didn't remember everything about the case, of course, so he told me he would look it up and call me back."

"Does Dad know you did this? Are you even speaking to each other right now?"

"Rolando and I haven't discussed this," she says. "He's still at work. I just heard back from Daniel this afternoon and he said some additional information was added to the file a few years after he last saw me. He said Juan didn't die when they shot him. He escaped to Costa Rica."

"So he's just . . . alive?" All of a sudden I feel like I'm drowning.

"We don't know. Daniel has no information past 1989, when Juan was on a ranch in Costa Rica, working to help the Contras. He said Juan got there with the aid of a CIA connection. Which I'm sure was Martín."

She does this: tells me stories about people I don't know as if I've known them my whole life. "Who's Martín?"

"Martín was Chucho's uncle. He had worked with the CIA in the sixties, when they were there trying to get rid of Castro. That's how we got the explosives."

"Explosives?" I manage to say. "What 'we'? What are you talking about?"

"I'm talking about what we did. Why Chucho and Juan were arrested."

"You said they burned a field." I pull out of the parking lot onto 87th Avenue and have to slow down right away because the traffic is so heavy.

"Yes, they burned a field. They burned many fields. That was the crime they were arrested for. But we did other things to undermine the government as well. We bombed a train station and a refinery."

"Are you kidding me?" I yell. My mother committed crimes? *Bombings?* Or maybe she didn't. But she sounds completely lucid. No dreamy, faraway voice, no mistaking me for someone else. "Mom, this is true?" I say. "You're telling me the truth? This isn't one of your . . . moments? You know you're talking to me, Mónica, in 2012, in Miami?" I put on my turn signal, hoping someone will let me over to the right lane.

"Yes, Mónica. I know exactly who I'm talking to. I know exactly what I'm saying. We were fighting for our country, trying to get it back. Someone had to. The '60s were over and people had resigned themselves to life under Castro. But we hadn't. We were young and strong and mad. We saw what that life had done to our parents." She's getting angrier. "My father's business that he had worked so hard to build was just gone—taken over by the government, nationalized, so that all the profits went to them. And Juan's father was *killed*. He fought in the Escambray rebellion and died a horrible death, suffocating in a supply truck after they captured him." Her voice gets softer. "Juan was eleven years old. Adelita was nine. Can you imagine?" She sighs. "The Revolution destroyed so many of us. In so many ways."

She's talked about Cuba before, of course, but never in this way. I've heard all about what a pig Castro is, how "el socialismo," as he calls it, is a joke. This is standard conversation at any party once everybody's had a few drinks. But I've never heard her talk like this, about exactly how Castro hurt her. I'm quiet for a moment, concentrating on getting into the right lane and trying to get the courage to ask her what I know I have to ask: whether she killed anyone in those bombings. I don't think I can handle knowing she did. I don't think I can handle knowing anything else about her I didn't know.

Thank God, the next thing out of her mouth is "We never hurt anyone. That was not our intention. We always did it late at night, when no one was around. We were trying to cripple the government's efforts at controlling everything, and to bring awareness to the people who believed in the Revolution."

I imagine my mom, young, her hair black and long like she wore it back then, sneaking into a train station in the middle of the night carrying a bomb. What does a bomb look like? I picture the little black box from the movies. The wires—black, red, blue. A digital clock, the green numbers counting down. Who knows if that's right? My mother. My mother knows if that's right. "Did you actually set the bombs?" I ask.

"No. Juan and Chucho did all the work. Adelita and I helped with communications, passing messages, organizing others to help. But they found us out, somehow. Well, they found *them* out: Juan and Chucho. By miracle of God, they never got *us*. Or Martín. He left right after. Came here through Mexico and started working with his brother at the dealership." Again, as if I know what she's talking about.

"What dealership?"

"Sosa Cars and Trucks. Right there on Flagler."

"The one from TV? From the commercials?"

"Yes. His brother owned it. Now it's his."

"You bought explosives from the guy who owns Sosa Cars and Trucks?"

"We didn't *buy* them. He *gave* them to us."

I finally make it into the right lane but I keep forgetting to press the accelerator. I'm right at Norman Brothers Produce, so I just pull in and almost hit a blond dad and his two blond kids riding the grocery cart. I hit the brakes hard, my heart slams into my chest, and I yell, "Oh my God!"

"¿Qué pasó?"

"Nothing. Keep going." I don't want her to stop. I need to know the rest of this. I don't want to, but I know I need to. I pull into the nearest parking space. No more driving right now. "So what about the ranch in Costa Rica where Juan ended up?"

"I was just reading about it on the internet. *People* magazine did a story about the man who owned it. His name was Frank Wall. He was an American guy who owned land down there and he was helping the Contras."

"The Contras, like—"

"En Nicaragua. Con Oliver North y el escándalo ese de Iran-Contra? They didn't teach you that in school?"

All I know about Oliver North is that he's some military guy and that my uncle has a signed picture of him hanging in their house. "He's the guy Tío Fermín likes? From the picture in the den?"

"Yes," she says. "The Contras were fighting the communists in Nicaragua. Oliver North was helping them. It was as simple as that."

There's no way it was as simple as that, not if there was a scandal, but I'm not getting into it. "So Juan was living in Costa Rica why?"

"He was hiding from the bad people who tried to kill him."

"The drug dealers?"

"It wasn't drug dealers. Well, not *just* drug dealers. He had gotten involved in counterrevolutionary activities here, too."

I put the phone on speaker and lay it on the dashboard. "What does that mean, 'counterrevolutionary activities'?"

"He tried to bomb a travel agency."

"What? Oh my God, Mom. This guy was a terrorist!"

"He was *not* a terrorist. He was supporting his beliefs, calling attention to the cause he believed in."

"Uh, hello?"

"Juan would never have tried to hurt anyone. Not ever. Daniel said they planted the bomb in the middle of the night, just like we did in Cuba. That travel agency had been arranging tours to the island, working with Castro to make money off people wanting to go see their families. The bomb was just to make a statement, to disrupt that business, which was supporting communists."

"So the FBI wanted him because of the bomb?"

"The bomb didn't even go off; they caught him before it blew. He agreed to become an informant to avoid going to prison. They were trying to catch other people doing the same kind of thing, but bigger and more violent. They were trying to get Gamma 99."

"What is that? A gang or something?" I turn the A/C down a little and angle the vents to my neck. The baby turns over and kicks me. I press on his foot. *I know, mijo,* I think to him. *This is insane.*

"There were these groups—Gamma 99, Beta Force—there were many, but those were the two biggest. They were doing what *we* had been doing: fighting Castro."

"In Cuba? They were in Cuba?"

"No, aquí."

"Aquí Miami?" My mind is reeling, I'm trying to keep track.

"Aquí Miami, aquí Union City, aquí Nueva York. They were in the news all the time, doing bombings and hurting people. They were organized and they didn't like it when people spoke against them. They did what Juan did to that travel agency, but with bigger bombs. And they killed people. They killed a guy from the UN. They blew up a plane. And they tried to kill one of the guys from WQBA."

"The radio station? Why would you want to kill a DJ? And how do I not know about this stuff?"

"They don't teach this in school, I guess. But they should. It's part of our history. He wasn't a DJ. He was a newscaster and he had been talking against them on his show, saying they were too violent, that it wasn't right, this wasn't the way to change things."

"And Juan was in the Whatever 99?"

"Gamma 99. No, no. He became an informant. To tell on them. You know, they have to pretend to be a bad guy and then report back to the police."

"Yes, I know how it works," I say. I put my hand on my stomach and think, *Mijo, I can't believe this. Who* was *this guy? And who is your abuela?*

"Mind you," my mother says, "I had no idea about any of this. By the time I found him in the English class, he was already working with the police. Daniel said Gamma 99 got involved with some drug people, to make money for the organization. That was why he said yes when I asked him if drugs were involved. But drugs weren't the main investigation. It was Gamma 99. They were trying to get the guy who ran it. He was a decent man, a patriot. He loved his country and wanted it back. Like all of us. His methods were just very extreme." I hear in her voice a reverence I don't understand. This guy was a murderer, for God's sake. How can she say he's a decent man?

"You said he killed people."

"Communists." This shocks me a little. It's not a complete disregard for human life but it *is* something like that, and it's chilling.

"Was the newscaster a communist?"

"No. He just didn't agree with him. That's what I mean. Extreme. Too extreme."

I'm quiet for a second. "And if he had been a communist? You're okay with this guy trying to kill him?"

"It's more complicated than that. The communists in Cuba killed many people. They killed Chucho. And they would have killed Juan eventually. The prisons are horrific. Juan said when he was in there, he wished they had shot him at the wall, the treatment was so horrible."

"So, did Juan get the information the cops needed to catch the Gamma 99 guys?"

"Yes, but the guys found out he was an informant. That's why he went to Puerto Rico. It wasn't just that his mother wanted to die on an island; it was because Daniel sent him there to hide and he took Adelita and his mother with him. Daniel needed Juan—to testify, you know. After Dolores died, Daniel moved him to Panamá for safety. But the bad guys somehow found him and shot him, and Daniel thought he died."

"So Juan actually got shot?"

"Yes. But the FBI's information source down there wasn't very good and he got the story wrong. The guy didn't know Juan survived the shooting and escaped to Costa Rica."

I hear the sink water turn on. "Are you up? Are you cleaning the kitchen?"

"Well, I'm just putting the dishes in right. Caro came earlier." The water whooshes and a dish clinks. "Listen, Mónica, we need to find him."

"Who?"

"Juan. We need to tell him. And you need to meet him."

My breath catches. "Why? *No.* No, I don't."

"Yes," she says. "You do." She turns off the water.

The baby kicks me in the bladder. "Mom, you don't even know if he's alive. And finding him is—" I can't even finish the sentence. It's bad enough to find out that my biological father is actually some revolutionary, or counterrevolutionary, whatever it's called. Some bomber who ended up on the run, but to think about meeting him right now? Forget it.

I say, "This is a lot to take in. Especially with you recovering from surgery."

"My recovery is going fine," she says in English. Then: "Esto es muy importante, Mónica."

"I know it is. But I can't do this. Not now. Please." I look up at the ceiling of the car and feel my neck muscles pull taut. "I have to go," I tell her.

"Wait. Are you coming over tonight?" she says quietly. "It's Friday."

"I don't think so." I hold my breath.

"Oh. Okay. Why not?" The hurt in her voice slices through me. I say the same thing I said to Robert: "I need to be on my own right now. I need some time to process everything that's happened."

As if she's channeling him—answering in English, even—she says, "You can't process it here? With me?"

"No."

She goes back to Spanish. "But I'm your mother. I'm part of this too."

"Mom, I don't think you understand what this feels like," I say. I press my palms into the steering wheel until it hurts.

She says, "I know it's difficult. But I'm trying to help you."

"By suggesting that I try to find him? I don't think so."

She sighs heavily into the phone and I hear the pain in it, but I can't bring myself to relieve that pain. I can't tell her it's all right. Because it's not. "I need to go," I say.

"Okay. Maybe I'll see you in a few days?"

"Maybe," I say, even though the thought of walking back into that house suddenly fills me with dread. That house with the pictures of the family I'm not actually a part of, all the reminders of the years I wasn't who I thought I was.

"Okay, hasta luego, mi niña," she says, and hangs up.

I sit there, trying to take it all in, but I'm unable to. All that information my mother just delivered is making me feel floaty and scared and like I don't know what's real anymore. I open the car door and step out. I just need to put my feet on the ground. I think about how Norman Brothers Produce has been here forever, with its big green-and-white-striped awning and its old-timey farm equipment outside. It's real. It's solid. I walk across the parking lot and put my hand on the warm metal of the tractor, feel the five-o'clock sun on my face. The sky is blue, the clouds are whispy and white, and, according to my mother, Juan is alive.

26

When I go to the front desk the next morning and ask about paying for another week, the guy tells me it's already been paid for, that a Visa with the name Manuel Rivera is on the account.

"Thank you," I say, and stack two miniature donuts onto a napkin. I know I should give the guy my card, but Manny can afford this way more than I can. And maybe he owes it to me, after leaving me over and over again for years. If he hadn't, I wouldn't be in this position. I would still be hearing my mother's voice in my head saying *Juan is alive* every ten minutes, but I'd be doing it in our house in Little Gables or the very edge of South Miami if we had found a deal. And the baby inside me would be his, not Robert's.

I take the donuts back to my room to eat them and Google laundromats. I think of my mother going to see Adelita at the laundromat where she worked. I wonder whether Adelita knew what her brother was up to, bombing a travel agency and then having to work for the police as an informant against Gamma 99. I looked up the group last night, and there was so much. Articles, websites, videos. I couldn't stop. It was stuff about Gamma 99, but also about the Bay of Pigs and John F. Kennedy. And some *other* mission after the Bay of Pigs where the CIA trained a bunch of guys down in the

Everglades but then never deployed them. Which, of course, pissed them all off. So then there were a bunch of angry CIA-trained Cubans running around, one of whom was the guy who ran Gamma 99, the patriot.

After he got trained for nothing, he and a few other guys started bombing shit. It was always people and places they thought were supporting Castro, like the Venezuelan consulate and some small newspaper where they thought the guy running it was a communist. And the newscaster from WQBA, like my mom said. He came out of work one night, started his car, and the front half of it blew up. It tore his legs right off. He lived through it, but not everybody they went after did. One guy was part of a group that had been negotiating with Castro to release some political prisoners, and they didn't like that. They drove by the guy's house and shot him dead right in front of his kid. I couldn't believe this. Who cares so much about a political cause that they kill a man right in front of his son? I hate Fidel just as much as everyone else in this city, but I wouldn't kill someone because of it.

They caught the leader of Gamma 99 three months after I was born, which means they had him by the time Daniel was over at my mom's house, doing the one-two-three. They didn't have the other members of the group, though. I read all this in the *Herald*, and when I got to that part of the article, I thought, *This is it. This is where Juan was connected.* I searched for his name over and over, but it was nowhere. There were mentions of informants, but mostly it was about how they were hard to come by because so many people either sympathized with Gamma 99 or were too afraid of them to tell on them. I guess nobody else wanted to get their legs blown off. Juan had to do it, though, to avoid jail for himself. The FBI eventually got them all, three years later, once my mother was back to her regular life, no FBI agents at the kitchen table, no bad guys to worry about, just cooking ropa vieja for my father, having coffee with Teresita, and trying not to think about the love of her life being shot dead.

Which, according to Daniel Fernández, never happened.

The website for Coin Laundry of America has a picture of a kid sitting at a table, doing his homework. I pick it for that reason, and because it's in Kendall, close to the Goodwill that Rack and Suzie told me about. On the way there, I stop at La Carreta for café con leche and eggs from the ventanita. I'm standing on the sidewalk, waiting for my order and staring at the giant rooster draped in the Cuban flag, when Caro texts, inviting me to a barbecue at her house tonight. *Your parents are coming. And I think Pablo and Maritza too,* she says. Hell no. I'm not going to sit on her patio eating a burger, pretending that Robert's just at the track tonight and that my mother didn't have an affair with her first husband and conceive me in the hotel where I'm now living. I text her back that I have plans with my friend Lisa. Lisa, who I haven't talked to for months. The woman at the ventanita calls my name. *Juan is alive,* my mother says in my head again, and I go get my order.

I eat while I drive, and Robert texts me just as I'm pulling into the parking lot of the laundry. *Sorry for how I acted the other night. Can we talk?*

I don't want to talk. Yesterday, when he showed up at the office to deliver the water for the waiting room, I went to the bathroom for twenty minutes. I sit there looking at the phone. "What do I do?" I ask the baby. I put the phone back in my purse and bring my laundry in.

Instead of texting Robert back, I text Manny. *Don't need a sugar daddy, but thanks for the room charge.*

He texts back right away. *Trying to be nice. Didn't want you worrying about that too. How are you?*

Found out yesterday Juan is alive. Also he was kind of a terrorist.

WTF. Call me?

I walk outside to call him. It's raining a little, so I stand under the overhang and tell him everything my mom told me about Juan: what they did in Cuba, what he did over here.

"Your mom, the manicurist, was involved in counterrevolutionary activity?"

"Just one more part of her secret past."

"Wait. Are you sure she was cogent? Like, it wasn't the brain issue?"

The sky looks darker now than it did when I drove in. "Yeah. I asked her question after question, and then I researched it all. It's true."

"Okay. Wow. So are you all right?" His voice is soft, concerned.

I sigh. "I don't even know what I am. The daughter of a terrorist?"

"Sounds like he was more of a narc."

"Yeah. But for terrorists." I tell him about the newscaster from WQBA and the guy they shot in front of his kid.

"Coñó. Was he involved with that stuff?"

"Actually, no, I don't think so. He wasn't into hurting people. Not like the other guys." The rain picks up a little. "Have you ever heard about those groups? The Alpha Beta Gamma whatevers?"

"Maybe. My uncle was in the Bay of Pigs and always yelling about Castro. He might have said something about it."

"A lot of the guys in these groups were part of the Bay of Pigs. One guy from the Beta group was actually former CIA."

"Sounds like Afghanistan," Manny says. "Those guys are invisible. And they stick their noses in everywhere. Did you know that the guy who captured Che was Cuban and a former CIA agent? The Bolivians shot him, but the guy who captured him was ours."

"How do you know this?"

"Read a book about it. Good info. Bad book."

"Interesting. Fun fact: the guy who saved Juan's life used to be in the CIA. Now he owns Sosa Cars and Trucks."

"The one right there on Flagler?"

"The very one." *Juan is alive*, my mother says in my head, and for some reason I repeat it back to the baby. *Mijo*, I think. *Juan is alive*. "Another fun fact?" I say to Manny. "My mother wants me to find Juan. To meet him."

"You're kidding me. Really? Is that what *you* want?"

The rain gets harder, and I have to step back against the building to stay dry. "I want none of this to be happening. I want to jump in a time machine and just go backward."

"Yeah," he says. And then, more quietly, "Tell me about it."

I want to ask him when he would go back to and why. But the rain is slamming the pavement now and I'm getting wet and my clothes are probably finished washing and I'm afraid to hear what he has to say. So I tell him I have to go and he says to text him later and let him know how I'm doing. Even though I shouldn't, I say, "Okay. I will." When I hang up, I stand there for a moment listening to the rain roaring out of the sky. I press my hands into my stomach. This time I don't just think it. I whisper it out loud: "Mijo, Juan is alive."

Rack and Susie were right about the Goodwill. I score a hot plate, a toaster, and a few pots and pans, all for fifteen bucks. Plus a small set of robin's-egg-blue dishes: three plates, three bowls, two mugs. And these two pewter mushrooms that I thought were just decorations but turn out to be salt and pepper shakers. On the way home I stop at Home Depot for a drop cloth to cover the sofa in my room. I can't take the dark blue with the gold flecks anymore. I'm at the checkout when Pablo texts me that Maritza has the maternity clothes from her sister, so I tell him I'll pass by in a little while.

When I get there, Maritza's wearing shorts and a jog bra and making smoothies. She hands me one. "I put extra protein powder in it," she says, glancing down at my stomach, which is about six times the size of hers.

"Thanks." It's horrible—both super sweet and super sour at the same time. I drink it anyway because it has protein and I haven't eaten since the eggs from La Carreta. And because it's cold. It's hot in their house. So hot that I'm sweating a little.

Maritza brings me into the dining area to give me a large Banana Republic bag full of the maternity clothes from her sister. "She said it's mostly tops."

"This is amazing," I say, looking through it. Everything in there is nicer than anything I've ever owned. "Please tell her thank you."

"I will," she says, and goes back to the kitchen to make a smoothie for Pablo.

He's in the living room, shirtless, in workout shorts, playing some first-person shooter game on their giant TV. Everything in here is giant: the black leather sectional, the coffee table, the chair they don't need on the other side of the coffee table. Scattered around the room is a collection of statues. Not angels or cherubs like Gladys has but nude women. They're all white, clearly by the same artist. Or from the same sale.

Maritza brings in his smoothie and puts it down on the table for him.

"Thanks, baby," he says without looking away from the TV.

"I need to take a shower. There's more smoothie in the blender if you guys want," she says, then heads upstairs, her chancletas slapping on the tile floor.

Outside the French doors, the sun is shining on the bay. They live right on Brickell, in a condo her parents bought her when she graduated from UM. Pablo's whole goal in life is to buy a boat and keep it in the private dock reserved for residents of their building. That's why he works sixty hours a week at the shady insurance company. Not that the life he has now isn't already charmed. He's the prince of the family who gets to float in and out whenever it's convenient and he's basically bankrolled by his rich girlfriend in her bay view condo.

He drinks his smoothie and I wait for his face to cave in from how sour it is, but it doesn't. He must be used to it. "So, what's up? How are you?" he says.

I sit down on the other side of the sectional. "Hot. Why is it ninety degrees in here?"

He rolls his eyes. "Maritza turned off the A/C. She read a thing where Gwyneth Paltrow says it's bad for your respiratory system. We only use it at night."

No wonder no one has a shirt on in here. I consider taking mine off too. Maybe there's a sports bra I can change into in the Banana Republic bag.

"So Mom and Dad told me who Juan is," Pablo says. He tries to shoot a robot/Transformer-looking thing in the game, but it gets away.

"What did they tell you?"

He explains what he knows, which is not much. They didn't even tell him that Juan and my mother had been married. And they conveniently left out Daniel Fernández and the FBI. I fill in the gaps for him. "So all that crazy stuff she was saying about the chickens and Adelita was all about living with Juan in Cuba."

He looks away from the screen for a second. "*Was* saying? Dude, Maritza took food over yesterday and she called her 'Adelita' the whole time she was there."

I let out a giant, exasperated breath. "Fuck. Are you serious? I thought it was over. I thought getting all that shit off her chest— telling me everything, telling Dad everything—would end it."

"Well, it didn't. Listen, I think it's stress. I think you guys just need to make up and you need to start talking to her and let's just get everything back to normal."

"You think we just need to make up?"

"Yeah."

I just stare at him.

"What?" he says.

"Do you know if Dad called about the psychiatrist?"

"She'll never go to a psychiatrist."

"But she needs to. Or a neurologist. Something." I fan my neck with my hand.

"That stuff happened so long ago, it's all done. It doesn't change anything." He shoots three more Transformers and runs into an abandoned building.

"What do you mean it doesn't change anything?"

"I mean, whatever, dude. Dad's still your father. He raised you. That Juan guy is nobody. We just gotta get past this and get back to normal." He looks at me for a second. "And you gotta, like, start talking to them again."

"I'm *talking* to them."

He shakes his head. "Mónica, you're about to have a baby. You can't just cut them out of your life. Mom's having a heart attack that you're not going over there. She's driving everyone crazy."

I pull the hair off my neck with one hand and fan my face with the other. "Everyone who?"

"Everyone."

"Do Gladys and Fermín know?"

"I'm pretty sure."

That feeling of embarrassment, of us—of me—being trashy wells up inside me again. "Great."

"They were gonna find out eventually."

"Yeah, I was just hoping maybe not so soon."

Two of the Transformers come jumping out of a building at him. "Shit," he says. "Are you going to Caro's tonight?"

"No, I have plans."

"With who?"

I wipe the sweat off my upper lip, take a sip of my smoothie, and swallow it as fast as I can. "Who the hell cares with who? I have plans, okay?"

"Okay, fine. Sorry. Well, you gotta go see Mom. Look, it is what it is. It was a long time ago and it's over. Let's move on."

"She doesn't want me to move on. She wants me to find him."

"What are you talking about?"

"She didn't tell you that part, either? She called the FBI agent and found out he wasn't actually killed. He's alive. And she wants me to find him. To meet him and get to know him."

He actually stops playing and looks at me. "What the fuck? Why?" He sounds angry and genuinely confused. He's frowning, shaking his head.

"Ask *her*. She's the one with all the answers." A boat pulls into the dock outside, the sound of its engine rumbling through the French doors.

Pablo shrugs. "Well, it's not like it changes anything. He's not your father. Dad's your father."

"Seriously?" I say. "It doesn't change anything? It feels like it's changed everything. Like, suddenly I'm an entirely different person with an entirely different story."

He gives me a face. "Mónica, it's weird and it sucks, but Dad's still your father. That's never going to change."

That's it. I can't sit here sweating and drinking a liquid Swee-Tart, listening to him tell me everything's fine and we just need to get back to normal. There is no normal anymore. "I gotta go," I say, my voice a little hard. He doesn't seem to notice. He's engaged in a giant battle now, trying to fend off a whole gang of the Transformer things. "Tell Maritza I said bye and thanks for the clothes. And the smoothie."

"Go see Mom," he says, without taking his eyes off the screen. "Please."

27

Robert texts me again on Sunday. And again on Monday. I know I need to text him back, but I can't. All I can do is think about Juan and decorate my room at the hotel. At lunch on Tuesday, I go to T.J. Maxx to look for maternity pants, but I don't even make it over to women's clothes. A display of throw pillows catches my eye and I end up buying two, plus a Marimekko-looking tablecloth that I want to use as a wall hanging. When I get home, I ask Suzie and Rack to help me put it up using pushpins I stole from work. Rack says he's friends with the woman who runs housekeeping and he'll make sure it's okay.

"Don't worry," he says, "I got your back," and takes off for a staff meeting at the lesbian club.

Suzie sits down at the little table in the kitchen area. She looks around my room—at the drop cloth covering the sofa, the red-and-yellow throw pillows, the plant Rack gave me arranged next to a fan of magazines on the coffee table, and now the giant wall hanging across from the bed.

"So, uh, you're really settling in here, aren't you? Planning to stay awhile or are you just nesting early?"

"What's nesting?"

"It's a thing at the end of pregnancy where you have the urge to fix up the house. Or make a bunch of food. My cousin made like five lasagnas and froze them the day before she had her first kid."

"I don't know. I mean, yeah, I like to decorate." I tell her about how I was going to school, hoping to eventually get a degree in interior design.

She picks up one of the pewter mushrooms on the kitchen table and puts it back down. "And now?"

I sigh. "Now I'm . . . here." What I want to say is that I feel so alone right now, so between worlds, that this is the only place that makes sense for me to be.

"Well, it looks good. Homey." She stands up. "Hey, I don't have any homework tonight and I was gonna go to the pool for a while. You wanna come?"

"I don't have a bathing suit."

"Who cares? Just come put your feet in. C'mon. I'm gonna go change. I'll meet you out there."

It feels strange to think about doing something besides going to work and coming back here to be by myself, but also a little interesting. "Okay. Let me just change into shorts."

When I get there, it's just her, sitting on the steps in the shallow end, drinking a cider, wearing a blue bikini top and black boy shorts. She has a little pooch but her legs are muscular. I sit down on the edge of the pool nearby and stick my feet in. Like Juan on his lunch hour. I try to imagine him: black curly hair, blue eyes, a mustache. That's all I know. I see him sitting here, his pants rolled up, his work boots a few feet away, the sweaty socks curled inside each one. He bends down to splash my mother, who would have been about my age, in that pink-and-green one-piece I've seen in old photos, and little Pablo, chubby and laughing in her arms. *Juan is alive. Juan is alive.* It's *my* voice in my head now, not my mother's.

"So, how were the midterms?" I ask.

"Brutal. But I think I did okay. Nursing school is hard as shit."

"I've heard that."

"I'm so glad my son isn't here. I could never do this and parent at the same time."

"You have a son?" The sun is starting to dip in the sky and shining right in my eyes. I have to shade them with my hand to see her.

Suzie takes another sip of her cider and waits for the two motorcycles flying down the street to pass by. The engines are so loud it's scary in that gut-clenching way. The sound fades, finally, and she says, "He's in Cincinnati. With my mom. We're trying to make it so he can visit this summer. And maybe move down once I'm all done and settled."

I want to ask what the story is, but I don't want to pry, so I just ask about job prospects. She tells me how they have job placement through the nursing program, how she might just end up working at Jackson for a while, since that's where she did her clinicals. "Especially if I can get something in the trauma center," she says.

A group of guys comes through the pool gate. They're white and sort of corn-fed, with ruddy skin. They're talking and laughing, bath towels over their shoulders and beers in their hands. They all have farmer tans and really red faces, like maybe they're on a construction crew and down here for a job. Or maybe they're just friends on a vacation and didn't know that the Quality Inn & Suites in Little Havana is nowhere near the beach. They put their stuff down at the table closest to us and then all jump in. The fattest guy does a cannonball.

"I should go do that," I say, rubbing my stomach. "I could probably make a bigger splash."

Suzie laughs and takes a sip of her cider. "If you do, they'll
probably invite you to get drunk with them."

"You have no idea how badly I need to get drunk right now."

She moves off the steps and into the pool, dips her head back
in the water to wet her hair. "Personal trouble or work trouble? Or
both?"

"Work's fine. I have a good job with good people. I just don't
care at all about insurance billing."

"You'd rather be buying throw pillows."

"Yep."

"So the main problems are personal. Let me guess. The fiancé
and the ex."

I tell her the whole Robert and Manny story. I get the feeling
she won't judge me for it, so I even tell her about kissing Manny
the first night at the hotel.

"Oof. Have you talked to Robert since my dad tried to strangle
him?"

I shake my head. "He's been texting me to death. And this afternoon he left me a voice mail. He wants to talk and work it out."

"And you don't?"

"Ugh. I don't know. What I want is to just pause my life for a
little while, you know?" The corn-feds are laughing and messing
around. One of them does a can opener and the splash is so big it
wets me a little.

"Sorry about that, miss," his friend calls out from the deep end.

"No problem," I call back.

Suzie nods her head toward her lounge chair. "Let's . . . ?"

"Yeah."

We get out of the pool and move our stuff down a few chairs. "So, yeah, I do know—the pause feeling," Suzie continues. "It's like you just want to regroup for a minute. Press Play again once you get everything figured out."

"Exactly."

Suzie squeezes the water out of her hair now. "I felt so discombobulated for years—back when my son was young. I was seventeen when I had him. You're doing it the right way. You've waited until you have your shit together."

I laugh. "I'm six months pregnant and living in a hotel."

"No you're not. *We're* living in a hotel. You have options."

I think about the baby's room, full of iguanas. "Yeah. I'm just not sure how good any of them are."

She looks out beyond the pool, over to the parking lot. "I pretty much sucked at being a mother. I did okay at first. I fed him and changed him and got up with him in the night. But once he started walking and potty training, I started going back out with my friends. I didn't want to be a mom. I wanted to be a kid. I left him home with my mother all the time. Eventually, she adopted him."

"Like, legally?"

She nods. "When she did that, I moved away. Talk about a pause." Her eyes look sad, like she's resigned herself to something she can't say out loud. "Took me three years to come back. But I still wasn't done being a kid. When my dad got out of prison, he called and said, 'Come to Florida and I'll help you pull yourself together.' So I did. In the process, I grew up. Mostly. I need a job and a place and then I'm hoping to bring Liam down to live with us."

"How old is he now?"

"Thirteen. Graduates from middle school this year." She gets her phone and shows me a picture. He's a skinny kid with pale skin, sandy brown hair, and a sweet smile.

"He's adorable," I say. "And what's up with his father?"

"He bailed immediately. Went away to college the following year, the whole nine. Liam found him on Facebook, wrote him, but he didn't write back."

"So you told Liam his name and everything?"

"I almost didn't—I was worried about what it would do to him if Brandon didn't want anything to do with him. But I also figured, hey, he's his father. Kid's got a right to know. And if Brandon can't live up to being a parent, that's his problem. But Liam wants a father, I can tell. That's why I want my dad to stay out of trouble, so he can be there for him." A car with a deep-sounding engine turns into the parking lot and for a moment I panic that it's Robert, but it's just a lowered Civic with really tinted windows. Suzie finishes off her cider and says, "My dad made me tell Liam about him going to prison." She lowers her voice, trying to imitate Rack. "'Listen, Suze. I am who I am. He's gotta be able to take me or leave me. Plus he can learn from my experience.'"

I laugh and think about telling her about Juan, but I can't. I can't say it out loud right now.

The sun is going down, the light around us changing. The corn-feds are still laughing and drinking. Two of them have decided to race, calling it the Olympics. "Let's figure out who the Michael Phelps is here," they say.

Suzie checks the time and says, "Oh shit. I gotta go. I'm supposed to call Liam at seven."

We gather up our stuff and walk back to our rooms, the guys at the pool yelling and cheering like kids, their voices getting farther and farther away. Meanwhile, the sun dips lower, turning everything around us that melty orange that's weird and beautiful at the same time.

That night before bed, I try to read the life-changing India book, but I can't. Instead, I look up nesting and then read the Week 30 chapter in the pregnancy book. "Mijo," I say, rubbing circles on my stomach, "you're the size and weight of a cabbage. Your brain is starting to get all crinkly. Your hands are fully developed. And, by the way, you're living in the hotel where your mother was conceived."

Then I just sit there in bed staring at my new wall hanging. It's really soothing to look at, with its black and white triangles and yellow dots. I know it's not normal to be decorating a hotel room. But the truth is I like it here. And I like Suzie. And even Rack. They're good with me being who I am, which, right now, is a mess. I guess it's because they've both been a mess—a worse mess—and they know what it's like. This is the thing Caro doesn't get. She called a couple of days ago and wanted to know when I'm moving out of the hotel and what my next steps are. As if I have next steps.

I talk to the baby for a little while longer, about the triangles, the new pillows, just so he can hear my voice. He hasn't heard his dad's voice in two weeks, and I feel bad about that. I pick up my phone to call Robert but I don't know what to say, so I just put it back down. Suddenly, I'm exhausted, like someone came and tied weights to my arms and legs. I turn out the light and fall into sleep.

28

Work is torture, with all the patients streaming in and out, and Sandra sitting five feet from me. I find myself wondering if people can see it on me. Do they know that I'm a totally different person? It's like what you feel after you get your first period or lose your virginity, when you're wondering if the whole world can tell you're different in a fundamental way. At the end of the day, I drive home and sit in the parking lot in a daze.

I feel in control of nothing, as if I have a mouthful of loose teeth that could fall out at any moment. I feel scared and alone, and scared because I'm alone. I want someone or something to help me. Of course, I think of Manny. But I also think of my mother, the first person ever to calm my fears, the person I have gone to all my life when I was scared. When I was in second grade and in the hospital with pneumonia, I was afraid of the oxygen tent I had to stay in, so she got in there with me. I wish there was some way she could do that now: get in here with me, put her arms around me, and hold me until this feeling goes away. Except she is the cause of this feeling. She and my father. I unbuckle my seat belt and just sit there, not even crying, paralyzed by this fear.

For the longest time, I thought Manny was the one person in my life who could bring me not only the most comfort but also the most pain.

Now I realize it's my mother.

In the hotel room, I use my new pots and pans to make picadillo and rice. I chop the green pepper for the sofrito and then start on the onion. I'm thinking about my mom, trying to figure out how to get her help, when my phone rings. Of course, it's her. She's such a bruja. She could probably feel me thinking about her.

I answer and she yells into my ear, "You're living at the Palmetto Motel?"

Fucking Caro. I knew she couldn't keep it to herself. She probably told Gladys, who told Fermín, who told my father. "Who told you?" I say.

"Robert just called me." Wow. How did I not realize this was a possibility? "What's going on?" she says in English. "Why did you move out from him?"

"I needed some space," I say.

"¿Pero space de qué? What are you talking about? Ay, Mónica, por favor. I don't need another thing on me. I have my heart and my blood pressure and now this." She's in full Spanglish, talking quickly, clearly agitated. "And you're pregnant, por Dios. You don't need to be living alone en un hotel."

I almost say, "I'm not alone, I have my friends Suzie and Rack," but I know what she'd say if I told her I'd befriended the homeless ex-con and his daughter next door. She doesn't mention Manny, so I guess Robert didn't tell her about the night he found him here.

Which is surprising. I'd think if he were going to tell on me, he'd *really* tell on me.

"Why are you there?" she says, going back to Spanish "Why at the Palmetto?"

I'm quiet for a moment. "I don't know. I can't live anywhere else right now."

"You should be living with Robert. You should be married to him. He loves you. He's the father of your baby. He said you didn't have a fight, that he just came home from Marco Island and found you packing. Why?"

I have her on speaker so I can keep cutting, and the "Why?" seems to echo out into the room. It seeps into me, into my skin, and I want to say, "It's none of your business why." I mean, who the hell is she to tell me who to live with, who to love or not love? And how does she not realize how devastating it is to find out your father isn't who you thought he was? And, frankly, that your mother isn't, either. I chop the end of the onion and try to find the right words.

"Mom, everything you told me, about you and Juan and Daniel and all of that—it's very hard to deal with. Can you understand that? It's not like you told me some family secret about someone else. This family secret is about me. This family secret *is* me. And I need time on my own to process that. Okay?"

She sighs quietly. "Mónica, please. Why don't you come over? We can talk more."

"I can't. I'm cooking."

"You're cooking?" she says in English. "How?"

I tell her about the kitchenette and the hot plate, the pots and pans. "It's nice. I like it."

"Ay dios mío. You can't cook con un hot plate!"

"I'm cooking con un hot plate right now," I say. I pour a circle of oil into the pan and turn the heat on to medium.

"What are you cooking? Eggs?"

"Nope. Picadillo y arroz."

She's silent, taking it in. "Well, don't forget the tomato sauce. You know you always forget the tomato sauce."

"I won't." I fold up the paper plate I've been cutting on and use it like a little slide to pour the peppers and onions in.

"Okay, listen, why don't you come over tomorrow? Tomorrow is Friday. We can eat dinner. We can watch *Abismo*."

I stir the sofrito. I say nothing.

"Please," she says, in a quiet, pleading voice. "You need to come."

Out of nowhere, the image of her in the coma appears in my mind. The ventilator in her mouth, the machines with all their ticking and hissing and beeping, the lights indicating that, thank God, she was still alive. Then those first few days after they woke her up, when she was just lying in the bed, still so weak, hardly able to talk or make sense. I think about Pablo's theory that if we can just get back to normal, things will settle down. She'll stop slipping out of this world and into the other one. I'm angry, and sad, and lost, but I do miss her, it's true. I miss our time together, our Friday nights. And, of course, I'm worried about her. I need to know if she's getting better.

"Okay, Mom," I say. "Okay. I'll come."

29

My father answers the door with a penguin dish towel over his shoulder. He looks tired, his eyes a little droopy, still in his black pants and button-down from work. "Hola, mija," he says, leaning in to give me a kiss on the cheek. *Mija.* How am I going to do this—sit with them, eat with them, talk to them like nothing happened?

I follow him into the house, past the entry table full of family photos, their wedding photo front and center, like a sick joke. Even worse, though, is the picture of the four of us on my first Christmas, all of us dressed up for Noche Buena, standing in front of the tree at Tía Gladys and Tío Fermín's. I'm a baby in a little red dress and black baby shoes. My father is holding me. And thinking what? That I don't belong to him? That I'm a stranger? I've looked at this picture thousands of times. Now, though, it's different. Now it's like *it's* looking at *me*, mocking me, calling me the fool who never knew who she was.

In the kitchen, my father unloads Styrofoam containers of food from the comida por libra place next to the optical. Masitas. Rice. Tostones.

"Mom still isn't cooking?" I say. I cross my arms and squeeze my biceps. My hands won't stop trembling.

"She gets tired if she has to stand up for a long time."

"Where is she?" I wonder if she's hiding from me, or from him. Who knows if they've even made up. Last thing I knew, he was standing over her, screaming about Juan and the FBI and then locking himself in the bedroom. After that, she was secretly calling Daniel, the FBI agent, which she probably still hasn't told him.

"She's reading," he says, pointing down the hall to the White Room.

I lower my voice. "Pablo told me she's still having those memories, talking crazy. He said she called Maritza 'Adelita' the whole time she was here the other day."

My father looks a little shocked, but all he says is, "Yes, well, she's been stressed and out of sorts with you not calling her." He pulls three plates down from the cabinet. "And you didn't come last week." His face looks pale and more drawn than usual. It reminds me of how he looked when my mother was in the coma.

"I've been needing some time to myself." It comes out colder than I mean it to.

He nods. "It's just hard for her."

I feel that in my gut, close to my spine. "It's hard for me too." All of a sudden, the smell of the food is making me a little nauseated. I take a step back from the counter.

"I'm sure this is very difficult for you to deal with." He says it in English.

"That's putting it mildly." I look away from him. "So did you ever get the appointment with the psychiatrist?" I say it almost accusingly, like this is one more thing they're doing to me: refusing to get her help.

"The doctor thinks she needs to see a neurologist. The appointment is next Thursday."

"What appointment?" my mother says from the doorway.

I spin around to face her.

"El neurólogo," my father says. He hangs the penguin towel on the stove handle.

I'm waiting for her to get mad or tell me again that she will not be seeing anyone, but she just nods slightly and comes into the kitchen to straighten the towel. She's moving slowly, and she looks weaker than I remembered, her reading glasses pushed up into her hair, more gray at the temples than the last time I saw her. It's been two weeks—the longest I've ever gone without seeing my parents, I realize, and this thought makes me feel more unsteady.

She's wearing an old yellow T-shirt. It's a V-neck and a little stretched out, so her scar is peeking out the top. The pain and fear from the hospital come slamming back, and, with them, the memory of the surgeon coming into the waiting room to tell us they couldn't extubate her, how I felt my own chest cave in with fear. Now, standing here with them in the kitchen, *that* fear is gone, replaced with the fear of whatever it is that's happening to her mind.

She gives me a kiss hello and looks me up and down. "How are you? Are you feeling okay?"

"I'm feeling fine," I tell her.

"Your back doesn't hurt? My back always hurt with both of you."

I open the fridge to get a glass of water. Inside is the Brita, a gallon of milk, a bottle of V8, and a couple of old take-out boxes. No ham, no cheese, no eggs. None of the Yoplaits my mom likes or the rice pudding she keeps for my father's late-night snack. I look around the kitchen. My father's two-liter of Pepsi is there, probably because he picked up that and the gallon of milk at La Vacita. But there are no tomatoes on the yellow plate, no bananas on the hook. Not even a loaf of pan cubano for breakfast tomorrow.

"You guys," I say. "You don't have any food."

They both look around, as if noticing this for the first time.

"How long has it been since you did groceries?" I ask. "What's going on around here?"

My father says, "I was going to go this week, but I didn't have time. I'm very busy at the optical, catching up from when your mother was in the hospital."

"But, like, what are you even eating for breakfast? Why didn't you tell someone?" I turn to my mom. "Why didn't you ask Caro to go to Publix for you? Or Teresita?"

She looks down and shrugs. "I didn't want to bother anyone."

"Teresita's your best friend! What the hell? What about Pablo and Maritza? They were here last week, right?"

"Last week we were fine," my mother says.

"And this week you're starving. Great." I shake my head, more upset about this than I should be, I know, but I feel guilty for taking off on them and angry that I can't take off on them without everything falling apart. "Okay," I say, clapping my hands against my thighs, "well, let's make a list and then I'll go to Publix."

"Tonight?" my mother says. "We'll miss our show. I don't want you to go tonight." She reaches her hand out to me but doesn't touch me.

"Mom, there's literally nothing for breakfast."

My father steps closer to me and puts his hand on my arm. "I'll go. Make me the list and I'll go. You stay with your mother. Please." He's trying to tell me to stop hurting her, to stop making things worse. Like Pablo, wanting me to just forget it all, so that everything will go back to normal. But how can it? The look on my father's face is almost pleading, though, so I say, "Okay. Fine. Let's eat and make the list."

My parents serve out the food onto plates while I go to get a piece of paper and a pen off the computer desk in the hallway. There, on the back of an FPL bill, it says *Daniel directo,* with a Miami number—the 786 area code, not the old 305. *Fuck, there's my life,* I think. *The life I didn't even know I had.*

We sit down to eat and, at first, no one says anything. Finally, I pick up the pen, gripping it as tight as I can because my hands are still shaking a little. "Ham, bread, hot dogs." I start writing down things I know they'll want, reading the list out loud so that at least someone is saying something. My mother, who is barely eating, I notice, just nods.

"What else?" I say.

My father looks at my mother. "Mirta?" He's probably never made a grocery list in his life.

She closes her eyes. "Let me think," she says. She opens them. "Get me some chicken thighs. I'll do them tomorrow night."

"Are you sure you can do that?" I point to my father. "Dad said you can't stand up for long."

"I can do that," she says. "I'll use the George Foreman. And he can make the rice. He knows how."

I look at my father. "You do?"

"You just use the rice cooker, right? She can show me."

The baby wakes up and starts going crazy, punching and kicking me, excited from the food, which I ate too quickly because I was nervous. My mother doesn't notice him moving, and I'm glad. I don't want to have to let her feel him tonight.

She pushes her masitas around on her plate but doesn't take a bite. "And what about you?" she says to me. "Are you still cooking at the hotel?"

"Yep," I say, without looking up from the list.

My father makes a small noise next to me. "I can't believe you want to be anywhere near that place." He shakes his head, closes his eyes. It's like he's mad at me for going there. My stomach tightens. I know I can't defend my decision—it's too weird—so I just say, "Well, it's working for me." I push my hair away from my face, sit up a little straighter, and press back on the baby to let him know I'm here and I'm taking care of us. "So, what else do you guys need? Dad, do you want cereal? Raisin Bran?"

When the list is finished, my father stands.

"You go ahead and go," I say. "I'll do the dishes." I make him take his cell phone, even though he hates it, so that he can call us with questions.

As I'm loading the dishwasher a few minutes later, my chest starts to burn. This is only the second time I've had heartburn this whole pregnancy and it's much worse than the first. I press the heel of my hand into my sternum and ask my mom if she has any Tums.

She shakes her head. "You don't need Tums. Just drink some manzanilla." She's already heading for the pantry.

"You're sure?" I ask, but I know the answer. Manzanilla is her remedy for everything. If I was bleeding from my eyes, she'd make me a cup of manzanilla.

"Of course," she says, handing me a tea bag. She touches her stomach lightly and takes a second one out of the box. "I'll have some too. No coffee tonight."

We take our mugs into the living room to watch *Abismo*, which opens with Armando making a secret telephone call to Jaquelín, trying to get her to rescue him. She's nodding and writing down everything he's saying about how to get the rest of the money from the bank and how to deliver it to him, but then the camera pans back and we see that she's not alone. Sebastián is sitting right next to her, smiling.

"Oh my God," I say. "Why is she doing this to Armando?"

"She's trying to pay him back," my mother says.

"For what?"

"For not loving her."

I try my tea. It's still a little too hot to drink but my chest is on fire. "It's not somebody's fault if they don't love you."

She looks at me. "But it feels like it is. That's why Robert is mad at you. He thinks you don't love him."

I fight the wave of guilt rising up. "Is that what he told you?"

"No." She swirls her hand in front of her chest. "But I could sense it. He's worried about you," she says in English.

"Yeah, right. Did you guys talk about how worried you both are?" I can just see it: her discussing my whole life with him, talking about how I need to get over everything and just go back home to have the baby with him.

"We talked about how he wants you to come home, how he's worried that you're pregnant and living in a hotel on Eighth Street."

I blow hard on my tea, which helps my heartburn a little, actually. "First of all, the hotel is perfectly safe. And second of all, he's not worried. He's mad."

"Well, what do you expect? Lo abandonaste."

I look at her. "I didn't abandon him."

"Well. Maybe *you* don't see it that way. But I think *he* does."

Thank God he didn't tell her about Manny at the hotel or I'd be getting an earful right now. The show goes to commercial and she turns the volume down. "Is it because of Manny?" she says, like she's reading my mind. "Your father told me he called you the day you fainted. He shouldn't have come to the hospital. He shouldn't be calling you. He needs to leave you alone. He had his chance and he didn't take it. So that's it. You're with Robert now."

"Ay, Mom, please," I say, raising my voice. "It's more complicated than it seems, okay? It's not that simple."

"Why not?" she pushes. "Why isn't it that simple? It looks simple to me. Robert is a wonderful young man. You're engaged." She points at my stomach with her hand. "You're having his baby. So what's the problem? You don't love him?" As usual, she cuts right to it.

"This from you, Mom? For real?" I yell.

She flinches, and a bit of her tea spills onto her shirt. She dabs at it with a Kleenex from the side table. "You might come to love him, you know." Her voice is softer now. "I did. After Juan left. After you were born."

I think of her in the years after Daniel told her Juan was dead, trying to get on with her life, eventually coming to love my father. She had no choice. But I do. Robert. Manny. Or neither. Just me and the baby, in some apartment.

My mother watches the muted commercial for a minute, her face turning sad. Maybe she's thinking about her choices, the ones she made so long ago. She's looking at the television, but not really. "Everything is so messed up," she says, and I think she's talking about everything with us. But then she says, "Rolando beat him too badly. And Dolores is dying. If she wants to go, they'll go. He'll never deny her."

"Mom," I say, reaching over to touch her knee. My stomach is in the way, though, and it hurts to lean out of my chair like this, so I get up and come to sit next to her on the sofa. I take her hands and look into her eyes. "Mom, you're gone again."

Her eyes are filled with tears and her hair is falling into her face. I squeeze her hands. "Mom, do you know that I'm here, that we're in Miami, that it's 2012?"

She nods, looking at me but not saying anything at first. She closes her eyes, takes a deep breath through her nose, and blows it out her mouth. Her glasses have slipped down from her hair almost onto her forehead. "Yes, yes. I'm sorry. They're just so vivid, these thoughts. It's like I'm there completely. And then I'm here."

I lean into her face a little, relieved to hear her articulate it. "You have to tell the neurologist that, okay? You have to explain it just like that."

She nods. "I will." She repositions her glasses, then gets the lemon pomegranate lotion out of the basket on the coffee table. I added it to her collection when she got home from the hospital. She puts some on, rubbing it in while she watches the commercials on mute. "You know, I knew something was going to go wrong. Before the surgery, I could feel it. That's why I told you about Juan. I was afraid that if I died, you would never know. Rolando certainly would have taken it to his grave. But you needed to know." She points to my stomach. "*He* needs to know. And Juan needs to know too." She looks into my eyes. "He has a right to know."

"What if he doesn't care?"

"He'll care."

"How do you know that?"

My mother rubs the lotion into her cuticles, pushing them back one by one. "Because I know Juan. He's a good man. A loyal man."

"That's who he was back then. People change." The thought of this man who is my *father*, a part of me, being out there somewhere is so scary. I don't know whether to hope he does or doesn't care.

My mother wags her finger in the air. "Loyalty is a quality that doesn't change in a person. Possibly he's married. He probably has children. That's fine. It doesn't matter. We need to find him. He needs to know that his first child was you."

"Do *you* want to find him? He was your first true love, right? Is that why you want to find him?"

"No. That has nothing to do with it."

I don't know if I believe her or not. I want to, but with the way she's talked about Juan, it's hard to believe she doesn't feel something for him still. "Does Dad know you called Daniel?"

"No, not yet."

"Well, you're not doing a great job of hiding it; his number's sitting right there by the computer." Just like with my father earlier, it comes out angrier than I meant it to.

She looks down. "I'm not hiding anything from your father. I just haven't had the energy to talk to him. I'm still very tired. And it's been hard for me to have you so mad at me." She looks up at me. "Please don't be mad at me anymore. I know I made a mistake. That's what I'm trying to tell you: it was a mistake. I should have told you from the beginning. I should have found a way to tell Juan. But I didn't. I was trying to just put it behind me." She shakes her head. "But that was not the right way to do things. I should have told him."

"You thought he was dead."

"No, before then. While I was pregnant. I should have tried. Somehow. Maybe I could have tried to call his cousin. If I had tried harder—"

"Then what?" I lean away from her. "Would you have wanted him to be a part of my life? Coming to my birthday parties? My graduation? You think Dad would have been into that? I don't think so."

She looks at the television. The show is back on, but she leaves the sound off. "I'm going to contact a professional. An investigator. Daniel said he could give me the name of someone."

I slide back even farther away from her on the sofa. "Are you kidding me?"

"Mónica, I need to find him. He deserves to know. You both deserve to know. I should have done it years ago."

On the television, Jaquelín is crying into her hands on mute. In the kitchen, the dishwasher switches cycles. In here, it's just the sound of me breathing, trying not to yell at her again. Finally, I say, "You know, Mom, this isn't just your decision to make. This is my life too. I know that's a foreign concept for you, but it's true."

She frowns at me. "What do you mean that's a foreign concept for me?"

"I mean the idea of me having my own life where I make my own decisions and do things the way *I* want to do them is not something you're into." I've never said anything like this to her before. I can't look at her. I look at the TV. Jaquelín is still crying.

"I don't know what you're talking about. I don't control your life."

Of course she sees it this way. I cross my arms and say nothing.

"Mónica, this is important. This is who you are."

Right now, I feel like I'm nobody's daughter. In some ways, not even hers. My eyes fill with tears almost without me realizing it. I look over at the pictures on the entryway table, all of them. Years of birthdays and Christmases, the four of us, but also Tío Fermín and Tía Gladys, Caro, her brothers, the kids, all of us, one big happy family, with no big problems, no big secrets. *Yeah, right*, I think, and the tears spill down my face.

My mother leans toward me. "Mi niña. Don't cry. Rolando loves you very much. He raised you. I just mean that Juan is part of your history, and it's important to know your history, especially now that you're going to have a family of your own."

I shake my head, blinking back the tears. "Well, I'm not ready. Like you said, it's *my* history. And I want nothing to do with this." I look at the front door. "You think Dad wants this? You think he wants you contacting your long-lost love to tell him he's the father of your child?"

"Of course not. Rolando is not happy about any of this. But it's time to finally have the truth out, all of it." Her voice sounds stronger than it has in a long time, since before the surgery. She sounds ready to prove that she's right.

My heart is hammering now at the thought of this, my voice getting louder. "You know what, actually?" I push myself up off the sofa, a repeat of two weeks ago, except instead of my father standing over her, yelling about Juan, it's me. "You know what?" I say again. "I'm done with the truth, and I'm not ready to find Juan and tell him. That's crazy!"

In the kitchen, I grab my purse and keys. My chest, which had felt better, is burning again. I hear my mom behind me, but she doesn't follow.

I walk out past those fucking pictures. I have to sit in the car, keys in hand, and breathe for a full minute until I'm calm enough to back out of the driveway. As I drive away, I hear it again: that voice in my head. Is it my mother's or mine? I can't tell. All I know is what it's saying, which is: *Juan is alive.* And now a new thing: *It's time.*

I miss the exit for Eighth Street and it takes me half an hour longer to get back. When I do, I don't even have the energy to wash my face or brush my teeth. The heartburn is gone but my whole body feels like it's made of wet sand. And I can't think. I stand in the middle of the room trying to remember what I need to do to go to bed. Finally, it comes to me: get a glass of water and plug in my phone. I do those two things, pull off my pants, and slide under the covers.

A few hours later, I wake up to Manny drunk texting me again. They're coming in rapid-fire.

1:21 a.m. I can't believe ur fucking preg w that guys baby.

1:23 a.m. Sorry I just cant tell you how much you mean to me

1:24 a.m. Why did this happen

I lie there looking at them. "Goddamn it," I say out loud into the dark room. Then I get up and go pee and don't text him back, mostly because I'm afraid of what I'll say if I do. I'm tempted to say, "Fuck you. You're too late." But I'm even more tempted to say, "Don't *tell* me how much I mean to you. *Show* me."

I'm awake for a long time after that, thinking and talking to the baby—about Manny and Robert and my mother and Juan. I turn on the TV but there's nothing on, so I turn it back off and just sit there in bed, looking at the triangles and trying to figure out the answer: How *did* this happen? All of it. And what am I going to do about it?

Mirta

I wish you hadn't stormed out once again, back to that place that I can barely think about. I wish you would have stayed to let me explain better how hard it is for me—the thought that he could be alive somewhere not knowing he has a beautiful daughter who has his hair, his hands. You are part of him, mi niña, and he is part of you, and you're about to have a baby, a little boy who might have those same long fingers or that same curly black hair. I know Juan would want to know. I know he would be angry with me if I didn't tell him. You know so much now, but you don't know this—this feeling of obligation.

He's a very loving person, and he did want to have children. We talked about starting a family one day, once things were better politically. We were afraid, of course, to bring a child into that situation, to have him or her educated in that system where children were indoctrinated by teachers who were loyal to Fidel. But we also wanted a child. We had talked about it, more than once.

And then we had one, only he had no idea. He has a right to know, Mónica. I told so many lies: to your father when I was with Juan, to you for your whole life. It's time to start telling the truth, all of it. If Juan is still alive someplace, I need to find him and tell him when he first became a father.

30

The donuts at the front desk this week are powdered, not chocolate. I put two on a napkin as I'm waiting for the couple in front of
me to finish checking in. Manny's drunk texts from last night are
still sitting on my phone. I *also* can't believe I'm fucking preg with
that guy's baby. *That guy,* who I still can't call, especially now that
he's ratted me out to my mother. The couple finishes and I hand
the guy behind the counter my credit card. "Another week," I say.
"On this card, please."

When I get back to my room, I call Manny to tell him I did it. It
rings and rings and I think it's going to voice mail, so I'm planning
my message, but then he answers, half-asleep.

"Sorry to wake you," I say. "I just wanted to let you know I paid
for the room this week, so if they charge your card again, it's a mistake." I'm not sure why I'm calling and not texting. Probably so I
can seem more assertive. But also probably so I can hear his voice.
And to see what he has to say to me about those texts.

"You didn't have to do that."

"No, I know. I just—I need to take care of myself." I take a bite
of one of the donuts and white powder explodes all over the table.

"Okay. Yeah. I get it." He coughs. "Ugh. My head."

"Hungover?"

"Yeah."

"I bet."

"What?"

"You texted me last night? Late?"

"I did?"

"Check your phone."

He goes silent for a few seconds, then comes back on. "Oh. Shit. Sorry."

"Robbins in town?" I wipe up the donut powder.

"No. I was hanging out with some guys from work. They came over to watch the fight. One guy's getting a divorce. We had a few beers. And then some shots. Bad idea."

"Ah. Well, I'll let you get back to sleep."

"No, no. I gotta get up. I got a million things to do."

"Like what?"

"Like I got no clean underwear and the truck is dirty and I told my sister I'd come look at her computer. What are you up to?"

"Same problem with the underwear. Gotta hit the laundromat. Also, it's one of Caro's girls' birthday. The party's at three and I have no present." No present and no desire to go. I can't imagine having to sit around eating cake while everyone pretends they don't know about Juan. All of this while my mom and I are in a secret fight about whether or not to try to find him.

Manny coughs again and I hear rustling. "Ow. Hurts to sit up. Hey, why don't you bring your underwear over here?"

"Excuse me?"

"Your laundry. Bring it over." He sounds more awake now.

"You got laundry at your place?"

"Yeah, man. I'm a homeowner, remember? A townhome owner."

This is an appealing offer. I'm over American Coin Laundry. It was fine, but my clothes smelled a little like feet afterward. I could try somewhere else or maybe take my stuff to Caro's if I asked, but I don't want to ask. Plus, I want to see him. I know that makes me an asshole, but it's true. "What time do you want me there?" I say.

"Are you bringing coffee?"

"Sure."

"Then right now."

I pass the pool three times before I finally find his unit. I ring the doorbell with my pinky because I'm carrying a café con leche in one hand and a cortadito in the other.

He opens the door. "Welcome to my humble commode," he says, doing an arm flourish thing, waving me in like a butler. He's drinking a Gatorade and not wearing a shirt.

"Thanks," I say. We kiss on the cheek—just friends. I hand him his cortadito and try not to stare at his chest, which is as toned and muscled as it was when we first met.

"Thank *you*," he says. "How much sugar is in here?"

I give him a look.

"Sorry, sorry. Just asking." He takes a sip. "Perfect."

I recognize the barstools and some of the art: the vintage Calle Ocho festival poster and the photo of the reef at Pennekamp he bought when we went down there for his birthday. And he still has the papasan chair that we tried to have sex in one night.

"Well," he says. "Ready for the grand tour?"

"Of course."

He spreads his arms. "Okay. So this is the living room." The blue sofa-and-chair combo is a little Rooms-to-Go but it's not terrible. He points three feet away to the area in front of the kitchen. "And that's the formal dining room."

"Beautiful. I love your china cabinet." The "china cabinet" is an Ikea bookshelf behind the dining table where he has a mixture of family pictures and books—mostly Stephen King and Tom Clancy, but also random stuff like *The Hitchhiker's Guide to the Galaxy* and some Buddhism stuff. His helmet and dog tags are also displayed, along with the pictures of his friends from each of his units. Some of them came home okay. Some didn't. One guy came home with one leg and no nuts. One guy can no longer feed himself or remember his wife's name. And three of them are dead.

I think back to the night he told me he was going to enlist for a third tour. I pointed to their photos. "Going back isn't going to bring those guys back, you know. They're gone. They're dead. And there's nothing you can do about it." I regretted the words as soon as they were out of my mouth.

He looked at me and his voice got really quiet. "You don't know a fucking thing about it, Mónica," he snarled.

I sat on the sofa, stunned and silent, feeling gut punched by the fact that he was going back, and guilty for what I had said. I also felt hurt. Really hurt. He had promised me his second tour was his last. He had promised me he would stay with me. "Listen," I said, "I'm sorry. And I know I don't know anything about it. But this is not okay. How can you think it is?"

"I know it's not okay. But I can't help it. I have to go. I can't live here, like this."

"Like how?"

He waved his hand at the door. "Like going to work, coming home. Not doing anything that makes any difference. Going over there is the only thing that makes sense in my life right now."

My eyes filled with tears. "Being with me doesn't make sense?"

"Yes, it does. Of course it does. But what difference does my life make right now? What am I contributing to the world?"

"Manny, I know you feel guilty, but—"

"Of course I feel guilty. I have a valuable skill that's not being utilized."

"So utilize it," I said. "Become a paramedic."

He didn't look at me. "I don't want to be a paramedic here. I'm not needed here. Not the same way I'm needed over there. I could be helping. It's killing me to know I'm doing nothing, Mónica. I can't do nothing. I have an obligation."

"You already served. Twice. You fulfilled your obligation."

He shook his head. "It doesn't feel fulfilled."

"And you think going back again will do that? It won't. Nothing will. You have to learn to live with this, okay? I don't know how. Maybe go see someone, get some therapy. A lot of vets get therapy. It's not just for pussies, you know."

"I know it's not just for pussies. It's just not what I need."

"Oh, okay. So what you need is to go back?" I yelled. "Again! And leave me here? Again!" My chest felt tight with anger.

He closed his eyes and shook his head. "I don't *want* to leave you here. I just can't take you with me." He sat down next to me on the sofa and drained his beer. "I'm sorry," he said.

"We've been together for four years. You've already done this twice. Do you realize what you're saying to me, what you're asking of me?" I was being selfish; I knew that. But so was he. The worst part—the part I could barely stand to think about—was how scared I was that he wouldn't make it home a third time.

"Of course I know what I'm asking. The problem is you don't

know what you're asking of *me*. Being here is torture, okay? *Torture.*"

It felt like he had hit me. I knew he didn't mean being with *me* was torture, but I also knew that there was something about our relationship that was too hard for him.

His face looked really sad. Tortured, even. He pulled his baseball cap off his head and held it in his hands. "Look," he said. "I know you think I'm running away. I know you want to move in together, get married, have kids. That's what people do. I know that. But I can't. Not right now. I need to do *this* right now and do the other stuff later."

"Later when?"

He shook his head. "In a year. Maybe two."

"And I'm just supposed to wait around, being terrified?" I'd imagined it a million times: the soldier showing up at his mother's house, his sister's voice on the phone. *Mónica, I have to tell you something.*

He looked away. "Yes."

We didn't break up right away; I couldn't do it. But a few months into his deployment, I started thinking about how things were when he was home—how he'd be fine for a while, but then, eventually, he would come over less often during the week, saying he was tired after work and had to get up early, and then on the weekends he'd invite Robbins to come down or say he was busy with family stuff. After a few weeks he'd circle back and be fine again—until he wasn't. I talked to Caro about it a little. I talked to my mom about it a lot. One day she said that thing about how a man like that can never fully give himself to you and that's what made it click. A few days later I Skyped him and said I thought it was best if we just quit.

Manny motions behind him to the stairs now, continuing the grand tour. "Two bedrooms, two baths upstairs." He leads me into the kitchen. "Kitchen. All the basics. And the best part is in here." He opens the door to the garage where he has a huge red four-wheeler.

"Wow," I say. "When did you get this?"

"Right when I got back. Got a great deal on it."

"You go riding a lot?"

"Yeah. I go by myself sometimes, down to the Everglades. It's meditative, you know? And me and Robbins go when he comes down. He bought one, too, and he brings it." He points to the washer and dryer. "So where's your dirty underwear?"

"In the car."

While my clothes are washing, we sit in the living room and eat bagels and cream cheese and finish our coffees. I think about Robert and how I still haven't called him. And how I paid for another week of the hotel, and now I'm here, doing this. Whatever this is.

Manny gets himself another Gatorade and drinks half of it in one chug. "So, how's it going with the guy next door?"

"Fine. He gave me a plant and some gluten-free bread the next day. And he wrote me an apology note."

He raises his eyebrows. "Are you joking?"

"He's harmless."

"He choked Robert."

"Yes. However—"

"However, he choked him harmlessly?"

I laugh. "Kind of." I think about how he drives Suzie to and from Jackson on the days she has her clinicals. "You know, I think he's just really protective."

"But why does he want to protect *you*? He barely knows you."

"I think he kind of wants to protect everyone. He's just one of those people. We've been hanging out a little—me, him, and his daughter. She's cool. And he's reading a really stupid book on anger management." I smile. "So it's all good."

He takes a bite of his bagel. "Whatever you say." His phone is sitting on the coffee table and it buzzes with a text. He looks at it. "Edgar, the guy from work. The guy who's getting a divorce puked in his car last night." He starts laughing and writes him back something. "Man, remember when you could drink all night and barely have a headache? That night we stayed up to watch the meteor shower that never happened, did we drink that whole bottle of vodka, just between us two?"

"I think so." I've always thought of that night as the best night of my life. We went out to some lake down in the Redland and sat in lawn chairs for hours, just talking and laughing and drinking. I knew then something was happening to me, something that had never happened before. It felt like my whole self was alive, like I was vibrating from the inside out.

"So you're pretty hungover, huh?" I point to my phone. "You really don't remember?"

He takes a drink of the Gatorade and looks away from me. "Sorry. No, I don't."

I nod. I don't say, "It's okay." Instead, I say something I didn't know I wanted to say until just now: "Why did you come to the hospital?"

"I wanted to make sure you were okay."

"You didn't seem to care how okay I was the times you decided to reenlist."

"I know," he says quietly. "I know. And now—" He waves his arm in the direction of my stomach.

"Now what?"

He sits up straighter, takes my hand. "I'm sorry."

"For what?"

"For everything."

I'm quiet, looking over his shoulder at a plant that really needs to be watered.

"I'm sorry for not being with you," he says. "For not staying. I just couldn't. Especially with the surge. I knew it was going to be bad, that they were going to need us so much more."

I pull my hand away. "You know, it wasn't just that. Even when you were here, you weren't here. I couldn't handle the possibility of you coming home and ignoring me one more time."

"I didn't ignore you." He looks at me pleadingly. "Mónica, I didn't—"

"You didn't commit, Manny. Remember when I wanted you to go to Jersey with me for Christmas? And you told me some bull-shit about work training? You know what that made me feel like? Committed boyfriends go on family trips with their girlfriends. Es-pecially girlfriends who waited for them to come home from war."

He's quiet, just looking down, nodding. Admitting to it, I guess.

I know I should stop, just shut up and let this moment pass. What does it matter now? It's over. I've moved on, like Caro said that day in the hospital bathroom. But for some reason I can't let it pass. Now I'm angry. "And how many times did we talk about tak-ing the next step? But every time, you weren't ready, you needed a little more time. And then you left. And came home and still weren't ready. And then"—my throat goes hard and my voice breaks—"then you left again." I turn my body away from him, al-most instinctually. "You didn't care about me enough. It's just that simple. I just wasn't important."

"Not true."

"I wasn't important *enough*."

He moves closer to me on the sofa. "Please. I don't know what to say to you."

"Say I'm right. Stop trying to bullshit me."

"You're right. I didn't value you enough. I loved you, but I didn't value you. And I was afraid. Of feeling too tied down. Of feeling the heavy feelings I had for you." This feels true. I could always sense that he was scared of something.

"Why couldn't you ever tell me that?" I ask.

He turns away from me now, leans forward, elbows on knees, his head in his hands. "I couldn't. I couldn't face it myself and I couldn't face telling you that I was afraid. Would it have made a difference?"

"Maybe. Maybe if I had really understood how scared you were. Or if you had been willing to talk about it."

He starts pulling on the hem of his shorts, just the right leg, over and over. "At some point I just stopped feeling anything, except the need to go back. I was basically flatlined. Especially after the second tour." He sits up and looks at me. "It's a thing. A defense mechanism thing. I read about it. It comes from spending nine months scared, living on edge. Then you come home and just shut down as a way of dealing. Meanwhile, all the people around you—your family, your friends"—he points to me—"your girlfriend—they're feeling things. Happiness, sadness, whatever. But you're just there, numb. Some guys notice it. Others don't. I didn't. I thought it was just being scared to settle down. And grieving my father. I thought that was probably fucking me up too. Which it was." He stops pulling on his shorts and just sits there, staring at the coffee table. "It still is. But the flatline thing—when I read about it later, after I came back last year, I knew that was me."

I think about everything he's just said. "Is it still you?"

He rubs his forehead with one hand and then turns to me. "No. That night at the hospital, when you walked in and I saw you like this? Man, you don't know what that did to me."

"Let me guess. It made you feel like I was choosing a whole different life over you?"

He looks away from me. Somebody starts a lawn mower outside.

"Seriously? It took this?" I look down at my stomach. "God, Manny. Really?"

He shakes his head. "I'm sorry. I really am. That's what I'm trying to tell you." He turns back to me, takes my hand again, and rubs his thumb over the back of my hand, back and forth, back and forth. "So, can I ask you: Have you talked to Robert? Are you guys working things out?"

"No. I don't know. I'm kind of in limbo on that right now." I feel the anger dissipate and something else take its place. A longing, it feels like. Like I want something I haven't been able to have.

"What do you want to do? Are you in love with him?"

I don't move. He's looking at me. Eventually, I close my eyes. "I'm not sure."

He puts his hand on my face. I lean into it a little and a second later I feel his mouth on my neck. *There is nothing I can do about this.* That phrase literally goes through my head. That's what it feels like: like I can't control this. Like I don't want to control this. This is what I want to be happening and it's happening and I'm letting it happen. We end up with our hands all over each other. I'm in his shorts and doing what I know he likes. He pulls my hand out and lays me back on the couch, pulls my dress up just enough but keeps my belly covered. He slides my underwear off and goes down on me. I leave myself, just float out of my brain. It feels so good I have no choice. I come and he comes back up, starts kissing my neck. I pull his waistband down and take him in my hand. He makes a sound from low in his throat, and then he starts breathing in that familiar way. It only takes a little and then he comes too. He lays his head on my chest and says, "Mónica, you don't know. You just don't know."

31

Of course, Caro's gone all out: there's a bounce house and a rented chick dressed up like the princess from *Brave* giving archery lessons. The plates and cups are all *Brave*-themed, the picnic shelter wrapped in pink and green streamers. Even the water bottles have custom pink and green labels. *Happy Birthday, Amanda!* they say. The exclamation point is in the shape of an arrow.

The guests are a mixture of kids and adults, many of them family friends, which means every person I say hi to asks where Robert is. And every time I hear his name, I picture Manny going down on me. I make my way over to where Pablo and Maritza are sitting by themselves in the back corner of the picnic shelter.

Pablo asks what's up with Robert. "He said he could get me tickets to a race, but he won't text me back. Is he mad at me?"

I open a *Happy Birthday, Amanda!* water bottle. "Um, I'm not really sure."

"What do you mean you're not really sure? Don't you live with the guy?"

I look over to the bouncy house. "Not right now."

Maritza leans in. "Oh my God. Did you guys break up?"

"We're taking a break. I just need a little space."

They're looking at me like they have no idea what I'm talking about. And they wouldn't, not with the way they're so pegado. I swear, I don't think Pablo's spent more than thirty minutes alone since they met. He has a small mountain of Cheetos on a *Brave* plate. He plucks one off the top and eats it. "Where are you staying?"

"At a hotel." I take a sip of water. "Are Mom and Dad here?" Usually, my father would be talking to Tío Fermín or my cousin Igor. And my mom would be with Tía Gladys, rearranging the napkins and talking shit about Caro's friends. But Tía Gladys is sitting with some woman I don't know and Tío Fermín is helping Mike pull burgers off the grill.

"I haven't seen them," Pablo says. Behind him, just outside the picnic shelter, the *Brave* princess is standing under a tree, showing a group of kids how to pull back the string on the bow.

"When was the last time you saw her?" I ask Pablo.

"Today. Earlier. I passed by there for a minute."

"No weird shit?"

"Nope. I mean, I was only there for like ten minutes. Why?"

I take down my ponytail, put it back up in a twisty bun. "I was there last night and she had another episode. Then, on the way here, she left me a weird voice mail."

"Weird how?"

I pull up the message and play it for him. "Not today," she says. "Maybe tomorrow when Teresita comes by." It's her crazy-talk voice: hushed and dreamy.

"Yeah, that's weird," Pablo says.

"And it doesn't make sense. Teresita's in Orlando, meeting Alex's new boyfriend." I look around for my parents again. "Shouldn't they be here by now?"

Pablo finishes off the soda in his *Brave* cup and rattles the ice. "You know Mom's always on Cuban time."

I check my phone. "It's 4:12. She's not usually *this* late. Especially to stuff like this."

Maritza says, "So call them," with a little thing in her voice, a little challenge. "Just reach out."

And then, almost as an afterthought, Pablo says, "I mean, fuck, dude, she's driving me crazy."

"What are you talking about?"

Maritza sighs. "We have to, like, go over there a lot."

"Oh yeah?" I can't help but raise an eyebrow at her.

"Yeah. She, like, always needs something. Her prescription, a new chair for the shower . . ."

Pablo says, "Yesterday she called me to complain about her pillows. I had to go to Bed Bath & Beyond between meetings to get her new ones."

"Right. This is my whole life."

"Okay, I know, but, like, you're used to it," Pablo says.

"So fucking what? That doesn't make it any easier."

He adjusts his sunglasses. "You know, she just wants you to be normal."

Maritza says, "She misses you. She's worried about the baby."

One of the kids hits the target the *Brave* princess set up and they all cheer.

I say, "I went over there last night, okay?" I look at Pablo and plant my feet on the concrete floor of the picnic shelter. "You can't understand why this bothers me? Doesn't it freak you out that I'm your half sister, not your real sister?"

He waves his hand at me. "Bullshit. You're still my sister. We still grew up together; we're still part of the same family."

"I don't know," I say. "I don't really feel like part of this family right now."

Pablo says, "Of course you don't. You're, like, desaparecida."

And this is when I get pissed for real. "I'm not desaparecida. I'm just having a little trouble being around the two people who thought it was a good idea to lie to me for my entire life, okay?" I get up from the picnic table, put my purse on my shoulder. "I'm sorry I can't come back and relieve you of your duties as their son."

He looks at me like he's surprised. "Damn. Relax already."

"Dude, this is what being their kid is. You just never knew it because *you've* been desaparecido for your entire *life*. I'm sorry having to be present is cramping your style so much. And I'm sorry I asked you to understand my position. It's obvious you can't do that right now."

He gives me an eye roll and a face and Maritza looks at me like I'm being a crazy bitch, which maybe I am, but I don't care. I walk away and go tell Caro that I'm not feeling well and to please tell Amanda I said happy birthday. By the time I get to my car, which is through a big grassy area and at the far end of the parking lot, I'm furious. At Pablo and Maritza, at my parents, at everything. Then my phone rings. It's Teresita. I almost let it go to voice mail but something tells me not to.

"Mónica," she says. "Thank God you answered. Your mother's at the airport. She's trying to take a plane to Costa Rica."

"What do you mean she's at the airport? How is that possible? No, no. That's—no."

"Chica, sí. I'm telling you: she called me and told me she was leaving to Costa Rica."

"Costa Rica? What the hell? Is she with my father? They're

— 281 —

supposed to be at Amanda's birthday party." I'm yelling into the phone.

"No, not with your father. I don't know where he is. Neither does she. They had a fight; he left the house. You need to call him, tell him she's at the airport. He didn't pick up when I called. She booked a flight. It leaves at five o'clock."

"She left by herself? Oh my God. How do you know?" The asphalt, hot under my sandals, the cars shining in the parking lot, Teresita, my mother's best friend since I was a baby, telling me my mother took off alone for Costa Rica—all of it feels like I'm dreaming this.

Teresita says, "She called me and asked me to watch you and Pablo while she was gone. She gave me instructions for picking you guys up from school. I kept trying to talk to her, to tell her that wasn't making any sense, but she just said not to tell Rolando where she went, and then she hung up. I tried to call her back but she won't answer."

I can feel my brain wanting to float away into disbelief. But I can't let it. I have to deal with this. I have to take care of it. "Let me call her," I say. "I'll call you right back."

I stare at my phone for a good five seconds, trying to remember how to call someone. Contacts. I need the Contacts list. I find the icon, find her name, press it. It rings forever, then goes to voice mail. Fuck. I leave a message telling her to call me, I'm worried, please, where is she? I go back to Contacts, which takes three tries because my hands are shaking. I'm looking for my father's number and I almost can't find it. I'm in *F* for father for ten whole seconds and then I realize, no, I need *D*. *D* for *Dad*. My dad. He's my dad. I almost start crying right then, but I don't; I hold it in because I cannot cry right now even though this feels horrible and so scary—

the thought of my mother at the airport alone, going to Costa Rica. Where Juan was. Where he still might be. My God, what is happening to her? What is she doing?

My father doesn't answer, either. Of course he doesn't; there's no way he has his phone with him, I realize. I call the house and then the optical. By now I'm a pro at using the phone. No answer at either. That's when I know I have to go back to the picnic shelter to tell Pablo. I start doing a half walk, half run back over there and call Teresita along the way.

"Did you talk to your father?" she says.

"I tried them both everywhere. No answer anywhere. Did she say anything else? What airline? Anything?"

"No. Nothing. Just what I told you. Ay, por díos. I kept telling her she was not okay. Every time she said one of her crazy things about Juan or Adelita or those days back when you were kids, I would tell her, 'Mirta, algo te pasa. You need to get checked.' I was going to call you next week to tell you that you have to take her to the doctor. And now this."

The walk-jogging is hurting my belly, so I support it with one hand, the other hand holding the phone to my ear. "I can't believe her. I can't believe this is happening. She must be out of her mind. Do you think she even knows what she's doing or what's happening? She cannot get on a plane to a foreign country right now."

"Pero, why would she go by herself? Why wouldn't she go with your father?"

"She's trying to find Juan. This must be part of it. I have to stop her," I say. "I have to stop her." At the picnic shelter ahead, it's cake time. Everyone is gathered around Amanda, singing. She blows out the candles and everyone claps and the happiness is the weirdest thing I've ever seen. It's the exact opposite of what I'm feeling. I tell Teresita I have to go.

It feels like it takes an hour to walk past the kids getting the pieces of green-and-pink cake, the parents hovering nearby, the *Brave* princess standing off to the side, smiling. Finally, I get to the back, where Pablo and Maritza are sitting. They clock me, panting, sweating, my phone in my hand.

"What's wrong?" Pablo says.

32

We take Pablo's car. I sit in the back and try not to puke from his driving. Maritza and I are both on our phones searching flights to Costa Rica that leave around five. "American is the only one," I say. "They have a 5:12."

Pablo says, "It has to be that one," and cuts off a black minivan. The driver beeps for like a minute straight.

"Why would she do this?" Maritza says.

"She's trying to find Juan," I say.

Pablo looks back at me. "How do you know?"

I tell them about her wanting to hire the private investigator.

"What the fuck?" he says. "Why can't anyone let this go?"

We pull up to the curb at 5:09 and only I get out. I guess they even have to park the car together. I jog into the terminal and check the first TV monitor thing I can find. American Airlines Flight 1017 Miami to San Jose, Costa Rica. Departed.

"Goddamn it," I say out loud. I bend over at the waist, hands on my knees to catch my breath and try to figure out what to do next.

The woman behind the counter is about my mom's age with dyed blond hair. Her name tag says Hilda. I speak to her in Spanish and ask her whether my mother—Mirta P. Campo—boarded the plane. I tell her all of it: the heart surgery, the medical coma, the brain problems. I almost tell her about Juan. She checks the computer and nods sympathetically. "Sí, mi vida," she says. "Ella abordó."

Shit. Oh my God. What am I supposed to do now? I look at Hilda. "Um. Okay. Is there any way to hold her at the airport when she lands? Will they do that?"

Hilda's supervisor is a short, round man named Eduardo who speaks to me in heavily accented English even though it's clear we both speak Spanish. He says they can't hold her at the gate without a doctor's order.

"Does it have to be in writing? Or can he call them? Please? If she leaves the airport, I don't know what she'll do. She's not thinking straight. And I have no idea if she has her medicines with her." This is true. I hadn't thought of it until just now. She needs her Coumadin and her blood pressure meds.

"Have the doctor call me," he says, "and then I will call the supervisor at the counter in San José."

"Thank you. Thank you so much." I look up the cardiologist's number and leave the message with his emergency service.

Right then, Pablo and Maritza come running up. Maritza's in three-inch cork wedges, so her run is more of a hobble.

"Someone has to go get her," I say. "Do you have a passport?"

"It's expired," Pablo says.

"Then it's me. Unless we find Dad before the next flight takes off."

Maritza looks up from her phone. "Which is at 7:23."

Pablo says, "I tried the store again. Nothing."

"Okay, I'm going to call Robert and ask him to bring me my

passport. I'll never be able to get to the house and back here in time for boarding."

I go stand by the Au Bon Pain to call him. My throat and mouth dry up, so I finish off the bottle of Amanda birthday party water I have in my purse. God, I don't want to do this.

He answers on the first ring. "Hey." He sounds more happy to hear from me than pissed. "How are you? How's the baby?"

I rest my arm on top of my stomach. "The baby's good. All good. But there's a problem with my mom." I explain everything, including that I'm pretty sure this is part of her neurological thing, that she would not have done this if she were in her right mind. "We can't find my father and Pablo doesn't have a passport. Is there any way you can bring me mine? I'm really sorry to ask. But there's no way I can get there and back in time."

He's quiet for a second and I think he's going to hang up on me. But then he says, "Yeah. Where is it?"

I tell him about the red box in the closet where I keep it.

"Okay, I'll get it," he says. "I'm sorry to hear your mom got so bad. I know things are wild right now. We can figure it out. I'll be there as soon as I can, okay?"

"Thank you. I really appreciate it. Just come to Departures for American and text me and I'll come out to meet you."

After we hang up, I stand there for a minute. The woman from Au Bon Pain is restocking the self-serve case. Orange juice. Water. Milk. All the bottles lined up perfectly, all the labels facing out. *We can figure it out. Things are wild.* Did he mean things with us or just all things? I put my face in my hands.

Eduardo gives us the bereavement rate for my ticket, but it's still $508.91. Pablo slides his credit card across the counter. "Dad better pay me back for this."

I tell him they need to go to my parents' house and bring me back whatever medicine is still there.

Maritza asks, "Can't she just take a dose tomorrow?"

They obviously haven't been helping out that much if they don't know this. "No, it's every day. If not, she could throw a clot." For a split second, I see fear on Pablo's face, like he's finally starting to understand the seriousness of this situation. This whole situation. I give him the key to my parents' house off my key ring, because of course he doesn't have one.

As soon as they're gone, I text Manny, and three seconds later he calls. "And your father's gone? Just off the map? No phone, no nothing?"

"He hates his phone, and this is his thing when they fight. He takes off. I'm sure it was about Juan again." I go sit down in the green chairs by the window. Two seats away is a couple with two suitcases wrapped in Saran Wrap, a microwave, and a bicycle.

"Okay," he says. "What airline?"

"American. Why?"

"I'll try to get a ticket."

"What? No. I'm fine. They're going to hold her at the airport for me when she gets there. We'll just be coming right back."

"Mónica, you don't know what kind of state your mother's going to be in. I told you: the TBI stuff is serious. It could be that, or it could be a psychotic break. Or at least something that looks like one. Let me come with you. Please."

"The tickets are a million dollars."

"Military discount. No big deal."

I think about the fact that Robert is coming here, to the air-port, and that they could see each other. But Robert's just pulling up for a minute, not even parking and getting out. It should fine, right? *Yes,* I tell myself. *It should be fine.*

The truth is I really don't want to do this by myself. I wish my father were here to do this with me. Or for me. "Okay," I say.

I put my hands on my stomach. *Mijo, I can't believe your abuela is doing this. She wants to meet you so badly. She already has a penguin for you and everything.*

When she gave it to me, she said, "It can be the first thing in his crib. And he can look at it every night and think of his abuela."

It's been on my dresser at Robert's ever since. I wish I had thought to ask him to bring it so I could show it to her when I get there and remind her: this is what's happening. This is what's real. I almost text him, but I can't ask him for anything else right now.

As I'm on the way back from refilling my water bottle, Manny calls saying he got a flight and do I want him to pass by the hotel to get anything. "Yes," I tell him. "Let me see if Rack can get you in."

I text Suzie and give her the abridged version. Just *My mom went crazy and jumped on a plane to Costa Rica and I have to go get her.*

Holy shit. Are you okay? she says. *Do you need anything?*

I need to get Manny into my room. Can Rack talk to housekeeping for me?

Def. Tell him to knock on our door. If we have probs, I'll let you know. Good luck. So sorry. XOXO.

Something about her text makes me feel better, more grounded, like there's one more person out there who knows and cares about what my life has become.

My mom's meds are still in the house, and Pablo and Maritza come back to the airport to deliver them. I meet them outside at Departures, like I'm going to with Robert when he gets here.

"So, um, Manny's coming with me," I say into Maritza's window.

Pablo says, "Manny, your ex?"

"Yes."

"Are you guys back?"

"No. Not like that. He's just helping me out. He has, like, medical training with this stuff." I feel like an idiot. I'm pretty sure I sound like one too.

"It's Costa Rica, not Afghanistan."

"I know. But he knows about the brain injury stuff. He thinks that could be what's up with Mom."

Maritza says, "Does Robert know?"

I don't even look at her.

Pablo says, "Dad wasn't home. I'm going by the optical now. I'll text you."

They drive away, and I feel a tiny bit of triumph for telling them Manny's coming, for owning my decision. Like: if I want to take my ex-boyfriend instead of my fiancé to go get my deranged mother from a foreign country, I will.

My phone buzzes: Robert. He's here, he says, inside, by the currency exchange place. Inside? Shit. He can't come inside. Manny's coming inside. My mouth dries up again and I chug the Amanda water.

He's holding his phone in one hand, his overnight bag in the other. I squeeze the water bottle so hard the plastic crumples.

"Look," he says, "I'm sorry I was so mad that night at the hotel. I'm sorry I called your mom. I just want to be with you. And you shouldn't do this alone. You're pregnant. I can go with you."

I can't believe he's doing this. But of course he's doing this. I'm carrying his child. He doesn't want me chasing my mother to Costa Rica alone. I close my eyes, then open them. "I'm fine going alone."

He shakes his head. "No. No way. This is a time of crisis." A woman with a dog in a stroller walks by. I want to jump in the stroller.

"It's okay. I'm just going to go get her and bring her right back. I've got it." I think about the money. Maybe that will deter him. "And it's expensive. Really expensive."

"It's fine. I'll put it on the new Mastercard. I need to get some points on there anyway."

Manny already bought the ticket. And even if he hadn't, I don't want Robert to come. I'd rather go alone. "You know, I just need to do this by myself. Okay?" My phone buzzes. It's Manny. *Just parked. Be there in a min.* Oh my God, how is this happening? My armpits start to sweat. "Thank you, for real, for offering. But I think if it's just me, that'll be better for her."

"What are you talking about? Your mom loves me." He's right about that. She'd much rather see Robert than Manny right now.

"I know. But it could be a psychotic break. She could be out of her mind." I blink three times, trying to think of what else I can say. "Listen, I'm going to need your support when I get back, for sure."

He steps closer to me. "Mónica, why won't you let me go with you? Why do you keep doing this?"

I look past him, then up at the ceiling for a moment. "Do you have the passport?"

"Seriously?"

My back is aching and Manny is on his way here and I just need to get this passport and he just needs to go. Now. "Do you have it?" I say again.

He crosses his arms and just stands there, bag at his feet. He looks out the big windows, at the people getting dropped off, hugging, kissing, saying goodbye. He's frowning, shaking his head. I've pushed him away one more time. Silently, he pulls the passport out of his bag and hands it to me.

I take it from him but he doesn't move, doesn't leave.

"Please," I say.

Finally, he picks up his bag and walks away. I try to look for Manny in the hundreds of people all around me, walking fast, walking slow, on their phones, dragging or cajoling or carrying kids and babies, pushing strollers and carts full of luggage. I scan their faces, their bodies, looking for Manny—his brown face, his Yankees cap, his beautiful arms and chest—hoping, for once, not to see him.

33

The flight is so packed we can't sit together. At least the guy in the aisle seat offers to switch with me. I spend the flight alternately walking up and down so that I don't get a blood clot in my legs and sitting quietly, willing myself not to panic about what kind of state I'll find my mother in. Manny convinced Eduardo to call the gate in San José even though the doctor hadn't called back. They're going to hold her when she gets there. On one of my last trips up and down the aisle, it hits me: I'm pregnant, on a plane to Costa Rica with nothing but a change of clothes and my toothbrush, trying to rescue my mother from her own mind. I stop at Manny's row and he gets out to talk to me. He must see that I'm on the edge of losing it. He takes both my hands and looks into my eyes. "We're going to get her and bring her home." He squeezes my hands. "Okay?"

I just stand there.

He squeezes again. "Okay?"

Once I nod okay, he walks me back to my seat and gets the flight attendant to bring me some pretzels. I somehow manage to sit there calmly and eat them. Afterward, I close my eyes—not to sleep but just to rest, so I can be ready to see my mother.

———

No one at the gate has even heard of a Mirta Campo who's medically unstable and needs to be detained. They think the person Eduardo talked to was probably Sylvia, but Sylvia's gone for the day.

Manny and I walk the airport, which is just like every other modern airport: rows of plastic chairs, moving sidewalks, giant windows looking out onto the tarmac. We walk and stop at every gate. I check every stall in every bathroom while Manny checks every restaurant and gift shop. We text each other:

Nothing. You?

Nothing.

We do it all one more time, knowing that once we go down to Baggage Claim, we can't get back up here.

We go down to Baggage Claim thinking—hoping—that even though it's been more than two hours since my mom landed, maybe she's still there, waiting for Juan to come pick her up. We scan the area and then watch the American Airlines carousel, which has the bags from our flight on it. Maybe, somehow, her suitcase is still on there, which would mean that she's still here, somewhere in the airport. I describe the suitcase to Manny. "It's green with three wheels and a wooden block where the fourth one should be." He gives me a confused look, and I explain about the wheel falling off on the way back from Jersey and my father replacing it with the wood.

We watch the carousel until the last bag is claimed. "Let's go to the counter," Manny says. "Maybe someone there will know something."

They don't. She hasn't booked a return flight with American or any of the other airlines that fly to Miami. We talk to Security, showing them the picture from her birthday in July, where she looked so relaxed and happy, holding up her mimosa and smiling. Who knew that three months later she'd be losing her mind after open-heart surgery, lost in a foreign country?

Outside Baggage Claim, we ask taxi drivers: Have you seen this woman? I show them the picture. "No. I'm sorry," they all say, and then ask me if I need a ride somewhere. "Not yet," I tell them. I'm afraid to leave the airport. And even if I wasn't, I have no idea where to go.

I need to sit down; I'm having pressure in the bottom of my uterus and my back is starting to ache. Manny sees me wincing and asks what's wrong.

"Normal stuff," I say, sitting down in one of the chairs against the wall. I also have to pee. I massage my lower back for a couple of minutes before I get back up to go to the bathroom, where I make sure to call my mother's name and check all the stalls before leaving.

"The police," I say to Manny when I come out. "We need to try them."

"Yeah. It might be too soon, but it can't hurt to ask." He takes my hand. Thank God he came.

We find a cop and show him her picture. He says I'd have to go to the station in San José and open a case to file it as a missing person. "I don't think they'll do very much tonight, though." The cop looks around the airport. "She's probably around here some-where. Or maybe she went to the beach. Everybody wants to go to the beach. You should call the hotels in Limón, or maybe Tama-rindo. I bet that's where she went."

So we do. Then we take one more lap around Baggage Claim,

one more check at the counters, one more check of all the bath-rooms. We go to the phone kiosk to buy SIM cards so our phones will work outside the airport, and afterward Manny goes to get us something to eat while I call Pablo and tell him what's happening.

"Are you kidding me?" he yells.

"No."

"Did you talk to a supervisor?"

"Yes."

"Have you looked for her? Have you walked around?"

"I've walked this entire airport. Three times. I've talked to every cabdriver here. I've been to every single counter, I've talked to Security, and the police, which were both a waste of time."

"I'm gonna sue that fucking airline."

"Yeah, well, in the meantime, I'm gonna call Teresita and see if she has any other ideas." I hang up on him. I'm scared. So scared.

Manny comes back with two Styrofoam dinner containers and a bottle of water shoved into each back pocket.

I eat three bites of food, then push it away and call Teresita. She can't believe they didn't hold her at the airport.

"I need to know if she said anything to you that would help me figure out where she went," I say.

"Bueno, I imagine she went to find the ranch where Juan lived when he was down there."

"That's what I think too."

"I'm sure it's near the border."

"Border with what?"

"Nicaragua. They were fighting the Sandinistas."

"And you don't know that guy's name? The guy who owned the ranch? My mother told me, I think, but I can't remember."

"I don't remember his name, but he was in the news when all the Iran-Contra stuff was happening. Búscalo en el Google."

I remember my mother saying she was reading an article about him in *People*. Manny Googles "American Farmer Contras" and there it is, six entries down: *People* magazine, July 1989, "Frank Wall, Friend to Oliver North and the Contras, Accused of Dealing Drugs." Manny speed-reads it. "Apparently his main ranch was in Muelle San Carlos," he says to me. "You think that's where she went?"

I tell Teresita.

"Try it," she says. "Go."

I get what a shot in the dark this is; she could literally be anywhere down here. But this is our only idea. So we do what Teresita said and go.

The drive is supposed to be about two hours but turns out to be more like three because of the giant potholes and the patches of fog we have to crawl through. Out the window is darkness and so many thick trees and, eventually, farmland for miles. I sit there anxiously waiting for cell service to return, and when it does, I call as many hotels and hospitals as I can before the service cuts out again. I realize one more time how glad I am to have Manny here. I imagine myself doing this alone: trying to read the GPS, which only works sometimes; driving these narrow, scary roads, not knowing where the hell I'm going. And I think about Robert showing up, his duffel bag at his side, ready to come with me. I'm such a horrible person. But I might not have been willing to drive out into the Costa Rican countryside at eleven o'clock at night with him. With Manny, who's literally been to war three times, I am. I turn to him in the dark of the car. "Thank you," I say. "I can't tell you how grateful I am to have you here."

He nods. "I wasn't gonna let you do this alone."

We come out of another patch of fog. "She must have gotten a taxi, I guess? Assuming she's not in some hotel in San José." She's not in any of the hotels close to the airport. I called all of them before we left.

We get to Muelle San Carlos at two in the morning. Ramón at the hotel greets us in English, but then we all switch to Spanish and I tell him I'm the one who called earlier to book a room and ask if Mirta Campo had checked in. "Can you check if she's arrived?" I ask.

He checks the computer. "No," he says. "There is still no one here by that name."

I look at Manny. "She has to be at the other one." I verify with Ramón that there's only one other hotel here in Muelle San Carlos. "El Hotel Arenal? Is that right?"

He nods and stifles a yawn.

I call El Hotel Arenal one more time and, one more time they tell me she's not there, so I hand Ramón my credit card and he starts checking us in.

"Is the hotel full right now?" Manny asks.

"We are almost to capacity. This week we are welcoming the International Bird-Watching Association." He points to a sign in the lobby that says *IBWA 2012. Eyes on the Prize!*

Manny says, "I'd like to reserve a second room, please, for Mirta Campo."

"Why?" I say.

He turns to me. He's already growing in a bit of a five-o'clock shadow and he looks tired. "Because if she tries to come here and they're full, she might go somewhere else. This is the closest hotel to Frank Wall's property. What if she couldn't figure that out tonight but she figures it out tomorrow?"

He's right, so I ask Ramón to book a second room. "My mother flew here from Miami and she's very sick and we don't know where she went," I tell him.

"Oh, I'm sorry to hear that. Should I reserve the room on the same card?"

Before Manny can answer, I say, "Yes, please." Ramón runs the card and I tell him I need to call the police.

He gets the number out of a booklet he has under the counter and writes it on a piece of hotel stationery.

I don't know how to explain the Iran-Contra scandal in Spanish, so I switch to English. "Do you know the name Frank Wall? He was an American rancher who helped Oliver North deliver weapons to the Contras in the 1980s." I realize how insane this sounds.

"The Contras in Nicaragua?"

"Yes."

He shakes his head. "No. No se nada de eso."

Manny says, "He had a ranch here in Muelle San Carlos. Close to the border. We think that's where her mom is trying to go. We really need to find her as soon as possible. Do you know anyone who might know how to find that guy's property? Is there a phone book, a directory of any kind?"

Ramón produces a phone book from behind the counter and we check it. Nothing, of course. "This man you're looking for—he still lives here?"

"I don't know. But it doesn't matter," I say. "I just need to find the house."

"Have you looked him up on the internet?"

"Several times," I say. "I've Googled him, I've Facebooked him, everything."

"You need to talk to someone who knows that area out there. I know someone, actually: a long-term guest of the hotel. She's a scientist doing something with the farms. She goes out there a lot. Maybe she would know that man's property."

I lean in. "And she's here? At the hotel? Now?"

"Yes. You can talk to her tomorrow; she always comes down for breakfast around eight. Come down then and I'll introduce you."

"Tomorrow? Is it possible we can contact her right now?"

"I'm sorry but I can't."

Manny puts a hand on my back. "Can you tell us her name just in case you're not here tomorrow?"

"Dr. Wellington. But don't worry, I'll be here. I can't leave until nine."

Manny gives me a look: it's two o'clock in the morning and there's nothing else we can do, so I let it go and we go upstairs to our room.

The room has one bed, of course. Neither one of us mentions it. We just put our stuff down and I call the police. The person who answers asks for my mother's name and a description and says he'll alert the officers who are on patrol, and that I should come tomorrow to file a report.

"Let's get some rest," Manny says. "We'll go tomorrow."

"Okay. I'm going to take a shower."

He opens his bag and hands me the few toiletries and the change of clothes I asked him to bring me. I failed to think about pajamas of any kind, so I'm just going to sleep in my shorts and T-shirt. "I'll shower after you," he says.

When he does, he comes out wearing shorts and no shirt, his hair wet, his shoulders covered in little drops of water. "I can sleep on the floor if you want," he says.

I'm under the covers, lying on my back, my stomach like a mountain rising out of the bed.

"Unnecessary," I say.

"You sure?"

"Yes."

"Okay." He slides in next to me. He smells like the hotel soap but also still, somehow, like him. Robert's face floats through my head. Not from today at the airport, though. From the day I left, when I was packing in the bedroom. When he realized I wasn't moving in with my parents, that I was going to the hotel. I close my eyes now, trying to shut it out, trying not to think about the amount of pain I'm actually causing him.

Manny takes my hand. "We're going to find her," he says. "I promise you."

I turn my face toward him. "You don't know that."

"I do. I can feel it."

"You can feel it? What are you, Walter Mercado?"

"Walter Mercado is an astrologer, not a psychic," he says. "I'll thank you to get it right."

"Yeah, but with those sparkly capes and that blond blowout, he can do anything."

"That's true," he says. "At least, according to my mother."

I can't believe I can laugh when I'm this scared. But somehow I can. "My mom watched him every day. I thought she was going to cry when he stopped doing the TV show. She still goes to the website every week."

"My mom too," he says, and I can hear that he's falling asleep. He squeezes my hand one more time and I don't say anything. A few minutes later his breathing changes into the slow rhythm of sleep. I don't know if I'll be able to do the same. But I lie next to him, more connected to him than I have ever been.

34

I'm awake before the alarm we set for seven, checking my phone for any news of my mother. Nothing. I try to get out of bed without waking Manny, but it doesn't work. As soon as he feels me stir, he makes a sound in his throat and I know he's awake. When I come out of the bathroom, he's dressed, shoes on, all packed up. He rubs my arm. "Did you get any rest at all?"

His face is still puffy with sleep like it always was when he first woke up, the thin scar above his left eyebrow more prominent. It's a face I haven't seen in years, and it hurts to see it now.

"Some," I say. "I kept waking up to check my phone. Also, I just couldn't stop thinking . . ." I shake my head.

He nods. "Of course. Give me a minute and then let's go down to meet the scientist."

The lobby is packed with white people wearing cargo shorts and T-shirts. Most of them have chunky black cameras or binoculars around their necks. It's the bird-watchers, preparing for the morning tour. Ramón spots us in the crowd and comes out from behind the desk. "Buenos días," he says, and guides us into the hotel restaurant, which is also full of bird-watchers. He takes us to a table over by the wall and introduces us to Dr. Wellington.

"I'm Eleanor," she says, getting up from the table to shake our hands. "Please, have a seat. Ramón told me you'd be coming down." She's British, with long, curly hair like mine, but blond. "So your mum is missing?" she says.

I explain the coma and the delusions and how we're pretty sure she came down here looking for her first husband. I don't say he's my real father.

"Oh God. You must be absolutely panicked. Have you spoken to the police?"

"I talked to them last night. We're going to the station after this to file a report. We think she might have gone looking for this guy Frank Wall's ranch. He owned a lot of property down here in the eighties, but his main ranch was here in Muelle San Carlos. That's why Ramón said we should talk to you: he said you work out in the countryside with the farmers and that you might know where it is."

"Frank Wall? Sorry. I've never heard of him, but if he owned that much property, I'm sure some of the campesinos knew him." Her pronunciation of *campesinos* is great—*com-pay-see-nose.* "We should start with my lab manager, Carlos. He grew up here and he knows a lot of the farmers in the area."

A bubble of excitement rises in my chest. "How can I get in touch with him?"

"We can call him in about an hour. He's at mass right now. His wife makes him go." I want to call him now. I want to get him out of church. But I don't want to piss him off. So far, he's the only hope I have. I fake a smile. "Okay, thanks."

The waiter shows up and asks us if we'd like menus. I ask him if we can get food to go. If we're not going to call Carlos right now, I want to go to the police station. But the waiter says no, they don't offer food to go.

I look at Manny. "Maybe we can eat somewhere else? Like, in town? We need to get to the police station. And I want to walk around town and show her picture to people."

Eleanor says, "It's eight a.m. on a Sunday. Nothing's open. All the shops and restaurants are closed until noon, if they even open at all. You should eat." She points to my stomach. "You've got to keep your strength; you're under a lot of stress. Have breakfast and then go find the police station." She takes out a pen and a slip of paper from her purse and writes her phone number on it. "Then call me from town and we'll figure out how to put you in touch with Carlos."

Manny says, "Yeah, you barely ate last night. Te vas a quedar con low blood sugar. It's not a good idea."

He's right. But I feel like I should be out talking to people, not sitting in a restaurant with a bunch of bird-watchers.

"Okay," I say to the waiter, who is still standing there. "Sí, café y el menú por favor."

Eleanor says, "You speak Spanish. I wish I did. I'm learning, but it's a slow go."

Manny says, "We're Cuban."

"You live there?"

This takes me a little by surprise. "No, we live in Miami. Our parents were born in Cuba."

And then we do all the background stuff. She's a professor of environmental science here on fellowship, which she explains is where they pay you to take time off from teaching to go work on your research.

"I study dirt," she says, smiling. "They have some of the richest volcanic soil in the world down here." The waiter delivers our coffees and menus. Eleanor points to my belly. "So, is this your first?"

I nod and touch my stomach. I push a little, just to let him know I'm here.

"I have three at home with my husband. All teens. All girls." She doesn't look old enough to have teenagers, but I don't say that. She asks me how far along I am and I tell her: thirty-one weeks tomorrow.

"Ah, the third trimester. The calm before the storm. She leans in. "Listen, it's all very doable. You just have to keep a sense of humor about the whole thing." She looks at us both. "You guys are going to do great, I can tell."

I can feel Manny shift in his chair. I stare at the table. "Thanks."

Doable. Suddenly, all my fears about parenting surface, and, along with them, a new one: the fear that I won't have my mom to help. While Manny and Eleanor eat and talk, I sit there silently, try-ing not to think about my mother having a heart attack in the cab on the way to Frank Wall's ranch, or throwing a clot and dying of a pulmonary embolism in the plane on the way home. I am trying to think of anything but the possibility of me having this baby and my mom being dead. But right now there is nothing else.

At the police station, we only have to wait a couple of minutes be-fore an officer leads us back to an office.

"¿Cómo los puedo ayudar?" he asks, and we tell him, speaking in Spanish as well.

He's skinny with pockmarks on his cheeks and a mustache he touches every few seconds. He takes down our information and tells us they can send someone to the public records office tomorrow to search for Frank Wall's properties. "I can send her picture out to the officers on patrol. That way they can detain her if they see her."

"Okay, great," I say. "But can you send someone out specifically to look for her? We need to look for her. She's sick. She just had surgery. She needs her medicine. Please."

"We have a limited staff today. It's Sunday."

Before I can speak, Manny puts a hand on my leg and presses. *Don't piss him off*, he's telling me, just like last night at the front desk. He speaks softly, sweetly. "Officer Salazar," he says. "Please. Is there no officer you can ask to help us? It's an emergency. A medical emergency. We're worried Mónica's mom could suffer a heart attack without her medication." He's good-copping the cop.

The officer sighs. "I'll radio the guy working Ruta 35. There's probably nobody out speeding today anyway."

Manny bows his head at him. "Thank you," he says, and then motions for me to give the officer the picture of my mom.

Officer Salazar leaves the room to go scan it. "Thank you," I say to Manny. "How did you know his name?"

He points to a plaque displayed on a bookshelf in the corner of the room. It says *Officer Felix J. Salazar, Superior Leadership, 2009.* Manny sees everything. In Afghanistan, they were trained to notice their surroundings. Especially medics, who, for a while, were being targeted. When he first came home, he couldn't go anywhere crowded—no street festivals, no concerts, not even walking around Wynwood—because he couldn't relax. He was always looking at the tops of buildings, in doorways, watching people's bodies, how they carried their bags and what they did with their hands.

Officer Salazar comes back in, slides the picture of my mom back across the desk to me. "I will also send it to the main office in San José. And to all the hospitals. And I will call you the minute I hear anything."

"Muchas gracias," I say. "Lo agradesco mucho."

"Con mucho gusto," he says, touching his mustache one last time.

As we're heading over to Eleanor's lab to meet Carlos, Pablo calls me for the update. He re-asks all the questions about everything I've done and not done. He wants to know exactly who the scientist is. It's all I can do not to tell him that if he doesn't like the way I'm doing this, he should get a fucking passport and come down here himself. Instead, I just ask if he's heard from my father.

"Nope. I left a message on the house phone and the optical phone."

"Where *is* he? Doesn't he just go sleep on the couch at work when he does this?"

We pull up to a red light. On the corner is a gas station that's connected to an auto parts store. Neither one looks open.

Pablo says, "I don't think he sleeps at work when he does this. I passed by there at eleven o'clock last night and his car wasn't there."

"You think he was out at a bar getting drunk or something?" I can't imagine him doing this, but I also couldn't imagine my mother carrying a bomb. At this point, I'm pretty sure anything's possible.

Pablo says, "He wasn't out at a bar getting drunk. Have you met Dad?"

"Maybe he's at Fermín and Gladys's."

"I talked to Fermín last night. He hasn't talked to him since Friday."

"What the fuck? This is crazy. Could he be at a hotel? Like cooling off from their fight? Or do you think something happened to him? Have you called the hospitals?"

"Yeah. Maritza made me call them last night. And then she called again this morning."

Manny looks at me for the answer. I nod yes.

"Okay, good," I say to Pablo. "So he's not dead."

"I'm sure he'll show back up for work tomorrow."

"Tomorrow is twenty-four hours away. I need him *now*. Mom's gone. She fucking disappeared into thin air. I'm down here getting ready to go meet another stranger to ask him if he knows how to find her."

"All right, Mónica. Calm down."

"I can't calm down, Pablo. We have to find her. And him."

Manny says, "Have him check the house for your father's passport. Maybe he came down here."

"Pablo, listen. Go back to the house and look for Dad's passport and his maleta. If they're gone, we gotta start calling airlines."

"How am I supposed to know where he keeps his passport?"

"Look in his dresser. Top drawer. It's where he keeps all their important papers. Citizenship, passports, all that shit." Something else occurs to me. "And, hey, text me the phone number that's on the FPL bill in the hallway. On the computer desk. You'll see it. It says 'Daniel directo.'"

He asks who that is.

I close my eyes, almost as a way of avoiding the answer. But I can't avoid it. Not anymore. I open my eyes. "It's the FBI agent Mom's been talking to about how Juan's still alive and we should find him. I'm going to call him and see if he can help us figure out where this guy's house is."

"Okay," he says. "Do you know if there are keys to the optical at the house? I want to leave a note on his desk at work."

"Also in the top drawer. Go as fast as you can," I say. "I need to call the FBI guy and see if he can help."

I hang up the phone and feel like I'm going to puke. "Pull over," I say to Manny.

He doesn't even ask why; he just does it. I open the car door and vomit the toast and fruit from breakfast into the street. I stare at the bits of glass and tufts of grass coming up from the concrete. Manny has my hair, which I didn't have a chance to put up before I had to puke.

He's saying, "Shhh . . . It's okay . . . It's okay, babe."

Babe. He hasn't called me that since the day I called him from the hospital to tell him about my mom. It felt so strange then. Now it feels right.

I finish up and sit back in my seat. "Fuck."

"You think you're sick?" Manny says.

"No."

"Nerves?"

"Yeah."

"Okay." He touches my knee for just a moment, then points to the bottle of water I brought with me. "Let your stomach settle and then drink water. You gotta stay hydrated."

I nod, wipe my mouth with a tissue from my purse, and we keep going, driving through town, looking for my mother or anyone who might have seen her.

We're in a different auto parts store/gas station that's actually open, talking to the guy who runs it about whether I should make posters, or try to use social media, or both. Pablo texts me that my father's passport is still there, but his suitcase is gone.

I tell Manny.

"Okay, so he wasn't planning on coming back last night. And he's not down here," he says.

"So he's in Miami. Or somewhere in the U.S." It occurs to me that maybe he took off for Jersey. Maybe he went to see the cousins. I text that back to Pablo and he says he'll call them. Except he doesn't have anyone's number, so I have to give him that information too. In return, he sends a picture of Daniel Fernández's number on the FPL bill. When my phone pings with it, I put my hands on my stomach. *Well, mijo,* I say in my head. *Now I have to call Daniel Fernández, the FBI agent who held me when I was a baby and did the one-two-three.* I step outside the store and dial the number.

No one's answering, of course—it's Sunday. Why would he be in the office on a Sunday? It goes to voice mail: "This is Daniel. Leave me a message and I'll call you back. Thanks." Daniel. Not Agent Daniel Fernández. Is this his cell? Did he give my mother his cell number? I leave a message. It's rambling and desperate, but it has my name and number and all the relevant information.

A minute later, he calls me.

"Mónica," he says when I pick up, "Es Daniel Fernández."

I take the deepest breath I can and bite the insides of both cheeks. Hard. So hard, I think I might be bleeding on one side. "Hola," I say, and then quickly switch to English because I'm nervous. "Thank you so much for returning my call. I'm sorry to call you on a Sunday."

"No problem," he says, switching to English as well. It's accented, of course, but less so than my parents'. "Tell me what's going on with your mother."

I tell him everything and ask him when he last heard from her.

"Not since last week. She called me and I found the information she was asking for."

"About Juan? The information about how he survived the shooting and went to Costa Rica?"

"Yes."

It's like a little bomb, that *yes*. It means that she wasn't lying or delusional. It means he's not dead. Probably. It's confirmation that Juan, my real father, is probably alive somewhere. I steady myself with a hand on the wall outside the auto parts store. It's not that hot out, and I'm in the shade, even, but suddenly my entire body is covered in sweat. I wish I could sit down.

"I think that's what she's doing down here," I say.

"You're there?" he asks. "You're in Costa Rica?"

"Yes. I came down when I figured out she left. I think she's stuck in a delusion, thinking it's the old days. My best guess is that she's trying to find Frank Wall's ranch. Is there any way you can help me figure out where that is?"

He's quiet for a moment. "The short answer is maybe. The long answer is my son got married yesterday and I'm in Connecticut. I won't be in the office until tomorrow." His son the lawyer.

"Okay," I say. "I'm sorry to bother you at your son's wedding." An old blue pickup pulls up to the gas pumps and a woman gets out to come into the building.

"It's no problem. I'll be in the office by 8:30 and I'll pull the record again and see what I can find. I also have a contact at the CIA—an old friend from Cuba. I'll call him right now and let you know as soon as I know anything. Is this the best number for you?"

I tell him it is and then he asks me several questions about who I've talked to down here. I tell him about Eleanor and Carlos and he says, "Actually, that could be your best bet. You want people who know the area, the locals. What about the local authorities?"

I tell him what Officer Salazar is doing.

"Okay, sounds like you've got your bases covered for now. I'll be in touch as soon as I can, I promise."

"Okay," I say. "Thank you. Thank you so much."

"No problem. I'm sorry to hear your mother isn't doing well."

"Thank you," I say again. I hang up and stand there for a moment. I feel a sliver of calm just from having talked to Daniel, and maybe from having someone tell me I'm doing it right.

Eleanor's lab is a brown one-story building between a hair salon and a restaurant called Iguanas. I think of Robert and the Hulk and feel guilty one more time for everything. Eleanor takes us into an office in the back with a big laboratory room off to the side.

I'm feeling a little like I did the day I fainted in the hospital, which seems like a year ago. I breathe as slowly as I can and sit down in the folding chair in the corner. Manny puts his hand on my back. "You okay?"

I nod.

"You nauseous?"

"Lightheaded."

Eleanor says, "I'll get you some water."

My phone buzzes in my purse. After another couple of breaths, I take it out. There's a text I missed from Caro asking what's going on, seeing if she can help in any way, and this new one is Suzie, checking on me. *You okay? How's your mom?*

Eleanor comes back in with water in a paper triangle cup. "Sip this," she says. "Slowly."

Manny pulls my wrist and takes my pulse. He nods when he's done. I guess it wasn't too bad. As I'm sipping the water slowly, a guy walks in. White shorts, yellow polo, sneakers.

"Carlos," Eleanor says, "please meet my new friends Mónica and Manny." We all say hello and shake hands and speak in English. I tell him how much we appreciate his being here.

"No problem," he says. "This way I don't have to go back for the eleven a.m. mass." He smiles and we all laugh a little.

"So," Eleanor says, "Mónica and Manny are looking for Mónica's mum, who might be wandering around the countryside."

I explain everything. He has no idea who Frank Wall is, but he agrees with Eleanor and Daniel that the campesinos might.

Carlos and Eleanor make a list of people to try: Jorge and María, Leonardo and Ana, someone named Doña Pancha. I finish my water and text Pablo the update, and then Suzie. *Haven't found her yet but I'm getting help. Thanks for checking.*

35

Doña Pancha isn't home and Jorge and María moved here in the '90s, so they have no idea who Frank Wall is. But when Carlos asks Leonardo and Ana, Leonardo says, "Of course we know Frank Wall. He saved my sister's life." We're standing in their living room because Ana insisted we come in. "She got an infection in her lungs and he flew her to the hospital," Leonardo continues. "Frank's not here anymore, though. He got into a lot of trouble. That man is a complicated person, let me tell you."

Carlos translates for Eleanor and, of course, she wants to know what he got into trouble for. I tell her what I read about him last night: "Back in the '80s he had an airstrip and the CIA paid him to fly weapons to the Contras in Nicaragua. Which was illegal."

Manny says, "And it wasn't just weapons flying off that airstrip."

"Drugs?" Eleanor says.

"Yep," I say. "The CIA knew about that too." I turn to Leonardo. "So you know where this guy's ranch is? You can give us directions?"

He says, "Yes, his son is living there now, running the ranch."

He looks at Ana for a second and she makes a face I can't quite figure out.

"Okay," I say. "Then let's go."

We drive for about twenty minutes on roads that, technically, are paved, but don't always feel like it. Trees and farmland are everywhere. As are the farm animals. At one point we have to stop for a herd of dark brown cows in the road. Carlos inches the car forward and they make a space for us to get through. Finally, we arrive at Frank Wall's property. In the *People* magazine article, it said Wall had to keep a guard dog because the Sandinistas kept trying to kill him. When we pull up to the gate, I find myself looking for that dog. Or any dog. Or guards or goons of any kind. But there's nothing—just a large metal gate. Carlos opens it and we drive down a long dirt road with fields on either side. On the left: cows. On the right: rows of fruit trees, citrus of some kind. At the end of the dirt road is the house. It's reddish-brown, big but not huge—kind of like something you'd see in Coral Gables, except with a wraparound porch. We park in a gravel driveway next to an old black Suburban and a green four-wheeler.

"Looks like you're gonna get along with this guy," I say to Manny.

We get out of the car and something screams. My whole body tenses up and I look at Carlos.

"Monos," he says, and points into the forest behind us.

"Damn, that's crazy," Manny says.

Eleanor sweeps her arm out to indicate the land around us. "That's how I feel all day, every day, about this place. It's thrilling." She smiles.

At the front door, Carlos takes the lead. He rings the doorbell and a guy answers. I'm hoping he's Frank Wall's son. He's tall, with a beer gut, older than me—about forty—with bags under his eyes and broken veins on his nose. He looks at all of us. "Yes?" he says in Spanish. "Can I help you?" He's looking at us warily, obviously surprised to see us, no idea who we are.

"We're looking for Frank Wall's son," Carlos says.

The guy frowns. "Why?"

I step up. "Hola," I say. "Me llamo Mónica Campo. Mucho gusto."

"Frankie Wall," he says.

I'm so relieved I almost say "Thank God" out loud. I'm filled with adrenaline, my legs twitching and my heart beating a little faster. I hold out my hand, smiling, and he shakes it but doesn't look me in the eye. He looks at Manny and Eleanor and then behind us, to the driveway, almost like he's checking for something. "Hola, Frankie. ¿Hablas inglés?" I'm thinking of Eleanor. Also, it's just easier for me.

He says yes and I explain in English: my mother is somewhere, lost, looking for a man she was in love with who might have worked for his father in the 1980s. "She had heart surgery a few weeks ago and needs her medicine. I need to find her. Did she come here?" I'm expecting him to say, "Oh yes, of course," and usher me inside to see her.

But he doesn't. He looks over my head, back out to the driveway again. "No. No one's come here." His voice is deep but quiet.

I want to burst into tears. I can't believe we came all this way, actually found this house, this guy—Frank Wall's son—and she's not here. How could she not be here? Where else could she be? I step closer to him. My voice is panicked. "She could have come earlier today, this morning. Or last night? Were you home all night?"

"I've been here since Thursday." Frankie keeps moving his feet, shifting his weight from one foot to the other, almost like he's nervous. Which makes *me* nervous. Now I start to wonder what's going on with this guy, why his vibe is so off.

Manny steps up next to me. "Look, we know she was coming here. Or trying to. Is there anyone else who would have seen her? Ranch hands? Employees? Anyone? Maybe your wife answered the door?"

"No," he says, emphatically, with a quick head shake, and somehow I know this whole thing just got worse. He's lying. Or isn't telling us something. Now I'm pissed. And scared. I'm in the middle of nowhere in a foreign country with Manny and two strangers I've dragged into this, and this guy is acting shady as hell. If he knows something about her, why wouldn't he tell me?

"Okay," I say, stalling, trying to figure out what to do next. I look at Manny and, with the tiniest movement of our eyes, we communicate. It's the way we used to say "This waiter is awful" or "Get me out of this conversation." Now we're saying "I don't trust this guy." I turn back to Frankie. "So, um, do you have any idea where else she might have gone to look for him? There are other farms around here, right?"

"Hundreds."

Carlos asks for directions to the next closest one. Frankie tells him how to get there and then starts closing the door.

"Wait," I say. "Can I give you my number? Please. In case she eventually shows up here?"

He glances inside for a second and then says, "That would be fine." He pulls out his phone so I can put my number into it.

"It's a local number. I have a SIM card."

He nods quickly but doesn't say anything else, and the silence is unnerving. I realize in this moment that we can't leave. I don't know anything else, but I know *this*.

I turn back to Frankie. "So sorry, but could I please use your bathroom before we go?" I glance at Manny and he gives me a nod only I could ever see. I take it to mean "Yes, do this. Get inside the house."

Frankie sighs. It's like he needs to be somewhere, and it's clear he doesn't want to let me in.

"Sorry." I look down at my stomach. "Sometimes I can't wait."

He says something that's a cross between a grunt and "Sure" and then opens the door wider. Just then a monkey screams again and I jump. He doesn't flinch.

As I walk through the house, I try to do Manny's thing and notice everything. We go through the living room, which is filled with dark, carved wood furniture. The sofa is against the wall. The coffee table, empty but for a plant, is a square. Two chairs face each other on either side of it. The art is all paintings, mostly landscapes and women. There is no TV. Just off the living room is a hallway with several doors on either side. "First one on the right," he says.

"Got it. Thanks." As I take my final look at the living room, I see, barely sticking out from behind one of the chairs, lying on its side, the bottom of a green suitcase with a little piece of wood in place of one of the wheels. What the fuck? My legs immediately feel weak and all I can think is *No*. I barely make it into the bathroom, lock the door, and lean against it, my arms and legs shaking uncontrollably. I try to find my text thread with Manny but I can't use my hands. I knew there was something off with this guy. But why? Is my mother still here? Where is she? Inside my head, there's a screaming sound, like the monkeys, over and over. Finally, my hands and my brain sync up and I text Manny. It's a jumble of words. *My mom here saw suitcase she's here he's lying.*

You sure it's hers? he says.

I take the biggest breath I can and try to hold the phone steady so I can type. *Positive. He's waiting for me. Watching me. What do I do?*

I look at the window and try to figure out if I should crawl out of it and try to get back to the car. But then I'll be out of the house. And my mother might be somewhere *in* the house. And I cannot leave without my mother, not even to go get the police. Not that any of this matters. The bathroom window is too small. I'd never make it out, not with my stomach this big.

Manny writes back. *Sending Carlos back to ask for more directions. When he answers the door, you can look around.*

This guy is bad. Call the cops.

Carlos knocking now. He answered. Go.

I open the bathroom door as quietly as I can. Sweat is running down my back. I hear Carlos talking to Frankie from the porch, asking for more information, keeping him there. I walk as silently as I can on the tile floor and open the first door I see. It's an office: desk, chair, computer, papers everywhere. The door across the hall is open: it's a guest room. The last room is the master, obviously. I crack that door and peek inside. I see nothing: the left side of the bed, a nightstand. I open the door another few inches, put my face in a little farther. And there she is, in a chair in the corner. She's breathing heavily through her nose, making small, almost humming sounds on every exhale. She looks terrified. She's wearing the 1980s outfit—seafoam-green pants, yellow shirt. It's pulled a little askew and her bra strap, thick and white, is showing. "Mónica," she says in a strangled voice, her eyes wide with surprise but also fear.

Sitting on the bed in front of her is a woman with black hair in a ponytail who turns and looks at me. She drops her head, almost like she's disappointed in me, and stands up. From the waistband of her shorts, she pulls out a gun. "Okay. Both of you, to the living room," she says in Spanish.

I almost collapse and have to grab on to the door frame to hold myself up. "What—what is this?" I say. "What are you doing?" My heart is beating harder than I've ever felt in my life. It's almost painful in my chest.

The woman looks at my mother and says, "Come on. Stand up, please. Let's go to the living room." She holds the gun pointing down at the floor. I can't stop looking at it.

My mother stands up. She walks slowly across the room. Her shoes—the white pumps—make a tapping sound as she moves across the tile floor. She's taking loud, ragged breaths.

"Mom," I say. "Are you okay? What's happening?"

"I don't know," she says. "I don't know what's happening." Her face is a mask of fear and confusion.

"She's okay," the woman says. "Come on. Let's go."

My mother makes it to the door of the bedroom. Behind her, the woman indicates with her arm that we need to walk down the hall. "Back to the living room," she says. The gun is still pointing at the floor.

My mother and I walk silently, shoulder to shoulder. My entire body is trembling. The places where my arms are attached to my torso feel tingly and almost cold. My chest is a cavern of anxiety and my mouth tastes like metal. We pass the guest room, then the office, then the bathroom. The whole time the woman with the gun is walking behind us and saying nothing.

Mirta

I'm so sorry, Mónica. I don't know what's happening, why they won't let me go, why they have guns, why they're treating me like this. They had me in the living room at first, and then someone came—a car pulled up—and the woman said, "We need to hide her," so she took me by the arm and pulled me down the hall. She made me sit down, told me not to make a sound, then showed me the gun. I'm afraid they're going to kill me. What else are they going to do with me? Oh God, they're going to shoot me. And I'll never see you again. Please know, mi niña, you are my heart, my life. You and your brother mean everything to me. And Rolando. His kindness and his patience have always been what saved me. I hope he knows how sorry I am, for all of this, for everything. Please tell the baby his abuela loved him.

36

Carlos, Eleanor, and Manny walk through the front door with Frankie right behind them. He's also holding a gun.

Manny's eyes are scanning the room wildly. They stop on me for a second and I see how scared he is. I'm having that tripped-out feeling where you know it's reality but you don't want it to be and all you want in the world is to go back in time to before you got that phone call or ran that red light or found your mother being held at gunpoint in the bedroom.

Frankie says, "None of you are armed?" He speaks in English.

They all say no. He points to Carlos and Manny. "Could you lift your shirts? Let me see your waistbands?"

They both do it, turning a small circle.

"Thanks. Okay, I need you to sit down. On the sofa. All three of you."

They sit down and the woman points to my mother and me. "Ustedes también." I'm not sure if she speaks English or not.

My mother and I sit across from each other in the chairs, the coffee table between us. She twists her hands in her lap, looking down at them, breathing those ragged breaths through her mouth. I sit with my arms folded across my belly as tight as I can.

When she looks up at me, I know she's feeling the same terror I am. I want to jump over the table and take her in my arms. But God knows what would happen if I did. These people are holding guns. *Guns.* So I look back at her, boring my eyes into her face, trying to send her messages like I do with Manny. She and I have our own language, too, after all. *I love you*, I say. *Stay calm*, I say. *Don't die*, I say.

Frankie says, "Okay. We need to figure this out. I can't believe—"

The woman walks over to him. "¿Qúe te dije?" She glares at him.

He continues in Spanish. "I know, Beatríz. But we still would have had these people." He sweeps an arm out across the room, indicating us people.

"No we wouldn't. They would have been gone in five minutes." She jabs a thumb in the direction of the back of the house. "Now it's too late. And don't use my name," she says, not quite under her breath. I don't know what she's talking about, why it's too late. But she's right about the names. Maybe he did it because he doesn't care if we know their names; he's going to kill us anyway. I watch the guns—his and hers. They look the same. Black, squarish, lethal.

Frankie says, "Maybe we can slow it down. Call him."

Beatríz says, "I am not calling him. We already have a problem there. This will only make it worse." She's older than Frankie, I see now. Maybe pushing fifty. Her hair is black but she's graying at the temples a little. She actually seems to be a little more in charge. "Que despiche," she says, rolling her eyes. I don't know the word *despiche*; it must be Costa Rican for huge fucking mess.

Frankie starts pacing back and forth, scratching the side of his head with the hand that's holding the gun. "Okay, let me think. Let me think."

Beatríz looks at Carlos, Eleanor, and Manny. And me. "Who are they?" she says in Spanish.

I answer back in Spanish. "I'm her daughter. I came to get her. This was all a misunderstanding. These are my friends. They came with me."

Beatríz looks Manny up and down. He's wearing cut-off camo shorts—tan, not green—and a pink tank top from Lucy and Ricky's, his favorite bar in the Keys. His tattoos are showing: on his left arm, the combat medic insignia; on his right, the Army star with the initials of his friends who died.

"He looks like a cop," she says to Frankie.

Frankie says, "You a cop?" in English.

Manny looks from Frankie's gun to Beatríz's and back. "Nope."

"Military?"

"I was in the Army."

"Are you her husband?" He looks at my stomach.

"I'm a friend."

I think of Robert and feel an actual ache in my chest. If he knew the kind of danger I'm in . . . My eyes fill with tears. I blink them away as much as I can but a few fall down my face. I cross my arms tighter and press my hands in on either side of my belly. *Mijo,* I think to the baby, *I will save you. Somehow, I promise, we'll get out of this.* My stomach starts to cramp and I need the bathroom. A wild thought floats through my mind: What if those aren't just stomach cramps? Extreme stress can cause preterm labor. *Mijo, no,* I think. *It's not time yet. Please.*

"And who are you guys?" Frankie says to Carlos and Eleanor.

"I'm an environmental scientist," Eleanor says, trying not to cry. She keeps inhaling and swallowing. "I met them at the hotel this morning. I offered to help them find Mónica's mother." She nods at Carlos. "He works with me. I asked him to come with us, to talk with the campesinos. To help us find your farm."

Carlos stands up and says, "Listen, I know you—"

Frankie steps toward him, gun up, shoulder height, but he's turned his wrist to the left, so the gun is pointed sideways. "No, no. You need to stay seated, okay? Please. This can't get any more complicated than it already is."

Carlos puts his hands up and sits down slowly. He nods. "Okay, okay."

Frankie lowers the gun. "Just stay where you are and let me figure this out." He explains to Beatríz who the three of them are and tells her that Manny is not a cop. So she must not speak English.

Beatríz turns to my mother. "So you know these people? This is your daughter?"

"Sí, ella es mi hija," she says, her voice low and shaky.

I lean forward in the chair, but I don't stand up. "We came to take you home, Mom."

My mother puts her face in her hands. "Yes, I need to go home," she says in English. Then, "Lo siento, mi niña. Me equivoqúe."

"I know. I know you made a mistake. It's okay. We're gonna be okay." This feels like the worst lie I've ever told.

She puts a hand to her chest.

"Mom?" I grip the arms of the chair. It's that stupid dark wood, carved into swirly designs. "She needs her medicine," I say to Beatríz, now that I know she's in charge. "Please, can I just give her her medicine?"

She looks at Frankie. "What medicine?"

He closes his eyes and shakes his head.

I say, "She has high blood pressure. She had heart surgery last month. It's very dangerous for her to be without her medicine. Please."

Beatríz palms her forehead. "Where is it?"

"In my purse. The brown leather purse in the back seat."

Frankie's phone dings with a text. He reads it. "They're ready," he says to Beatríz.

"Tell them we'll be out in a few minutes," she says, and then goes outside to get my mother's medicine.

Frankie writes the person back and then starts doing that thing where he shifts his weight from one foot to the other. "You people are causing me a lot of trouble," he says.

"I'm sorry," I say. "I'm sorry we interrupted you. We can just go. We can just leave."

Eleanor takes a deep breath. "Excuse me. Listen, if my husband doesn't hear from me tonight, he'll worry. He'll call the consulate. I'm a British citizen. There will be an investigation. I know you don't want that. We've found Mónica's mum. We can go now. You'll never hear from us again." She takes another deep breath, as if she used up all the air she had saying that.

"Sorry. That's just not possible. Not now." He looks around at all of us. "Look, we're going to get you guys out of here. We just need to figure out the best way to do it." This gives me no comfort. This guy's already lied to us once. Who says he's not lying to us now?

I tighten my arms around myself again and look at my mother. Her breathing sounds better but she still has her palm to her chest.

Manny is stock-still except for his left leg, which is vibrating. Without Beatríz here, he's focused only on Frankie. And, I notice, the ways in and out of this room. There are only three: the front door, the opening into the hallway, and a set of French doors that lead into what I think might be the den.

Someone comes through those doors now and I see Manny flinch. It's a fit-looking guy wearing a black Nike shirt and a gray baseball cap with sunglasses sitting up on the brim.

He stops, takes in the scene, frowns in confusion. "Who are these people?" he says in Spanish. He looks at the gun in Frankie's hand. "And what the hell are you doing with that?"

"What are *you* doing in *here?* I told you we'd be out in a minute," Frankie says.

The guy does not have a gun. At least, not one that I can see.

Frankie points to my mother. He continues in Spanish. "This woman showed up looking for her ex-husband. Some guy who used to work with my father. And we told her he wasn't here. But her taxi had left and things were already underway. I told Beatríz let's just keep her here until later, then call her another taxi. She wanted to do it right then, but I didn't want anyone else coming around right then. Thirty minutes later"—he looks at us—"these people show up."

"Wait. What?" the guy says. He looks completely confused.

Frankie points to Manny and me. "These two are her family." He points to Carlos and Eleanor. "And these two are some . . . scientists?" He shakes his head. "God, I don't even know. This is—"

The guy takes off his baseball cap and his sunglasses clatter on the floor. The sound is like gunfire. He picks them up and hangs them off the front of his shirt, puts his cap back on. "I don't believe this. How are we supposed to even prepare anything with these people here? Much less execute." Weirdly, I'm pretty sure, from his accent, that he's Cuban. "Where's Beatríz?" he asks Frankie.

"Outside, getting her medicine."

"Whose medicine?"

Frankie points to my mother. "She has a heart problem, apparently."

"Me cago en la mierda," the guy says. Now I *know* he's Cuban. No one else uses that expression, at least that I know of.

The front door opens and Manny flinches again. Beatríz comes back in with my purse. Her gun is now in the waistband of her Bermuda shorts. She has a little bit of a belly and the fat of her stomach bulges out around the gun's handle. She puts the two prescription bottles from my purse on the table.

My mother says, "Could I have some water, please?" and something about the way she says it—softly, like a child—breaks me.

Beatríz goes to the kitchen and comes back with a glass of water. My mother's hands are shaking so badly she spills it a little. She can't get the bottle open.

Beatríz helps her, asks her how many to take.

My mother closes her eyes, trying to remember.

"One," I say. "One of each."

The Cuban guy in the Nike shirt says, "Okay, we have no choice. We have to proceed as planned and figure out what to do with these people in the meantime. Does Raymond know anything about this?" Oh God, another name.

Beatríz doesn't get mad, though. She just says, "No, he doesn't. And I don't think we should tell him."

Nike says, "I agree."

We're all sitting silently, just listening to them. My mother has closed her eyes. She's speaking softly to herself, touching the fingers of her left hand as if she's counting on them. I hear her say, "Ruega por nosotros pecadores," and I realize she's praying the rosary, using her fingers as beads, just like she did on the boat the night they came from Cuba and she thought they would all die.

I say my own small prayer that we live through this, even though I don't know how we're going to. I think of my father, of my brother. Of Juan, for some reason. Will I die without ever meeting him? Maybe my mother's right. Maybe I need to meet him. I think of the baby growing inside me. Will I die without ever meeting *him*? Will he die without ever meeting Robert? My eyes fill with tears again. I blink them away as fast as I can so I can keep watching Frankie and Beatríz's hands.

Now Beatríz gets a text. She looks at Nike and nods at the back of the house. "I'll go explain that we're delayed," she says, and goes back through the French doors.

Nike checks his watch and says to Frankie, "We have to get them out of here. It's gonna take us at least an hour to load, and they cannot be here when that happens."

An hour to load. Must be drugs. Just like his father.

Frankie says, "I know. But what are we going to do with them?"

Nike walks over closer to him. They lower their voices to discuss this and I look at Manny. He's watching them too.

Frankie nods and says, "Okay, I'll call her and tell her we're coming over."

He walks down the hall to make the call and Nike turns to us. "Do everything I say and you will not get hurt." He's speaking in perfect English. So he must be Cuban from Miami, not Cuban from Cuba. He looks around at each of us slowly. When he gets to Manny, he stops. "No heroics. Nothing like the movies. Okay?"

Manny just looks at him. He's sweating and his face is completely still and focused.

"Okay?" Nike says.

Manny says, "Okay."

Frankie comes back in. "She's home. Let's go." He motions for all of us to stand up, but then his phone rings. He shows Nike the number. I guess he's learned not to say names.

Nike says, "Let me get it." He turns to all of us. "Everyone: Silent."

We all do as he says. I look at Manny and he gives me a look I've never seen before. There's the fear, but there is also a love so strong I can feel it from where I'm sitting. He's never looked at me that way—not the night we went out to see the meteor shower, not any of the times he deployed. He won't take his eyes off me. He looks down at my stomach. I put my hand there and close my eyes. When I open them, he's still looking at me, and he has tears in his eyes.

Nike walks out to the front porch, trying not to talk too loud, but there must be a bad connection, because every time he lowers his voice, he has to repeat himself. As a result, we hear it all: "Twelve monkeys, thirty-two parrots, two tigrillos. Confirmed. Airstrip three. Confirmed." So it's not drugs. It's animals. He finishes the call and comes back in. "Okay, let's go."

37

We walk out onto the porch and Nike stops us. "I need your phones," he says, and everyone except my mother hands them over.

"I don't have mine," she says. "It's at home. In Miami." She looks out into the patchy front yard and over to the fields to the left of the house. It's like she's looking for Miami.

"That's fine," Nike says. "Let's just get in the car."

I want to ask where they're taking us, but I'm too scared to.

Frankie leads us down to the Suburban parked in the driveway. It's black and covered in dust with the tires caked in mud. He points to Eleanor, my mom, and me. "You three in the back." Then he points to Manny and Carlos and tells Nike, "We should keep them close, where we can keep an eye on them."

Nike says, "I'll drive." He nods at the gun in Frankie's hand. "You manage everyone."

Eleanor helps my mother into the car and I slide in last. It feels so much worse in here. We're more trapped. At least in the house we could have tried to run out the door. I remember what Nike said about how, if we just followed directions, we wouldn't get hurt. It's all I have to hang on to right now. I take my mother's hand and press it between both of mine. She's looking straight ahead, her eyes closed, her lips moving slightly, no sound coming out. "We'll be okay," I say. "We'll be okay."

Frankie gets a call and walks a few feet away to take it.

Carlos repositions the second-row seat and gets in. Manny is about to come in behind him, but then a car comes flying up the driveway. It's a white SUV with two—no, four—men in it. Then another SUV, exactly the same, pulls up behind it.

The men in the cars jump out and start yelling "¡Policía! ¡Paran ahora!" They're in regular clothes with bulletproof vests and matching dark blue baseball caps. Some run toward the car, some run straight up to the house.

Nike's sitting in the driver's seat. "Shit," he says, in English. "Get down!"

"What?" I say. It feels like a movie. I'm so scared I can't process what he means.

"Down!" he yells again, and then he's out of the car holding a gun too. I'm frozen until I hear the three loud pops. I hear people yelling, the front door slamming open and shut. My mother is already on the floorboard, pulling at my shirt. She's making sounds that aren't words. Eleanor is down there with her. Carlos is crawling across the floorboard and Manny is stepping up into the car, but then I hear more pops and Manny groans. It's wordless, just sound. I feel it in my spine. He crumples to the ground.

"Manny!" I scream. "Oh my God, Manny!" I'm trying to look out the door. I can see him from the waist up. He's lying there, blood all over his arm and his chest. I can't feel anything in my body; I can't think. The police are yelling, Manny is moaning, there are more pops, and my mother is next to me, screaming, "¡Madre mía! Madre mía!" I try to fold myself over her, to protect her in any way I can. Eleanor and Carlos are both shouting something, I don't know what. All I know is Manny was shot and he's on the ground, bleeding.

The shooting is moving farther away now—inside the house, or maybe out in the fields. We're still huddled in the car, and Nike comes running up. "Help me get him!" he yells. He pulls Manny's torso up by one arm. Carlos gets out to help but Manny's able to stand long enough to collapse onto the floorboard behind the driver's seat. Carlos crawls in over him and Nike starts the car. "Everyone stay down! Do not get up! Stay down until I tell you!" he shouts. He does a three-point turn, hitting both Carlos's car and the four-wheeler on the way out. I hear a few more gunshots as we're driving away.

Manny is holding his arm now, yelling "Goddamn! Goddamn!" and grunting loudly as the car bumps over the gravel. There's blood all over him—on the hand that's holding his arm, on his arm, on the pink tank top, which is now mostly red. I reach up between the seats and stroke his cheek. It's clammy. "Babe, oh my God," I say. "Oh my God. I'm so sorry." Next to me, on the ground, I hear my mother praying to San Judas, asking him to watch over us, to help us, to keep Manny safe. I hold my stomach, press on it. *Mijo, are you okay?* I say to him. *I love you. Abuela loves you. She's right here. We found her.* I realize I've said this out loud, but I don't care. I use my other hand to touch my mother's back and try to move even closer to her.

As soon as we hit the dirt road leading away from the property, Nike picks up his phone and speaks in Spanish. "This is Special Agent Joe Ramos. I'm working with Capitán Herrera. I need an ambulance to meet me in Muelle San Carlos." He gives them all the information: five hostages from the operation—two adult males, three adult females.

Special Agent Joe Ramos. With a Cuban accent and perfect English. I wonder if he's FBI. Do they do this kind of thing? Whatever this is. Exotic animal trade?

He listens to the person on the phone, then says, "One casualty. Shot in the arm." He turns back to Carlos. "It's just his arm, right? Nothing else?"

Manny nods, his face scrunched up, his lips curled inside his mouth. He's breathing heavily, stifling a yell with every exhale.

"Just the left arm," Carlos says to Joe. To Manny he says, "Hang in there, man."

Joe reports that it's only the left arm and says, "But I've also got somebody with a heart condition. And a pregnant woman." The person says something else and Joe calls back to me, "How many weeks are you?"

"Thirty-one."

"Thirty-one," he says into the phone.

He hangs up and tells us we can sit up now, that we're safe. Eleanor helps me get my mother off the floor and into the seat. "Everything's okay now," she says to my mother.

My mother says nothing, just puts a hand over her mouth and shakes her head. She's looking at Manny. He's rocking a little now, to the left and right, holding his arm and making a kind of *hmm-hmm-hmm* sound over and over. "El pobre," she says. "El pobre."

I'm crying and rubbing my mom's arm. I say, "Manny, should we do anything? To help you? How can we help you?"

"Don't do anything," Joe says, almost shouting. "Let the paramedics handle it."

"He was a medic in the Army. In Afghanistan," I say. "He knows."

Manny's still making the *hmm-hmm-hmm* sound but he transitions to a seething noise to be able to talk. "Pressure. A bandage."

Carlos says, "Okay." He asks Joe if there's a first aid kit in the car.

Joe shakes his head. "No idea. It's Frankie's car." He checks the glove compartment. "Nothing. Maybe the back?"

"I'll look," Eleanor says. She climbs over our seat into the back area to look into the compartments back there. "No kit here, either."

"What about a shirt?" Carlos says. "Would that work?" Manny nods, and Carlos pulls off his shirt. Manny moves his hand off the wound, which I see now is a nasty round gash about the size of a dime. "Just press on it, hard," he says. Carlos presses his shirt to Manny's arm. "Harder," he says, so Carlos leans forward to put his weight into it. Manny yells, "Fuck!" and Carlos jumps back. "No, keep it. Just like that," Manny says.

Carlos does it again—leans forward and presses down—and this time Manny closes his eyes and screams with his mouth closed, nodding the whole time.

A minute later Manny opens his eyes and says, "Mónica." I come out of my seat and sink down to the floorboard. I'm still shaking. He looks at his arm. "This is gonna be okay."

"You sure?"

He nods and I feel myself calm down by one notch. Not a lot, but just enough to think.

I sit back in my seat. "He's okay," I say to my mother. "He's going to be okay." I look into her eyes, trying to get her to believe me. I'm not sure she does.

We come out of the farmland and into the mechanic shops and little restaurants and strip malls of town. I'm looking for the ambulance that's supposed to meet us. Joe says, "I'm really sorry you guys ended up in this."

"Are you an FBI agent?" I say.

My mother looks out the window. "I knew Daniel would save us."

I don't correct her.

"Fish and Wildlife. I've been working this operation for two years. Everything was supposed to go down at three today, but the captain must have called it in early. I was getting you guys out of there, over to my colleague's house; you would have been safe with her." He shakes his head. "I can't believe this. What are the chances?" He looks over his shoulder, trying to see Manny. "How's he doing?"

"Hurry," I say, looking at Carlos's hands, which are all bloody, his shirt completely soaked now.

"The ambulance is meeting us in five minutes," Joe says, and I try not to count them down one by one.

38

Twenty-four hours later, we're back where we started: Baptist Hospital, seventh floor, Heart and Vascular. At the hospital in Quesada yesterday, they didn't rush Manny off to surgery as I had expected. They didn't even remove the bullet. "Eso es puro Hollywood," the nurse told me. They just cleaned the wound, stitched him up, and gave him pain meds. Meanwhile, my mother was having chest pains and shortness of breath. And her blood pressure was way too high. They did an echocardiogram and found a leak in the suture line in her heart. The doctor called her cardiologist and he said he wanted her to come home and get it repaired here, by him. So she stayed in the hospital overnight for observation, then flew home and went straight to Baptist by ambulance.

Now we're all here again—my father, Pablo, and I—in the room with my mother. I'm filthy, Manny's blood on the sleeve of my shirt, my hair in a ponytail with a halo of frizz. I've slept maybe six hours in two days, if you count the nap Manny and I took in the hospital waiting room last night. He's here, too, out in *this* waiting room.

My father offers me the pink pleather chair, but I'm too amped-up to sit down. My mother is the opposite of amped. She seems to have fallen into a near-catatonic state where she's barely speaking. My father and Pablo keep trying to talk to her, to ask her questions about what happened, why she decided to get on the plane, but she won't answer. She just sits there, her eyes unfocused and dead looking. Finally she says, "I made a mistake."

My father says, "I should never have left you. I don't know what I was thinking." He strokes her hand. "Lo siento, Mirta. Lo siento mucho."

Even though I'm mad—about so much—I feel a little surge of love for him. I know he's scared to death. I know he thinks he could have prevented this by not taking off after their fight. But who knows? He's never been able to prevent her from doing anything she wanted to do. And if he had been the one to go down there to get her, would he have found Frankie's house? Or would she *still* be down there, the blood leaking out of her heart? Or worse: Would she have been shot dead in the living room when the cops showed up for the raid? Maybe it's good that he made a mistake and I went down instead.

I turn to him. "Dad, there's no use beating yourself up. Who knows how all this would have turned out if you hadn't left? You were angry. You weren't thinking. It happens."

Pablo nods. "Yeah, it happened; it's over. Now we just gotta get Mom better and get out of here."

The nurse comes in to check vitals and give my mother more blood pressure medicine and a tranquilizer. The doctor thinks the borderline catatonic state is a trauma response and that it's not helping the BP issue. Tomorrow she's scheduled for a procedure to seal the leak. It's not actual surgery, thank God: it's done in the cath lab by her cardiologist.

It's too crowded in here now, with the three of us plus the nurse and her vitals cart, so I tell my father and Pablo that I'll be back in a little while. "I need to go check on Manny," I say.

I touch my mother's shoulder. "I'll be back, okay, Mom?" She doesn't respond. I'm gutted. How could we have done all this— flown to Costa Rica, found her, brought her back—and now she's worse?

In the waiting room, it's just Manny and an older white guy who reminds me of Rack. He's sitting over by the TV watching Brian Williams. Manny is sitting on the floor up against the wall, his head leaned back, his eyes closed, his left arm in its big white bandage propped up on the seat of the chair next to him. He's supposed to keep it elevated above his heart anytime he can. They gave him Percocet for the pain but he's only taking half the dosage. He's also filthy, the five-o'clock shadow darker, wearing the same camo shorts as yesterday and a white T-shirt a nurse was able to find him last night because his tank top was ruined.

I walk up quietly in case he's asleep.

"I'm awake," he says, but doesn't open his eyes.

"Go home," I say.

"Not going home." His eyes are still closed. "How is she?"

"Gone. Like, pretty much not talking."

"Still? Even after seeing your father and Pablo?"

I lower myself to the floor, mostly by crouching and then plopping down because of my belly. "Jesus Christ, I've never been more tired in my life," I say.

"It's good practice for the baby. You won't be getting any sleep then, either." He scratches his face, his eyes still closed.

"Oh my God, the baby better be easier than this."

"Is your mom awake?"

"Yeah, but they just gave her Ativan, so probably not for long. They're trying to calm her down. It's so weird, because she doesn't look agitated at all. She looks the opposite."

"How's her blood pressure?"

"Still bad. 177/115."

He opens his eyes. "Shit."

When it's clear there's nothing more to do, Manny drives me home, neither of us talking. We *will* talk. I know that. But not right now. For right now, we're just together, alive, hurt, but healthy. I watch him to make sure he's not falling asleep, that the Percocet isn't making him even more drowsy. He looks okay.

When we pull into the parking lot of the hotel, he takes my hand and rubs his thumb over the back of it. "You okay?" he says.

I nod. "Are you?"

He nods. "Go sleep. And call me when you wake up."

We don't kiss or hug. He just holds my hand for a long minute. He squeezes and I squeeze back and I step down out of the truck. He waits until I'm inside before driving away.

Mirta

My God, I've never been more scared in my life. Knowing you were in harm's way. And the baby. And then Manny got shot. I can't stop thinking about him lying on the floor of the car, making those sounds, bleeding. What if it hadn't been his arm? What if it had been his chest? It was so close. He was so lucky. But what if he hadn't been? Or, worse, what if it had been you, with the baby inside you? What if you had lost the baby? What if you had died? I can't stop thinking that. You could have died. We all could have died. And it would have been all my fault.

39

Instead of rushing to get to the hospital the next morning, I go to the front office for a cup of coffee. For some reason, even though it's Tuesday, not the weekend, there are donuts. I take three instead of my usual two.

On the way into my room, I run into Rack and Suzie. She's in her scrubs, her giant backpack over one shoulder. "Hey," she says. "I didn't want to knock. Wasn't sure if you were up."

I tell them how my mom is doing.

"Oh my God," Suzie says, when I tell her about the bleed in her heart.

"I know," I say. "I know. And they're working on getting the BP down so it doesn't happen again. And so she doesn't have a stroke."

She holds her arms out to hug me. I hug her back with the coffee in one hand, the donuts in the other.

In my room, I sit down and eat my donuts and drink my coffee, just me. No Mom, no Dad, no Manny, no Robert. Robert texted me yesterday and I told him my mom's home and the baby's fine and that's pretty much it. I didn't tell him what I need to tell him, which is that I can't go back to him. And it's not because of Manny. It's because I'm not in love with him. I should never have moved in with him. Keeping the baby, raising him together but separately—that's what we need to do. I know that. I just didn't have the courage to do anything about it. But after all of this, I know I need to live my life the way I want to. And Robert deserves someone who will look at him the way Manny looks at me. I finish my donuts, then I text him. *Hey, will you be home tonight? Can I come over to talk?*

He texts back immediately. *Training with the Daytona 500 guy tonight. Home tomorrow by 6:30.*

I text back *See you then.*

At the hospital, I ask my mother a series of questions: How did she sleep? Did she eat breakfast? Would she like to take a shower? She answers none of them, just sits there silently, as if she hasn't heard a word I've said. It's frustrating, but mostly it's scary.

Finally, she looks away from Kelly Ripa on TV and stares at the wall. "We need to find him," she says. "Daniel can help us."

I think about how she went all the way to Costa Rica looking for Juan, endured that horrifying experience, and still doesn't know anything more than she knew when she left Miami. "Do you want me to call Daniel? Is that what you want?" I ask.

But she doesn't answer, just looks back at the TV, and I decide to leave it alone for now.

Just as Kelly Ripa goes to commercial, there's a knock at the door. It's Dr. Layne, the doctor who looks like Kobe and is married to the marathoning oncologist. When my mom hears his voice, she looks over but doesn't say a word. She just sits there while he says hello to me and holds up his stethoscope. "Mind if I take a listen?" he says.

When she doesn't respond, I say, "She's not really talking much right now. She's been through a lot."

"I heard," he says. "Must have been harrowing."

I nod. "Yeah. Harrowing." I've never used that word in my life.

"So sorry to hear it." He asks my mom if she's still having chest pressure.

She looks off as if she's remembering the answer, not delivering it for the first time. "Yes," she says finally.

"Okay. I can help with that." He explains that they'll do the procedure this afternoon. "We might have to leave the catheter in your heart for a couple of days just to make sure we get all the fluid drained, so we'll need you here for that. But more importantly, we need to get that blood pressure down."

As he's checking her heart and lungs, my father comes in with Pablo behind him. He's wearing shorts and a T-shirt and holding a Starbucks cup. I'm shocked he's here. And not even in work clothes, which I guess means he took the day off.

Dr. Layne finishes up and pats my mom's hand. "You take care, Mrs. Campo. Just relax and we'll get you out of here as soon as we can."

Afterward, he talks to us in the hallway. He's worried about her blood pressure, which he says is borderline stroke level. When he says that, I feel a clawing in my chest. "We're treating it with medication, but we need to watch her stress level," he says. "That means minimal visitors and lots of rest. I've also ordered a psych consult."

The psychiatrist is Dr. Reyes. She says my mother is pretty shut down, probably due to the trauma more than anything else. If she doesn't get better, though, she wants to transfer her to the psychiatric floor for therapy and medication.

Pablo says, "So, like, you've seen this kind of thing before?"

She nods. "It's very common."

I say, "What about the other symptom: the delusions?"

"Not *as* common, but not unheard of, particularly after being in the ICU. I think it's a coping mechanism. The brain is feeling overloaded and is just trying to find a way to unload the stress. Sometimes leaving the current situation in favor of a different one—even if it's imaginary—is how we do that." She smiles and I can feel my body relax by one level.

My father runs his fingers through his hair. "Well, can you start the medication now? Maybe she can just get better without having to go to the psychiatric unit."

"She's getting a benzodiazepine, so in a way we already have. I'm hoping that in a few days, after the pericardiocentesis, she will start to become more responsive and we can avoid having to transfer her altogether. I would, of course, recommend therapy and possibly medication no matter what."

My father says, "Yes, yes, she should do therapy. But the psychiatric ward"—he shakes his head—"she would not do well in that environment."

"Seriously," Pablo says. "That would not be good for her."

Dr. Reyes nods and clicks her pen. "I understand. But I wouldn't recommend sending her home like this."

In the waiting room later, my father sits down next to me. "I wanted to talk to you yesterday, but there was too much going on. Listen, I'm very sorry I left and didn't call you guys." He's holding a Pepsi with two hands, almost cradling it in his lap.

"We figured out that you had gone somewhere," I say. "We just didn't know where."

He looks me in the face. "For twenty-nine years, I have felt like a fool, ashamed that he's your father, not me. So when she told me that she was going to look for him with a private investigator, I got very angry, and I needed to be by myself."

There's no one else in here, thank God. I touch his arm, rub it a little. "I understand," I say. "I've been feeling the same way."

"And then I got the message that she flew to Costa Rica, and that you had gone to get her. And when I called Pablo back and he said there had been a shooting—" He shakes his head, looks down at the Pepsi in his hands again. His face is getting redder, and I think he might be crying. When he speaks again, I know he is. "May you never know that feeling, mija. That fear is like nothing in the world. And on top of it, it was my fault." He takes off his glasses and runs a hand down his face. He might look five years older than he did last week, the creases around his mouth deeper, his crow's feet more pronounced. "I should have been the one down there looking for her," he continues. "Not you. I failed you. And I failed your mother too. I should never have left her alone. I knew she wasn't all right. She was dressed up in those old clothes, talking crazy, and I just said 'Forget it' and left."

I reach over and rub circles on his back. "Dad, you had no idea she would do something like that. None of us did. Mom's unbelievable. She's like . . . unstoppable sometimes." I smile a little.

"I know, but now I think she might be losing her mind. And I don't know what to do to help her."

"I do," I say softly.

He looks up at me.

I'm afraid to say it and I can't look at him when I do. I look at the swirls in the red paisley carpet. "Let's try to find Juan."

He nods. "It's what she wants. Maybe it's what she needs." He opens his Pepsi and takes a sip. "Is that what *you* want?"

"Yes and no. But I think I at least need to know if he's alive or not. And so does Mom."

"Yes, I understand," he says.

"I talked to the FBI agent when I was down there. I called him for help finding her. He can give us the name of the investigator. I'll call him and ask."

He leans forward and puts his head in his hands. "Okay," he says, his voice so soft and sad. What is this doing to him? I don't know if he can stand it. I don't know if *I* can.

I put my hand on his knee. "Hey, are you sure? Are you sure you're okay with this?"

"Mónica, I'm afraid for your mother. And I think talking to Juan could help her. So I have to be okay with this."

"And what if they talk and, you know, something crazy happens?"

He's still hunched over, head in his hands. "Something like they're still in love? God willing, it won't. But if it does"—he shrugs—"I have no control over that."

A nurse walks in for a second but then walks back out.

"I don't know how you can be so calm about this," I say.

He chuckles just a little and sits up. "I have not been calm for two months. Ever since she came home from the doctor saying there was something wrong with her heart. I just want her to get better. I want all of this to be over." I look at him and see the pain of a man whose worst nightmare has come true. The secret he never wanted revealed is out and it's destroying his family, just as he knew it would. But maybe finding Juan will help. Maybe, bizarrely, finding my biological father will bring my family back together.

I pull out my phone and call Daniel Fernández, tell him what's happening, and ask for the private investigator's number. He says never mind the PI. His old friend from Cuba, the one who was in the CIA, is a better option. Daniel's going to contact him and let me know as soon as he finds something.

I hang up and then hold out my hand to my father. He takes it. I think about all the ways he's sacrificed for my mother—the times, as she said, he's saved her. If this works, if we can find Juan, this could be one more. We stand up, still holding hands, and walk back to my mother's room.

40

By day three, word gets out that my mother is back in the hospital and the Cuban National Convention starts to pack the place. Nobody can go in to see her because of Dr. Layne's orders, so everyone just hangs out in the waiting room eating pastelitos and gossiping. I float in and out, barely speaking to any of them, and then escape to the gift shop to buy my mom another tube of the lemon pomegranate lotion. She's going to be here for at least another couple of days. The procedure went well, but they want to keep her under observation for her blood pressure.

I'm standing in line at the gift shop when Daniel Fernández calls. Apparently, they thought they had found Juan, but then the guy was too young. "But we're not done looking," he says. "My friend is working on it. It's just a very common name, you know. I think the way we'll find him is through connections, so we're trying to find family members, friends, et cetera."

When he says *connections*, I remember: Martín. Their CIA connection. He's how both Juan and my mom managed to make it to Frank's farm. I tell Daniel about him.

"You know how to contact him?" Daniel asks.

"He owns Sosa Cars and Trucks."

"The one that advertises on TV? Right there on Flagler?"

"Yep."

"Bueno, I'll have my friend call him. Better the call comes from him than me."

I hang up feeling a mix of dread and not exactly excitement but something positive I can't name. Maybe a little curiosity. And the smallest bit of hope that if we find him it will help my mom get better.

When I get back to the waiting room, everyone is still there. Including the Stars, who must have arrived when I was downstairs. They have the fanny packs on but no tote bags this time, though Chichi does have a big denim purse slung over her shoulder. I wonder if they came on their own or if someone called them in special. Sure enough, I hear Gladys say, "Thank you for coming so fast."

This floor is intermediate care, not the ICU, which means the Stars can just walk down the hall and slip into my mother's room while the nurse isn't looking. Once they're in, my father keeps watch outside the door. They stay in there for about thirty minutes and when they're done, they come straight for me.

Chichi takes my arm and leads me to the other side of the waiting room, where no one is sitting. "Mónica," she says, moving the denim purse from one arm to the other, "you need to bathe yourself." Yeya is standing right next to her, nodding.

I take a step back, a little afraid. I don't have any experience, really, with this stuff. "What does that mean?"

Yeya explains that I need to get in the shower and pour a full bottle of Cuban cologne—Kolonia 1800 if I can get it—all over myself while "scrubbing" with a large bunch of basil. "Preferably one that's flowering." She says the bath will clear the bad spirits. And it needs to be me who does this because I'm the person most connected to this ailment that my mother is suffering from. I am the child who came from Juan, who she must let go of.

"She told you about Juan?" I say.

"No," they say in unison.

My father, who I didn't know was behind me, says, "I did."

An hour later I'm standing in the shower at the hotel, rubbing a basil plant all over my legs, my stomach, up and down my arms. I didn't think I believed in this shit, but everything's so broken that now I don't know what I believe in. I splash a little of the cologne into my hand and rub it on my shoulders. It's lemony, citrusy, crisp. As I go, I get more and more paranoid that I'm not doing it right. And what if not doing it right means my mom won't get better? They said to put a lot on, so I dump some directly onto the basil and re-scrub my legs, almost whipping them. Then I dump what's left of the bottle over my head and stand there letting it drip all over me. Out of nowhere, I remember one time when I was nine or ten years old, in the tub in my parents' bathroom, a fever burning through me, and my mother pouring cup after cup of tepid water over my head, the look of fear and concern on her face as I shivered, freezing and sick. I turn on the shower now and rinse myself, but not very much. They said I need to keep myself "clean," hoping that whatever bad mojo or vibes I've been carrying around for however long—my whole life, maybe—are now swirling down the drain and away from me, away from all of us.

Afterward, I lie down on the sofa, my swollen feet propped up on pillows. I fall asleep like that, talking to the baby, telling him I'm trying very hard to help his abuela get better.

When I get to Robert's that night, I smell like a bottle of cleaning solution, but also kind of fresh and green. I park behind his RX-7 in the driveway and sit there for a good minute or so, trying to calm down. I'm so nervous I can't do anything but take these little staccato breaths in and out. I hate so much that I have to do this. The only thing that makes me feel any better is the fact that it's the right thing to do, so I make that a mantra in order to get myself out of the car. *It's the right thing to do. It's the right thing to do,* I say. At the front door, I say it one more time before I knock.

The door opens and there he is, still in his uniform: dark blue shorts, light blue polo with the Deer Park logo on the chest. He's carrying the spray bottle for the iguanas in one hand and the Hulk, who is much bigger now—almost as long as his forearm—in the other.

"Hey," he says. "Come in. I'm spraying them."

I follow him into the house, which looks messier but not trashed: a couple of pairs of sneakers thrown in the living room and some clothes on the sofa, mail and a pizza box on the coffee table. The plants are looking good, though. He must be remembering to water them.

"So I guess Laz never showed up?" I say.

"He shafted me. But Flaco knows a guy who might want them. He's coming to see them on Saturday." His voice is flat, like he can't get the energy to have this discussion. In the iguana room, he gets the Hulk to walk up to his shoulder. All the other iguanas have grown much bigger too.

I think I might die if I can't find somewhere to put my hands. "Do you want me to help? I could use the gloves and help you get done faster."

"Nah. I'm good. I like it. It's, like, an activity, gives me something to do."

It's the right thing to do, I say in my head. I lean against the windowsill. It's low enough that I can almost sit on it.

"So," he says. "How's your mom?"

"Back in the hospital, actually. Her blood pressure's so high it caused a leak in her heart. They fixed it, but they can't get the BP down. And she's traumatized from Costa Rica." I decided on the way here to keep it simple. I'm certainly not going to tell him the whole story with Manny going and getting shot.

He opens a cage and feeds the iguana a lettuce leaf. As it chomps on it, I watch its scaly dinosaur mouth, its weirdly human pink tongue. "I'm sorry," Robert says. "What does the doctor say?"

"They need to get the heart stuff resolved. Then she might go to the psych ward."

"Damn. Maybe they'll help her in there, though."

"I'm doing everything I can to make sure she doesn't have to go," I say. And then, for some reason, I tell him. "I'm trying to find Juan. My biological father. She found out he might still be alive and she really wants me to meet him. So I'm looking for him."

He raises his eyebrows at me. "That's . . . a lot."

I take a deep breath. "Yeah, there's been a lot going on. I've been doing a lot of thinking."

"Let me guess. A lot of thinking about us. About how you're not coming back." He's not yelling, but I can hear the anger in his voice.

I lower mine to almost a whisper. Not on purpose—it just comes out that way. "Robert, I want you to be a father to this baby. To be in his life." I can feel the blood in my ears, my heart thumping in my chest. "But I don't think we can be together. I love you as a friend, as the father of my child. But I'm not *in* love with you."

He says nothing, just puts the top back on the cage and moves on to the next iguana. He spritzes it twice. "Are you in love with Manny?" he says, without looking away from the cage. The Hulk is still on his shoulder, looking around, then looking at me. "Are you in love with the guy who fucked you over however many times and now he's your knight in shining armor? Coming over to check on you and bring you food? The guy you're shacked up with in a hotel?" Now he's raising his voice a little.

I press one palm into my stomach, the other into the wood of the windowsill. "I'm not shacked up with him."

"Oh, really?" The Hulk is still looking at me. Now Robert looks at me too. "You're certainly doing something with him. I saw how he looked at you. Is that who you're in love with? *That* guy?"

The blood pulsing in my ears feels stronger, louder. How do I answer this? I cannot answer this. Not honestly. And the honest answer doesn't matter; my feelings for Manny have nothing to do with my feelings for Robert.

"My feelings for Manny have nothing to do with my feelings for you," I say. "They're totally irrelevant."

"Totally irrelevant. Yeah, I'm sure." He palms his chest with both hands. "Sounds like *I'm* totally irrelevant."

My throat thickens. "Robert, you're not irrelevant at all. I'm so sorry. You're not irrelevant. You're this baby's father. And a really good guy. And I feel like such a piece of shit for doing this."

Neither one of us says anything for about five seconds. My eyes are stinging and I'm blinking away tears and he's just standing there holding the spray bottle.

Finally he says, his voice flat again, "How long have you known this wasn't going to work, that you're"—he waves his hand in front of him—"not in love with me? I mean, did you know it when we moved in together? Did you know it when I proposed? Why say yes? Why take the ring?"

Someone's car alarm goes off for a few seconds, then stops. I swallow, trying not to cry. "I think deep inside I've known it all along, but it was hard to see because we worked so well together. And then I was pregnant and we were keeping it, and it just made sense. There was no reason not to say yes."

"And now Manny's back. How long has that been going on, by the way? Were you cheating on me before your mom's surgery?"

I shake my head and wipe my eyes. "No. I had no contact with Manny before my mother's surgery." I look him in the eye. I want him to believe me. "And I didn't move out of here because of Manny. I moved out of here because I was losing my mind and something told me I needed to be alone." I take a step toward him. "I promise you that Manny has nothing to do with this decision."

He huffs. "Hard to believe that one."

"I know. But it's true. I shouldn't have agreed to move in with you. I should have had the guts to tell you right then. But, honestly, I think I was in denial."

"I was too."

"What?"

He talks into the iguana cage, not to me. "I've been afraid of this the whole time. I was hoping you were just scared because we were moving so fast with the baby and everything."

"I *was* scared of that, and I was letting myself believe it was just that. But then everything with my mom and Juan and all the shit that's going on has helped me see that—"

"That you don't love me," he says, cutting me off. "I know. I don't need to hear it again." He tears off a few pieces of lettuce and drops them into the cage. "Well, I love *you*. And this is pretty much the worst thing that's ever happened to me."

My chest is aching with sadness. I take off the ring and put it on the windowsill. It makes the tiniest sound of metal on wood. The Hulk looks over at it, but Robert doesn't. "I'll get you this month's rent as soon as I can," I say. I don't know where the hell I'm going to come up with an extra $600. Maybe Pablo and Maritza can lend it to me. But I feel so bad about everything that's happened that I cannot leave him hanging. "And I'll text you about coming over to get the rest of my stuff. Maybe one day when you're racing."

He nods. "Yeah." The look on his face is completely devastating.

Mijo, your father is so sad, I think. And then I ask Robert if he wants to talk to the baby.

He bites his upper lip and I realize he's trying not to cry. He nods and puts the Hulk back in his cage, leaves the spray bottle on the ground.

He squats down in front of me but doesn't touch me, doesn't lift up my shirt. "Hey, Taz, this is your dad." He stops, looks down. I can't hold my tears anymore. They're pouring down my face and I wipe them as fast as I can. "Taz, I'm gonna see you in a few weeks, okay? I'm here waiting for you, and I'll see you soon. Be good." He stands back up and walks away, back to the other side of the room, picks up the spray bottle, and sprays the next iguana.

"I'll text you after every appointment," I say. "I promise."

He nods and, after a few seconds, I walk out, that dark, ugly guilt swirling inside me. In the car on the way home, I realize that swirling alongside it is a kind of lightness, as if a valve has been opened and some of that ugly darkness is being released.

41

Two days later, while Dr. Reyes is in with my mother, Daniel calls. My father and I are sitting in the waiting room alone; the nurses shut down the Convention for good yesterday, saying it was just too much.

"I have some news," Daniel says. His CIA friend was able to use information from Martín to figure out that Adelita is living in New Jersey. And that Juan, as my mother said, is still alive. And living here. In Miami.

I grip the wooden arm of the chair. It's good I'm sitting down. "He's here?" I say. "Are you sure?"

"Positive. I just texted you his number."

My phone dings. "Okay. Wow. Thank you so much for your help," I say, and we hang up.

I turn to my father. "So . . . he's here. Alive. In Miami."

He nods and exhales deeply, processing. I put my hand on his knee. "So. We tell her, right? We don't just get him to call her out of nowhere? That's too much."

"We need to tell her and see what she wants to do." He nods at me. "And what you want to do."

"What do *you* want to do? Are you still okay with this?"

"Sí, mija," he says, right away—no hesitation, which makes me feel like we're doing the right thing.

Dr. Reyes agrees. She says hearing from Juan could help my mother, but that we should make sure to tell her in advance. "Mirta doesn't need any more surprises."

I go into my mom's room alone. My father thought she would feel more comfortable that way. "Mom," I say, and she barely turns her head. The television isn't on. She's just sitting in silence. "Mom, listen, I need to tell you something."

No response.

"I called Daniel and asked him if he could help us find Juan. And he did. He's alive."

She nods slowly and says, "I knew he was alive. I could feel it." It's the most she's spoken in five days.

"I have his phone number. He's here in Miami, actually. I was thinking about calling him."

She looks at me. She actually looks at me. "He's here. Not in Costa Rica." She says it as a statement, not a question. As if she's telling herself.

"Yes."

"Okay, call him." She's still looking at me.

"Would you like to talk to him? Should I ask him to call you?"

She's quiet for a moment. Then she says, "Yes. If he would like to talk to me, yes."

I'm so happy to see her responding that all I do is smile and rub her arm and tell her okay, I will, that I'll call him right after I get something to eat, which is not true. I couldn't eat for a million dollars right now. I just need a reason to get away. "I'll be back a little later, okay? Dad's here. He's coming right in."

She shakes her head. "I need to take a nap."

"Okay. I'll tell Dad." When she closes her eyes without saying anything else, I just squeeze her arm and leave.

In the hallway, I tell my father everything and I can see his relief. "Okay," he says, nodding, a little excited. "Okay. That's good."

"So I'm going to call Juan. Okay?"

"Okay, mija." He takes off his glasses and cleans them with his cleaning cloth. He looks overwhelmed, and I'm wondering if he might need a moment to himself as well.

I ride the elevator all the way down to the main floor and go straight out to the fountain. I sit on the bench and watch the water shoot out the top of the big blue pineapple. I need to make sure that I can do this—that I can call Juan and tell him what my mother has wanted to tell him for years.

A giant swarm of everything I've been trying not to feel descends upon me, and I let it. From the moment my mother, high in pre-op, said the words *Your father is Juan,* I've been hiding. But I can't hide any longer. And, more important, I don't want to.

I sit there for a good ten minutes. People come and go, in and out of the automatic doors. I open Daniel's text and look at the number. Juan's number. This is how we might get back to our life. Not our old life full of lies but this new one full of truth and light. I close my eyes and listen to the fountain for a minute before I press Call.

42

Tonight, one of Sebastián's goons is driving an SUV, and Clara, still dressed as a nun, is bound and gagged, lying in the back seat. A briefcase full of money is on the passenger's seat, and beside it is a gun. I can't look at it. I have to focus on something else: Clara's beautiful face grimacing or the goon's chiseled jaw. I look at my mother to see if she's okay. She looks exactly like she's looked for the last five days: gone.

Though when I told her that Juan is coming to the hospital tonight to say hello, she gave a sigh of relief. And after dinner she asked for wipes to do a face wash. Then she wanted her hairbrush and her makeup bag.

"Well," my father said, smiling, "you're fixing yourself up for your boyfriend, I see."

"Juan no es mi novio," she said.

I smiled at my father to let him know it was okay that she didn't get the joke and that I appreciated his attempt at making this less weird.

When Juan picked up my call earlier and I told him who I was, he almost couldn't speak. "¿Qúe? ¿Pero como?" he stammered. "¿De verdad?"

"De verdad," I said. *For real,* I thought, not to the baby but to myself. *Juan has a daughter. I am his daughter.*

At 8:15, my phone buzzes with a text from him. *Estoy aquí.* My stomach bottoms out like I'm on a roller coaster and we've just hit the drop.

"Dad," I say to my father. He's sitting in a folding chair the nurses gave him, doing payroll on his laptop.

He looks at me and I hold up my phone.

"Mom, Juan is here at the elevator. We're going to meet him and bring him in, okay?"

She looks away from the TV but not at me. She looks at my father. "He needs to come."

"I know, Mirta. I know. It's time."

I take my father's hand for the walk to the elevator. I want him to know that I'm loyal to him, that I forgive him for insisting they don't tell me, that I don't want this to be happening any more than he does but I know it needs to and I'm ready for it. I hope he can feel all of that in the way I squeeze his hand and then let it go right as the silver door of the elevator slides open and a man in jeans and a red polo steps out. He's about my parents' age, medium height, medium build. Black curly hair like mine, shot through with gray. Glasses with no bottom rail. Eyes the color of the water in Varadero.

I remind myself to breathe and not to lock my knees.

"Juan?" I say to him. He nods and I hold out my hand. "Hola. Yo soy Mónica." He takes it, shakes it like so many men shake a woman's hand: softly. I want to examine his fingers, to see if they really do look like mine. "Nice to meet you," I say, continuing in

Spanish. I know from the phone call earlier that his English isn't great. My God, this feels insane. It's like meeting a character from a book you're reading.

He looks at my stomach and smiles. "Congratulations. You didn't tell me over the phone."

"Well, we had a lot of other things to talk about."

"Boy or girl?"

"Boy."

He nods, looking from me to my father. "I'm sure you will be a wonderful mother. If you're anything like Mirta."

I turn to my father, put my hand on his upper arm. "This is my father, Rolando." The last time they saw each other, they were young men, and my father was beating him with a stick while he was curled up on the ground, making sounds like an animal. Does he have scars from that? I wonder. A part of his leg that always hurts when it rains? I hope not.

My father holds out his hand to Juan. "Thank you for agreeing to come. We appreciate it very much."

"Of course," Juan says. "How is Mirta doing?"

"The blood pressure is still a problem," I say.

"¿Y el cerebro?" He points to his brain.

My father takes this one. "The same," he says. "We're hoping your visit will do something to help with that." His voice is steady— steadier than mine—but strange sounding. Maybe a little higher than normal. He points to Juan and me. "Why don't you guys talk a minute. Mónica, you can fill him in on everything that happened in Costa Rica." It's like he's trying to escape. He looks away, down the hall, and pushes his glasses up. "Take your time. Come in when you're ready." I want to reach out to him, to take his arm and say, "Dad, no. Don't leave. Please." But he walks away quickly.

"Is there a place we can sit down?" Juan asks.

We go into the waiting room, which is empty except for a dad and two teenage boys in the corner. All three of them are wearing earbuds and looking at their phones. As Juan lowers himself into a chair, I look at his left hand. Wedding ring. Good.

He smiles, then looks down at the floor, away from me, I guess because he's nervous. Or maybe he's trying not to get caught doing what I'm doing, which is scanning his face, looking for myself—the curve of his nose, the angle of his forehead, his jaw. Finally, I find myself in his eyes, which are shaped exactly like mine.

He looks at me. "I—I still can't quite believe it. When you called . . . you can imagine. And then when you said Mirta had a child who was mine . . ." He widens his eyes.

"It's shocking," I say in English, because I can't come up with the word for *shocking* right now. I feel like I can't come up with much.

He nods. "Sí. Muy shocking."

"I didn't know anything about this until a few weeks ago. She told me the morning of her heart surgery and I didn't believe her. I told myself she was just talking crazy because she was on drugs. But she wasn't talking crazy." I squeeze my hands together. I feel almost short of breath. I can't believe this is happening. This is actually him. Juan. Juan from all the stories. Juan from the farm. Juan who set bombs and burned fields and got caught and sent to prison but got released somehow and sent to the States, where he tried to set more bombs and got caught again and, in order to not go back to prison, had to pretend to be someone else. Juan who found my mother in English class and took her to Tamiami Park because he couldn't take her to their favorite park in Cuba anymore, because Cuba was gone and now they were here, in Miami, where she was a wife and a mother and all they had was that one hour a week to be the people they used to be. And in that one hour, without realizing it, they made me. Me, Mónica Campo, Mirta and Rolando's daughter. Juan's biological daughter.

He shakes his head and plants his fists on his thighs. "My God, I wish I had known."

I look away from his face to the gold cross around his neck. I want to say thank you but I don't know if it's okay to say that. But that's what I feel: overwhelming gratitude that he wishes he had known, that I'm not automatically some freak he wants nothing to do with.

I tell him my mother feels bad that he never knew and his eyes go sad. He looks down. "Yes, well, that's not her fault. I'm the one who left."

I tell him everything else: about the coma, the delusions; how, for my whole life, she thought he was dead but then found out two weeks ago he might not be. And then I explain Costa Rica and what happened at Frankie's.

His face cracks open with shock, his eyes wide and unblinking.

"It was awful," I say. "For all of us. But maybe this will help her, you know? Maybe if she sees you, and sees that we've connected, and talked, she'll feel like she did what she was trying to do. Like she finished what she started. I hope."

"Well." He blows air out of his mouth, maybe involuntarily, to psych himself up. "Let's go see her, then."

We walk down the hall side by side. A current—metaphysical, spiritual, something—is running between us. I can't explain it, but I can feel it.

I want to ask him how and why he left Costa Rica, where he went—whether he came here or went somewhere else after that.

I don't, though, because I don't know how much he wants to tell me about his life. I don't know what kind of invasion it would be, especially after everything I've already asked of him today. We've come this far and I don't want him to back out or decide it's all too much and turn around and leave. So I stay quiet.

"I hope this will help her," he says.

"Thank you again for coming."

"Your mother was very important to me at one time. I know it hurt her very much when I went to prison, and then when I left, a second time, to go to Puerto Rico. It hurt me too. When you lose someone and get them back, then lose them again, it can be almost unbearable."

Like me losing Manny over and over again. "I know," I say.

At my mother's door, I want to ask him if he's ready, but again I don't want to pry. And, really, I know the answer. How could he be ready? No one could be ready for any of this. So I just knock on the door.

"Come in," my father calls.

I push on the door and as it slides open, she comes into view: sitting up in bed, her hair brushed, a bit of mascara, a bit of gloss. Nothing major but, given where we've been, she looks like Miss America.

"Mom," I say, approaching her bed. "You have a visitor."

Abismo is still on. Clara is now sitting on Sebastián's sofa, her arms tied behind her back, scream-whispering about what a horrible person he is. My mother mutes the TV, looks at me, then looks behind me, at Juan. He steps forward, into the room, and then here we all are, one happy little family. My father is trying to look okay. His face is neutral—almost no expression. Which is somehow worse than if he were scream-whispering at my mother about what a horrible person she is.

Juan says, "Mirta."

At the sound of his voice, her eyes fill with tears. "No lo creo," she whispers.

I look at my father. He's looking at her. I imagine he's thinking, *Am I losing you forever right now?*

Juan says, "It's been a long time, hasn't it?"

"Yes, it has," my mother says.

"How are you feeling?"

"My heart is bad."

"Rolando and Mónica asked me to come and see you. They said you've been wanting to get in touch with me."

"Yes, for a while now. You live here, in Miami?"

"Yes. My wife and I live with our son in West Miami. Not far from where I lived with my mother and Adelita when we first came here." The apartment where my mother would hang out with Adelita, drinking coffee and practicing English in the red spiral notebook. The apartment where she last saw Juan, with his leg up on the table, bruised and bandaged, the result of the beating my father had given him. It's all flashing around in my head, a movie sped up. I wonder if it's doing the same inside hers.

She seems okay, nodding and possibly processing what he said. "So you live here. Not in Costa Rica."

He puts his hands in his pockets. "I haven't been there for many years."

My father steps toward me, puts a hand on my elbow. "Why don't we let them talk?"

I can't speak. I just let him lead me out the door.

We walk a few feet down the hall and stand there, neither one of us saying anything. The patient door we're in front of is half-open and I can see only the man's legs. They're big and hairy. I look away immediately. I count the tiles from my left foot to the wall. I look at the water fountain a few feet down. I look anywhere but at my father. Then, without knowing I'm going to, I say, a little too loudly, "He's not my father. Okay? He's not."

My father doesn't say anything.

"Okay?" I say again, leaning toward him.

"Yes. Okay," my father says quietly.

"You are my father. You have always been my father. You will always be my father."

He nods.

I point to my stomach, and that's when I start crying. "This is your grandson." I try to lower my voice, but I can't. "You are this baby's abuelo, okay? End of story."

Now his face begins to redden. He nods as his eyes fill with tears. "Sí, mija, sí."

I point down the hall to my mother's hospital room. "I don't care what goes on in there. Nothing changes here. I mean, he's a nice guy. That's obvious."

"It was very good of him to come." He's choking back tears.

I hold up my index finger at him. "But nothing changes here. Everything here is just the same as it was before." It's like I'm angry, but I don't know at who. I'm not mad at him anymore. Or my mother. Maybe what I am is sad. Maybe I'm grieving all the years of pain they went through. And the pain *I'm* currently going through as I try to understand and accept all of this. "Nothing changes," I say again, pointing back and forth between the two of us. I want him to know that he has nothing to worry about, that what we have is never going to change, no matter how angry I was that they never told me. He is my father, the man who has been a constant for me, through everything—through my mother's moods, through the years when I was trying to go to school and the years I was trying to get Manny to love me, through this year, trying to get myself to love Robert. He is my father, my baby's grandfather.

He tries to wipe his eyes without taking off his glasses. I don't even bother with mine. I just let the tears spill down my face and I tell him, "Dad, I don't know how you're doing this. I don't know how you've done this for twenty-nine years. I know it was horrible for you. And I'm sure part of the reason you didn't want to tell me was to spare me the pain of having to deal with this."

"It was a decision I made in the moment. I probably should have taken more time with it. I probably should have let your mother tell you a long time ago."

"It's okay with me that you didn't, though. That's what I'm trying to tell you." I wipe my face, pull my hair back, and tie it up into a bun.

My father says, "Listen, Mónica, I understand if you would like to have a relationship with him. You should feel free to stay in contact if you'd like to, if you feel it's important."

I'm not sure what to say. I want to say thank you but I don't want him to know that I'm as interested in that idea as I think I am. So I just say, "Okay. I don't know if I will. But okay."

We stand there for another minute while a cleaning cart goes by and someone pages Dr. Stein, and then he says he needs to go call the cousins, that he hasn't updated them since yesterday. I'm pretty sure he just needs to get away, so I say, "Why don't you go call them downstairs? And if the cafeteria's open, maybe bring me back a pudding in a little while? No rush. I'll say goodbye to Juan for you." I squeeze his shoulder and run my hand down the length of his arm to squeeze his hand. Then I pull him into a hug, turning my cheek to rest against his chest.

He sighs and I can feel all the weight of his fear in that sigh. "Okay, I will. Thank you, mija."

"Thank you, Dad," I say.

43

On the way home, I call Manny and ask him if he wants to hang out. "I can come over," I say.

He says he wants to come to me. "I'm so over the corner of my couch. I gotta get out of here. I'll elevate at your place, I promise."

"You sure?"

"Positive."

"Okay, but bring something good. Something salty and something sweet."

He shows up with Combos and chocolate ice cream. And Heineken and Diet Dr Pepper. We serve the ice cream in my blue Goodwill bowls and sit on my sofa. He puts his arm up with two of my T.J. Maxx pillows under it for support.

"Should you be drinking?" I say.

"Haven't had a Percocet in two days." He takes a bottle of Motrin out of his shorts pocket and rattles it. "So how you doing?"

"I don't know. I feel insane. In the past five days, I've been held at gunpoint and met my biological father, who I didn't even know existed. And officially become homeless."

He looks down at his ice cream. "You're not moving back in with Robert?"

"I told him it wasn't going to work out between us."

He points to my left hand. "I wondered."

I feel weird talking to him about this, but I want him to know where I am. "I plan on sharing custody as much as he wants. He's a wonderful guy; he really is. And he totally loves this kid already. He's just . . . you know, he's not the wonderful guy for me."

He finally looks up at me. "So does that mean you're officially back on the market?"

My heart jumps a little in my chest. "I am. Know anyone who can handle this hotness?" I lift up my shirt, show him the dark brown line down the middle, the bulging belly button. Right then the baby starts kicking, jamming his foot into my side.

"Ow," I say.

He leans in. "You okay?"

"It's fine. Touch this." I point to where the foot is.

He puts his hand there and the alarm is gone from his face and now it's just happiness and wonder. "Oh, man. You're amazing."

"I'm not amazing. *This* is amazing. It's the coolest thing in the world to grow a person inside you."

He puts his bowl down on the table and turns to take both my hands. He even uses his left arm. "Mónica, you *are* amazing. And I have been a fool and an asshole. I totally want this hotness and I'm sorry it took me so long to figure that out."

"You know I'm pregnant with someone else's baby, right?"

My stomach is still out, bulging right under his face. "Hard to miss."

"And, like, Robert's going to be around. He deserves to see his kid." I drop my head. "I feel so bad. The least I can do is let him be a dad."

"No, for sure. I get that."

"And I need to take this really slow. I need to make sure you're serious. That this is real—that you really do want to be committed here."

He looks into my eyes. "Mónica, when I was lying there on the ground, before they got me into the car, my only thought was you. I wanted you to be okay." He points to my stomach. "And him to be okay. And I wanted me to be okay so that if there was any chance of us being together, I would be alive for it."

In my head, I hear him scream, see him fall back into the gravel, see him bleeding, bleeding, bleeding. "Same," I whisper. "All I wanted was for you to be okay. So that we could try again." I lean in and kiss him.

"Hey, I've got room at my place. We could put the crib in the second bedroom."

"What? I just told you I need to take things slow and you're asking me to move in?"

"Joking." He moves my hair back from my face and looks at me. "But, like, maybe someday?"

I lean over and kiss his mouth, his neck, his jaw. I inhale deeply and smell his soap, his body. It smells like home, of course. I hold the scent in for a few seconds.

"Maybe," I say. "Someday."

Mirta

We talked about what happened after he went to Puerto Rico. I told him how sorry I was that I never found a way to tell him about you.

"You would never have found me," he said, which made me feel better.

We talked about our lives. Our families. Adelita is living in New Jersey. She's married to a Puerto Rican man. They own a restaurant where they cook Cuban and Puerto Rican food, and they have three children—a girl and two boys. The girl's name is Dolores, after their mother, and she works at the restaurant with them. The boys are younger—twins they had by accident after they thought they couldn't have any more children. They're in college at Rutgers. I asked about Adelita's husband, whether he was good to her, and Juan said, "Sí, es un hombre decente." I was relieved to hear that. She's a very loving person—like you—and she deserves a good man.

As he was leaving, he said, "Would it be all right if I gave you a hug?" and of course I said yes. We held on tight for a long minute. It was a minute filled with pain and sadness, but also joy. The joy of knowing he was okay, that Adelita was okay. It felt very nice. Not the same as it did all those years ago; that passion is gone. In its place is love for an old friend, one who helped make me who I am.

44

She's not miraculously cured after seeing Juan, but she *is* different. She's still not talking a lot, but over the course of the weekend, she asks me how much the baby is kicking and calls me by my name for the first time since before Costa Rica. She also asks me how Manny is. Her blood pressure comes down some and the EKG they do on Sunday morning looks much better. The doctor says if it keeps going like this, he'll release her in a couple of days, pending a positive report from Dr. Reyes.

On Monday afternoon I go to my thirty-two-week appointment a week late. As soon as I get in the car afterward, I text Robert. *Just saw the doctor. BP is good, baby heartbeat good, fundal height 33.* He texts back immediately *Good, thanks,* and that's it. That swirly guilt rises in my gut again and I drop my head onto the steering wheel. "Fuck," I say out loud, and squeeze my hands together as hard as I can. *It's the right thing to do,* I remind myself as I put the car in drive.

When I get back to the hospital, my mom is watching *Primer impacto* while Pablo and my father do work on their laptops. I wait for a commercial to say, "So, um . . . I wanted to tell you guys something."

They all look at me. Even my mother, which is great.

"I broke up with Robert."

My father tilts his head to the side. "Oh."

"I'm not in love with him." Before I can talk myself out of saying it out loud, I say, "I'm in love with Manny."

Pablo gives me an eyebrows-up look, like *What's up with the life proclamations?* And honestly I don't know. I just know I need to say this to them. To tell them what's happening with me and to ask them to stay out of it.

"I just needed to tell you guys, and I'd really appreciate it if you could keep your opinions to yourself. I'm going to find another apartment and move my stuff out of Robert's as soon as Mom is better."

My father says, "Okay, mija."

Pablo says, "No problem," and goes back to his laptop.

My mother nods and says, "Bueno." It's a nod of understanding and, I think, approval. She's been here before, and didn't get the chance to do it this way.

On Tuesday afternoon my father pulls the car around to the pineapple fountain and Pablo and I help my mother into the front seat for what—please, God—will be the last time. We get her buckled in and I hand her her purse. There's no suitcase to put in the trunk this time; it's probably still in Frankie's living room behind that chair. I've already decided that I'm getting her a new one for Christmas. Maybe I'll get them both a whole new set, just to start fresh.

That night I eat with my parents in the kitchen and then my mom and I watch *Abismo*, drinking our coffee and eating the cheesecake Caro dropped off earlier. It's my mother's favorite American dessert.

Armando is finally out of the dungeon. In an unexpected twist, Jaquelín and one of the guards have fallen in love, and together they freed both Clara and Armando. He got his surgery and has miraculously recovered with almost no physical therapy. Now he and Clara are on the run, hiding in a mountain village.

I take a bite of cheesecake and let it melt on my tongue. "There's no way they're going to get away. I'm sure Sebastián is going to find them. Don't you think?"

My mother doesn't answer at first. Then she shakes her head and says, "I couldn't figure out how we were going to get away from them." She puts her fork on her plate and just holds it in her lap, not eating. "I thought we would die. I really thought we would die."

"Me too," I say. "But we didn't. We're okay now."

"When they started shooting . . ." She doesn't finish. She has her reading glasses up on her head, pulling her hair back off her face. Her gray is really prominent now—it's her whole hairline— and it's disconcerting. She looks a little like a different person, which I guess she is. We all are. She's still a little foggy at times, but it's been days since she's fallen into the past. She speaks to us in sentences now. Sentences that make sense.

I squeeze her hand.

"I'm so sorry, mi niña. For everything. I'll never forgive myself for getting on that plane. Never."

"Well, I do." She looks at me and I look back. "I forgive you for getting on that plane. I forgive you for never telling me. I forgive you for all of it. You never meant to hurt me, Mom. With any of this. I know that. And even though you did hurt me, it's okay. I want you to know that." I look right into her eyes. "Mom, I forgive you, okay?"

She scrunches her eyes closed. "My child. I nearly killed my child, and my grandchild."

"No you didn't. *They* nearly killed your child and your grand-child. And *they* shot Manny. And not even on purpose. He was just in the way. It was all a horrible accident."

"I never should have gotten on that plane."

"No, you shouldn't have. But you were out of your mind."

"I never should have gone back to that English class. I wasn't out of my mind then."

"He was the love of your life. Who you thought was *dead*. Of course you went back to that English class. I would have too." I think about how I basically did just that. I called Manny that first night at the hotel. I kissed him. And I chose to keep it going. Now I'm so glad I did. "Listen, Mom, all that matters is that we're here. We're alive. You're getting better. I know the truth about who I am and I met Juan. Just like you wanted me to. Right?"

She nods. "Right."

I squeeze her hand once more, kiss her cheek. "Okay. Good."

Quietly, I ask, "And how was it seeing him?" I'm terrified to hear the answer, but I know I need to.

"He asked a lot of questions about you."

"Did he ask questions about you?" I ask. "Are you going to stay in touch?"

She shakes her head. "He has his life. I have mine." I feel the relief in the back of my neck. "But you should make him part of your life. If you feel it's the right decision."

"I'll think about it," I say.

By the time the show ends, Clara and Armando are living in their own mud house in the village, wearing traditional clothes and learning to cook without a stove. My mom yawns and rubs at her eyes.

"Go to bed," I say. "I'll get the plates."

"Okay," she says. But then she doesn't move. A moment later she takes my hand, puts it to her cheek, and closes her eyes. We stay like that for a good minute. My throat is hard, my eyes burning with tears. *She's back* is all I can think. *Thank God. She's back.*

Acknowledgments

When you've been writing a book for as long as I've been writing this one, you end up having to thank the entire Cuban National Convention, and then some. So here goes:

First, my family. Thank you, Mom and Papi, for backing me up, always, in this endeavor. I've been a writer since I was a kid, and your support throughout my life has been invaluable. Thank you also to Estrella, my wonderful stepmom, for all your encouragement. Nati, this is my Osama bin Laden. Thank you for always telling me I could do it.

Next, to the two people who literally changed my life, my agent, Brettne Bloom, and my editor, Marysue Rucci: I don't have the right words to explain how special our connection is, but I know Nina would be so proud and happy for us all. Brettne, your immediate love of these characters and this story floored me and buoyed me. I'm so grateful for your dedication to the manuscript, especially in those early days. Marysue, thank you for taking a chance on this book. Your ability to see Mónica, to show me sides of her I hadn't yet seen, made this story everything it is. You have guided me in a way no one else in my writing life ever has.

Giant thanks to the people at Marysue Rucci Books and Simon

ACKNOWLEDGMENTS

Element who helped make it all happen. These folx include, but I'm sure are not limited to, Andy Tang, Emma Taussig, Ingrid Carabulea, Laura Levatino, Allison Har-zvi, Jessie McNiel, and Elizabeth Breeden.

Jenny Meyer, friend and foreign rights agent extraordinaire: Thank you for your early support and all your help on so many things, book-related and beyond.

I'm indebted to Jon Baker for all his advice (personal and professional!) and for reading this manuscript with his sharp, knowing eye and giving it the facelift it needed.

Many of my friends have read this book for me, some fellow writers, some not, and I owe them all muchísimas gracias. John Duberstein and Jennifer Cazanave, thank you for your friendship and love, for your feedback on the book, and, most of all, for giving me the come-to-Jesus that made me finally send it to Brettne. I owe you forever for that.

Thank you to Cristina Henríquez, who has been my sounding board, my advocate, and my cheerleader. I'm truly honored to be your friend and colleague and humbled, always, by your kindness and compassion.

To my oldest and bestest friend, Tony Martínez, thank you for keeping me afloat in so many ways for so many years, for allowing me to borrow details from your world to make this one, and for reading the manuscript (like a pro, I might add) and helping me make it right. Wapondoo.

And a special thank-you to Tony's beautiful, loving mother, Lourdes Martínez, who was, even if she wasn't aware of it, a guide of the highest order as I wrote this book. Her voice and her spirit will be here, in this story, forever.

Jorge Jiménez, papi chulo of Long Island, thanks for all your

ACKNOWLEDGMENTS

love and support. Your feedback on the book helped more than you know.

To Alyssa Walker, thank you for reading and for always offering to help in any way you can. You're a treasure.

My good friend Doug Smith read the manuscript right before he left this world for what I hope is a better one. I'm forever grateful for his wise words about writing and teaching and life.

A big shout of thanks to the Ventana group at Lit Camp 2019 for your excellent advice on chapter three and all your encouragement about the project. A special thank-you to Julie Freedman for her medical knowledge and her sweet spirit.

Speaking of knowledge, I owe a huge debt of thanks to the people who helped with research. Drs. Michael Cooper and Kevin Steinl provided information about cardiology and gunshot wounds, respectively. Terry Wagoner, BSN, CNOR, CRNFA, schooled me on heart surgery pre-op procedures. Dr. Angela Van Trigt fielded my questions about cardiac complications. Dr. Peter Van Trigt literally helped me plot parts of this book, and then graciously answered all my questions about pericardiocentesis.

Many thanks to my cousin Alex Pérez for sharing the story of his and his family's journey to the US via the Mariel boatlift.

Finally, I want to shout with a bullhorn my appreciation for Jake Mattocks. Jake, thank you—first for your service to this country, and second for sharing with me all those details about deployment and military life, and, most important, about what it's like to come home and live a life very few of us understand.

Next up: my in-town crew of friends and chosen family who helped make this project possible. First, my amazing parenting village: the Sedgwick/Bufters, the San Georges, the Spira/Piklers, and the Kennedys. Thank you so much for supporting this book via carpooling my children, hosting so many playdates, and the many playground/sidewalk talks about our kids, our lives, everything. A very special shout-out to Liz for being my/our right-hand person, always.

To Allison, purveyor of emollients and writer of the best texts ever; to Jen, most thoughtful human and maker of the best birthday mixes; and to Jess, my favorite walk-and-talker: Thanks to each of you for your love and kindness, and for keeping me sane enough to finish this book.

To my faraway chosen family: Beth and Vicki, beautiful angels, always; Kelly, with your excellent hallway vision; and Cassie, my ride or die from way back when. Thank you to all of you for believing in me these many years.

Many thanks to Elon University for its support of the Creative Writing program, which has served as a home for me and for my students. Thank you to my students, whose encouragement and enthusiasm keeps me going back to the desk. Kevin Boyle and Cassie Kircher, thank you for being amazing friends, colleagues, and partners in crime. Thank you also to my new colleague and partner in crime, Shaina Jones, whose writing and teaching I admire and learn from every day.

I've received support of one kind or another from a few excellent local institutions: the Green Bean coffee shop, where I wrote much of this book; Scuppernong Books, whose owners, Brian Lampkin and Steve Mitchell, do so much to support writers, readers, and thinkers in my community; and the North Carolina Arts Council, a grant from whom made it possible for me to move out of the coffee shop and into a room of my own for a couple of years. Gigantic thanks to all of them.

ACKNOWLEDGMENTS

A big thank-you to the whole Perry family, far and wide, but in particular to my in-laws, Tom and Judy, who have kept the faith with me all the way through this. Your support and love mean so much.

And one more shout into the beyond: To Nina Riggs, who left this earth way too soon, thank you for teaching me how to live. How I wish you could have read this for me and given me some notes. I know they would have been brilliant.

Finally, to Tomás and Nico: Without you, there is no me. Thank you for loving me and being patient with me. DP: I literally could not have done this—not this way—without you. Thank you for all the things, especially for helping me block out the scene at Frankie's house with Nerf guns. I love all three of you twenty-five a lot.

About the Author

Tita Ramírez grew up in Miami, the daughter of a Cuban exile and a Kentucky native. Her fiction and nonfiction have appeared in *LitHub,* the *Normal School, Black Warrior Review,* and elsewhere. She currently lives in North Carolina with her husband and their two sons and teaches creative writing at Elon University. *Tell It to Me Singing* is her debut novel.